Copper Dragons

Some doorways to the mind should never be opened...

Timothy Cole

authorHOUSE®

AuthorHouse™
1663 Liberty Drive
Bloomington, IN 47403
www.authorhouse.com
Phone: 1-800-839-8640

© 2010 Timothy Cole. All rights reserved.

No part of this book may be reproduced, stored in a retrieval system, or transmitted by any means without the written permission of the author.

First published by AuthorHouse   8/2/2010

ISBN: 978-1-4520-5812-2 (e)
ISBN: 978-1-4520-5811-5 (sc)
ISBN: 978-1-4520-5810-8 (hc)

Library of Congress Control Number: 2010910711

Printed in the United States of America
Bloomington, Indiana

This book is printed on acid-free paper.

Prologue

We readily accept any sound that can be confirmed by viewing its origin. In the light of day, visual confirmation makes sounds more palpable, while all other sounds fade into the static of background noise until we ignore them. However, when we are robbed of our vision, our hearing operates at a heightened awareness. Even the slightest of sounds arouse our interests.

There is always a logical explanation for each sound we hear; right?

The supernatural world churns around us in constant activity every minute of our lives, but it cannot be seen. However, its presence can be sensed and its occasional influence on the physical world can be heard... especially when the lights go out.

The dull streetlights shining through the display window cast an eerie glow on the pale and pasty faces of the store's mannequins. Their arms and hands twisted into ominous poses and their facial features were hauntingly vacant. Darkness crept about the floor like a sea of tar, shifting when the lights from a passing automobile brushed it back into the corners like a recoiling black tide. The department store was devoid of all things living and animate.

The oppressive hum of solitude rung in Jennifer's ears until it was muffled by the clicking echo of her high heels against the walls of the house wares' department. Jennifer always viewed a crowded room with mild distaste due to untreated anxiety. However, this vacant store felt overwhelmingly oppressive. She walked hesitantly with her arms wrapped tightly around a box of display items. Her eyes shifted from side to side with each passing aisle. She had never set up a display when the store was closed, and the hair on the back of her neck stood up in protest of her current attempt.

She moved to the back of the store where the shelves that lined the wall were full of bathroom accessories. The color of the towels and wash clothes were impossible to determine in the darkness. A grouping of metallic toothbrush holders and soap dishes slightly amplified her available light. The line of shelves broke momentarily for a five-foot glass case that was pressed against the back wall. A door was hung with metal hinges and secured by a combination lock that had been guided through a hasp. The lock had three numeric dials. Jennifer placed the box on the floor in front of the case and attempted to open the lock; suddenly realizing that she was uncertain of the combination. She attempted several series of numbers unsuccessfully - until she dialed six-one-two, the month and date of her son's birth. The bar sprung free of the lock, and she pulled it up through the ringlets allowing the door to open.Kneeling on the floor to open the box of display items, she began to remove its contents. She uncovered the protective foam sheet from the first item, revealing a porcelain angel. She paused for a moment, admiring the craftsmanship of the statuette. The face of the cherub was strikingly resplendent to her. The eyes were piercingly real; the cheeks were roseate and full of life. She ran her fingertips over its features before placing it delicately on the top shelf.

She reached back inside the box, withdrawing a papier-mâché heart that had been crushed by the weight of the other items. She could not recall where she had acquired it, but she knew it was very old and dear to her. The sight of it, smashed beyond repair, gave her an overwhelming sense of regret. She wished that she had been more careful with it. She gently placed the heart back into the box and pulled out the next item; a large glass sphere, nearly the size of a bowling ball and ten times the mass. The sphere was filled with air bubbles that were suspended within the glass. She wondered what had possessed her to bring such a large object for an obviously delicate display. The glass case could never bear the weight of the sphere.

She balanced it with the fingers of both her hands, raising it up to meet her gaze. She stared at the strange air pockets inside, varying in size and placed selectively by craftsmanship or randomly frozen in time by chance.

She had nearly escaped the discomfort of the immense darkness of the unlit showroom when she heard the sound of a faint cry. She slowly rose to her feet, still holding the glass sphere in her hands. Pausing, she waited through the silence for the cry to direct her to its location. The voice returned, but this time in a sobbing whimper.

Jennifer followed the direction of the voice, walking slowly with the sphere now clutched to her chest. She had made her way to the edge of the house wares section when she realized the voice had stopped. She stood quietly, wondering if the clicking of her heels had drowned out the sound. Her eyes peered hopelessly through the dimly lit store. Her heart began to race, thumping hard against her ribs. As she pressed the sphere ever tighter against her chest, she struggled to breathe. Her arms began tingling with numbness under their own grip.

"It was an accident, and accidents are not anyone's fault." The voice quivered, whimpering in a barely audible whisper.

Jennifer turned left and walked cautiously down the main aisle toward the women's clothing section. The main aisle seemed like a vast empty void, much larger than she recalled. It enhanced her feeling of isolation from the outside world. The outer walls of the department store seemed miles away as they echoed the voice back to her.

She pushed her way in between circular racks of blouses, brushing away the silken cloth as it grazed her. The feel of the cloth brushing her skin could not have made her shudder more if it possessed eight tiny legs and multiple eyes. She heard the voice repeat the irrational phrase as she made her way through the clothing racks. "It was an accident, and accidents are not anyone's fault."

As she entered the aisle for ladies' accessories and turned the corner, she came face to face with a young girl. Jennifer released a startled gasp as she stumbled back away from the child. The child's hair hung in tangled clumps in front of her face. However, Jennifer could still discern her tear-soaked cheeks. The dress of the prepubescent girl was sopping wet and stained with mud. She held a drenched kitten, which hung limply like a wet towel in her arms. The cat's chest remained still, without the slightest heave of breath. The bones of its hips had manifested through its skin and scant fur with no muscle or flesh to cushion its protrusion. The smell of dilapidated animal flesh drifted into Jennifer's nostrils. The young girl stared up at Jennifer, sobbing as she spoke, "I'm sorry, Mommy."

"I'm not your mommy, honey," Jennifer said softly. Her attempts at calming the child were betrayed by her eyes unblinking fixation on the small intruder and her cat. She attempted to subdue the feeling of panic which cloaked her like an unsavory layer of skin. "Why are you in the store? We're closed."

"It was an accident, and accidents are not anyone's fault." The girl whispered, ignoring Jennifer's inquiry.

"Did something happen to your kitty? Is that what's wrong?" Jennifer asked, wishing the child would speak reasonably without repeating herself.

But before the child could respond, Jennifer was startled by a raspy voice from behind. "What have you done to my child?"

Jennifer turned to stare into the aged and sun-worn face of an elderly woman. Her hair sprawled out in unruly tangles about her head. Her eyes peered at Jennifer above a snarling face. Her thinning lips were replaced with a line of lipstick on her skin. Her teeth were raven black, charred with stain and decay. Her breath was foul from the rot, and the stench made Jennifer's stomach churn with queasy acid.

"I didn't do anything. She had an accident and …" Jennifer stammered, shifting her weight back on her heels.

"There's no accident here, Lass," the woman snapped. "The child is afraid of the crystal ball you carry. She can see the bleak future it foretells. You need to get rid of it."

"You misunderstand. It isn't a crystal ball. It is for a display."

"I said, get rid of it!" The old hag barked in a slurred, drunken tongue.

"But I can't, it is part of a display that I'm doing." Jennifer motioned in the direction of the glass case from the house wares department.

"I don't care what it's for, you little bitch. I said get rid of it!" The old woman snapped.

Jennifer tried to speak, but no words could escape her throat. Her mouth was cotton, and her lungs heaved as though they were starved for oxygen. She clutched the glass sphere, staring at the old woman in amazement.

"Did you think you could get off that easy? Get through this while blaming everyone else without looking at your own faults? The old woman's face became flush with anger as she spoke the words. In the distance, a low howling erupted like a harsh wind through an icy canyon. The woman paused. Her face waned with fear and then a smirk stretched across her putrid lips. "Better run now, Lass. The Incubus is coming."

"I don't understand." Jennifer began stepping back slowly away from the strange woman. Her backward retreat was hindered before she could get herself clear of the old woman's hideous smile. She pressed her back against a display case or clothing rack; her wobbly knees thankful for the support. Whatever she had pressed herself against was not as solid as she would like. It had a give to its structure. In fact, it seemed to rise and fall like the expansion and contraction of lungs. Startled, she spun to see another intruder staring into her eyes. The man's features were difficult to distinguish in the dark of the store. His face bore fewer visages than the mannequins, but his raspy voice came clear to her. "Get rid of it!" He grunted in conformity with the old woman's demand.

Jennifer tried to scream, but the air that had filled her lungs could only escape in a slow and hollow wheeze. Her eyes frantically searched for any possible route of retreat. She did not know who these people were or how they managed access to her store in the middle of the night, but she knew she had to get out as quickly as possible. She walked swiftly toward an open aisle, but before she arrived in the clear her path was blocked by several more people. Her eyes were fixed solely on the movements of their chests and hips, unable to bring herself to look up at their faces – terrified of what she may or may not see. She tried to move to the left of the crowd, but they stepped in unison with her, as though they were already aware of her chosen course.

"Get rid of that thing!" The strangers spoke the words in a chorus as they pressed forward closing off any escape that Jennifer had left. She burst through the crowd and began running for the front door. Her legs felt heavy and arduous to move - her pace slowing as her feet could no longer operate under their own weight. She could hear the footsteps from behind. Her pursuers were closing in. She could feel their warm breath brush against the nape of her neck.

The front door now appeared in Jennifer's sight. She shifted the sphere into her left arm so that her right hand could reach the door's handle. She grabbed the handle and pulled, but instead of the door coming back at her, she was pulled forward into the door. It was locked. She turned to face the crowd as they descended upon her. The glass of the door, cooled by the midnight air seeped through her blouse to bite at her skin. Her eyes deduced the escape route and her legs instinctively carried her in that direction.

She quickly darted to the left and down the cosmetics' aisle. The echo from the clacking of her heels and the thumping of her heart was almost deafening now. She could no longer hear the approaching footsteps, but she did not fancy the idea of slowing her pace. She pushed forward, exiting the cosmetics' aisle and running back into the women's clothing section where the confrontation had first ensued.

She was nearing the main aisle once again when the little girl appeared in front of her, allowing Jennifer almost no time to stop her forward momentum. The girl stood holding her dead kitten in outstretched arms to Jennifer, who lurched backward, struggling to keep her balance and shaking her head in disbelief.

"This can't be happening," Jennifer cried as she gasped for breath.

The crowd now began to surround her once again. Their faces no bore distinction. Their eyes were as void as corpses as they collapsed around her. There was no place left to run. She was trapped.

"This can't be happening," Jennifer repeated. "It doesn't make any sense."

Jennifer felt a hand placed gently on her right shoulder. For a moment she was startled, but this touch was unthreatening. She turned to see a handsome faced man with jet-black hair. His smooth skin shone with a bronze complexion, and thick eyebrows that accented soft, deep brown eyes. He stared down at Jennifer with a warm smile on his face, like a visit from a long forgotten friend. His presence cast a subtle glow around himself and Jennifer, as they gazed into each other's eyes.

The terror that had gripped Jennifer so tightly had now subsided into a feeling of immunity. She felt a genuine love in his presence, and a familiarity in his eyes. She remained silent for a brief period, wrapped in the cloak of his gaze.

"This doesn't make any sense," she managed to speak through a lump in her throat that caught the projection of her voice, leaving it nothing more than a whisper.

"Of course it doesn't make any sense to you." His hand gently brushed back the hair from Jennifer's face. "You are dreaming, Jennifer."

"How do you know my name?"

He answered her question with a broadening of his smile as he placed his hand against her cheek. "It is time to wake up now."

Reality

Hope in reality is the worst of all evils because it prolongs the torments of man.

-Friedrich Nietzsche

Reality is a sliding door.

-Ralph Waldo Emerson

Chapter 1

'Jerked to Jesus', these words were used in the late eighteen hundreds to theatrically describe the hanging of a felon on the gallows. Beyond a Governor's stay of execution, this was the most the condemned could hope for - a sudden jerk of the rope as the body fell, resulting in a broken neck. If the neck did not break, one was destined to endure a slow and brutal strangulation.

Yet even still, hanging somehow seemed accessible to Rachel. A rope and a chair was all that was needed. Death would come quick, provided she carried out her plan flawlessly. Though, Rachel's life had been far from flawless. For twenty years she had suffered at the hands of Adam Simmons, the man who had once vowed to love her now relentlessly abused her.

Out of a dark and helpless existence there was a light; a pinhole of illumination within a shroud of pain - a chance to be free from the anger and brutality of the man who controlled her every move.

A flash of her husband's fist, pure white knuckles, and the strong smell of alcohol wormed its way into her thoughts. She brushed it aside and tried to relax, focusing on the surrounding aromas of twenty scented candles which she had placed around the interior of the garage to induce positive memories; the rich confection of French vanilla, the floral rejuvenation of lilac, the quietude of chamomile.

She curled her bare toes around the edge of the chair, playfully testing their grip. Soon, all would be well when she was at last in the arms of the one who truly loved and appreciated her. All she had to do was cut herself free from her husband - release the marionette from the autocratic puppeteer. The thought of hanging the marionette to free her, brought about ironic amusement. *A string to cut the strings.*

Timothy Cole

She shifted her weight upon the balls of her feet, pushing herself higher, and then rested back on her heels. The next time would be the one. Her knees bent and her body weight shifted over her hips. Something was wrong. She felt helplessly off balance. Her weight was too far forward. The chair eased out from under her, sliding on the smooth concrete as her toes struggled to maintain their grip. Her body weight settled down slowly. *This was not right. There should have been more force.* She had missed her chance to jump. She struggled to regain her footing on the chair, but only managed to tip it over. She clawed at the chords of the rope in desperation. The sudden jerking snap of the rope had never come - instead an irritation about her neck increased to a sharp pain. Her lungs burned as she desperately tried to inhale despite her mind's intentions. This was going to take awhile.

She released a groan, as did the support beam as the coarse rope imposed its will. She began kicking her feet wildly; perhaps something would give; not because of a change of heart, but to allow herself another attempt - a chance to do things properly. But both the beam and the rope held strong.

As her muscles began to ache for oxygen, her thrashing subsided. She knew there was nothing she could do now, except wait. Slowly her consciousness faded from her. And when she heard the voice of the angel, it was as though a sigh had been shaped into words.

Chapter 2

"It's time to wake up now," the voice started out faint but grew in its intensity.

Jennifer regained complete cognizance from her slumber, and she became instantly aware of a beautiful pair of azure blue eyes gleaming down at her. Those eyes were set in a round face with handsome boyish features, outlined by curls of chestnut brown hair. Jennifer's mood was always lighter whenever she awoke to the face of the person that she loved so much it seemed nearly heartbreaking. Her five-year-old son, Arlen, had the face of a cherub and the spirit of a sprite.

Arlen was the wondrous product of six long years of elevated hopes and repeated disparagement. Jennifer and her husband, Sean, attempted to conceive for four years, delving through countless fertility books. They tried BBT charts to track Jennifer's Basal Body Temperature in order to determine her exact ovulation schedule. They purchased Ovukit from the Med Swift Pharmacy. Ovukit tested Jennifer's urine for the LH or luteinizing hormone surge to predict her ovulation. Each time a blue dot appeared Sean had to drop anything he was doing and attend his wife's bed. To this day, Sean had fond memories of that time.

By the fourth year desperation set in. Jennifer even attempted standing on her head following intercourse. A suggestion provided to her by an old friend of Sean's mother. Then the couple decided to try their luck with a fertility clinic. The doctors' concerns about Jennifer's ability to carry the baby full term ranged from anemia to a heart murmur she displayed from a birth defect. Jennifer was born with two holes in her heart, which caused a back flow of blood. The back flow resulted in low oxygen levels giving her skin a slight blue appearance: a condition commonly known as "Blue

Baby." Jennifer was to undergo surgery to repair her heart after she turned thirteen; however, the holes had healed before the surgery was needed.

The clinic attempted In Vitro Fertilization and Embryo Transfer despite her history of health problems, but all attempts failed. When all hope seemed lost their family physician, Dr. Conahan, told Jennifer about something he called Hypothalamic Pituitary Dysfunction. He explained that the body reacts to stress with surges in respiration, blood pressure, and heart rate. The same gland that produces the hormones that control ovulation also triggers stress reactions. Jennifer had a history of anxiety related stress.

Dr. Conahan told her of a study done at the Infertility Program at Harvard's Deaconess Hospital in Boston in which infertile women attended stress management classes. Some had to overcome depression, while others battled with exhaustion or aggression. The program produced pregnancies in one-third of the participants within six months. The odds seemed low, but Jennifer signed onto his idea. With Dr. Conahan's guidance, she conceived within eight months of attending classes on stress management.

She could remember the nine long months anxiously carrying the child until the final glory of his birth, as if it happened yesterday. And now, five years removed from their quest, the gift of the journey was growing more precious to her with each passing year. Arlen became the ribbon of love that bonded her and Sean together in a marriage made of love, faith, and child. She told Sean that God gave her two holes in her heart and then filled them with her husband and son.

Jennifer gazed into Arlen's face and gave him her best look of total bewilderment. "Who are you and what are you doing in my bedroom?"

"Mom, it's me, Arlen," the child replied with a giggle. "I'm your son, silly."

"Arlen," Jennifer said thoughtfully. "I don't know anyone named Arlen."

"Mom, me and Dad cooked breakfast," the little child pleaded.

"You can't be my child; my child would know proper grammar."

"Dad and I. Dad and I. Now come on, get up." Arlen commanded as he grabbed Jennifer's hand and pulled. His soft little hands pressing against her skin was a touch of solace to her.

"Tell Daddy I will be downstairs in a minute."

Jennifer sat up in bed as Arlen ran from the room and bounded down the staircase. Her lips momentarily curled into a frown as she remembered that her job awaited her. She had received a college degree in interior design and was now working near Philadelphia for an upscale department store. A job that now seemed dull and mundane. Her father had been right; she chose the wrong major. He never realized the decision was a sacrifice that Jennifer made for him.

She breathed in deeply. An aromatic wind swell of freshly brewed coffee and cinnamon French toast flooded her nostrils. Sean was a master in the art of breakfast. The morning sun sliced through the slightly parted, sheer burgundy drapes. She glanced outside at the layer of frost that had blanketed the lawn. Autumn had arrived in the town of Honey Brook and winter was following swiftly.

Honey Brook was located in Chester County, in eastern Pennsylvania. The town rested atop fields of coal and slate buried beneath the earth, surrounded by rolling plains and low mountains. Forty miles to the south, the winding Susquehanna River, the artery of the state, pumped its contents into the Chesapeake Bay. Approximately forty miles to the north, the Blue Ridge Mountains etched their way up from Maryland and through the central part of Pennsylvania. The distant mountain range displayed a soft bluish green hue, while the nearby hills changed from a lush green in the spring and summer to brilliant shades of gold and reds in autumn, as the maple and oak leaves turned colors before dropping from their trees. Pennsylvania was the perfect location to enjoy all that autumn had to offer. And it was at this time, while attending junior high school, that Jennifer Gray met a handsome Irish boy named Sean Bergin. Sean was the brother of her best friend Arlene. Sean and Arlene, the two youngest of four Bergin children, lived with their grandparents after being orphaned by the death of their mother. But it was another tragedy in Sean's life that drew Jennifer to him romantically.

Jennifer sat on her bed quietly structuring her day, creating small goals and gaining confidence as she reassured herself that she was in control of her life. Jennifer was one of millions of people suffering from panic disorder. In Jennifer's case, any deviance from her structured routine left her feeling helplessly vulnerable to any and all of the dangers the world possessed; both real and imagined. Her only hope of curtailing the anxiety attacks was to maintain control of her life through scheduled behaviors and actions. Even a misplaced bottle of body wash or shampoo could set off a day long battle against her attacks. It only took one occasion for Arlen to learn - never touch Mommy's soap.

She drew in a deep breath and gathered her composure as she ran her hands through her long waves of reddish-brown hair, shaking the strands free of each other. She released a sigh, slouching on the edge of the bed; she could feel the morning gravity as it attempted to pull her back under the covers. However, seeking additional sleep would be futile with Arlen on the prowl.

She exited the bedroom out into the hallway and retrieved a towel from a linen closet on her right. The entrance to the bathroom was directly across the hall.

She brushed her teeth, pausing in the mirror to pull back her deep red locks from her neck and shoulders to examine her bare skin. The midnight blue nightgown she wore gave her creamy complexion a subtle glow. She was thirty-four-years-old, but showed little signs of aging. Her five-foot two inch frame was still firm from her four-day workout regimen. She managed to keep her weight stable at 120 pounds; her full hips accented any flowing dress or gown she wore. The beauty of her face came from no distinct features, only a youthful softness which was perpetuated by the presence of sparse freckles that extended downward to her breasts.

She was retrieving her robe from a plastic hook on the door when her eyes were captured by the copper colored solid glass sphere from her dream. The sight of the sphere resting on a towel on the edge of the sink reminded her of the strange dream from which Arlen had awoken her. She was to use the decorative piece for a display of women's leather gloves. The sphere was the size of a baseball, but it weighed nearly three pounds. Air bubbles of assorted sizes were suspended in position within the mold and highlighted by reflected light from above and given dimensions from shadows below. They hung like planets in a frozen galaxy, forever trapped in the compression of the transparent copper glass.

Arlen had become enamored by the sphere the previous night as he watched Jennifer pack a box of antiquities and assorted items for the display she was to complete the following day. Arlen fancied the sphere to be a giant marble. He had pleaded with his mother to keep it. For a short while, she was able to stand her ground, rebuking the precious child's request by warning him of the sphere's unexpected weightiness. She attempted to avert his interest with one of his baseballs. But it was difficult to turn the heart of a stubborn Irishman once he chose his path. Especially considering this Irishman was three and a half feet tall and as adorable as a puppy in a field of clover. In the end, they reached a truce. Arlen would maintain possession of the sphere for the evening and return it to his mother in the morning.

Jennifer surmised that Arlen had left it on the bathroom sink after brushing his teeth for bed the previous evening. She wondered if Arlen's attachment to the sphere induced her department store dream. She made a mental note to retrieve the paperweight before she left for work as she put on her long cotton robe, tied the sash, and walked from the bathroom. Unaware that like a fortuneteller's crystal ball, the same sphere would later reveal a haunting truth in her life.

Chapter 3

Jennifer descended the staircase, sliding her hand along the wall until it opened up to a balustrade and a panoramic view of the dining room. She ran her fingertips along the deep rich mahogany finish of the balustrade rail.

Sean had renovated the home using as much of the existing nineteenth century interior as possible. The archways still displayed the original Australian red mahogany trim, adorned with rosettes. The plaster walls rose to meet a ceiling which hung ten feet above the hardwood floor of the dining room. Jennifer recognized the potential of the house when the couple viewed it seven years ago, and Sean was able to elicit the rustic charm of the original decor. The spirit of the homestead, warm and benevolent, connected with Jennifer. It was the first time in her life that a house truly felt like home. Jennifer was subsequently diligent in the home's upkeep, much to the chagrin of the male occupants. Obsessive cleanliness was an inherited trait that Jennifer tried to curtail. The brutality of desired perfection haunted her to this day. She had a skeleton closet full of memories of a woman's twisted obsession that left her broken and frightened as a child.

Sean removed a frying pan, with three pieces of French toast, from the electric range. When he awoke, Sean had slipped into some comfortable sweat pants and his favorite grey sweatshirt, embroidered with the words Penn State in dark blue letters. His bare feet against the laminate floor foretold the drop in the temperature outside.

He placed one piece of the toast on each of the three plates that rested on the table and put the pan into the sink. He opened a utility drawer, which nearly released from its glide track to spill the contents. It reminded him for the hundredth time to repair the drawer's catch. The contents slide to the front as it lurched forward. Balancing the drawer, he retrieved a knife from inside before banking left then right to push the drawer shut. He then sliced a grapefruit in half and placed each on saucers, putting them at two of the place settings.

He turned to see Jennifer enter the kitchen and quickly wrapped his strong arms around her, gazing lovingly into her face. Eight years of marriage could not erase his awe for Jennifer's beauty. His pulse still increased and his stomach still fluttered each time he held her. He delighted in the feeling as she rested her head against his chest, and her hands gripped his broad shoulders.

Sean had only admired Jennifer passively from a distance until an untimely event in Sean's life engendered their union.

He had just completed his bachelor's degree for business and landscaping when his grandfather, Thomas Bergin, died of complications brought on by black lung disease. Thomas Bergin was a man Sean deeply loved and respected. He enjoyed listening to the full-blooded Irishman reminiscing of his life as a miner in Honey Brook's coal region. Thomas' speeches would begin in his Irish brogue, thick tongued, but decipherable. As the heat of the conversation wore on, he would slip into a Gaelic dialect and was scarce to notice. Thomas told Sean stories about his own grandfather, the late John T. Bergin, who was allegedly a member of the now infamous Irish clan known as the Molly Maguires, but managed to escape prosecution when the secret society was brought down by the world's original private-eyes of the Pinkerton Agency. The Molly Maguires were a band of immigrant workers who terrorized the mine owners and their supervisors in the late 1800s. The Irish had come to America seeking refuge from the brutality they had suffered at the hands of the Welsh in Ireland, only to find themselves slaving for little pay amidst harsh conditions in mines that were managed by Welsh immigrants. A small group of the men banded together to form a terrorist group, using guns and dynamite to intimidate the mine owners into improving their working and living conditions.

Sean was devastated by the loss of his grandfather, yet his grieving found solace in Jennifer's nurturing arms on the night of the funeral. She held him gently and listened as he described the man he loved so much.

Timothy Cole

The night of caring friendship transformed into a weekend of romance and passion. A passion for a woman that still burned strong in his heart.

Sean had a ruggedly handsome face with prominent features, most notably a defined square jaw. His cheeks displayed dimples even when he didn't wear a smile. His skin bore a slightly bronzed complexion from exposure to the sun in his landscaping business. His hair curled in waves of deep auburn, and his bright emerald eyes glowed with fiery Celtic passion.

"Morning Lass, breakfast is served," Sean said.

"I like waking up to this. What's the occasion?" She slid from his arms and sat in her chair.

"I thought we would be kind and feed you before we sent you off to earn our money," Sean said, taking a seat. A flame danced atop a red tapered candle that was pressed inside a small glass holder and placed at the table's center. The queer sight of its presence at breakfast caught Jennifer's eye. She glanced to her right, realizing Arlen was smiling at her. "Did you light a candle just for me?"

The child responded with a nod of his head.

"That was very thoughtful," Jennifer related. "Thank you. My, you guys really went out of your way for me this morning."

She took her napkin from the table and spread it across her lap. "You would not believe the strange dream I had last night. I must be having a lot of underlying anxiety from this job lately."

Sean's shoulders shook with a sudden chuckle, "If you keep analyzing everything, I'm going to take back your book on Sigmund Freud. You know, it seems like you have bizarre dreams every night. I never dream. Or at least I don't remember them."

"Oh, I don't mind the dreams - they're fun," she replied. "And for your information, I am not reading my Freud book right now."

"So, what is it now?"

"The Tao of Pooh."

"The Tao of who?"

"The Tao of Pooh."

"Do you mean Winnie the Pooh?"

Jennifer nodded.

"Are you serious?" He exclaimed. "Does Winnie kung fu the shit out of Christopher Robin after he meditates?"

"Very funny," Jennifer sighed. "And watch your language around Arlen." Sean rolled his eyes. "Lass, this Christmas I'm going to buy you a crocheting kit. You need a hands-on hobby; give your brain a rest."

"Oh, I see. And what do I get for my birthday, a rocking chair?" Her eyes opened wide in a playful glare.

"There, you see? You even twisted crocheting into me suggesting that you're old."

"I like Pooh and Freud. And if you keep it up, I will start reading Dr. Laura Schlessinger's book again. Remember how strict I was during that ordeal."

"What am I going to do with you, woman? Ya know; I've never been able to cope with the fact that you learned to meditate from a book on Celtic shamanism."

"At least that brought me in line with your Irish heritage."

"So basically you practice psychology through philosophical mysticism?" He posed.

"I think we should analyze the fact that your favorite color is gray," she narrowed her eyes. "Why do you suppose that is? Emergent brooding from some deep seeded repressed memory, perhaps?"

"What's the matter with gray?" He retorted. "I like gray."

"You must get really depressed when the sun shines."

Sean decided to let the comment pass uncontested. "Do you think you could escape from work a little early today?"

"I suppose I could be finished by three o'clock. Why? Did you want to meet in the city for dinner tonight?"

"I thought Arlen could skip afternoon kindergarten and come with me into the city after his dentist appointment this morning," Sean said, pausing to spoon some grapefruit into his mouth.

"Wow! Can I, Mom?" Arlen became immediately animated at the thought.

"I suppose it couldn't hurt for just one day. But you're back to school tomorrow with no complaints," Jennifer ordered.

"Okay, I promise. Thanks, Mommy. Thanks, Daddy."

"It looks like I'm going to have quite a lot of down time over the next couple weeks," Sean spoke over the rim of his coffee cup, "unless I get lucky with some early snow, so I can make extra money by plowing. I don't have many landscaping jobs left this year. But it will be great to finally get some quality time with Arlen. I worked so much this summer I was afraid the two of you might forget what I look like."

"Mommy forgot what I looked like this morning," Arlen interjected.

"I have an idea." Sean lifted his head from the coffee. "Why don't you stay home with us today?"

"Baby, I have to finish Christmas prep. I have two other large displays I have to start by the end of the week. Besides, it's good that you get to spend some time alone with him."

"Okay, but we will meet you for dinner." Sean paused for a sip of coffee. "By the way, do you have forty dollars? I need a case of beer for later on tonight."

"Sean, I thought we agreed you'd drink only on the weekends," Jennifer said in a soft, yet persuasive voice.

"Chill! I won't overdo it. I have some time off; I just want to relax a little."

"Daddy, you are not supposed to drink." Arlen narrowed his eyes. "It's not good for you."

"Stooge," Sean warned, "I told you before, if it's above your head …"

Arlen joined in finishing the phrase, "it's above your concern."

"There's money in my purse," Jennifer said, shaking her head and casting a glance toward Arlen. She had conceded in words, but in her heart she agreed only to end the conversation for the sake of her son.

Arlen finished his French toast and pushed his plate aside. "Can I go play now?" He sprang to his feet before receiving a reply, and began to dart for the living room.

"Excuse me," Jennifer spat. "Take your dish to the sink and rinse it off."

"But Mommy, I need to play my *Star Wars* video game," he whined.

"But Mommy!" Jennifer mocked. "I will remove your butt if you don't do as I say."

"Mommy," Arlen pleaded.

"Arlen, that's enough. Taking five seconds out of your day to rinse a dish won't stop your world from turning."

"Yeah, but Darth Maul could take over the world." Arlen rushed his plate over to the sink, stepped up onto the stool his Dad had made him and allowed a quick flow of tap water to rinse the center of the plate before placing it in the dishwasher.

"I swear, child, your brain will cease to operate if you keep playing those video games all the time." Jennifer yelled after him as he darted from the kitchen.

She finished the final bites of her breakfast and carried her own dishes to the sink to rinse them. She returned to the table and stood in front of Sean, who was still seated. She untied her robe and pulled his head into her bosom. "I guess I will go upstairs and remove my clothes," she uttered with a passing sigh of apathy.

"Slowly I trust," Sean breathed, "with your hips swaying ever so gently."

"Oh my, are you a little horny today?"

"I fed you breakfast this morning and tonight I'll be your midnight snack," he said, clutching the collar of her robe, pulling her head lower to meet his. He kissed her soft full lips then eased back into his seat with a satisfied smile.

Jennifer returned the smile, enjoying the way his eyes roamed over her as though their honeymoon had never ended. Sean was always respectful and attentive to her, and the strength of his passion could still make her legs delightfully weak. She straightened herself but remained fixed in their passionate gaze. "I don't know if you'll survive," she uttered coyly, "I have a ravenous appetite."

"Well, if I'm not enough," Sean pivoted his head and waved his hand, "I could always get the woman next door for you."

Jennifer leaned down and placed her hands gently under his chin. "You are the typical male, aren't you? Contrary to your belief not all women have lesbian tendencies. You know, I can remember what a romantic gentleman you were when we first started dating."

"I'm still romantic, in a perverted sort of way."

"And what would Father Thomas think of your twisted fantasy?"

"He already knows; I've gone to confession."

"Oh really, and when was the last time you went? Was it last summer when the church lost its electrical power for half the day when lightning struck the transformer?"

"Yes, I confess that was I."

Jennifer chuckled and kissed his lips, "I love you; even though you are a little pervert. I have to go upstairs and get showered now. Tonight you can have me, but only me."

"That is always enough. You know that." The fire in Sean's green eyes cooled, "God, I love you. Maybe tonight, we should start trying for another child. Arlen needs a playmate."

"Sean," her face slackened in defeat.

"I'm just saying we try. No pressure. No clinics. Arlen wants a baby brother."

"How do you know we would have a boy? What's wrong with another Jennifer in the house? I could use a little back up."

"Wow. There's a thought. I don't know if I could survive another you."

"Sounds like fear."

"I don't care if it is a boy or a girl. I just think it's time."

"You just want an excuse to have sex more often."

Sean considered the thought. "No, but that's an added bonus. So let's start with a romp in the shower and see…"

"Daddy," Arlen shouted from inside the family room. "The TV's not working right!"

"I believe that was your son bellowing," Jennifer said under the press of one final kiss, and then released him from her embrace. She turned from him to exit the kitchen as she uttered fair warning over her shoulder, "Keep it warm, you will need it for tonight."

Sean watched her sway as she exited the kitchen. His hands could almost feel the softness of her bare skin, as he longed for what the night would bring him. His thoughts were disturbed as Arlen called for him once again from the family room.

"Yes, child, I am coming." Sean rose to his feet, tucking the image of Jennifer's nude body away for the moment.

Chapter 4

Arlen raced up the staircase and paused outside the bathroom door. He could hear the water from the showerhead as the spray collided against tile. He still had time. His mom would have to agree to play their story telling game with him before she left for work. He simply would not accept "no" for an answer.

He ran into his bedroom and pulled the comforter up to his chin tucking himself into his bed. He waited until he heard her in the adjacent bedroom getting dressed. "Mommy," he called in a faint voice, "come into my bedroom when you're done."

His mom walked into his room inserting her earring. "Yes, my little one." She said pausing as her eyes surveyed the situation. "Why are you back in bed?"

"I want to play Copper Dragons." He said with a sly smile.

"Honey, that's our bedtime game." She stared into his eyes and recognized how much he missed her. "I know you don't like Mommy working, but I have to do this. I wish I could spend all of my time with you, but mommies also have to work."

"I guess, but I still miss you a lot while you're gone." He reached up, wrapping his arms around her neck and held her in a tight embrace. He closed his eyes and drew in deep breaths of the fragrance he had come to know as Mommy.

"I miss you too. But you and Daddy are coming into the city today. We'll go to a nice restaurant and have dinner. Maybe Daddy will take us to the museum. Would you like that?"

"That would be great!" The excitement came to Arlen in a rush like the feeling he got while dropping from the top of a roller coaster. He loved

Timothy Cole

exploring the exhibits at the museum. "Can I see the dinosaur bones?" He quickly added.

"You can see anything you want, but now Mommy has to get to work."

She bent down to kiss his cheek, but he blocked her by placing his hand over her lips. "Mommy, can we please play just one game!" He knew his mother could not resist his charm.

"Okay, just one. But then Mommy has to go to work."

Arlen reached over and grabbed three pennies that rested in their own private space on the corner of his nightstand. He began shaking the pennies with his two pudgy little fists cupped together. He slapped the pennies quickly on the table with both his palms down, covering them.

"Fair maiden," he recited, addressing his mom. "I met a copper dragon on a stony road in Wales. If you can tell me what he looked like, I will tell you all his tales."

Arlen's mom smiled and leaned down toward his ruddy little face. "Let me see. Your copper dragon has two heads and only one tail." She responded clutching her lower lip between her teeth.

Arlen slowly peaked under his hands and then threw them both in the air displaying the coins. Two of the coins lay heads up and one was tails up. "You guessed right," he said, disappointedly.

"Okay brave sir knight; you owe me one tale."

"Okay, let me think. Once upon a time the two heads of the dragon were... eating breakfast," Arlen said with a giggle.

"I pray you, sir, continue." She said with a laugh, as she sat down next to Arlen on the bed.

"The dragons had eaten all their food, but their milk got spilt before they could drink it. So one head said to the other head, '*You spilled the milk you stupid dragon.*" Arlen tried his best to create a deep dragon voice.

"And the other head said, '*I didn't spill the milk you did. And now I have nothing more to drink!*' And he growled through his sharp teeth."

"That's scary," She uttered. "So what happened to the dragon?"

"They got so mad that they never spoke to each other again."

"Over a glass of spilled milk?" She questioned astounded.

"Those dragon heads were really mad and really thirsty."

"He sure was a silly copper dragon, wasn't he?"

"Yeah."

"Okay, now it's my turn brave sir knight. I met a copper dragon on a stony road in Wales." His mom spoke as she shook the pennies in her

16

hands, and then slapped them down on the night stand. "If you can tell me what he looked like, I will tell you all his tales."

"Uh, let me think," Arlen said, pausing to raise a finger to his chin. "Your copper dragon has three heads and no tails."

"Are you sure you want to guess that?" She mockingly warned him.

"Yes, fair maiden, I am quite certain," Arlen said firmly, attempting to sound older than he was.

"If you guess three heads and you're wrong, you automatically lose."

"But if I guess three heads, and I'm right, then I automatically win," Arlen rebutted.

She lifted her hands slightly so that only she could peek at the coins. "Oh boy, now you've done it."

"Come on Mom, let me see."

She revealed the three coins with each of them facing heads up.

"Yeah, I won!" Arlen gloated.

"Yes, you did, brave sir knight." She touched the tip of her index finger on his tiny nose. "Listen. Mommy really has to get going. We'll play again tonight at your real bedtime. Now, I want you to get out of that bed and have a good day with Daddy. But I want you to behave yourself."

"Yes ma'am," he responded.

Arlen paused, searching for any subject that would prolong his mother's stay. She was stepping toward the door when he uttered the first thing that came into his mind.

"You like dragons, don't you Mommy?"

"Yes," she gave him a self-effacing smile, knowing the intention of the question. "Dragons are like a symbol of everything we don't understand. We love them and fear them, all at the same time."

"You mean like God?"

She decided upon a diplomatic answer. "Some people may feel that way."

"Mommy, did Jesus know He was going to die?"

"Arlen. Honey. Why would you ask a question like that?"

"I don't know," he answered quietly, "I'm just curious."

Jennifer sat down on the edge of his bed and released a deep breath, "Yes, He did."

"How did He know?" He asked.

"God told Him."

"Do you think He was scared?"

"Honey, is everything alright?" Jennifer's brow creased.

Arlen shrugged, "I just wanna know."

"Jesus was very brave," she continued. "If He was afraid, He didn't show it. He knew He had to be crucified so that we would be forgiven for our sins. He did it because He loved us so much. I suppose His love helped to keep Him strong and brave."

"Does He ever speak to us?"

"He speaks to us through our faith. And sometimes God will send a messenger angel."

"You tell me that I'm an angel," Arlen implied.

"You are to me," Jennifer replied. "But the angels I'm talking about are the ones that the Bible calls a seraph."

"How do you know when a sheriff comes to visit you?"

Jennifer chuckled, "It's called a seraph, Honey," she said, pronouncing the word slowly. "Your faith will tell you it's a seraph." She searched Arlen's tiny face for any sign that would reveal the intent of his questions. "Are you sure that you're okay Pumpkin?"

"I'm okay Mommy," he said, "I'm curious. I'm not scared."

"Well, that's good because you have no reason to be scared."

"I know," Arlen spoke with a smile that spread across his face and glistened in his eyes.

"Are you sure nothing's wrong?" She questioned.

"Positive."

She leaned forward and kissed him gently on the cheek. "You promise?"

"I promise."

"Okay, don't forget to get a bath and wash those ears, or do you like walking around with a potato farm in your head?"

"I'm not growing potatoes!" He argued, covering his ears with his hands.

"Okay, but if you're not going to clean those ears out, you may want to talk to Daddy about getting some harvesting equipment, just in case there's another potato famine." She placed a hand on Arlen's head and tossed his hair; her touch was like the kiss of an angel to him.

Jennifer exited her home, stepping out into the sun, which was trying to take the chill out of the cool autumn air. The morning breakfast with Sean and Arlen should have set a pleasant tone for the day; however, anxiety knotted her stomach. She rationalized the feeling as being guilt for not staying home with Arlen. But her attendance record at work was less than perfect, so staying home was out of the question.

The sun's rays reflected from the hood of her burgundy Taurus sedan, helping to warm her face. She reassured herself as she steered the car out into the street. *Today is just another normal day in reality. There's nothing to worry about.*

Chapter 5

Father Thomas Morelli had been startled from a deep slumber by the ring of the telephone. He was still shaking free from the cobwebs of sleep when he placed the receiver to his ear and uttered a raspy hello. He had recognized the person on the other end as a member of his parish. The female voice quivered and her sentences were broken with passing sobs. Following a brief five minute conversation she apologized for calling so early, and then, despite his objections, abruptly ended the call.

Now, thirty minutes later, he found himself stepping onto the weather worn porch of the Simmons' house. The home was painted gray and dulled by years of neglect. He opened a tattered screen door that nearly released from its hinges into his hand as he rapped lightly on the front door.

Father Thomas had served Saint Anthony's parish for over six years. He resided over ceremonies of joy, conviction, repentance and sorrow. It seemed each joyous time for one family was paralleled by tragedy in another. He prayed for the best, but prepared for the worst. Priesthood brought a constant swirl of emotions that were both fulfilling and exhausting. He possessed the passion for his faith and the compassion to help those in need. Wearing the collar had allowed him to pursue both. He hoped that today he could help Mrs. Simmons. He had first been drawn to her plight from the consistent pattern of bruising and injuries. On several occasions, he attempted to persuade her to open up - but to no avail. It was when he attended her hospital bedside following a particularly brutal battering that he knew his suspicions were correct. However, he had never been able to coerce her into telling him the truth about the abuse. Nor would she seek help, despite him opening the doors to many agencies for her. This morning was different. She had nearly spoken the words, repeating "I won't let him..." several times before hanging up. Today, he was determined to get her into a shelter for battered women - far from the reach of Adam Simmons.

Father Thomas was relieved to see Adam's truck missing from the driveway; relieved that there would be no confrontation. Adam worked at a lumber mill outside of town, and he usually left for work before sun-up.

After a second knock brought no answer, Father Thomas tried the door. Locked. He attempted, unsuccessfully, to peer inside through the smeared windows of the living room. But he could barely make out the shapes of the furniture within. He walked down from the porch, heading toward a small garage that was attached to the side of the home. If he could enter through the garage, he could access a door which led directly into the kitchen. He gripped the handle and was relieved to feel the knob turn and the latch pull free of the frame. He opened the door cautiously and thrust his head inside to call out her name to announce his arrival. But the word never escaped his lips. Instead the scene inside the garage brought a wave of nausea and made his mouth dry instantly.

Chapter 6

Sean tiptoed into the living room to see Arlen with his nose nearly glued to the forty-six-inch television screen. Quietly dropping to his hands and knees on the carpeted floor, he crept up behind the unsuspecting child. He lowered himself flat on his stomach just behind Arlen's head. He was just about to scare his son when Arlen began verbalizing his thoughts.

"Oh no, Qui-Gon Jinn is in trouble!" The young child's speech paused, as he frantically worked the buttons of his video game controller. "You can't beat me. I'm the greatest Jedi Knight ever. Hey no, that's cheating. God! This game cheats so bad! Damn it!"

"Hey!" Sean called a warning in a firm, but calm voice.

Arlen somehow managed to lift his butt off the ground from a seated position and perform a quarter-spin in mid-air, while never releasing his grip on the game controller. He chanced a look over his shoulder at his father, as he landed. "I'm sorry, Daddy," the startled boy's face grew redder with each passing second, "but this game keeps cheating."

"Well, I understand that, but that does not give you the right to cuss, now does it?" Sean was striving to be firm, but the amusement of his son's tirade curled the one side of his mouth in an involuntary smile.

"No."

"Obi-Wan Kenobi having a little trouble these days, huh?" Sean said, allowing his son free from the hook he seemed to be on.

"Yes. I hit that guy with my light saber three times, Daddy, and he didn't die." Arlen said, attempting to plead his case of the fraudulent game.

"I suppose those games can be cruel like that. You really love this Star Wars stuff, don't you?"

"I want to be king of the planet Naboo and marry Queen Amidala." Arlen's eyes opened wide, threatening to leap from their sockets at any moment. He, at last, had an audience to speak to about his passion. "I love Queen Amidala. She's hot!"

'Arlen," Sean said with a chuckle, "you're a little too young for using 'hot' when you're describing a girl. Besides, girls have Cooties, remember?"

Sean placed his hand on Arlen's back, rubbing gently, "Listen, Daddy has to go upstairs and get a shower. When I'm finished, I'll call for you. You need to come up and get your bath."

"All right, but I can still play right now?"

"Well, yes. I didn't say you had to come up now, did I? You little stooge." Sean pressed his fingers under both sides of Arlen's ribs and began tickling him. Arlen rolled around on the ground in uncontrolled laughter, as he struggled to catch his breath in order to speak.

"Okay, okay, I'm a stooge." Arlen giggled. But as soon as Sean released his grip, he added, "But you're a fart sniffer."

Sean dove in for another tickle attack, but this time he directed his assault on Arlen's tummy. The pair rolled about on the soft shag carpet, laughing, as they both attempted to achieve the upper hand. Arlen ended the struggle by sitting proudly on top of his Dad's chest and pinning his back and shoulders to the ground.

He placed one hand on either side of his father's face and lowered his head until they were nose to nose. Arlen's eyes inadvertently crossed, as he tried to focus on the eyes of his dad. The tide of the battle had now turned, as Sean was the one who could not control his laughter.

"Listen buddy," the cross-eyed boy warned, "I am the best Jedi Knight who ever lived."

"I throw myself at the mercy of the council." Sean answered.

"Let me see what Yoda thinks." Arlen straightened up and turned his head away from Sean's sight. "What say you Master Yoda."

Arlen's Yoda voice was more comical than clever, "Release him, you shall."

Arlen turned his head back to face Sean, "Okay, I'm gonna get up now. Don't try anything funny."

"I promise." Sean said, raising a palm in the air, "No more tricks."

Arlen rolled off his dad, managing to scoop up his controller, as he rolled back into a cross-legged seated position. Sean turned back onto his stomach and kissed the child on the cheek, but he had already lost Arlen's attention to his video game. "I love you, Stooge."

"I love you, too." Arlen muttered as he struggled to concentrate on the action unfolding on his television screen.

Sean rose to his feet and headed for the staircase knowing the battle would continue later, or as soon as the child lost interest in the video game.

Jennifer was ten minutes into her drive and immersed in thought, when she suddenly glanced down at the fuel gage. The needle was balanced slightly above empty, and already in the red zone. Her face flushed with anger; she recalled asking Sean to fill the gas tank for her last night. The man forgot everything she placed in his brain. Football stats were no problem, but anything he deemed inconsequential was destined to die of loneliness up there. He had been extremely forgetful over the years; from birthdays and anniversaries, to misplacing the keys to the car - so she always tried to be patient. She knew his memory was a source of frustration for him, so she rarely made it an issue. Although, she often wondered how he managed to operate his own business.

If she stopped to get gas, she would devour all of the time she used as a safety net to arrive at work. She had already been late for work twice this month and a third time could mean disciplinary action. She was also concerned about jeopardizing her ability to leave with her family at three o'clock.

She conceded to finding the nearest gas station and hoped the remainder of her drive would unfold without hindrance. She steered the car off Interstate 76 via the first exit with an available convenience store.

As she entered to pay for the gasoline she would pump, she was greeted by the scent of coffee. She decided to take advantage of the opportunity and purchase a cup of their French Vanilla before reconnecting with the highway.

After pumping her gas, she eased behind the wheel and started the engine, noticing the time as it popped up on the display of her stereo. Only ten minutes had expired off her drive time, but that time could be easily lost in heavy traffic or new road construction. She rejoined the interstate and pushed the car a little faster than she would normally dare to drive. The speedometer hovered near eighty as she took control of the passing lane. She sipped her coffee and tried to relax her nerves. The aroma of the brew was better than the slight bitterness of its taste. A disingenuous smile spread across her lips as she shook her head in disgust. Her life had always carried a slight bitterness to it. She wondered why she had not come to expect it by now. She had apparently inherited her father's flare for misfortune. Even through her childhood, circumstances frequently arose at the most inopportune times to taint the positive.

She was the only child of Sue Ellen and Donald Gray, a prominent English teacher and a speech therapist, respectively. Donald was a seraphic gentle soul who cared for the happiness of others long before he considered his own. In his youth, he was an accomplished concert pianist, who could have achieved greatness until his father intervened and forced him to relinquish his dream. His father expected the soft-spoken young Donald to be more masculine, and to apply his talents to college and collegian sports. He struggled for years to ascertain his own identity until his father died when Donald was twenty-seven. Donald worked for the local school district as a speech therapist when he met Sue Ellen who was teaching high school English.

Sue Ellen was held in high regard amongst her peers until allegations of abusive behavior toward the children and a nervous breakdown left her unable to cope with her teaching duties. Jennifer and her father spent most of their time appeasing Sue Ellen during Jennifer's youth. Sue Ellen was critical and demanding, although her eyes showed a feeble weakness of defeat, as if the loss of her teaching position had drained her final ounce of dignity.

Jennifer could recall a Sunday morning when she was ten years old; Sue Ellen had been in control of her emotions that day. The family had returned home from church following a rare appearance by Sue Ellen. They had also enjoyed a wonderful breakfast at a local restaurant. Jennifer could remember how well her mother looked that day, carrying herself with her previous eloquent grace. She could remember how beautiful her mother looked in her flowered summer dress, and how she could never recall a time when her parents looked so much in love with one another.

After they arrived home, Jennifer went searching for her kitten that had been missing since the previous evening. Still wearing her peach colored cotton dress, she searched the edge of the woods near the family's home in hopes of finding the feline. The tall grass and dandelions slowly turned to underbrush and peat moss as she drudged deeper into the woods. The soil had been saturated from rain the previous two days and the moisture released the sweet aromas of the vegetation.

The trunks of the large maple and pine trees cascaded upwards to meet a powder blue sky. Their branches fanned out into brooms of green leaves and pine needles. The canopy cloaked Jennifer into a world she ruled. Guarded by tree gnomes and guided by the sparkle of pixies. Wild jasmine arose in the slight breeze that moved beneath the ceiling of branches. Rays of sunlight broke through the partitions above, shining down to project a welcoming glimmer on the ferns that were strewn about the ground. Scores of broken twigs and pinecones crunched beneath her tan leather sandals.

She had traveled nearly half a mile into the dense brush and trees when she heard the cat crying from inside a sinkhole. The kitten had been unable to claw its way up the near three feet of muddy earth to safety, so Jennifer laid flat on her stomach to rescue the tiny kitten. Jennifer wrapped him gently in the frill of her dress and carried him back to the house. She had rescued the kitten, marching out into the clearing as the heroine of the forest; eager to tell the tale of her good deed to her parents.

As Jennifer reached the edge of the front lawn, her mother exited the house with her father in tow. When Sue Ellen saw Jennifer's dress, slightly torn and heavily soiled, her eyes glazed over with fury and a haunting detachment. Don attempted to calm Sue Ellen, as she stormed across the front lawn and grasped the child by the arm. He tried to explain that it was an accident and Jennifer was not at fault, but Sue Ellen began screaming at the child as she pulled her toward the house. She could still remember the raspy voice of her mother shouting, "Look at you! You filthy little girl! Do you know what happens to filthy girls? The Incubus gets them!" As Jennifer was being drug into the house, her kitten leapt from her arms and ran beneath the front porch as Sue Ellen continued her very embarrassing public tirade.

Even now, Jennifer could still picture the look in her mother's eyes, wild and bulging hideously from their sockets, as Sue Ellen dragged her into the house. She could still hear the threatening words that screeched through the otherwise calm air on that Sunday morning. She could still see the red fury flowing through the whites of Sue Ellen's eyes.

Red that she suddenly realized was the breaking lights of the silver Mitsubishi Eclipse in front of her. In the freeze-frame of an instant Jennifer's heart sank into her stomach. Wheels locked. Tires squealed. But the distance between the vehicles continued to close.

Chapter 7

For a brief moment Father Thomas stood frozen, his mind unable to accept what he was witnessing. But soon, he was rushing into the garage in a desperate attempt to quell the situation.

A glowing slit of sunlight from the parted garage door sliced across the concrete floor and up the length of Rachel Simmons' body as it swayed eerily like a pendulum in the throes of death. Her skin had already begun to take on a bluish hue. The muscles controlling Rachel's foot, which had been twitching only seconds ago, now softened. *Perhaps there was still time to save her.* A thick rope was wrapped around her neck in a figure eight noose. The rope ran back across two support beams and had been tied off on the leg of a workbench. A kitchen chair rested only inches away from her bare feet.

"For the love of God." The words nearly caught in his tightened throat.

Rachel had suffered physical and psychological abuse at the hands of her husband until death appealed to her as the only escape. Hanging herself in front of Adam Simmons' workbench, where he spent hours rebuilding used chainsaws and drinking himself into a rage must have seemed fittingly macabre to her. The odd presence of jarred candles placed about the greasy cogs and gears had been her way of taking over what he guarded as "his space."

Father Thomas rushed past Rachel's body and worked frantically to untie the knotted rope from the leg of the workbench. The thick rope had been pulled tight by the weight it supported, and his thin fingers lacked the strength to uncoil the knot. His mind raced unable to process a quick solution. Wrapping his arms around Rachel's legs, he lifted her body, hoping to ease the stress the noose was placing on her neck. His heart throbbed in his temples as his eyes surveyed the mass of wires, beams, and lawn tools that covered the interior walls. The noose was still choking her airway; soon there would be no hope of resuscitating her.

"Dear God, help me," instinctively the words parted from his lips. "Please, help me." His plea to the divinity soon became a repeated shout of distress to anyone within the range of his voice. It was Harold Eckley who, at last, answered the call. Eckley lived across the street and was leaving for work when a shout of desperation reached him.

The large man burst into the garage. After two tours in Iraq and one in Afghanistan, he had seen enough carnage to be sickened by it, but not paralyzed with fear. Without hesitation, the former Marine grabbed a handsaw hanging from the side of the workbench and cut through the rope. Suddenly the full weight of Rachel's limp body shifted into the arms of Father Thomas, who stumbled backwards, awkwardly trying to keep his balance. He managed to press Rachel's head against his chest before his back came crashing down upon the concrete. He rolled the body off his and loosened the noose. He shouted, "Call 9-1-1," but Eckley had already burst through the kitchen door in search of a telephone.

Chapter 8

Jennifer's foot jumped instinctively on brake pedal at the sight of the glowing taillights in front of her. The squeal of the rubber tires on pavement jerked Jennifer from the depth of her thoughts. She pulled the steering wheel. The car turned to the right, avoiding the edge of the bumper on the Mitsubishi Eclipse by inches. The front tires slid to a halt on the shoulder of the highway in a spray of stones and dust.

Her stomach quivered as though the stress had set off some gastro-earthquake that extended out to her extremities to include her knees and hands. Her palms were slick with sweat as she continued a death grip on the steering wheel, gazing through the windshield at the line of cars extending out along the highway for nearly a mile. Their red brake lights all glowing as an alert to the traffic that followed them, this morning's commute had come to a halt. Jennifer placed her forehead on the top of her steering wheel and tried to catch her breath. Her coffee cup lay on the floor in front of the passenger seat, and the remaining coffee within now spilled across the gray carpet. She quickly reached down and set the cup upright. Glancing over at the Eclipse, she could see the look of disgusted astonishment on the driver's face. It was a young man behind the wheel who lacked the decency to check to see if she was alright. *Humans can be so self-centered.*

She turned her gaze back to the line of cars ahead of her. There was nothing she could do now except call and hope that her supervisor, Jonathan Schinse, was in an understanding mood. She straightened out her car and flipped the turn signal on to indicate her intentions of re-entering the roadway. She reached for her cell phone and dialed the number for Reiman-Fromme, an upscale department store, in the King of Prussia mall where she worked.

Arlen laid back into the tub, submerging his head until the edge of the water surrounded his face, and tickled the corners of his lips. Shampoo suds floated around him. He could feel his hair becoming more buoyant as it was released from the weight of the soap. His ears filled with water, muffling the sounds of the splashing. He rubbed his hands through his hair before he sat up. Reaching for his action figures on the edge of the tub, he submerged them in water. He stared at the figures with curiosity. The water magnified their images and their faces blurred under the ripples of the waterline. He pulled them out of the water and studied their appearance, before plunging them back under. The room was silent except for the intermittent synchronicity from the dripping faucet. He reached under the water and grabbed a bar of soap, lathering the hair of the Queen Amidala figure.

"Okay, Amidala hold your breath." He instructed the figure, his voice echoing in the surroundings of the bath and shower walls. The echo, extremely ominous and disturbingly isolated, gripped his stomach and twisted it like a knotted shroud. He looked up from his toy at the open bathroom door that lay far from his reach.

"Dad?" He waited, but as the seconds of silence passed a chill ran up his little spine. The absolute quiet left him disconnected and alone. A peculiar sense of seclusion suddenly overwhelmed Arlen's sensitive heart. He submerged the Amidala figure's head under the water, watching a halo of lather form around her. He wished he were tucked safely inside the arms of his mother. He lifted the action figure of the Queen up to his face. The eyes of the figurine painted blank and beautiful, stared back granting him a shawl of reverent warmth.

"I bet you're a seraph," he whispered.

Suddenly the voice of his dad, coming from the bathroom doorway, startled him, "Stooge, have you washed up yet?"

Arlen gave his dad a vacant look, "I washed my hair," he uttered.

"Well, come on Arlen, we're running out of time." Arlen's dad commented. "We have to get you to your dentist appointment; we can't be late."

"Sorry," the boy said, meagerly.

"What have you been doing all this time?" His dad snapped. His nostrils flared. His face flushed. Arlen knew this look all too well.

"I don't know," Arlen's voice quivered."I hate it when you screw around like this. Where's the soap?" His dad asked as he stepped into the bathroom. As he squatted down at the edge of the tub, his feet slipped out from under him on the wet tile. His knee crashed into the side of the tub with a bone cracking thud. His dad growled in pain, uttering something about his bad knee from between clenched teeth. Arlen watched his dad's face tighten with exasperation - those green eyes glaring wildly at him.

"How many times have I told you about getting water all over the floor?" His dad spat - his face now boiling with rage. He began looking around the room as Arlen slid back against the far edge of the tub.

Jennifer was pleasantly surprised how understanding Jon was about her dilemma. She was more relaxed as she listened to a talk radio program and kept watch for any break in the gridlock. The traffic had been creeping at a snail's pace for nearly thirty minutes, and now the reason for the delay had become painfully apparent. Jennifer could see what appeared to be a three-vehicle accident on the opposite west bound lanes approximately one hundred yards ahead. A hunter green Ford Explorer and an old maroon Chevy Nova, with a good portion of the paint chipped from the hood, were resting in the passing lane with their bumpers interlocked. The third vehicle, a gray Fiat, appeared to have flipped over the far guardrail and rested on its roof in the gravel with its front end hanging over the brim of the interstate.

Jennifer reached forward and slowly turned off her car radio as she peered across the road at the twisted metal remains and the emergency vehicles in attendance. The attention of the paramedics and firefighters seemed to be focused on the overturned Fiat. A paramedic lay flat on his stomach with his arms, head, and shoulders inside the shattered passenger's window, while two firefighters attempted to open the mangled driver-side door from the vehicle with the 'Jaws of Life.'

Shards of glass were scattered across the road, oil blending with antifreeze, the smell of exhaust, the cries of despair. Lives that were considered routine only moments earlier were now distorted into nightmares that those involved could not awaken from.

Jennifer could see two attendants working on one of the victims inside an ambulance, as she drew within twenty yards of the scene. She had shifted her eyes to the other side of the road as she drove past the Fiat when she noticed a small boy standing on the outside of the guardrail near the rear of the inverted car. She stared closely at the features feeling her heart pause as the recognition of the face took hold; standing beside the car was Arlen. Her jaw dropped open and her foot twitched to completely depress the brake to an absolute halt, until she realized she was actually staring at a teenage girl, not Arlen. The girl was made short by her crouching stance giving her a childlike appearance. The teen gazed wildly at the vehicle she had once occupied - the vehicle which now held a loved one, trapped within its wreckage.

Jennifer blinked her eyes and gazed at the person once again. Her heart threatened to explode as it thumped hard against her ribs. She had been positive that she discerned the face of her little boy. But, there was the young girl baring little resemblance to Arlen. A female paramedic arrived at the teenager's side and wrapped her in a blanket, attempting to comfort her as best she could. Jennifer heard the engine of the vehicle in front of her rev to a higher speed. She shook her head clear of the image and reluctantly increased her speed to match the flow of the eastbound traffic, questioning her own sanity. She reassured herself that Arlen was safe at home, safely spending time with Sean. Stress was playing bizarre games with her imagination. Or maybe it was the caffeine."I guess I have to lay off the French Vanilla coffee. Evidentially, it makes me hallucinate."

The sound of her own voice helped to calm the racing of her heart. She pushed the car forward, and locked in the cruise control at the appropriate speed limit. Seeing the site of the accident reminded her of the dangers of aggressive driving. The ability to arrive for work on time was important, but not quite as paramount as arriving at all. She turned the radio on once again and switched the tuner from AM to FM. The sound of Tom Petty vibrated from her speakers and soon she was adding her voice to the chorus of 'Running Down a Dream.' She considered telling Sean her story of mistaking the young girl for Arlen, but rescinded the idea. He maintained enough ammunition against her in his warped sense of humor. Telling him would only give him another reason to mock her.

Chapter 9

Junior climbed from his black BMW and schlepped across the street to the Bergin house. His day was starting early; too early for his liking since he preferred to sleep at least until noon. But his options slimmed as his father's request had quickly become a demand. He could never understand the older generations. *Why was everything driven by some dire sense of urgency?*

Upon first introduction, Domenic Marconi Jr appeared as a cartoon caricature of every Italian-American stereotype, giving one the impression he had discovered his heritage by watching The Sopranos. However, his close friends recognized it as a deliberate posture to foment his personality. The act seemed egregious given a physical presence that alone, demanded attention. Junior was a burly hulk of a man, packing two hundred and ninety pounds onto a six-foot-five frame.

He rang the doorbell and stepped back, folding his hands across the bulge of his belly. Glancing down the street, he wondered where Michelle Kenrick lived. She was only a freshman when he graduated, but was already showing great promise for filling out a bra.

He was about to knock when the door suddenly swung open and Sean Bergin stepped out onto the porch. Sean looked frazzled, his eyes unusually wide, and his face unusually red. The cuffs of his sleeves were wet as he finished rubbing his hands dry in a towel.

"Hey Sean-o," Junior stammered. "Did I catch you at a bad time?"

Sean cast a quick glance back at the door, "No. It's okay. What can I do for you?"

"Listen, I'm sorry to have to bother you, but Pops is having a fuckin' herd over the landscaping at the Distributors." Junior and his father,

Domenic Sr, were the proud co-owners of the only beer distributor within a thirty mile radius. *DJ Beverages, where parties brew.*

Sean cast a pained glare, "Why didn't he just call me?"

"He said he did;" Junior retorted. "Seven times since August, to be exact. I know we are not a big account, but..."

"That's not true. Every customer is important to me."

"Well," Junior continued, "he insisted that I come over here this morning before your work day started. He was hoping to get a trim before the snow covers things up. Ya know what I mean?"

"I know," Sean gazed down the street in an abnormal look of confusion, appearing to struggle to simply remain focused. "Look, I'm kind of locked in with my family today, but I'll call Earl Hales and see if he can cover this one alone for me."

"Yeah." Junior responded sympathetically. "He wouldn't have to do much; just do enough to shut-up the old man."

"I appreciate you backing me on this one, Junior," Sean interjected, "but your father's in the right. I did keep forgetting about him."

"Well, see what you can do."

"Don't worry. Earl will get to it today." *Even if it meant doubling his pay,* Sean thought.

Junior nodded and stepped down from the porch, but turned back, unable to let go of Sean's disconcerted behavior. "You sure you're okay, Sean-o?"

"Yeah," Sean replied, nodding to the house, "the kid's just getting on my nerves a little this morning."

"I understand," Junior said, smiling. "I do that to Pops all the time."

Sean waved as he watched Junior's car disappear around the first intersection, then he released a deep sigh. The vapor from his warm breath dissipated as it drifted above his head. The air had chilled quickly this year and smelled of an early snowfall. He tried to relax the tension in his body, remaining in a moment of contemplation until his bare feet reminded him of the temperature outside. With one final glance down the nearly dormant street, he retreated inside to call Hales.

Chapter 10

Jennifer entered the large storage room of Reiman-Fromme and placed her box of display items on her work counter. It was less than an hour before the store opened its doors for business and she was looking forward to getting a jump start before the shoppers began milling through the aisles. She could hear Trina Rathburn entering the room after a brief moment, but her focus remained entangled in her own thoughts. She could not let go of her encounter with the accident along the road and the face she was certain she recognized.

Trina worked in the cosmetic's department and was the closest thing to a best friend for the introverted Jennifer. Trina was 38-years-old and the single-parent of three children. She was a woman of strong resolve who protected Jennifer with maternal tenacity. Her wavy blonde shoulder length hair was tossed about as she bounded up to her friend and placed both of her hands on Jennifer's shoulders. Her full lips broadened into a sphinx-like smile as she leaned forward and whispered into Jennifer's ear.

"Steve Reeser is in the building," she said smacking her lips like she had just finished devouring a triple fudge sundae.

Jennifer's eyes looked toward the ceiling, as she forced the conflicts within her mind to bury themselves into the depths of her subconscious. She summoned her lips to curl up into their best imitation of a smile. "And what pray-tell is our little hottie wearing today that has you so ravenously heated?"

"Well, today Steve is wearing a fine gray double-breasted suit from Gucci and the latest fragrance from Hugo Boss. I wonder if he would consider dating an older woman with multiple kids. I think he would love my children. Someone has too; their father never seems to want to see them. Can you believe he missed his visitation again last weekend?"

"Oh no, you're kidding, those poor little people. They're going to think they can't rely on anyone except you; he's going to give them a complex." Jennifer responded.

"I know Jen, but what am I supposed to do? I can't force the kids on him, but I don't feel right pulling them away from their father either. God, they get so heart broken when he doesn't show to pick them up. And half the time, he never has the guts or decency to pick up the phone to tell them he won't be coming. I cannot believe I married someone like that. I never saw this coming. I spent fifteen years doing everything I could to please him, and he returns the favor by bailing on us for some little tramp." The final word had no sooner escaped Trina's mouth as the storeroom door flung open and Shawana Terrell barged into the room.

"Did you girls get a whiff of Steve this morning? He smells like an angel on testosterone," Shawana stated as her strut carried her impudently toward them.

"We know," Trina and Jennifer said in unison as they looked over their shoulders at the young black woman approaching. Shawana was the 25-year-old manager of ladies' wear. Her deep brown eyes had been replaced by hazel contact lenses, and her long black hair was straightened into larger flowing curls.

"I'm telling you that man is fine," Shawana continued, "If one of you girls don't get some of that soon, you're gonna force me into breaking my marriage vows."

"Marriage leaves me out, too," Jennifer stated. "Trina, it's all on your shoulders. You need to take one for the team." The laughter from the three ladies carried to the fourth person entering the storage area. This time a tall male figure stood in the doorway.

Vincent Michaels was six-foot-five with black hair and a mustache set upon the lip of a handsome face. "Let me guess; our topic in this morning's discussion is Steve, Mr. Assistant Manager."

"Steve is on the menu for breakfast, lunch, and dinner." Trina commented.

"Well, you ladies need to realize you don't stand a chance with him," Vincent blandly stated. "I am the only one of us that carries the equipment he wants."

"You freak me out when you talk," Shawana uttered. "No man as big as you should like other men; it's just weird. Do you have any idea how many women in this place would love to get their hands on you? They talk about you as much as they do Steve."

"I'm among very sexy company then." Vincent replied with a chuckle.

Shawana turned her attention back to Jennifer and Trina, "One of you girls needs to straighten this boy out."

"I would love to, but I have my Sean," Jennifer stated proudly.

"Your husband is so laid back. Mister Smoothie." Shawana commented with a smile.

"He has his emotional struggles just like everyone else does." Jennifer rebutted. "He just doesn't wear his heart on his sleeve. Actually I think he keeps his heart somewhere near his groin."

"Does his flirting bother you at all?" Trina intervened.

"No, I trust Sean. He is not at all like he portrays. He is loyal. He just likes to tease for fun."

"Jen, you are in denial as much as he is. I see the way he looks at me," Vincent boasted. "That boy is dying to come out of the closet into my living room."

"In your dreams, Vincent."

"No offense, Jen, but that man can put a hurting on me anytime he wants to."

"No offense taken. Coming from you, I will consider it a compliment."

The group was interrupted when the door opened slightly and the smooth-skinned face of Steve Reeser slipped in through the aperture. "Excuse me Trina, but you have an urgent phone call."

Trina's face blushed, but it was the blush of fear. "I hope the kids are okay," she muttered to Jennifer as she followed Steve out the door.

Shawana and Vincent decided it was best to return to their respective work areas, but not until they instructed Jennifer to inform them if anything was wrong with Trina's children. Jennifer assured the two she would contact them and then returned to her display preparation.

Steve led Trina back into the management office, motioning toward a telephone, which hung on a pillar at the northern half of the room. Trina lifted the receiver and placed her hand over the mouthpiece as she turned to Steve, "Thank you."

"You're welcome," he responded, "I will give you some privacy."

Trina watched as Steve left the room, closing the door behind him. The greeting she spoke was hesitant and quivering.

"Trina, its Sean," the voice on the other end sounded uncharacteristically weak to her.

"I'm sorry. They told me I was wanted on the phone." Trina replied confused.

"I did ask for you," Sean seemed to be laboring for breath as he spoke, but not from physical exertion. It was the kind of laboring that accompanies terror. "I have to tell Jen something, and I need you to be with her for me." His voice trailed off into a gentle sob, "I'm sorry to do this to you Trina, but I need you right now."

Trina's lips quivered as she fought back her tears, "It is okay Sean. I'll get her to the phone," she could not bring herself to ask what was wrong; something deep in her gut had already told her.

She placed the telephone down, allowing it to dangle from its cord. The walk to the storage room seemed like miles as the knot in her stomach slowly tightened. The pumping of her heart intensified until it threatened to burst forth from her throat. She struggled to regain control of her emotions, drawing in a deep breath before she entered the room.

"Jennifer, can I talk to you in the office."

Jennifer turned with a look of compassionate concern, "Sure Trina." She emptied her hands of their toil and followed Trina out of the storage room. The friends did not exchange words or glances as they walked back to the office where Trina had left the phone. Both could sense an emotional storm approaching and neither wanted to endure what was to unfold. They entered the office, and Trina lifted the receiver and slowly extended it to Jennifer, "Sean is on the phone." Trina could no longer hold the tears that filled her eyes. Jennifer's hand trembled as she accepted the device and lifted it to her ear.

The air seemed to be sucked from the room as Trina watched Jennifer's expression of confusion transform into anguish.

"No, he wouldn't do that ... He wouldn't take my baby from me. Trina! Why would God take my baby away from me?" Jennifer wailed, as she staggered backwards. "My baby's gone." She careened into the pillar behind her, which retained the wall unit of the telephone. The receiver slid from her hand and dropped to the floor, as she collapsed to her knees before at last curling into a fetal ball of wrenching sobs. "No, Arlen ... please ... don't leave me. Please, baby, don't leave mommy... ."

Trina stood in shock as her own tears soaked her cheeks. They filled her eyes and blurred the image of her best friend crumbling helplessly at her feet. She could hear Sean sobbing through the receiver, repeating endlessly "I'm so sorry, Jen. It was an accident." Sean's voice rattled through the phone line in a hauntingly agonizing chant.

Trina's mind swirled, dizzying her to a near faint. She silently prayed for the strength to help the friend she loved so much. But where would she begin? She herself, at this moment, did not possess the capacity to pull Jennifer back to her feet. She could barely manage to stiffen her own wobbling knees. She knew that she could never even begin to resolve Jennifer's question 'why a parent must lose a child.' A question no one will ever comprehend the answer to, perhaps not even God himself.

Chapter 11

Father Thomas lit the last of two special candles he had placed at the Alter and then knelt in prayer. The day had been the most trying and devastating of his tenure at Saint Anthony's. The lives of two families from his congregation had been altered forever. Rachel Simmons was now in the intensive care unit at St Joseph's Medical Center, her condition - comatose. The doctor had called it cerebral hypoxia. There was brain damage from oxygen deprivation. He had been too late to stop her suicide attempt, but not too late to save her life. It was in the hands of God now; he could only pray for her recovery.

No sooner had Simmons been admitted to the hospital, he received word of a tragic incident involving the son of Sean and Jennifer Bergin. The child had lost his life in a bizarre household drowning. Father Thomas was not certain if Jennifer had realized his presence in the house. The sounds of her wailing from the upstairs bedroom still rang in his ears and unsettled his stomach. His prayers provided little solace to the family. That wound would never heal.

He rose to his feet, an effort that made him suddenly realize how exhausted he was, and entered a corridor leading to his living quarters. His stomach growled, reminding him that he had not eaten since breakfast. The mere thought of food now made him cringe. He removed his collar, rubbing the back of his neck as he walked the length of the hallway. To both his right and left, photographs hung of the clergymen that had served St. Anthony's Parish before him; rows of eyes that watched over his efforts and comforted him when he needed their strength. He paused at the final photograph and stared into the gentle eyes of Father Anthony. The picture was taken at a time when the priest was more robust. A time before a personal tragedy left him drained of his now famous optimism.

Father Anthony had concluded his service three years before Thomas was assigned. Father Jonathan had served in the interim. Before he arrived at St. Anthony's, Father Thomas had heard of the passing of the beloved Father Anthony. A memorial service was held in the church, and from all accounts, the entire town had attended, including those not of the faith - so was the reach of the man's service.

From the death of Father Anthony, a great swell of admiration rose, followed by a greater swell of speculation into his personal affairs. Thomas was never certain of the details surrounding the personal tragedy in Anthony's life. He had only heard the whispers among the elders of the congregation - whispers of sin, of the dead body of a nephew and of long-held family secrets.

At times, St. Anthony's Parish appeared to Father Thomas as a lightning rod of tragedy. But where else would the strength of his faith be better served?

He touched the face of the painting, asking Father Anthony to watch over the Bergin child who had been taken so suddenly from the loving arms of his parents. He thought of the coming holidays, and how difficult it would be for Sean and Jennifer to endure. With a deep sigh, his hand slid down the photograph until it dropped to his side. *Faith and time*, he thought. *The healing would take faith and time.*

Chapter 12

Jennifer reached inside the microwave oven and wrapped her hand carelessly around the mug of steaming water. She carried it to the sink, unresponsive to the burning in her palm from the hot ceramic. She placed the mug on the counter and stirred a teaspoon of sugar into its contents before dropping in a bag of Earl Grey Tea. She stared out of the kitchen window at the swing set nestled in the backyard snow. A thin layer of the frozen crystals shimmered beneath the radiance of the midday sun, but the beauty was undiscerning to her as she gazed at the chains of a swing that supported the midair quiescence of its seat. A swing that portrayed anguish as it remained undisturbed by wind or by child.

It had been nearly four months since Arlen died, three months and nineteen days to be exact, and following a tormented holiday season Jennifer felt as though she had been drained of her emotions. The Christmas gift of flowers for his grave seemed absurdly inadequate, but she was diligent in tending the site. It was only on those occasions that she granted herself freedom from her home.

The circumstances surrounding Arlen's death seemed to be gnawing at her now constantly queasy stomach. Arlen was found slumped over from a seated position in the bathtub. The coroner reported that Arlen received a slight blow to the head that knocked him unconscious, causing him to slump forward into the tub, where he inhaled enough water to asphyxiate him. Forensic investigator, Jeff Hubbard, surmised that Arlen had attempted to stand up and slipped on the soap that had been left in the water. He believed Arlen had hit his head on the edge of the tub. The force of the blow was moderate, but hard enough to render him unconscious.

The police had interviewed both Domenic Marconi Jr. and Earl Hales. They had collaborated Sean's story, releasing him of any suspicion. The death was subsequently ruled an accidental drowning.

Jennifer could not help but wonder how Arlen was found slumped forward if he had indeed fallen backwards to receive the blow to his head; however, she was too afraid to say anything or to speculate further. Too afraid of discovering something that she was not prepared to face. She knew that Sean loved Arlen. She had no previous cause to suspect he was the least bit abusive toward him; nevertheless, she was aware of Sean's quick temper, and a piece of the puzzle seemed to be missing.

She had listlessly drifted over to the kitchen table and slipped into a chair as her thoughts continued to churn. She stared into the depths of the dark tea, praying that Arlen did not feel anything when his lungs were laboring for oxygen. Squeezing her eyes shut, she pushed back the image that was taking form in her mind.

Jennifer's psyche had become so friable following Arlen's passing that the events that proceeded seemed distorted and confusing to her. The memories were gray and fragmented with no hope of ever placing the past three months in chronological order. Arlen's viewing was an agonizing homage to her son as she attempted to hold tight to her last ounce of strength. It was painful to endure, but important for Arlen to know how much everyone loved him.

His ivory and gold casket was displayed in front of the southern wall; an area heavily adorned with sprays of flowers. A line of plush burgundy chairs had been placed at the eastern wall of the funeral home for the immediate family. The people in attendance walked down the aisle, pausing to grieve with the parents, before saying a final goodbye to Arlen and being seated. Sean's grandmother, Meagan Bergin, was the first in the line of the immediate family. She and her husband Thomas had raised the young Sean, but only she remained as Sean's living parent. Jennifer's father, Donald Gray, had been seated next to Meagan, followed by Jennifer and Sean.

Jennifer had walked to her seat clutching onto Sean to bring stability to her trembling legs. Her eyes were red and irritated from days of nearly constant weeping, her lids heavy and darkened from lack of rest. She had pulled her hair back into a ponytail, with no desire for any attempt at beauty. Sitting quietly staring at the casket, she hoped Arlen would soon awaken her from her nightmare. She could almost hear the words, "Mommy, wake up," as they crossed his lips.

No creature of God could ever hope to replace what she had lost. She longed, now more than ever, to see his serendipitous blue eyes and the innocuous smile. The tiny angelic face had always possessed the ability to draw Jennifer from the depths of any depression into a light of contentment. Tears streamed from her eyes, mercifully blurring her final image of Arlen, as he nestled into the hands of God.

She had released a tormented sigh as a hand pressed gently upon her shoulder. She had looked up to see Sean's elder brother, Neil Bergin Jr., and his wife Suzanne, the first to arrive with their condolences. Neil had knelt in front of her and held her tight.

"I'm so sorry, Sis." His voice was rasp and his eyes rheumy. "Are you going to be okay?"

Jennifer had held onto him trying to draw from his strength as her sobs now became hauntingly audible; it was a sound of painful despair. Sobs that lift the hairs from the back of the human neck and made one's stomach instantly twist. Neil released his embrace and stepped back to allow Suzanne access to Jennifer. The couple had then spoken to Sean, hugging him and reminding him to call if he and Jennifer needed anything, before quietly moving on toward the casket.

Jennifer's sobs had no sooner begun to ease, as Sean's sister, Colleen, and her husband Curt Anspach arrived in front of her. Colleen knelt beside her and gently stroked the back of her hand - whispering in a tone so soft that Jennifer could not hear the words she spoke. She had merely nodded politely until Colleen moved on.

The next to arrive was Sean's sister, Arlene, a woman that Jennifer had adopted as the sister she never had. The pair became instantly inseparable from the moment they met, and Arlene became the namesake of Jennifer's son. Jennifer rose to her feet and clutched her arms around Arlene, as they shared the grief of their loss. Sean, who had been standing to hug Colleen, rubbed his hand gently over Jennifer's back.

Aunt Arlene was the obvious favorite when she visited the child. Even as a baby, Arlen would not accept anyone else holding him if his Aunt were in the room. Arlene stepped back from Jennifer and embraced Sean as the line of people continued.

Jennifer cried with each person in attendance as they arrived at her side. Her sobs increased every time a new familiar face came into view. Many of the people Jennifer worked with had come to show their support.

Copper Dragons

Trina Rathburn, Vincent Michaels, Shawana Terrell, Steve Reeser, and the manager Jonathan Schinse, all arrived together, some bringing spouses with them. The Bergin family doctor, Alexander Conahan, had been in attendance with his wife Nancy. Dr. Conahan, who had stayed with Jennifer during her struggle to become pregnant, had taken Arlen's death surprisingly hard. Jennifer remembered seeing tears on his cheeks as he passed through the procession.

Jennifer stood to greet June Eckley and her seventeen-year-old daughter Angelia, who coordinated their available time to baby-sit Arlen any hours they were needed. June would watch Arlen during school hours and Angelia would watch him on the weekends. The three embraced and cried together. June's husband Harold watched them, shuffling his feet uncomfortably, unaware of what to say at these times.

Gail Harris, who was the best friend of Sean's mother Ilene, was the next to be received. Gail had become Sean's surrogate mother when Ilene passed away. Wendy Parks, who was a part of Sean's graduating class and dated him in the ninth grade returned early from the Philippines to attend. She was now a nurse and had been donating some of her time overseas. Sean seemed genuinely thankful that she attended, as the two embraced. Dylan Lucas attended with his wife Mallory. Dylan had played high school football with Sean and was now the local pharmacist. Earl Hales, who was accompanied by his wife Tricia, appeared to be burdened by grief as he clutched Sean in a strong embrace. Junior Marconi and his father paid their respects with their presence and one of the largest flower arrangements. Wayne Tibbens, the owner of a quarry and mulch company where Sean purchased mulch and landscaping stones, was in attendance along with Evan Kershaw, the owner of the Honey Brook Shopping Plaza.

Jennifer cried with each person while each extracted more of her strength. Her feelings of gratitude toward those in the procession turned into a tired frustration as she found herself longing for the people to stop coming. She became exhausted, feeling she could not endure bearing their grief along with her own. She could see the pity in their eyes as they embraced her. She could hear them speak, but did not comprehend their words, as they passed by in what she began to perceive as a mawkish promenade.

Father Thomas Morelli performed the service and led them in prayer. When all was finished, those in attendance filed out, while Jennifer and Sean approached the casket one final time. A thin powder blue blanket was folded neatly down at Arlen's waist. Jennifer reached in and pulled the blanket up to his shoulders, as though she were tucking him into bed. She ran her fingers through his hair and across his brow, gently kissed his cheek and held his hands through the blanket. Sean placed the action figure of Queen Amidala on Arlen's chest and stared at his serene face, peaceful and resting.

"Daddy's going to miss you so much." Sean said, breaking the silence of his tears.

"I can't do this," Jennifer's head bowed as she wept. She gripped Arlen's hands and buried her face into his blanket. "I can't go on without him, Sean."

Jennifer turned her head and looked up at Sean. When Sean witnessed the pain and helplessness in her eyes, the last of his spirit broke. The couple knelt on the floor in front of their child's casket, weeping together as they embraced. Their sobs echoed out into the otherwise silent room and were absorbed into the walls of the parlor, joining the many cries that had sounded before theirs. Cries which resonated from the mouths of mothers, fathers, children, and spouses for the loved ones that had been taken from their lives before they were prepared to relinquish them.

Jennifer's thoughts of the past faded into the numbness of the present as she sat at her kitchen table staring blankly at the wall. Tears now stained her cheeks, but, otherwise her face remained placid, void of color and of crease. She closed her eyes and placed her lips to the cup of tea, sipping several times before placing the cup back on the table. Her hair was still pulled back into a ponytail. She could not remember the last time she had washed it, nor did she care. She longed to feel normal again, to go to work, eat, and even sleep like a regular person, but the flames of her will had extinguished. There was nothing left of life, but to live it. Only to finish the journey, so she could be reunited with her son.

Sean stepped onto the porch, hearing the ice between the boards cracking under his weight. Snow had fallen through the late hours of the evening. He had arisen at four in the morning in order to plow the lots before the stores opened for business. His snow plowing operation boasted eleven clients, plus a free plow for the local volunteer firehouse; an act of goodwill which, today, concealed an ulterior motive. His home had become oppressively dark and the longer he was absent from it, the more comfortable he felt. These graying walls were slowly swallowing what remained of his life.

Jennifer had not worked since Arlen's death. In fact, she had rarely left the house since the day of his funeral. She barely spoke to Sean, and she showed no signs of affection. She was quietly drifting away from him.

He had called Jennifer's father, Donald, several weeks ago for some advice on how Sean could reconnect with Jennifer. And while Donald offered sympathy, he seemed remiss on advice.

"I know what you're going through, Sean." Donald had told him. "Jennifer has always been introverted with her feelings. She buries her emotions deep within herself, allowing things to boil over before she releases them. Her mother was the same way. I never was able to console Sue Ellen when she got upset either. I love the woman dearly, but she tested my love every day. And poor Jennifer went through so much with her Mom - God bless her."

"I know, Dad."

"You have to be patient with her. Arlen's death was devastating… ."

"It was for me too."

"Jennifer cannot cope with things as well as you. The poor girl has been through so much."

Sean remembered feeling frustrated after that conversation. Her father had acted as if Jennifer lost a son and Sean was merely a witness to the fact. Sean's outward calm was no more a testament to his inner turmoil than his marriage was a testament to bliss.

Sean paused in the living room to hang his coat in the closet and remove his boots. He took a deep breath and began walking through the dining room. As he entered the kitchen, Jennifer displayed a look of utter indifference as she lifted her attention from a cup of tea.

"Hi, Lass," he spoke the words in a near whisper. He leaned down to Jennifer's back and wrapped his arms around her chest, placing a gentle kiss on the top of her head. "Did you sleep okay last night?" No response.

He made his way to the counter and poured a cup of coffee from the pot he had made before leaving. The coffee tasted stale as he sipped, but it was warm enough to lift the chill the frigid temperature had left on his skin.

He sat across from her and cast an occasional glance in her direction. *She is remaining deliberately silent*, he thought, *and avoiding eye contact.*

The couple sat quietly for nearly ten minutes, sipping at their drinks, and casting blank stares at alternating walls. Their home felt more like a hollow chamber that they were locked in, and the same could be said of their marriage.

"Hey, why don't you go up and get a shower and we'll go out for lunch?" Sean said, finally breaking the silence.

"Sean, I can't."

"Why not?"

Jennifer sat in silence, avoiding the question, until at last she attempted to divert the subject. "If you're hungry, I can make you something to eat."

"No thanks. Wendy came by while I was plowing the Plaza parking lot and brought me a breakfast sandwich."

"Oh, well, wasn't that thoughtful of her," Jennifer answered. Her eyes flashed an emotion that evaporated before Sean could discern its intent.

"She has been really great through this. She has been there for me when I needed her." Sean stated with a snide undertone.

The conversation fell silent as the seconds ticked by like years. The words bit at Jennifer until they gnawed their way into her swelling resentment. She quelled her jealously and lashed out in an alternate direction.

"If we go out, you know as well as I do, we're going to run into people we know. I just can't face anyone. I'm not ready yet. People like to gawk and ask a lot of questions; they can be irritating. I'm just not ready for humans right now." Jennifer released a long sigh and continued. "I feel so empty. I wish that I could cry. I wish I could scream out in anger. I want the emotions out of me, but I can't release them. I can't smile; I can't laugh; I can't cry."

"Lass, I'm worried about you. You're not eating right. I wake up when you get out of bed in the middle of the night. It seems you wake up every hour. And I know you're going into Arlen's bedroom. Maybe we should try to pack up some of his things."

His suggestion was met by a wild glare, "We are not packing anything."

"Okay." He paused for a moment with his head down, trying to structure his next sentence in a conciliatory fashion. "Lass, listen, I spoke with Dr. Conahan the other day. He gave me a number for a psychologist," Sean reached into a pocket in his jeans and produced a slip of paper with a telephone number written in ink. "His name is Jonathan Bomboy. He is a personal friend of Dr. Conahan. Conahan thought it might be a good idea for you to talk to him." He slid the paper across the table to her.

She picked it up and examined it for a moment, before floating it back onto the table. "I don't need a psychologist; I can fix myself. I just need some time."

"How much time? Lass, it's been nearly four months. Life isn't always a magic garden, Lass. But you have to keep living. You have barely left the house. You refuse to go to work. I can't believe they're still holding your job for you. I'm the only one who's bringing money into this house, and the bills are starting to get backed up.

You barely speak to me anymore. Not like you used to. When was the last time you told me that you loved me? No touching, no kissing, no intimacy."

"I can't believe you just said that." Jennifer looked at Sean in exasperation. "Is this what this is about, Sean, your libido? You're concerned because you're not getting enough sex?"

"No." His voice rose in protest. "I just want to feel normal again."

"Why don't you get your precious Wendy to take care of that for you too?" Jennifer spat.

"You're being ridiculous. Wendy has been there as a friend; something that you should be doing."

"Well, I'm so sorry I'm not as calloused as you are. I'm sorry I can't live up to your standards." Jennifer's eyes flared with anger, anger that had been boiling inside of her for nearly four months, waiting to erupt.

"You act like I don't feel the same pain you do. Arlen is gone, Jen. But we have to live on."

"I lost my son for Christ sakes!" Jennifer hissed through clinched teeth, her eyes now glazed.

"I know!" Sean yelled. "Well, guess what? I did too!"

"Yeah, with one big difference; one of us was there to stop it."

"Where the fuck are you going with this?"

"I don't know, Sean. Why don't you tell me."

"I was giving him a bath and the fucking doorbell rang!" Sean shouted, pounding his fist on the table.

"Did the doorbell ring before or after he drowned?"

Sean's hands slapped against the underside of the table sending it flipping through the air until it crashed into the counter. He leapt to his feet and stood over Jennifer with his fist pulled back, poised to swing. She could feel the beat of her heart, thumping in her throat. She remained seated trying to portray ambivalence, though her fear grew from the fury that burned in Sean's eyes. His nostrils flared and his face grew a deep shade of red. A torrid moment suspended in time for which those who bear witness conceal the memory deep in their minds in an attempt to never think on it again.

"What's the matter, Sean? Can't you control your temper? Go ahead and hit me! The pain will be a fucking relief!"

"I don't even know you anymore," Sean's voice eased as he lowered his fist. "Don't you think I have tortured myself enough? The guilt I'm carrying … "

Sean paused as his mind replayed the argument until reaching a conclusion that knotted his stomach. "You think I murdered our son, don't you?"

"I think my baby is gone, and some things just don't add up."

Sean's jaw slackened as he backed away. "I can't believe this," he managed to utter. He did not halt his retreat until he reached the archway leading into the dining room. "I don't have to explain my actions to you. You should know me better than that by now."

"I wish I could say that I did," Jennifer stammered, as she became painfully aware of what she had said. There was no turning back now; her suspicions were no longer secret. She rose from her chair, and now tears were cascading from her eyes. She stared at the man she thought she knew. She tried to read his reaction, searching for a flinch or a twinge of guilt in his eyes as they avoided hers. But his stare remained locked onto her without aversion. Her hands shook uncontrollably as she fought to remain strong.

"I have to leave," Sean's voice rattled in confusion. "I'll send someone over to get my things. I can't stay in this house another minute with you."

She could see the pain on his face, and she wondered if she had made a grave error. The nightmare of Arlen's death seemed destined to continue for her.

Sean raised both his hands and ran them over his brow and through his hair. "You just characterized me as some sort of monster. Right now, I am too sick to my stomach to be angry. But when this sickness wears off, I'm gonna be angry. Oh, believe me, I'm gonna be fucking furious. And you're not gonna want to be anywhere near me. Ever."

He turned and retreated from the room. Jennifer stood with her hands covering her quivering lips. Tears drenched her cheeks. A part of her wanted to stop him from leaving. Perhaps apologize for what she had said, explaining her actions away as those of a grieving mother. But the damage had already been done.

She could hear Sean rummage in the closet for a brief moment before she heard the wood splitting sound of the door slamming shut. The argument had taken only a moment to transpire, but it seemed to take years to unfold. She was lost amid her own confusion, not knowing what was real. She had allowed her pain and anger to envelop her thoughts and assume control of her speech.

She walked slowly and methodically from the kitchen to ascend the staircase. She entered her bedroom and stretched across Sean's side of the bed. She could remember the love that she felt for the two men in her life, but only the love for one of them remained; the one she could no longer hold in her arms. She had loved Sean dearly, but she could not dismiss the doubt which ultimately devoured her feelings. An emotional storm grew within her until it could no longer be subdued. Jennifer became liberated from the apathy that had concealed her feelings. Any self-restraint that remained within her had been spilled about the kitchen floor with the contents of the table. She released a long and tormented wail of anger, pain, and sorrow.

The anguish that had been buried within her now released in loud sobs that shook her small frame. She wept without restraint, without shame of the volume of her cries. She pleaded to God for forgiveness. She pleaded to Arlen for strength as she clutched Sean's pillow to her face smelling the remnants of his cologne. Her cries went on for what seemed like hours until her sobs faded into sleep.

Dreams

Who looks outside, dreams; who looks inside, awakens.

-Carl Gustav Jung

Our dreams are firsthand creations, rather than residues of waking life. We have the capacity for infinite creativity; at least while dreaming, we partake of the power of the Spirit, the infinite Godhead that creates the cosmos.

-Jackie Gleason

Dreams are the wanderings of the spirit through all nine heavens and all nine earths.

-Lu Yen

Chapter 13

Jennifer dug her bare toes into the cold, soft grains of sand. The beach stretched out on either side for what seemed an eternity. No man-made structures were visible, and neither time nor history held status here. She could not sense any source of life other than her own. The sand and the ocean seemed to be her only companions. The beach contained a few large rocks, and a host of seashells strewn about the carpet of sand. The ocean licked the edge of the beach with jagged white wash foam that rose from the torrid waves. The degenerate sky was smeared in gray by a storm that thundered its anger above the ruffling water line. A strong wind tossed Jennifer's hair about in its propulsion, yet despite the wind and the cold sand chilling her feet, her body remained warm and her soul calm.

She was dressed in Capri pants with a white blouse that she had tied mid-waist, exposing her stomach. The blouse billowed in the fresh, salty air.

The agitation of the waves drifted to her ears in one continuous roar that blended with the distant intermittent rumble of thunder. Those sounds remained dominate until a soft voice whispered in her ear.

"The ocean sounds much more serene in here." A familiar black-haired man stood next to her with his hand extended, offering her a conch shell. He gazed at her through a handsome smile as he bid her to listen. His deep brown eyes softened the strong etching of his cheekbones, with thick, lush eyebrows to accent all.

"There's a storm coming," Jennifer stated in confusion, as she reached out tentatively to accept the shell.

"No," the man answered reassuringly with his finger tapping the air in the direction of the storm. "That storm is moving away from you."

Jennifer looked up at him like a lost child with all of the questions of the universe swirling within her head. "Is the storm over?"

His smile broadened, "Well, it's obviously not over you any longer, but it is still there."

"Will it come back?"

"I can't answer that, Jennifer," he responded. "No one can. Storms arise and they pass on, just like most things on God's Earth. Things begin and things end; some graciously, some painfully, and some mercifully. And sometimes, when we pray hard enough," he paused with a sigh, "Sometimes things can even end happily." His lips were relaxed, but Jennifer could see a warm smile dwelling within his eyes.

"You know my name and you look familiar, but I don't know your name." She raised the conch shell to her left ear and listened intently.

"My name is Nicholas," he responded. "This is a beautiful beach you have here."

"Oh, it's not mine; my parents brought me here. We come here every year for vacation."

He pointed out to sea. "So that must be the Atlantic Ocean."

"Yep. Daddy says if you sail straight out, you would run into Spain."

"That's right, and near Spain is my original home, Italy."

"Is that very far?"

"It's not close enough to cast a stone, but the world is never so big that you can't visit home. Why are you out here all by yourself?"

"When Mommy gets upset, I like to come out here and listen to the waves talk. They speak quietly. They don't shout too much - not like Mommy. But they're shouting a little bit today."

"Is that what the waves are doing right now, they're shouting?"

"No they're just sort of grumbling. I think the ocean is mad at the storm. The ocean wants it to go away so that the sun can shine again."

Nicholas placed his hands gently on both of Jennifer's shoulders and turned her toward him. Her red hair tossed about the creamy skin of her neck and her body bore the fruits of a mature woman, though she spoke like a child. He gazed into her eyes, remaining silent for a brief moment, struck by her beauty. Her fair skin glistened like that of a porcelain doll, and her eyes were sultry, and yet filled with innocence. "The sun will shine again for the waves, but only you can make that happen."

"I don't know how to do that," Jennifer's voice seemed to mature in response to his passionate gaze.

"Well, perhaps we can discover a way together."

Jennifer allowed a slight smile to appear on her face, "Okay." She felt warm and welcomed in Nicholas' presence. His touch enticed her into accepting his offer.

Nicholas slid both of his hands from her shoulders and allowed one to grip her hand. He sat down on the sand and gave a gentle pull to request her to do the same. Jennifer knelt beside him, gazing into his eyes for a moment, before turning toward the ocean and sitting down in front of him. Nicholas placed an arm around her waist, drawing her back to rest her weight against his chest. They stared out at the storm as it began to drift ever further from the beach.

"You know," Nicholas whispered with his lips at the tip of her ear; "I can actually smell your hair and your body spray. It's so sweet it nearly dizzies me."

Jennifer smiled at the compliment, "It's called Midnight Expressions; I'm glad you like it."

"I like it very much." Nicholas paused, snatching up a handful of sand, and raising it up to his face. He allowed the grains to slowly run through his fingers as if to feel its texture. "So, do you and your father ever visit this beach now?"

"We did come here once about seven years ago, but it was never the same without Mom. We stayed for an afternoon and discussed getting hotel rooms over night, but Daddy wanted to head back to Pennsylvania. He likes being at home and close to his work. I guess he likes to keep himself busy so that he feels needed."

"Did you ever visit this beach without him?"

"No. I think about doing it sometimes." She turned her head back to look into Nicholas' face. "My husband and son never..." her voice trailed and her brow creased with a look of dread. "Oh my God, Arlen!"

"Jennifer ..." Nicholas attempted to speak as she quickly rose to her feet. Thunder clapped with a deafening tone that rang steadily in their ears. The ominous clouds that had pushed their way out to sea now swung back toward the beach.

"He must have been out here with me," Jennifer's eyes darted right to left in confused panic. "I have to find him. What if he wandered out into the ocean?"

Nicholas rose to his feet and attempted to calm her, "Jennifer listen to me. Arlen is fine."

Her eyes flashed with anger, "No! He is not fine! I have to find my baby. Arlen!"

Jennifer began a quick pace down the beach as the waves rose up and struck her bare feet. Lightning streaked from clouds to ground, meeting in the charcoal sky and flashing with the brilliance thousands of flashbulbs.

"Arlen!"

The waves upon the water crashed together in high peaks. The foam rolling on the beach stiffened like quicksand and caused her feet to be suctioned down into the muck. She struggled to increase her pace, and with every shout of her son's name, the strong wind blew the thrust of her air back into her lungs to muffle her voice. Her chest heaved and her muscles burned.

"Arlen! Arlen!"

Nicholas ran to her side, "Jennifer, listen to me, please. Look at me!" He tried to turn her toward his face, but she pushed him aside and continued down the beach.

"Arlen! Please, answer Mommy!" Jennifer shouted as the wind now whipped the sand into the air. She tried to shield her eyes from flying debris as she ran.

Nicholas finally managed to grip Jennifer by her arms and turned her toward his gaze. He looked into her eyes with loving concern. "Jennifer, you are dreaming. You have to wake ..."

The final two words that Nicholas spoke rang in Jennifer's ears as she peered through the darkness of her bedroom. "...up, now."

She remained still, trying to regain control of the motion of her body. She could hear no sounds for what seemed like hours, except the echo of Nicholas' final words which lingered in her mind. Suddenly, she could hear the hum of the furnace, then the roar of a car engine as it approached and then dissipated down Arch Street in front of her home. The glow of the passing headlights cast subtle shadows on objects in her room.

She twisted to look at the green light from the digital alarm clock display. It was 7:05 p.m., and the sun had long since set, placing her in darkness. She rubbed her eyes and released a long sigh. Her mind began to re-enact the events of the final hour before she fell asleep. Her heart rate elevated at the mere thought of her confrontation with Sean. The acid in her stomach rose up into her esophagus, reminding her that she had also failed to eat for the entire day. But now she felt too ill to even think of food. She sat up in bed and liberated her hair from its ponytail. Her normally vibrant locks settled listlessly about her neck and shoulders.

After sleeping the entire day away, she would have no hope of a normal night's rest. The tension from the loss of Arlen, the allegations against her husband and his departure from the home would most certainly rob her of any further slumber. This was the first time since their marriage that Jennifer was the sole occupant of her home. She was alone. The emptiness of the thought seemed to swallow her soul. *It was going to be a long and sleepless night*, she thought. Her tears returned to fill her eyes, and began trickling down her cheeks. It seemed she had spent most of the past few months crying. "Here we go again," she whispered in helpless exhaustion.

Chapter 14

Sean eased back into the velvety thickness of a burgundy reclining chair, as he inspected the pictures that hung on the wall of Gail Harris' living room. Some familiar faces, some he was certain he had seen before, yet failed to identify. A photo in a tarnished gold frame caught his eye. It was his mother, Ilene, holding the infant Sean in her arms at his baptism. She was standing outside of Saint Anthony's church with Gail by her side. Gail was holding Sean's tiny hand through the receiving blanket as she smiled warmly for the camera. Ilene was tall and slender with only a hint of a post-pregnancy tummy showing through her peach colored dress. Her eyes were a piercing emerald green. Her features were adorably attractive. The picture came at a time before the surgeries, before the radiation therapy, before the countless trips to the hospital.

When Sean was a teen, he watched helplessly as breast cancer drained his mother's life. He could still remember the look of defeat in her eyes when she surrendered her fight. Her eyes became void of all emotion, and mercifully void of the pain that he knew racked her body.

But the nightmare of her disease held no significance in the photograph from outside the church. She was still a vibrant woman, and he was still a naive infant. A moment he would never remember with a woman he would never forget.

Gail was in the kitchen preparing a cup of tea. She still carried herself with a youthful exuberance at the age of 66. She described herself as a strong-headed survivor of the sixties. She was a 'flower power' child who renounced peace and free love for responsibility and accountability.

Gail's parents had disowned her for being engaged to a black man when she was in her early twenties. The turn of the decade was a time when many walls of prejudice were being demolished, but change presented itself slowly. Gail had fallen deeply in love with Reggie Harris, a truck driver from Alabama. Reggie was a highly intelligent man who could have better served his community as a doctor or a professor. A brilliant mind lost in the racial shuffle of society.

The couple became married for a period of three years. And Ilene Bergin was the only person in town who remained, undaunted, at Gail's side.

Gail and Reggie lived in a small bungalow outside of town, leaning on each other for support. But the pressures of married life, compounded by the social tensions they faced became too much to bare. The couple parted ways amicably, with Reggie returning to the south where he eventually remarried. Gail never recovered. She never remarried, choosing instead to live the rest of her life alone. On occasion, Reggie's job brings him to town. At those times, he and Gail meet for lunch. The laughter and the conversation is the same, but the stares that they receive have somewhat diminished. Reggie was saddened, but tolerant of the bigotry, while Gail hated society for destroying her marriage to the only man she ever truly loved.

The loss of her marriage drew Gail closer to Ilene. They spent many of their days coddling young Sean and many evenings on the telephone discussing social and political views. When Ilene lost her battle to cancer, she made Gail promise to watch over Sean in her absence. She visited him as often as she could, and as the years passed, Sean's love and admiration grew for the woman he called Mama Gail.

Gail entered the parlor as her parrot, Sweetheart, greeted her with a squawking 'hello' from his perch at the far corner of the room. She paused to offer the bird a kiss on the beak. Gail's short gray hair curled tight from a recent perm, and her eyeglasses were large by the day's standards. She had a warm smile and a resolve that could make those close to her feel more secure. And each room she entered was a better place in her presence.

She sat down on the sofa, next to the recliner, and placed her cup of tea on the heavy oak coffee table in front of her. She looked at Sean, following his eyes to the picture that had caught his gaze.

"I remember that day. Your parents were so proud to have their baby boy; showing him off to the congregation and the world. What a pure gift from God, you were." The wrinkles surrounding Gail's lips nearly disappeared as she smiled at the memory. "You never cried through the entire ceremony. And when the father brought his finger up to bless you, you grabbed it and tried to stuff it in your mouth."

"I was trying to bite him." Sean commented glumly.

Gail dropped her chin and looked at Sean over the top of her eyeglasses. "You were a very good baby, and you are a very good man, now."

"I guess someone forgot to tell Jennifer that."

Gail's eyes softened and she released a sigh of pity for her godson, "I'm certain she didn't mean what she said. The two of you will patch things …"

"No. I'm sorry Mama Gail, not this time. Jen really ripped my heart out today. The way she was looking at me. She was waiting for me to crack and spill out a confession." Sean paused as he crossed his legs and rubbed his chin. "I could have hit her. God help me. I wanted to."

"Sean Michael Bergin! If I ever hear that out of your mouth again, I'll sew your lips shut. Your mother would not have tolerated that kind of talk out of you and neither will I."

Sean sighed and stared out of the window near his chair. A light snow was falling in sparse flakes that drifted slowly and silently to the ground. The flakes shimmered like crystals as they passed through the soft illumination of the streetlights. The allure of watching snow fall was in its peaceful lethargy, it was in no hurry to reach the ground. The street was dim and deserted as it awaited the coming of another sunrise. The surreal scene only added to the hollow feeling that was swelling in Sean's soul - a hollow feeling of remorse and incomprehensible pain.

Sean had always struggled with his emotions. Never knowing how to react, or release what he was feeling in a proper manner. Most often, sadness was expressed by anger. And now his mind was entangled in a deeper struggle, a guilt he was not yet prepared to confront. His emotions were draining him. He needed to escape.

He looked back at Gail who had picked up her crocheting needle and began to create a new afghan. He walked over to her and placed a kiss on her cheek.

"I appreciate you putting me up for a while," he said. "You have always been so good to me. I'm glad my mom bequeathed me her best friend. And I'm glad you were there for her, as well.

I have to take a little walk. I need to clear my head. I may be a little while, so you don't have to wait up for me."

Gail looked up from her knitting. "Are you sure you're okay?"

"I will be fine."

"Well, if you need any more blankets tonight, there are a few left in your closet. I don't believe these old hands will have this afghan done by the time you get home." She was pleased to hear a brief chuckle escape from Sean's lips. "And when you get up tomorrow, I will have a nice breakfast waiting for you."

"You don't have to spoil me like that, but don't stop." Sean gave her a grin and another kiss on the cheek. "Thanks Mama Gail, I don't know what I would do without you."

He pulled on his coat and stepped from the house into the frigid January night. Hunching his back against the cold, he started down the street. A torrid scene twisted inside his mind. What happened with Arlen inside of the bathroom was tearing through his senses. He was angry with himself for not controlling his temper, and angry with Jennifer for betraying him.

Yet even through the anger he could not deny his love for her. His heart had somehow become a black hole that was swallowing the rest of his being. He longed to run back into her arms, but at the same time he wanted to scream at her. Give her back the pain that she had inflicted upon him.

The thoughts in his head refused to cease, and he refused to deal with them any longer. The only answer he could devise was to subdue his mind with alcohol until his nerves could feel nothing. He directed his steps to McKinney's Pub, vowing to not stop drinking until he could not feel the bitter cold against his skin. The brisk smack of a frigid wind caught his breath, slamming him head-on and nearly freezing him in stride. His body shivered. The temperature was low enough without the crisp whips of wind. He reasoned that if he could make his body numb to this cold weather, then he would certainly anesthetize his emotions. Or at the very least pass out from the attempt.

Chapter 15

"Someone looks pretty rough this morning," Gail commented. Her face appeared to Sean through a squint. Bright light split through his lids and burned his eyes like cinders. His normally perfect vision was displaying a slightly watery version of his second mother. Gail, the mariner.

He attempted to exhale, abruptly holding it before the air could completely escape his lungs. He placed his hand on the top of his head, groaning in pain. "Someone FEELS really rough. My head hurts when I breathe." He paused to swallow, but the cottonmouth he was experiencing would not allow him the luxury of saliva. "Even my hair hurts."

"Darn 'morning after' flu anyway," Gail said with a smile.

He tried to gently clear his throat, but the grimace on his face exposed his lack of success. Lying on the living room couch, he was not quite certain how he had arrived in this location. He looked up at Gail who continued to wear a facetious smile upon her face. "Well, I guess I didn't make it to my bed." Sean uttered weakly.

"No," she answered, "I suppose you didn't. Although I figured you were probably lucky to have made it to the sofa."

"What time is it?"

"It's 8:35. I thought you might want some breakfast."

"As long as it's preceded by a couple of aspirins," he uttered. He suddenly realized he was wearing nothing except his underwear. He reached down quickly and snatched his jeans from the carpeted floor. He clutched his head as he popped back up vertically then quickly pulled his jeans on from a seated position as he spoke, "I have to get over to the Plaza. I'm doing some work for Evan Kershaw. I have to put some finishing touches on the interior of the new store that he's building."

"You are a jack of all trades," Gail commented.

"I do whatever it takes to pay the bills," he responded flatly, thinking of how he struggled to maintain his household finances for the past two months while Jennifer refused to work.

Gail giggled. "That's what you head needs, the nice sound of a pounding hammer."

"You are a little sadistic when someone's in pain." He peered up at her through a squint and a smile. His hand gripped the back of his neck in hopes of alleviating some of the tension in his head.

"I'm only sadistic because you inflicted it upon yourself. I don't have a headache this morning. Of course, I was not drinking until God knows when. You should feel fortunate I didn't wake you up by banging two pans together."

"Well, thanks for the small favor, I guess." Sean paused, remembering a very important detail regarding his morning. "I had asked June Eckley to gather some clothes and toiletries from my house. Did she happen to drop them off?"

"Her daughter Angelia did." Gail replied, as she exited the living room in the direction of the kitchen. "I put your things up on the bed that I prepared for you. You remember; the bed that you never quite made it to last night. By the way, I love those lobster boxer shorts that you're wearing; very sexy."

Sean laughed, shaking his head ever so gently, at Gail's candid charm. "I will have to call Angelia and June to thank them." He rose from the couch and stumbled slightly as he made his way toward the staircase.

The Honey Brook Plaza was located east of town on a section of Route 322 called Horseshoe Pike. Sean steered his light blue, wide-bed pickup truck with the words 'Bergin Landscaping' on the driver's door, into the first entrance. The front of the truck bore the black attachment rack for the snowplow. Stains of road salt and dirt covered the body beyond each tire.

Inside, a travel-mug of Gail's coffee was secured in a cup holder in the middle of the console. The enticing scent of Columbia's finest blended with the smell of gasoline and exhaust fumes that permeated the cab of the old truck. It was a blend of smells that Sean had become accustomed to until they were nearly comforting to him. The landscaping business had created its own problems for Sean; however, it also provided a refuge from the pressures of home.

He drove around to the rear entrance and parked the truck. Grabbing his coffee mug, he hopped down from his vehicle and entered the large brown metal door that had been placed in the middle of the concrete block building.

The door opened into a large rectangular vacant room with an entrance hallway placed slightly to the right on the far wall. The drywall crew had finished the day before. Protective plastic was still strewn about the smooth concrete floor with remnants of joint compound tubs, putty knives, and sanding tools. Sean walked through the aperture, which led into a ten-foot long hallway. The smells of fresh cut pine filled his nostrils. At the end of the hallway, the walls opened up into a spacious storefront, which contained three more adjacent rooms. A long room with dividers protruded from the front section of the wall to his right, while two other rooms were located in the corners of the rear of the storefront. The store was lit by a few overhanging florescent lights and the sun, which entered through the large display window at the store's front.

Three men were surveying the building's interior as Sean entered. Evan Kershaw, the owner of the plaza, appeared to be giving the other two men a brief tour of his latest creation. One of the men was Dylan Lucas, who had come over from his pharmacy, located on the far side of the plaza. Dylan was of average height with a lean torso. His blonde hair was cut short, disguising the swirling, natural curl it possessed. His heart-shaped face bore large blue eyes as its distinctive feature. He was wearing a white dress shirt with a striped tie under an equally white lab coat.

The third man elicited the biggest surprise. Sean walked up behind the husky man whose face bore the same handsome, rugged features with a few more lines and creases. "Don't tell me I have to deal with you critiquing my work all day," Sean gibbed.

His brother, Neil, and the other two men turned to face Sean as he walked casually up to them.

"Hey, little brother," Neil responded in a welcoming tone. "A few items were missing on Dylan's last order, so I thought I'd drop them by myself." Neil now managed the same paper supply company that he had worked for as a teen. "I heard Evan had a temporary lapse in judgment and hired you to do some interior work."

"Sean's the best in town," Evan intervened on Sean's behalf. "I don't know why he wastes his time on landscaping. He could be making a fortune in construction."

Sean arrived at his brother's side and shook his hand, staring at him with a gratified smile on his dimpled face. "You see, I have fans outside my family."

Neil pulled Sean closer with his handshake and leaned in toward Sean's ear. "I heard about you and Jennifer separating. Are you okay?"

"Yeah, thanks Bro. I'll be fine."

"If you need anything, call me. You should be calling me more often than you do anyway." Neil added with a firm look of concern.

"Are you going to The Pub tonight?" Dylan asked Sean.

"I don't know. I had a really good time there last night. Clear up to the point when I woke up this morning," Sean responded.

"You have to come - tonight is Mincy's birthday party." Neil added.

"Like I want to put up with Mincy?" Sean commented with a chuckle. Nevin Mincemoyer was more obnoxious sober than most people were drunk. Anything that entered Mincy's mind was prospect for vocalization. Mincy made enough money to get by, although no one was certain how. They could never determine the truth from the lies. Mincy had never made an honest dollar in his life.

"No! It's going to be funny. Come on, Sean; we can watch him get shit-faced and throw up all over himself," Dylan pleaded. "Besides he put up the first two hundred dollars for beer."

"In that case, I'll be there," Sean conceded.

"Alright! I think it starts at eight, so I'll see you there at seven," Dylan continued. "If I'm going to attend that asshole's party, I want to be there for my share of the first two hundred dollars."

"I have to get back to the store," Neil said, "I'll see you tonight." Neil placed a hand firmly on Sean's shoulder as he stared at his younger brother with loving regard, "Okay?"

Sean smiled, "I'll be there."

"I have to get going, too." Evan chimed in before reminding Sean what he wanted done.

"I didn't count on my memory so I kept the list you made me," Sean responded.

Dylan watched as the other two men exited before turning his attention to Sean, "I missed you at my annual Super Bowl party. I was really hoping you'd show."

"I'm sorry," Sean explained. "Things have been pretty tense at the house. I was afraid to leave."

"Pittsburgh and Minnesota put on a good show. I thought for certain that Pennsylvania would win a title," Dylan added.

"I guess Minnesota's offense was too much for 'em," Sean commented, making small talk. He enjoyed being with Dylan and needed his friendship now more than ever.

"You and I should be out on that football field," Dylan commented. "Okay, maybe not me, but you should have been. When we played in high school, nobody hit as hard as you did. You were the best linebacker in the state. I remember when you hit that one kid from Central. He would not get up. He just laid there and cried."

"I can still hit pretty hard," Sean announced. "But the difference now is that you hear MY bones popping."

"I know what you mean on that one. My shoulder aches like hell when the weather gets bad. It's a good thing I have access to painkillers."

Sean chuckled. "You had a good arm. If it wasn't for that shoulder separation, you might have pulled down a scholarship."

"Thanks." Dylan accepted the compliment blandly. "I enjoy being a pharmacist. It doesn't hurt as much."

"Those were great times; not a care in the world. I don't know what the hell happened."

"I can't even begin to imagine how you must feel." Dylan gripped Sean's arm, "Listen, if you ever need to talk I'm here for you, okay? You know that, don't you?"

"I know."

"You need to let those emotions go; don't let them get bottled up inside. Something like that can eat a man alive."

"Thanks, Dylan, I appreciate the offer."

"Are you sleeping okay?" Dylan asked. "I can get you some Ambien if you need it. That will help you sleep."

"No, I'm okay." The two men stood quiet for a few moments, lost for what to say next.

At last, Dylan broke the silence. "Well, I guess I better let you get to work. I need to get back to the pharmacy. There are sick people in this town and I have the drugs to fix them."

Sean watched his friend exit through the front door. He sighed, wishing the conversation could have lasted longer. He could tolerate Mincy's antics as long as Dylan was at the party. Placing his coffee on the floor, he grabbed his tape measure and began taking readings of the doorways of the interior rooms.

Chapter 16

Sean entered McKinney's Pub, the scene of the previous night's tirade of drinking. The pub had been built in the early 1900s, but it had been remodeled several times since its inception. The dark walnut bar matched the color of the original hardwood floor. A sign behind the bar counted down the number of days until Saint Patrick's Day.

The pub was decorated in the theme of the region's coal mining history. Small picture frames surrounded a glass case on the wall next to the door. The case held a miner's helmet, several chunks of coal, and a newspaper article recounting the poor working conditions that the miners had to endure. The surrounding black and white photos were of the coal miners during their rare times of relaxation and personal time.

A row of five cherry wood tables each with four wooden chairs, lined the right wall. Old mining lanterns had been transformed into overhead electric lights above each table, illuminating the smoke in the room with a dim yellow glow. A soft country ballad eased from a jukebox in the far corner.

The pub was occupied by approximately twenty people, one of which was Dylan. Before Sean could remove his coat, Dylan was at his side. "It's 7:55!" Dylan stated admonishing. "You almost missed the start of the free drinks."

Sean stretched his neck upward searching the room, "Where's Mincy?"

"He has Ed trapped in the back room bragging about how he's buying the first two hundred dollars worth of beer again." Dylan said, referring to Ed McKinney, a Navy veteran and the owner of the bar. Ed was a descendant of the pub's founder and now held the responsibility of keeping its historic tradition alive. "I'm telling you, Sean, this is going to be fucking hilarious."

"I bought a birthday card from your pharmacy and put money in it. I had no idea what he likes other than beer," Sean stated, as he began walking down the bar with Dylan.

"That's all I did," Dylan responded. "Neil's at the other end of the bar."

Sean responded with a nod as he approached the man seated at the first barstool. "Hey, Junior. How are you?" Sean asked.

"Hey, Sean-o!" Junior exclaimed as he spun his large frame around on his barstool to face his friend. He extended a huge hand to shake. Sean held out his hand reluctantly, with his wrist still tucked against his stomach. Junior's hand shot out at it, gripping it like a vice and shaking it vigorously. Sean grimaced beneath his smile - loved the man, hated his handshakes.

"I'll be talking to you, big guy," Sean promised, patting Junior's back as he walked away. Sean continued down the bar, saying hello to the pub's regulars until he decided on a seat near the middle of the bar. He leaned back on his stool to wave hello to Neil at the far end.

Dylan placed himself on the stool next to Sean and slapped his palm on the top of the bar. "It's eight o'clock! Where the fuck is Mincy with my free beer?" His comment induced laughter from the other men.

Sean plucked a pretzel from the nearest bowl and focused his attention on the television screen above the back of the bar. A sports channel was reviewing the finer details of the upcoming college basketball tournament. He was immersed in the commentary when two hands gripped his shoulders.

"You made it!" It was the unmistakable raspy voice and foul breath of Nevin Mincemoyer. Sean turned and looked up at Mincy's droopy, unshaven face. His thin black hair was slicked down flat on the top of his head by gel or natural body oils. His eyelids were dark and puffy as though he suffered from insomnia. It was clear to Sean that it was one of Mincy's better days.

"Happy birthday, Mincy," Sean said as he handed him the card he had purchased.

"Sean, now you shouldn't have done that. I know you're having troubles of your own." Mincy spoke in a consistent exhale. He wrapped his arm around Sean and moved in fretfully close. "But Arlen's in a much better place."

"I know," Sean responded civilly, but his teeth clenched in disgust.

"You know, I never got my invitation to the funeral." Mincy continued.

Dylan jumped off his stool and put his arm around Mincy, pulling him away from Sean. "Mincy, you do realize you're a dick, don't you? Please tell me you're not that stupid."

Mincy chuckled. "I love you too, Dylan. You're always funny and stuff. I'm glad you're here."

"Mincy, I want you to know, you can count on me anytime you're buying," Dylan promised.

Mincy stuck his thumb in the air and winked, "I got you, buddy."

"Yeah, you got something, Mincy, and I don't want it. It looks incurable." Dylan put his hand on Mincy's back and gave him a subtle, yet suggestive, push to start him on his way back down the bar. Dylan then returned to his stool next to Sean, remaining in silence, searching for something to say. "I'm sorry about that, Sean."

"No sweat; he means well. It's his birthday. I guess you have to overlook the stupid shit he says," Sean muttered with a deep sigh. Finally the amusement of what Mincy said brushed back the painful memory. "He never got the invitation." Sean said as he began to laugh.

Dylan joined in the laughter. The discomfort of the previous moment made him laugh harder than he normally would - laughing until his eyes filled with tears. Dylan wiped the corner of his eye, "Oh, shit, Sean," he finally managed, "I am so thankful I have you."

"I'm glad I have you, too. Just make sure I get an invitation to your funeral, or I'm not fucking coming." Sean continued to chuckle.

The hours passed as the beer flowed. Mincy became more unstable with every passing drink. He pulled off his shirt at ten o'clock and stood atop a chair to perform a loutish belly dance for the crowd that had swelled to forty people. At eleven o'clock he slipped on beer he had spilled earlier and fell hard into the jukebox. The music stopped and the lights slowly faded out. Ed came from behind the bar and checked to make certain it was still plugged in. Everything appeared proper except the machine's operation. Ed threatened Mincy to stop the party unless he calmed himself.

Sean mingled occasionally, pausing several times to harass Neil as he passed him to go to the bathroom, but mostly he spent the night talking to Dylan. The two men spoke of their jobs and reminisced about their days in high school until, inevitably, the conversation turned toward Sean's separation from Jennifer.

"I tried to talk her into getting help," Sean commented. "You know, seeing a psychologist."

"It hasn't been that long," Dylan responded. "Do you really think she's losing it?"

"I hate to say it Dylan, but I really think she's going crazy."

The smell of body odor born of stale beer became apparent as Mincy pushed his way between Sean and Dylan. Mincy looked at Sean with glassy, red eyes, above his crocked smile. "Well, I say, Jennifer can be as crazy in the head as she wants. As long as that hot little bitch is crazy in my bed; it's okay with me."

Like fingernails scratching across a chalkboard, it was not the sound of Mincy's voice that raised the hair on the back of Sean's neck; it was the impudence of his words - a combination of the wrong words spoken at the wrong time. The level of Sean's frustration went from zero to intolerable within the span of a single phrase. Dylan could see Sean's nostrils flaring and his eyes widen as Sean hopped down from his barstool. Dylan jumped up, but he could not reach Sean around Mincy.

The wild and transfixed look in Sean's eyes never registered danger in the alcohol-enriched brain in Mincy's head as he continued to laugh hysterically at his own joke. Sean often stated that there were two different kinds of men in this world. Those who talk about fighting and those who fight. Sean was never one to talk.

The broken-toothed gaping smile on Mincy's face failed to remove itself before Sean's fist slammed into the nose above it. The fist clutched nearly four months of torturous pain and carried rage in between each whitened knuckle. The force of its blow sent Mincy stumbling backwards into Dylan. The two men fell onto the table behind them, sending splintering wood and shards of beer coated glass into the air as the table gave way under their weight.

Before Sean could take another step, Neil had navigated his way down the bar and slammed his shoulder into his brother's chest. Neil locked his arms around Sean, driving him out through the front door and into the cold winter night.

"What the fuck are you trying to prove!" Neil shouted as he stood face-to-face with his younger brother.

Sean reared his fist back, poised to attack.

"I'm going to forget that you did that." Neil stated firmly as Sean cautiously lowered his guard.

"I'm warning you, Neil; don't push me," Sean spat.

The two brothers stood inches apart, wondering if each would actually hit the other. They had many fist fights as kids, but never as men.

"I know you're hurting, Sean, but your loss does not constitute heartbreak for everyone else. You can't expect people to always watch what they say around you. You came here knowing that this was Mincy's night. You knew he would be hammered and at his worst. Well, if it's a dog, it's gonna bark."

"Did you hear what that fucker said about my wife?" Sean shouted, pointing toward the pub. He paused trying to control his temper. "I will not let anybody get away with that."

"You have to watch your temper. You always had a problem with..."

"Ah, spare me your fatherly lecture. You never quite filled the shoes."

"Hey! I tried to help raise you the way Pop would have wanted. I am sorry if that inconvenienced you."

Inside, Mincy lay on top of Dylan as he repeatedly shouted, "What the fuck did I do?" A crimson flow of blood poured from both of Mincy's nostrils. His eyes displayed a drunken glaze, but the alcohol could not subdue the pain that seemed to vibrate throughout his entire head.

"You pissed him off, you stupid shit!" Dylan snapped as he struggled to slide out from under Mincy, his legs still trapped under Mincy's upper torso. "Now get the fuck off of me before I hit you, too! Ah, Christ, Mincy! You're bleeding all over my new pants!"

Mincy struggled to his feet and stumbled into the arms of Ed. "Let's get you back into the bathroom and check that nose of yours," Ed told him. "I think it might be broken."

Dylan got up on his feet and looked around for Sean, "Where did Sean go?"

"Neil took him outside to cool off," Junior commented.

Dylan started to head for the door until Junior grabbed his arm, "Stay in here. It's a family thing now. It's best we stay out of it. Let Neil talk to him." Dylan nodded in agreement.

Outside, Sean responded to Neil's statement, "I'm getting tired of your constant criticism of me! You're always half way up my ass about everything I do. Let me ask you a question, Neil. Have I ever done anything right in your eyes?"

Neil softened his stance, knowing that he had been hard on Sean in the past. "Do you want to know the truth, Sean. Before tonight, I have always looked up to you." Sean's clinched jaw slackened. "Yes. I wish I were half as popular as you are. People love you." Neil paused for a moment and then continued. "I guess I push you too hard sometimes, but I'm just trying to help you. I feel guilty that I have memories of Dad, and you never had his guidance in your life. I'm only trying to teach you what he taught me."

Sean stepped back and stared down the dark street, searching for the right words to say. His hands, no longer clenched, rested on his hips. "You did well by me, Neil," he finally managed.

"Hey, I love you, little brother."

"I love you, too," Sean said, turning his gaze back to Neil.

"Man, you really inherited Pop's temper," Neil stated with a smile. "You can sure as hell through a punch like Pop could. That looked like a Barry Bonds home run in there." The two brothers now stood together in laughter. "Lucky for Mincy, Dylan played air traffic controller and, at least, helped him land."

Sean laughed for a moment then spoke, "Ah, shit, Neil," he sighed, "do you think I should go back in there and apologize to Mincy?"

"I think Mincy would wet himself if he saw you walk back in that bar. You head on home. I'll go back in and clean up this mess. I'll tell Mincy you're sorry and that you'll talk to him tomorrow."

"Okay. Tell Ed I'm sorry about his table, and I'll pay for it."

"Don't worry about it. You go home and get yourself some sleep. Stay out here for a minute; I'll go in and get your coat."

Sean nodded his head and stared, once again, down the vacant street, "Yeah, don't mind if I do." A shiver down the length of his body reminded him of the frigid chill in the air. The invasive cold stung his flesh as it permeated through the wooly cotton of his grey Penn State sweatshirt. Mincy's blood now dotted an elliptical pattern surrounding the letters ATE.

Neil returned, handing Sean his coat. Sean shrugged into the sleeves and walked toward his truck as he pulled his keys from his coat pocket.

"Isn't Gail's house within walking distance?" Neil yelled after him. "I think you had too much to drink. Why don't you leave your truck here?"

Sean tossed the keys slightly in the air, bouncing them against his palm. The thought of walking back in the morning cold to retrieve the truck was not appealing, but he was not in any mood to discuss the matter further. "Okay. If it makes you happy, I'll leave the truck here. It's a nice night for a walk."

Copper Dragons

Neil smiled and nodded his approval before he disappeared into the bar. Sean tucked his hands inside his coat pockets and walked down the street. His mind began to replay the past. He was frustrated with himself for not being able to control his temper. The anger he had felt toward Mincy had now turned inward. It was not anger for what he had done at the bar. Mincy had clearly provoked him. Sean was punishing himself for the last moments of Arlen's life. His mind played it out in fragments. A strobe of images began flashing through his thoughts. The burning wave of rage that took control of his rational thought. Flash. The look of terror in Arlen's eyes as he cowered inside the tub. Flash. His son's body hopelessly submerged. Sean shook his head in a desperate attempt to clear what was forming in his mind. But the memory played on, burrowing deep into his conscience. Sean knew that sleep would not come easy. He decided to stop and purchase a six-pack of beer before turning in. *I need this to help me sleep.*

Chapter 17

The morning sun rested on the eastern horizon, casting an orange hue upon the wintry sky. The rays slanted across the snow covered lawns, transforming them into glittering urban crystals. Only a few of the rays entered through the slit in the curtain of Jennifer's bedroom window, drawing a thin line of shimmering gold across the carpet and upon her bare feet. Jennifer wiggled her toes briefly, allowing them to bask in the light.

She was seated on the floor of her bedroom, curled into a ball with her knees against her chest and her arms wrapped about her shins. She stared incessantly at the disheveled pile of blankets and pillows stacked in the center of the king-sized bed. She was not exactly certain when it happened, but her bed had changed from a rest haven into a limbo of sleep deprivation during the past fifty-nine sleepless hours. The nefarious mattress tempted her with a desire that she could not fulfill. The pillows mocked her heavy head and the blankets tormented her tired body.

Her eyes, wide and unblinking, stung from their lack of slumber, and her hands set about the task of wringing together to pass the time. She had counted a thousand sheep one hundred times over in her attempt to sleep, with each cycle they changed color; white, brown, black, red, royal blue, magenta. The eight hours she spent watching television merely exasperated the situation. Even the warm milk left her with nothing more than an upset stomach.

Her mind played a lurid game of insomniac displays, repeating horrid images and events of her recent past. Her nerves were frail and her lips felt numb as she struggled to remain rational. She cried several times during the past days, visiting Arlen's room and stretching her body out on the floor next to his pristine bed. She wandered about in the night like a ghost in her own home, and her pale reflection in the mirror seemed to substantiate the conjecture. Worn to the point of exhaustion, her mind was unable to focus on the most mundane of tasks.

The situation could become dangerous if she did not sleep soon. She pulled herself to her feet and sulked over to the nightstand to withdraw the telephone book from its drawer. Her tired eyes ached, barely able to focus on the fine print as she searched for Dr. Conahan's number. She dialed the number, vowing to herself, as she waited for the tones to become a greeting, that no matter how busy he was, he would arrange to see her immediately.

Ninety minutes later, she walked through the automatic doors in the medical building that housed Dr. Alexander Conahan's office. The world outside the walls of home had seemed nearly foreign to her. The air was bitterly cold, yet refreshing upon her face.

The shower she had taken before leaving her home had helped her to relax. However, she was still far from sleepy. Her saving grace was not far away; she would be sleeping soundly come nightfall. Dr. Conahan was like a shroud of protection to her. He knew how difficult it was for her to perform the simplest social tasks with the anxiety with which she lived. She knew he would understand and provide the answers to her problems.

She approached the receptionist's window, recognizing the face through the glass as the door slid open.

"Hello, Jennifer." The woman behind the desk greeted her.

"Hi, Pam. How is little Sara doing?"

"Oh, she's a terror as usual. You can have a seat. Sharon will be out to get you shortly." The receptionist instructed, referring to Dr. Conahan's nurse.

"Thank you," Jennifer muttered as she turned to face a deserted waiting area. Rows of chairs lined the walls with an end table tucked between every fourth one. Pamphlets and magazines were abundant on each stand. A television was mounted in the corner directly across from the receptionist window.

She decided on the chair closest to the door that she would enter into the access hallway for the examination rooms. She removed a housekeeping magazine from the end table next to her and began thumbing through the pages. Less time ticked away than her perception insisted, but then again, perceiving anything on fifty sleepless hours was futile. She read about the bright color selection in post-holiday décor. Apparently, it prevented depression during the long final months of winter. A tickle brushed the back of her neck. At first she thought that something was crawling on her and swiped her hand across her skin. When it happened a second time it accompanied a chill that edged down her spine. It was not eight-legged freaks on the march; it was the fine hairs on her neck. Next came the uneasy feeling of being watched. That was followed by a gnawing paranoia. Slowly, she raised her head from the magazine.

In the far corner of the waiting area sat an elderly priest. A delicate and warm smile curled his lips as he nodded hello. The white hair surrounding his face only served to enhance his pasty complexion. Jennifer's eyes quickly darted back to the pages in front of her. She had not been prepared to actually see anyone, despite her overwhelming need to check. Her eyes widened and her breath increased, as she drew the courage to look back at him. His eyes were warm and welcoming, but a cold chill crept across her skin at his unrelenting gaze. Once again her eyes dropped back to the magazine. Her mind tried to rationalize how she could have missed him at her first inspection of what appeared to be an empty waiting room. He looked innocuous, but his presence bore an eerie presage.

Only months ago, she thought she had seen Arlen along the road on her way to work; her eyes had played tricks on her that day. Perhaps, it was happening again. She gathered her thoughts and looked up a third time from her magazine. The priest remained seated with his eyes fixed directly upon her. Jennifer swallowed hard, with perspiration collecting in her palms and the race of her heart threatening to burst forth from her chest; this time she returned his stare.

"It's really cold out there today, isn't it?" She had hoped that some casual conversation would break the tension. But the priest continued to stare at her without a word spoken. "Did you want something?" She asked, her voice rising slightly, quivering in confused frustration.

The priest responded to the question by a broadening of his smile, continuing to remain locked in his stare. Jennifer slowly rose to her feet, her eyes remained fixed on the pale priest who sat with perfect posture in the corner chair. His smile was unbroken and his eyes had a twinkle of either pureness or evil - Jennifer could not resolve which.

She walked over to the receptionist window and turned her attention to Pam. "Pam, who is this priest over here," she said in a whisper; "he keeps staring at …" She stopped her sentence as she turned to see the empty chair he had once occupied. Like a dip in a nice vat of liquid nitrogen - time froze, and for a brief second so did the beat of her heart. The chair was empty. She knew that the priest was there and she had not provided him with enough time during the diverting of her eyes to escape through the door. Everything else in the room, including Pam, had suddenly become insignificant to the point of nonexistent. The empty chair seemed to grow in stature until it engulfed the entire room. Her cotton-dry mouth drew in a deep breath. She became light headed as her mind struggled to believe what her eyes had seen - or did not see. Her body began to tingle until at last it convulsed in an involuntary shudder.

"What priest are you talking about Jennifer? There's nobody else here," Pam stated in confusion. "You're the doctor's last patient."

"There was a priest sitting over there just a minute ago," Jennifer insisted. "He kept staring at me. I don't know, he …" Jennifer's voice trailed off in a stammer, her brow creased upon her ever paling face.

"Jennifer, I have been right here at this desk since an hour before you walked in. There was no priest in this office." Pam paused with a look of concern, as she could see the dazed fear in Jennifer's eyes. "Are you all right?"

"Yeah," Jennifer uttered softly, her eyes seemed to be searching the floor. "I guess I'm just really tired." She turned away without reconnecting with Pam's eyes.

"Dr. Conahan will be with you shortly." Pam stated in a wary tone. Jennifer acknowledged Pam with a nod of her head as she slowly returned to her seat. She silently prayed that her hallucination was merely a derivative from her insomnia.

She knew she was in the throes of a deep depression, but the thought of losing control of her sanity frightened her beyond comprehension. The memory of her mother's condition still held the bite of degradation. All of the fear and confusion housed in Sue Ellen's eyes like a wild animal with the burden of understanding its own mortality. Sue Ellen's condition had deteriorated until she lived in a world that only she could see, always alone, even amongst a crowd. *I would rather be dead than to live that way,* Jennifer thought to herself.

Jennifer's head snapped up quickly at the call of her name, the windswell of her thoughts apparent in her eyes. Sharon, Dr. Conahan's nurse, stood above her and placed a hand on Jennifer's shoulder.

"You can come back now," Sharon offered, holding the door open, which led into a hallway lined doors, each leading to an examination room. Jennifer complied without a word as she stepped into the passage and then waited for Sharon to take the lead. A few paces down the hall, they stopped at a large scale, which Jennifer stepped on at Sharon's request. Sharon penned a note in a file that Jennifer had lost ten pounds since her previous visit. She then led Jennifer into one of the examination rooms and checked her blood pressure, noting in her file that it was slightly elevated. Jennifer sat up the examination table, feeling the cold vinyl even through her jeans.

"You are having trouble sleeping?" Sharon asked.

Jennifer responded with a nod of her head and then turned her eyes downward. "Don't worry," Sharon reassured her, taking Jennifer's hand in hers. "We will get you all fixed up."

Jennifer looked up at her like a child with a scratched knee, nodding at Sharon with tear filled eyes. Sharon smiled warmly and released Jennifer's hand. "Dr. Conahan will be in shortly." Sharon exited the examination room leaving Jennifer to stare at the posters and charts on the walls.

Jennifer learned on the Body Mass Index Chart that she was of average weight for her height. She attempted to memorize the names of the valves and chambers of the human heart from a poster that hung next to a window. Through the window, she stared at the roof of the adjacent hospital, watching the steam rise into the cold sky from the warm air vents. She read advertisements for medications ranging from sexual performance aids to relieving the symptoms of allergies. She stared at a jar of tongue depressors that rested on a desk attached to one of the walls in the room. She reassured herself that the doctor had no reason to use one on her. At last, the door opened and Dr. Conahan walked in, greeting Jennifer with a warm hello.

Alexander Conahan was a thin man with a full brown mustache that bore intermittent gray. A strip of hair ran from ear to ear encircling the back of a primarily balding head. Despite his show of age, his features were still strikingly handsome. He seated himself at the desk and began to review Jennifer's chart.

"Why don't you tell me a little about what's going on?" His voice was smooth and calming. Jennifer had always welcomed the sound. It was as though his words were a Lilly pad that could flow across the top of a pond without creating a ripple. Jennifer often wondered if he hypnotized her with it during each visit.

"I haven't been able to sleep in almost three days. My anxiety is getting so bad that at times it feels like I can hardly breathe."

"Uh-huh," Dr. Conahan shook his head slowly in a gesture of sympathetic understanding. "Are you still experiencing feelings of depression?" He had examined Jennifer not long after Arlen's funeral. Sean had insisted on the appointment. While she complied with Sean's request, Jennifer had refused medication. This time Dr. Conahan recognized a different look in her eyes. She was clearly at a breaking point.

"Oh, yeah," Jennifer replied as tears began trickling from her eyes as if upon command.

He rose from his seat and stood in front of her, "I'm going to listen to your heart and check you over a little bit." He began to feel her glands on her neck. "I'm concerned over your sudden drop in weight. Have you been eating properly?"

Jennifer shrugged, "I guess I eat when I think of it. I don't have much of an appetite lately."

"I know it can be difficult, but you have to maintain a proper diet; especially when you're going through these emotional times."

He used his stethoscope to listen to her heart and her lungs, requesting a few deep breaths. He looked inside her ears and at her throat, thankfully without the use of a tongue depressor. He placed the palms of his hands under hers checking the color of her fingernails and cuticles. And finally returned to his seat at the desk and began typing notes in her computer file.

Jennifer shifted on the table; the crinkling of paper seemed to echo in the room. "Can a lack of sleep cause a person to see things that are not really there?"

"Three days is a long time to go without sleeping. If our brain is unable to go into a REM or dream state, we will often experience dream-like images while we're awake. Are you experiencing hallucinations?"

"I just had one in your waiting room." Jennifer answered blandly.

He nodded. "Well, that can be a symptom of sleep deprivation. It can become difficult to tell the difference between reality and the visions you have because your judgment becomes compromised. It is good that you came in when you did. Are you taking any medications right now?"

Jennifer waged her head.

"Any over the counter medications?"

Again she replied with a shake of her head.

"Is there anything else I should know about?"

"Sean and I have separated," she admitted.

"I am sorry to hear that. Sometimes it can feel as though everything is crashing down on us all at once, huh?"

Jennifer answered with a sobbing 'yes' as the tears ran down her cheeks. Dr. Conahan sat patiently quiet, allowing Jennifer to release her emotions. He pulled a few tissues from a box on the desk and offered them to her.

"Once we get your body feeling healthy again, you will find yourself heading in the right direction emotionally. I want you to take this one step at a time.

I am going to give you two prescriptions. The first one is called Clonazepam to help ease your anxiety and help with your depression. I want you to take one tablet three times a day. The second one is 400 milligrams of Trazodone to help you sleep."

"So, I have to take sleeping pills?" Jennifer questioned with a frown.

"If you want to get some sleep. You need to pay your sleep debt. This will help you get started. Contrary to popular opinion, sleeping pills are nonaddicting. They are perfectly safe if you take them in moderation and as prescribed."

"Okay."

"Take one tablet of the Trazodone every night before bedtime. I'm going to give you one month of the Clonazepam, but only one week of Trazodone." There was a family history of suicide attempts, so he decided to error on the part of caution by limiting the number of Trazodone in her house.

"This stuff is going to make you drowsy, so I don't want you operating a vehicle." He paused, looking up from the file to achieve a visual confirmation of her understanding. She continuously nodded her head like a toy dog in the rear window of a car. "Jennifer, I will refill the Trazodone only on the condition. You have to schedule a couple of sessions with a psychologist. I don't believe what you're experiencing right now is due to any chemical imbalance. You are in a very serious depression and it's manifesting itself in you physically. It is not going to subside on its own. This is something that you need to work out with a professional. Okay?"

Jennifer implied her understanding with a nod, as she regained her poise.

"I want you to get some rest and make sure you're eating three good meals each day. I am going to refer you to Dr. Bomboy. He is a psychologist in the Reading area. I think you will find yourself very comfortable with him. I want to keep an eye on your progress, so I need to see you back here in one week. If anything comes up in the meantime, I want you to call the office immediately."

"Okay," Jennifer answered as she wiped the tears from her cheeks. Dr. Conahan gave her a smile and a pat on the shoulder as he left the room. A few minutes later Sharon entered with prescriptions and instructions for their use.

Jennifer left the building with something she had not felt in months; hope. She left with the hope of restoring her life back to something similar to normal. A brief stop at the drug store was all that stood between her and a restful sleep.

Chapter 18

Michelle Kenrick thanked the woman for her purchase and placed the change into her elderly palm, giving the customer her warmest contrived smile. Michelle was porcelain pretty, in the early months of her nineteenth year; a face beautified by nature with a mind cynical with conceit. No sooner had the elderly woman turned away with her prescription bottle Michelle averted her eyes to the clock on the wall behind her. The final hour of her work shift had slowed to a crawl. Her head snapped back around to face forward, frustration apparent in her eyes.

She worked at the Med Swift Pharmacy primarily on the weekends. Her current shift was one of few evenings. She hated working on a school night. She was a senior in high school and anxiously awaited her collegian academics in Social Sciences. She looked forward to the courses and the inevitable parties that accompanied life on campus. Time, at every stage in her life, was moving far too slowly for her liking. She enjoyed the first part of her senior year, but her abiding state of mind had turned impatient since the Christmas recess. Wasting her time at work was certainly not helping her frame of mind. There was homework to do, tests to study for, friends to call. The vision of her boyfriend, Seth, in his military uniform suddenly popped into her head. Two days had passed since she had been with him, and she longed to see his eyes fixate on her; the passion in his gaze. His rugged demeanor was no match for her long legs and full breasts. In her presence, the big soldier boy was nothing more than an obedient dog; except, of course, for the humping problem. But through months of patience, she had managed to harness that energy in ways more useful to her needs.

She heard the single tone from the door alarm to inform her of a customer who had just entered the store. Her eyes remained staunchly fixed forward until the redheaded woman maneuvered herself directly in front of Michelle's stare.

"Can I help you?" Michelle inquired, following a brief, but significant sigh.

"I have a couple prescriptions," the red-haired woman stated, despondently.

Michelle stood silent during the customer's pause, awaiting further information. Following a wait of what seemed like hours, she realized no further information was going to be given forthright. Michelle lowered her chin and shook her head mockingly as she spoke with snide venom, "Do you have the prescriptions with you, or was it called in earlier?"

"Oh, yes," the woman seemed to suddenly awaken from a disoriented state, "I have them here, somewhere." She rummaged through her purse and withdrew two papers.

Michelle glanced to her left to see Mr. Lucas, the pharmacist, move to her side as she accepted the prescriptions from the woman.

"Hello," Mr. Lucas spoke uncharacteristically sheepish to the customer.

"Dylan," the woman spoke his name in an emphatic professional tone, as she nodded her head with absurd refinement.

"It will only take me about five minutes," The normally self-assured Lucas lowered his head and shuffled away without another word.

The woman turned away and began exploring the products on the shelves of the pharmacy. *What a shame to see such an attractive woman acting so weird,* Michelle thought. This woman was obviously mentally disturbed, like half the population in this insignificant town – just another eccentric this job has exposed her to. In thirty minutes she would be free of this place and all of the quirky people within it.

Four minutes later, Michelle knew the exact expiration of time from her many glances at the clock, Mr. Lucas returned to her side. He called the woman by name and informed her that the prescriptions were ready.

Michelle waited until the woman returned to the counter to ring the sale into the cash register. "Are the prescriptions all that you needed?"

"Yes."

"Do you have any questions for the pharmacist regarding your prescriptions?"

"No."

Timothy Cole

"Are you a member of our preferred customer discount program?"

"No."

"Would you care to sign up for it?"

"No. Thank you."

"Okay, that will be seventy-nine dollars and ninety-seven cents."

The woman reached into a wallet within her purse and produced eighty dollars. Michelle took the bills from her hand and completed the transaction on the cash register. The cash drawer flung open with a slight 'ding.'

"Your change is three cents. Thank you for shopping at Med Swift." Michelle recited as she placed three pennies into the woman's palm. She watched as the woman clutched the coins in her fist, and then slowly opened her hand to examine them. Michelle was appalled that the woman would check her accuracy for a measly three cents. She had definitely given her three coins; of that Michelle was certain. She had always been excellent at math and giving the proper change.

The three pennies rested in the woman's right palm as she suddenly placed a fingertip to her quivering lips.

Tears swelled in the woman's eyes. "Two heads and one tail. Which one of you spilled the milk?"

Michelle stood quietly dumbfounded as the woman lifted her eyes. She appeared to be embarrassed that she had spoken the words aloud. Snatching the prescription bottles from the counter, she made her exit with a hurried 'thank you.'

"Okay," Michelle spat. "That lady has some serious mental issues."

Jennifer's attention was too preoccupied to comprehend what the young pharmacy clerk had said, but judging by the tone of Dylan Lucas' voice it must have been derogatory.

"Michelle, watch your mouth," Dylan spoke in a furiously audible whisper. "Show some respect. I can't understand why you want a career in social work with the attitude that you have toward people."

Jennifer was too tired and too heartsick for a confrontation, choosing instead to continue her exit from the store. She had never intended to display her lamenting publicly. Or perhaps her sudden display of rue was a cry for help. The memory of her Copper Dragon game with Arlen had caught her off guard. She desperately needed someone to understand her pain, and moreover, someone to ease it. The feeling of hope that had radiated within her as she disembarked from Dr. Conahan's office had now dwindled. The emotional roller coaster continued on.

Jennifer paused outside her car when she recognized the light blue pickup truck at the opposite end of the plaza. She had forgotten that Sean was working for Mr. Kershaw during the winter. Before she could disconnect her gaze, Sean had stepped from the building. Whether it was a moment of chance or fate – Sean had casually glanced down the parking lot in her direction. The two became locked in a stare. She felt miles apart from Sean, but at the same time inches away.

Her ears flushed and her face burned despite the cold. She wanted to run to him, and at the same time she wanted to run away. The strength of her accusations had now faded in her mind amidst lingering doubt. Truth seemed to be foreign to her now. Healing was all that mattered.

Sean stood stoically, looking directly at her before retrieving a tool from the truck cab and disappearing back into the building. Had he seen the longing in her eyes? Had he sensed it? For a moment, her gaze was glued to the truck. An apology would be simple. She desperately wanted to end all of this, but she was familiar with Sean's resolve and his temper. She would be alone again tonight, and perhaps forever.

Chapter 19

Jennifer directed her car into the driveway and entered the house. Evening had descended upon her during the drive home. It was just before six o'clock. She could see the glow of a lamp light through her living room window. She must have left it on absentmindedly until the opening of the front door revealed the presence of her father, Donald. He was walking from the kitchen as he shrugged into his heavy suede coat.

"Dad," Jennifer exclaimed in subdued surprise, "what are you doing here?"

"Hello Princess. I came to check on you. I left you some groceries in the kitchen. I figured you might need some. I already put the milk away, so it wouldn't spoil."

"You didn't have to do that." Jennifer pulled her coat off and hung it in the closet.

"By the looks of you, it's a good thing I did. Are you eating anything? There's almost nothing left of you."

"I'm eating."

He lowered his head and stared at her over the top of his eyeglasses. "You were never good at fibbing to me. You have to eat to keep up your strength, Princess." He sighed with a shrug, "Well, I'm glad to see you left the house for a while, at least."

"I went to see Dr. Conahan. I haven't been sleeping since Sean …" her voice trailed off to avoid the subject.

"I'm really disappointed with Sean; leaving you when you needed him the most."

"There was more to it than that, Dad. It was not all Sean's fault."

"Whatever. What is the doctor going to do for you?"

"He gave me a prescription for sleeping pills."

She did not have to wait for her father's response. She could tell by the expression on his face. It was that judgmental look of concern. It was the dogmatic Daddy look.

"I know what you're going to say, but Dr. Conahan said that they are nonaddicting and safe."

"Well, you remember what happened to your Mom when … ."

"I'm not Mom," Jennifer interrupted, "I don't abuse things."

"I just want you to be careful." Don fell silent, recognizing that fiery look of petulance in his daughter's eyes. The two remained quiet for a few moments as they set new boundaries for the discussion.

Jennifer enjoyed silence, but not in the presence of someone. "Dad, did Mom ever have hallucinations?"

"Your mom experienced a lot of things. She talked about people that could not have existed. Sometimes, it was almost as if she carried on entire friendships without my knowledge. There were other things, but you know I don't like talking about that. Your mother is a good woman, she's just not well. The sickness of a mind is frightening, but there's no shame in it. Why are you asking?"

"I was just curious. Just a book I've been reading."

Don looked at her suspiciously, but chose not to pursue the subject further. "I was just heading out to visit your mother. Why don't you come along with me?"

"I can't."

"You haven't visited your mother since I last summer."

"Dad, don't lay a guilt trip on me, okay." Jennifer interrupted sharply. "I'm really tired and I need to get some sleep. Besides, I just can't deal with her right now."

"Your mother can't help the way she is. She has an illness - not a character flaw. It is nothing to be ashamed of or embarrassed by."

Jennifer dropped her head and bit her lower lip. "I know. I know." Her palms dutifully patted the air. "I'm sorry. I didn't mean it that way. I haven't slept in three days and I'm getting a little testy, that's all."

Don threw his hands up in surrender. "Okay. Maybe next time you can come along; if you ever feel up to it."

He had to get his last little dig in. She was too tired to argue. She loved her father dearly, but at this moment he could not leave her house fast enough to satisfy her. She hugged him and kissed his cheek. Her lips pressed briefly against wrinkled skin. The sensation of which made her suddenly realized that her father was growing old. She had not truly noticed it before. She had been so busy over the past years; her time dominated by raising Arlen, working full-time, playing maid and chef. Her father had taken a back seat to the other men in her life. He had always been a strong presence to her; gentle, yet exuding a calm self-assurance that always made Jennifer feel safe. She pulled back, staring into his face and giving him a warm smile. The confidence still shined in his eyes, but the flesh around it had weakened. She suddenly looked at him in a different light, as she placed a palm to his cheek. He looked frail at that moment; more than any other time she could remember. Perhaps he needed her protection more than either of them would care to admit. "I love you, Dad."

"I love you too, Princess. You get some rest. I will tell Mom you said hello."

"Believe me I'm going straight to bed. Thank you for the food."

"You are welcome."

Jennifer held the door open and watched as her father walked to his car. His image dissolved into the darkness. She made herself a promise as she heard the car engine rumble to life and saw its headlights illuminate the pavement - she would spend more time with him as soon as she gathered herself together. She owed him that much. He was solely responsible for every good memory that she had of her childhood.

She closed the front door and secured the deadbolt. After gathering her prescription and a glass of water, she ascended the staircase and entered the master bedroom. She swallowed one of the sleeping pills with a few sips of water and sat down on the edge of the bed. The blankets were still in the same tangled pile that she had left them. She had no motivation to make the bed, so she tugged one blanket free of the pile and fluffed her pillow. Resting her head back onto the pillow, she felt the center softly give way as the edges wrapped about her ears. The moment she had spent three days waiting for was at hand. A sigh eased from her lips and her heavy lids shrouded her tired eyes. Five minutes passed quietly with scarcely a sound, except the rhythmic expansion and contraction of the air filling her lungs. *Why am I still awake?* Her eyes popped open. This was not going to be as easy as she hoped.

She spent the next fifteen minutes avoiding negative thoughts, attempting to fill her mind with images of comfort. She conjured an image of spreading her body across a sandy beach on a warm summer day. *Had she remembered to lock the front door?* She tried envisioning herself sipping latte at a cozy coffee shop in Venice. *The wind chill made the temperature feel like it was below zero today.* Sitting in a steaming hot tub in the Swiss Alps as the water jets massaged her body. Her mind began to drift amidst a cloak of serene black, though remaining remotely active with swirling thoughts. Thoughts that grazed across her conscious from the rebuking of Freud's theory of dream analysis, to if she had remembered to turn the living room lamp … and then nothing.

Jennifer's body jolted suddenly as if she had awoken from a dream of falling. Her eyes sprung open to see the priest from the doctor's waiting room with his face inches from hers. His features had substance, yet she could see the details of her room through them. She scrambled back to the headboard until she had no room left to retreat. His brow turned down in a look of great concern as the words rolled from his tongue, "E beheld un'altra bestia che esce in su la terra; ed ha avuto due corni come un agnello ed ha parlato come drago."

She could not assimilate the words, but she recognized the language and dialect as Italian. His face stared intensely at her and then as suddenly as it appeared, the face vanished. She scrambled from her bed and backed into a corner of the room. The image was so vivid; surely she had not imagined it. Her back slid down the wall until she crouched on the floor holding her head, her eyes shut tight. Her heart was a drum against her ribs and her breathing came in rapid heaves. *God, no! Not this!* Struggling to maintain her grip on reality, she took inventory of her senses, hearing the distant hum of her furnace and feeling her bare toes curled as they dug into the carpet. *This is real; that was not.* She repeated the phrase over and over in her mind until she spoke the words aloud. She replayed the moments leading up to the priest. She could remember her thoughts up to a point and then she had lost her consciousness to sleep. The priest must have been a dream, a very real one, but a dream none-the-less.

She reassured herself that everything would be okay. The priest was simply a derivative of her tired and overworked mind playing tricks on her. *My sanity is safely intact.*

She crept across the floor and slipped under the blanket on her bed. She laid back into the pillow with her eyes staring wide at the ceiling. She relaxed her body and consciously slowed her breathing. Everything was under control. She closed her eyes. A deep slumber would only follow many minutes of self-soothing.

Chapter 20

Sean arrived at Gail's house under the threat of admonition for his absence from the dinner table. It was nine in the evening, and he had not taken the time to warn her of his tardiness. The time had passed so quickly that before he realized his error, it was too late. He closed the door behind him. The lingering chill of the winter winds emanated from his coat along with the smell of alcohol.

Gail's parrot, Sweetheart, squawked its disapproval at the intrusion of frigid air entering the living room. The floor boards creaked above his head, announcing Gail's whereabouts.

"Sean?" Her voice came from the top of the staircase.

"Yes, Mama Gail. It's just me."

"Where have you been?' Her voice quivered. "I've been calling everywhere for you."

"Junior came by the plaza after I finished work. He wanted me to see the new location for DJ Beverage."

"Neil called," Gail stated as she negotiated the final step. Her eyes were fixed in a grave and staunch stare. A cold chill ran up Sean's spine and erupted in a sudden shudder. He knew the news was bad. "They have your grandmother at the hospital."

"What's wrong? Is she okay?"

"She fell and broke her hip."

"Oh, God. But she's going to be okay?"

"At her age, a broken hip can be serious. She is going to be in the hospital for quite some time." Gail paused with a deep breath. "Sean, it happened two days ago."

"What? Why in the hell did it take so long for Neil to call me!?"

"He just found out himself. He went to her house and found her unconscious on the floor. Evidently after she fell, she couldn't reach the phone to call anyone. The poor girl laid there suffering in pain. She couldn't move. They have her in ICU."

"Christ!" Sean spun and headed for the door.

"I will drive you to the hospital," Gail offered, following close behind.

"That's okay Gail; I can drive myself."

"Sean, you've been drinking. I'll drive you there."

Sean sat in silence during the ten minute drive, answering Gail's occasional questions with a nod of his head. He was oppressed with guilt. He had neglected an important duty that had been entrusted to him and soon, he would have to answer for it.

They entered the hospital's ER and followed the signs to the Intensive Care Unit, then entered elevator B to proceed to the fifth floor. The sudden lift of the elevator gave Sean's stomach the sensation that it had remained on the first level. The hallways on the fifth floor were marked with large color-coordinated dots, placed in a line on the floor. The dots were designed as a guide in directing visitors to the unit they desired. The dots for ICU were a pale medium blue. Sean thought the color must have been selected for its calming effect. It was not working. His heart thumped heavy with every passing step and every passing dot.

A large set of oak doors, with small windows of thick impenetrable glass, were hung at the end of a long stretch of hallway. Gail was struggling to keep up with Sean's rapid pace as each footfall bounced a quick echo back to her. She glanced up intermittently at Sean's face. His eyes were fixed forward, as if the doors were the only thing left in his world. Six feet from the set of double doors, a lone doorway stood as the only break in the white walls to the right. Sean glanced in the room marked 'ICU WAITING,' as they passed. He saw Neil and Arlene sitting on a couch together. He stopped abruptly and entered the room. "How is she?"

Neil rose from the couch to greet him. "She's in very rough shape. We almost lost her, Sean. After they brought her in, she had a drastic drop in blood pressure."

"Can I go in to see her?"

"We stepped out while the doctor was examining her. They said we could go back in shortly. Colleen stayed in the room with her."

Sean turned, staring out of the doorway. Neil continued his briefing, "They have her stabilized. She's resting comfortably with the morphine intravenous. She's pretty doped up - drifts in and out of consciousness. But she'll know that you're in the room. The doctor is concerned about any internal bleeding. There doesn't appear to be any signs of it at the moment."

"God, Neil, I watched how they reset a broken hip on television. She must be in so much pain."

Sean walked out into the hallway. Neil walked up behind him and rested a hand on his shoulder. He stared down at the end of the hall opposite the doors. "She was severely dehydrated." Neil rubbed a hand across his mouth and let it slide down to his chin. "Her heart stopped at one point, but only for a few seconds. They were able to bring her back."

Sean turned to face Neil with a glaze of tears in his eyes. "I have to get in there to see her."

"It shouldn't be too much longer." Neil withdrew into the waiting room allowing his hand to slip from Sean's shoulder. Sean was left alone to acclimate to the situation.

Five minutes had passed when the doors opened and a doctor exited the ICU. As he strolled down the hall, Sean stepped aside to allow him clear space and nod a greeting. The doctor returned the gesture continuing on, disappearing around a corner. A brief minute later the doors opened again and Colleen stepped into the hall.

"How is she?" Sean asked. He wanted to hear good news, and he would ask that question a thousand times until he achieved the desired response.

Colleen embraced him, her quivered from sobs, "She's resting."

Those were not the words of comfort that Sean had wanted to hear, but he responded to her embrace. He released her, kissing her on the cheek. The discerning look on her face as she pulled away from him foretold of her detection of his alcohol aroma. She turned abruptly toward the waiting room. "Neil, I need some coffee. Why don't you walk downstairs with me?"

Neil and Arlene rose at the same time. "I'll go with you," Arlene interjected. They exited the room leaving Gail sitting alone.

"Do you want to go back with me?" Sean asked Gail from the hallway.

"No, you go ahead. I'll go back with you a little later. You need some time alone with her."

Sean turned and pushed his way through the double doors. The central control area to his left consisted of a few desks, each with a computer monitor and keyboard behind a four-foot high counter that encircled the large station in an oval shape. The patient rooms lined the three walls starting to his right. The beeps and clicks of the monitors blended with the discussions of the attendants. The abrupt sound of a loud tone prompted a nurse to enter one of the rooms. An uneasy feeling descended upon Sean. But within seconds, the tone ceased and the nurse emerged from the room. Sean caught her attention as she walked past.

"Could you tell me which room Meagan Bergin is in?"

"Are you a member of her family?" The nurse questioned.

"Yes. I'm one of her grandsons."

"She is in room six." The nurse eyed Sean for a brief moment before returning to her duties.

As Sean entered the room, another nurse, this one tall with thick auburn hair cascading over her shoulders was checking the digital readings of the BP unit. The nurse moved with a familiar grace.

"Wendy?" Sean inquired.

The nurse turned displaying the fair skin and large, sultry, chestnut eyes that were unmistakable to him. "Hello Sean. How are you holding up?" Wendy replied. Sean had known Wendy Parks throughout most of his life. She had lovingly supported him through the solemn months following Arlen's death. Wendy was blessed with an uncanny ability to assess the needs of those in physical or emotional distress. She was highly adept at listening and nurturing, and was unassuming in the advice she delivered.

She was a woman of elegant beauty and intelligence. A devout activist who was quick to assign her skills to any child related cause, although she never desired children of her own. Wendy had moved to West Virginia shortly after acquiring her nursing degree and there she married a physics professor. She filed for divorce five years later after returning home to find him in bed with one of his students. She quickly returned to Honey Brook and immersed herself in her work.

"I'm okay," Sean responded. "How's Gram doing?"

"She's doing fine. She's a strong Irish woman. It's going to take a lot more than this to slow her down. She's still just as feisty as ever. We're having a real time trying to keep that oxygen line in her nose. She does not want it, and she's damned determined to let us know that."

Sean glanced at his grandmother, quietly sleeping, and then turned back to Wendy and mustered a slight smile. "I didn't realize you worked ICU."

"I've been on this floor since I got back from the Philippines. Did you stop by the waiting area? Neil, Colleen, and Arlene are here."

Sean nodded.

"Well, I have a few things to do before my break. Dr. Stanton will be meeting with your family soon. It will probably be around ten o'clock." Wendy approached the door to exit, but Sean was standing in the doorway. She paused, looking at him with a smile. He graciously returned the smile before realizing that her smile was one of amusement. He was blocking her path out of the room.

"Oh, I'm sorry." He chuckled at his own inattention, as he stepped aside to allow her passage. "Thanks, Wendy."

Sean approached the side of the bed and leaned in to kiss his grandmother's cheek. He was happy to finally see her, despite the monitors and tubes. He gently brushed the fine white hairs back from her eyes. "I'm here now," he whispered. He took a seat in a vinyl chair next to the bed and closed his eyes. He was tired and stressed. He longed for a break in his life. Even the warmth of the coming spring would be an improvement over his current conditions; anything to uplift his spirits. As he remained in the darkness of his sealed lids, he slipped past exhaustion. He realized he would easily fall asleep if he failed to get his eyes open. He leaned forward in the chair and rubbed away the sleep. Then realized his grandmother was awake and staring wildly into his face.

Startled, he reached for her hand. "Grandma?"

"I died today, ya know." Meagan's dialect bore a slight Irish accent.

"Huh?"

"I died. But I came back."

"Who told you that?" He wondered why they would tell her of the heart arrest while she was still in critical condition.

"I died, and I saw it."

Sean reached over and patted her coarse, wrinkled hand. "Saw what, Bright-eyes? You are not making any sense."

"The dragon."

"What?"

"He told me about you."

"Gram, I don't understand what you are saying."

"The dragon with the two heads. One of the dragon heads had Arlen's face on it. The other face - I never saw before. It wore a cloak of righteousness, but its heart was black and evil. He will use your son to get what he wants."

"Gram, settle down. What are you talking about?" It was chilling to witness the rational mind of such a strong woman disintegrate before his eyes. Goose bumps stirred up his spine and lifted the hairs from the back of his neck.

"He will try to tempt you." Her eyes grew panicked as she attempted to sit up in bed to reach for Sean.

"Just calm down. It was only a bad dream." Sean tried to push her back into bed, but found her resistance remarkably strong.

"He will try to tempt you!" She pulled the intravenous needle from her arm in a faint crimson spray. The blood dripped from her arm and spread thin as it soaked into the white bed sheet.

She continued repeating the warning, clutching the sleeve of Sean's coat until her knuckles changed from pale to white. Her heart monitor increased until at last a warning tone sounded. Sean desperately tried to loosen her grip and return her head to the pillow. Foamy drool ran from the corner of her mouth. Her blood pressure now dropped rapidly, and her heart rate turned from swift to drastically slow. Her strength weakened and her body became limp in Sean's hands, rigid muscle faded into frail bones and sagging flesh.

"Wendy!" Sean had barely called her name when Wendy ran into the room, followed by another nurse.

"What the hell just happened to her?" Sean's voice slid from the depth of its normal legato tone into a near shriek.

A man in green scrubs entered and pushed Sean back from the bed to gain access to Meagan. He turned to Wendy and barked an order, "Get him out of here!"

Wendy calmly placed a hand on Sean's chest and nudged him toward the door. "Come on Sean. Let us take a look. I promise we will do everything we can for her."

"What just happened?"

"I'm not sure, but we are going to find out. Now go out into the waiting area and I'll come out as soon as I can."

Chapter 21

The conference room contained a large rectangular table surrounded by eight blue plastic molded chairs. A small refreshment center, equipped with an automatic coffee maker, Styrofoam cups, and condiments, was placed in the far corner. Wendy offered the Bergin family coffee, but all refused. She informed them that Dr. Stanton would be in to speak with them shortly.

She placed a gentle hand on Sean's back, prompting a sharp glare from Arlene. Arlene was a small, yet feisty woman; the spirit of a wild stallion with a quick temper that matched Sean's.

Wendy asked if they needed anything further before exiting the room. They graciously declined. The room was left in silence. Colleen cleared her throat. Neil shifted in his seat.

"How's Jennifer?" Arlene finally asked.""

"I wouldn't know," Sean replied flatly.

"You mean you haven't checked on her since you left?"

"No. Why should I?" Sean snapped back. Arlene glared until at last turning her head in disgust.

Neil leaned toward Sean, who was seated next to him and whispered in his ear, "I want to talk with you after we finish here." Sean responded with a nod as a thin, bespectacled man entered the conference room.

"Good evening everyone, I'm Dr. Stanton. I know you're all concerned about Meagan's condition so I won't waste any time." Stanton sat down in an empty chair at the head of the table.

"Meagan is a very sick girl, but there's no reason to think that her situation is not manageable. The x-ray showed a fracture of the femoral bone. It's a mild break, but the area may have to be structurally reinforced.

From what I understand, she was found approximately 48 hours following her fall. When we received her in the ER, she was extremely dehydrated with mild delirium. She had an arrest while she was still in the ER. The attendants were able to resuscitate her and started an immediate intravenous drip to re-hydrate.

In the past hour, she experienced another drop in blood pressure and an irregular heartbeat. We are running a few tests, starting with a blood test, which was taken in the Emergency Room. We found her potassium to be low and have addressed that through the intravenous. Potassium is an important electrolyte in the body. It can be dangerous if we allow it to drop too low.

Her white cell count was slightly elevated also. I have prescribed some antibiotics as a precaution. I re-examined the area of the injury and noticed a curling bruise – sort of dragon-shaped that was not there before. The bruise could very well be a result of the low potassium; that can be one of the side effects. But we are doing an MRI scan this evening, to be on the safe side. That should give us a really good picture of the damage to her hip and the surrounding tissue. The low potassium also brings up concerns of her kidney function, so we will be monitoring her urine output. Although I will say, at this point, she has no other signs of any kidney failure, so I expect her output to be normal. I believe the low potassium was simply a result of the time that elapsed without food or fluids."

He went on to explain the course of treatment for the hip fracture, including the possibility of surgery before offering to answer any questions they may have.

"I was in the room during that spell." Sean spoke up. "I was concerned over the way she was speaking. She was not making any sense."

"Well, like I said, she is a very sick girl. We also have her on morphine which can have some bizarre side effects on rationale. I would not be too concerned about that." Dr. Stanton said with a reassuring smile. He raised his eye brows and glanced at each of their faces in a permissive gesture, "Any other questions?"

Following the shaking of their five heads, Dr. Stanton rose from his seat. "If any questions do arise, make certain you ask one of the nurses, and they can relay them to me. I will be around in the morning to discuss the results of the MRI. I think we have her stabilized for the evening. The best medicine for her is bed rest. You folks should also try to get some sleep. You are welcome to stay as long as you like; otherwise if any problems arise throughout the night, we will certainly telephone you." He shook Neil's hand and gave the entire group a casual wave, then disappeared from the room. Colleen stretched in her seat and released a mild yawn. "Well, I guess I will head home. Curt's working third-shift and needs me there with the kids. If anything comes up, make sure I get a phone call."

"I need to head out, too," Neil added. "Sean, are you staying?"

"I don't know. It's up to Gail - she's driving."

Convinced the ordeal had sobered Sean, Gail said, "If someone can drive me home, I can leave my car with you."

Arlene offered to drive Gail home and the two followed Colleen out of the conference room, leaving Neil and Sean alone. Neil stared across the room at a bare wall, trying to clear his thoughts. When he released a long sigh, Sean knew a lecture was coming.

"Sean, I hate to bring this up, but ... "

"I know, we take turns checking on Gram and this was my week to keep in touch. I'm sorry. My mind is so distant lately. I can't focus on anything."

"I know," Neil paused for another sigh, "but this was important. She's getting on in her years, and this is why I was worried about her living alone." Neil paused shaking his head. "Look, I don't want to make you feel guilty." He rose from his seat. "I just hope you can pull yourself together soon. I don't know what else to say to you."

Sean kept his head down to avoid eye contact with him. Neil could see Sean's anger from the clinching of his jaw and knew the conversation was over. He exited the room closing the door gently behind him.

"Fucking self-righteous bastard," Sean mumbled beneath his breath. He sat drumming his fingertips on the table briefly before exiting the room. The conversation with Neil had left him feeling frustrated. He decided to visit the cafeteria for a cup of coffee before returning to the ICU.

Chapter 22

For Sean, attempting to find solace in the black depths of a coffee cup seemed contradictory. The coffee was visible only on the surface. It was a dark well; the perfect analogy for his life. *Well, at least the aroma is somewhat soothing.*

The timing of Neil's lecture was heinous at best. He felt guilty enough for not checking in on Gram. He blamed himself for her injuries, or at least their severity; and he certainly did not need Neil to point that out to him.

Life had Sean off balance, and his recent actions were keeping him that way. He was continuing an Irish tradition of guilt; guilt for Arlen; guilt for his Grandmother. But the knife that made the deepest cut was Jennifer's. The only woman in the world who really knew and understood him, no longer trusted him. Sean imagined a conspiracy by Neil and Jennifer to undermine his self-esteem. Recently, every road he chose was a wrong turn, and every action taken was a miscalculation. The only person he had left was Gail, who was now showing signs of disappointment in regards to his drinking habits. Everyone he was close to seemed to eye him with such adjudication.

"Hi. Would you mind if I join you?" The voice pulled Sean from the depths of his self-pity. He looked up to see Wendy looking down at him with a cup of coffee and an engaging smile.

He quickly rose from his seat, the result of his Grandfather's persistence in providing manners to a young man.

"Hey, Contessa, have a seat. I could use a little company." Sean had a habit of assigning those close to him a nickname. Wendy became 'The Barefoot Contessa' during their years in high school.

Wendy was a beautiful girl who became a radiant woman. But despite her apparent interest in him, Sean never pursued her, an oversight he never quite understood. Their history consisted of a three month, juvenile relationship in junior high school. They parted close friends and maintained that relationship throughout their lives. She was close enough to Sean's family to be adopted and considered Meagan Bergin her grandmother as well, although was never quite able to win Arlene over.

"Is everything okay with Gram?" He asked.

"Yes. She was resting comfortably when I left. With everything that's going on, I'm getting my break in a little late tonight."

"What time do you get off work?"

"I have a double shift; I'll be here all night. Why?"

"Oh, I was just asking."

Wendy nodded her head, shifting her eyes away from the conversation. Silence.

"Sean, try not to worry. Gram is getting the best care. Dr. Stanton is one of our finest critical care physicians I know. I've seen a lot of these cases, and quite often the person heals more rapidly than everyone expects."

"It's not just Gram; it's me. I've really been struggling lately."

Wendy reached across the table and placed a loving hand on his. "I can only imagine how you must feel. You've been through so much in the past months."

Wendy's skin was the texture of fine silk. Sean had nearly forgotten how soft and purely gentle her touch was. A touch so soft - it was as though her skin never truly touched his. A sensation that always sent swells of engaging tingles through his body. Wendy had both a visible and metaphysical aurora about her. *Pure radiance*, he thought.

"Sean, you have my telephone number. Why don't you ever call me when you need to talk?"

"I don't want to burden you with my problems. I'm sure you have your own."

"Listen, I'm your friend. I'll always be here for you. Always. If I'm working, leave a voice message. I would love to hear from you. It lifts my spirits, no matter what the reason for the call."

Sean put his head down and nodded. "I will call next time."

"You promise?"

"I promise."

"Yeah, well, you promised to take me to the prom also. Of course, you never did." Wendy uttered through a teasing smile.

Sean chuckled. "How long am I going to be punished for that one?"

"Until you take me to a prom."

"We could always crash this year's prom."

"Works for me."

"I could see that. The kids would be dancing to rap music and we'd be yelling for Poison and Motley Crue."

"I was not exactly a Motley Crue fan in high school. I was reading poetry, remember?"

"Ah, yes. Keats and Dickinson."

"And you were engaged in the poetry of Vince Neil and Tommy Lee. I guess we were like *La Belle Dame* and *Dr. Feelgood*."

"I'm sorry, I can't handle poetry. I'd need an anti-diarrhetic if I tried to read the stuff you do."

"You read the poems that I wrote - sitting out on my front porch. You never complained about it then."

"I had ulterior motives then." Smiles replaced their conversation. Sean stared into Wendy's eyes. "Those were good times."

"Yeah, they were."

"Have you ever considered trying married life again?"

"I considered it, but nothing beyond that. I suppose I'm waiting for the right man to ask me."

Sean averted his eyes as he nodded. "You just haven't found Mr. Right."

"Oh, I found him. He just hasn't asked me to marry him, yet."

Sean looked up to see the mischievous smile spreading across her face. Her eyes were of the deepest brown, and the white surrounding them bore the brilliance of snow. The combination made her eyes piercing. "Well, I suppose time can bring about all manner of revelations."

Wendy leaned in, resting her elbows on the table. She cradled her chin on her petite fists. "If a dream is worth keeping its worth waiting for."

The sweet scent of her perfume drifted across the table. The smell was subtle, but enough to dizzy him. It stripped away inhibitions as it permeated his senses. Everything about her was soft and subtle, except her striking beauty. Each sound of her voice was like silk against his skin, each motion, each breath, each touch and every gaze.

Sean's comfort level was beginning to reach its limits. Perhaps Wendy had sensed it when she announced she had to return to her nursing duties.

"Well, I better get myself back to work."

"Yeah, I guess I should visit Gram."

"How long will you be staying?"

Sean shifted in his seat, his focus drifting between his coffee and Wendy. "I don't know. Perhaps all night,"

"I guess we will be seeing a lot of each other tonight." There was a satin to her voice and a depth to her eyes that was drawing him in. Welcome. Come in and experience what is offered.

He watched her as she rose from the table and glided gracefully away from him. He loved her full round shape. The sight of her walk allowed him a brief reprieve from the troubles that ravaged him. Perhaps life was not all bad. He watched her hips as they swayed. *That's my kind of poetry,* he thought.

Chapter 23

Jennifer rested back into the chair as she examined her surroundings. She was seated at a table of a small outdoor café. An awning stretched out from above the entrance, providing shade from the midday sun. Beyond the cobblestone walk of the café, the street was narrow enough to discern great details of the opposite side. The sidewalk across the street ended in the lush grass of a courtyard enclosed by a low sandstone wall. In the center, the wall rose to form a great arch with a black, wrought-iron gate, the doors of which were open to allow access to the loose stone pathways lined with precisely trimmed shrubbery within the courtyard. The Swiss Alps' mountain range rose from behind the building, forming snowy peaks against the clear sky. The Mediterranean Sea was not in Jennifer's view. However, she could smell it and feel its moisture in the warmth of the gentle breeze.

She picked up a cup of coffee from the table when she suddenly realized that she was not alone. A young gentleman was seated across from her.

"I've seen you before," she commented thoughtfully.

"I believe you remember me from the beach."

"Nicholas?" She smiled. "I am so happy to see you again."

"I am happy to see you, as well. And, might I add, this setting appeals to me much more than the beach."

"It is beautiful here," she stated as she glanced down the street at the Tower of Pisa in the distance. From the café, the distant structure was perceived no larger than an average Honey Brook apartment building.

"Where are we?" Nicholas questioned.

"Come on Silly, you know we are in Naples."

"Oh, I see."

"I've never been to Naples before," Jennifer commented.

Nicholas glanced over his right shoulder and then his left. "That is amusingly obvious to me. I never realized Pisa was so visible from Naples."

"I thought you were from Italy?"

"Oh, I am. But I must confess, I have never seen it," he paused as he continued to survey the landscape, "quite like this before. Actually, I was born in Sicily. My mother was from Venice. My father was born in the United States, but he came to Italy to attempt to establish a winery. The wine business has been in my family for generations."

"Do your parents still live in Italy?"

"They died when I was ten years old. My grandfather brought me to the United States to live with him. He had inherited a winery in upstate New York. He was my legal guardian for about five years. Eventually, I ended up on my Uncle Anthony's doorstep."

"That is so tragic. How did your parents die?"

"They died in a house fire."

"Oh, dear God! I am so sorry."

"I was the only one who made it out alive. For awhile I wished that I hadn't." Nicholas released a hollow breath. "But that was a lifetime ago."

"Where do you live now?"

"Everywhere;" he answered coyly, "wherever you are."

"Hey," Jennifer whispered, leaning in toward Nicholas. "Do you see those two people in that courtyard over there?"

"Where?" Nicholas searched the horizon.

"Across the street. They're standing in front of the courtyard entrance."

"Oh yes, I see them now."

"That's Liv Tyler and Jeremy Irons."

"Yes, I suppose it is."

"I bet famous people visit here all the time."

Nicholas shook his head with a chuckle. "You are adorable."

"What?"

"Never mind."

They stared quietly at each other for a few moments. Jennifer delightfully absorbed the ambience of the country and her newly found friend; astonished at the depths of her primal desires for him. Staring into his face made her feel alive and rejuvenated. His deep brown eyes danced with intrigue within his satiny bronze skin.

"Say something," Jennifer requested.
"Like what?" Nicholas smiled in amused confusion.

"Anything. I love to listen to the sound of your voice. It's like an old familiar song; it comforts me. It tells me that you will always be there for me." She smiled and averted her eyes like a young girl with a crush. "Your accent is beautiful and so are your eyes. I see the innocence of a child and the wisdom of a man in them."

"I will always be here for you. Anytime you need me. You are very special to me. Anything you want of me; all you have to do is ask. Besides, how could I refuse such a beautiful woman?" He smiled. "And I believe that word fits you far better than it does me. I wish my eyes could see nothing but you."

"Thank you. I feel safe when I'm with you."

"That is what I am offering you; perhaps not the world, but at least my own little part of it. You can come to me anytime you wish; stay as long as you like. And when the time comes that you want to stay with me forever, I will welcome you with all my heart. You can always trust me."

"I do trust you, Nicholas."

"I know you. I know your pain, Jennifer. I can help you, if you let me. Surrender your trust and soul to me, and I will heal your emotional wounds. Do you want me to help you?"

"Yes."

"Do you surrender yourself to me?"

"Yes. I do"

"Then you must say it," Nicholas giggled with childish abandon.

"I surrender myself to you."

He gently pressed his palm against her soft cheek. "That's my girl."

"You are the gentlest man I have ever met. I have so much pain. It has twisted my life into a nightmare. I miss my son."

"I know. Love can be more beautiful than life itself. The problem is it can be just as tragic."

"I feel so alone without him, Nicholas. I loved him so much."

"There is no reason to stop loving him. His spirit lives on. Believe me, I know. But, Jennifer, you must also love yourself. Arlen loves you, and he wants you to take care of yourself." He leaned ever closer to her face. Jennifer could feel the sweet warmth of his breath against her lips.

"Continuing your life does not diminish the importance of his. I want to teach you how to live again."

Her mouth parted and her tongue moistened her lips, nearly bridging the distance to his. She could feel the phantom sensation of their touch. They began to close the gap between them when a couple walked by. A voluptuous young woman and a middle-aged man sat down at an adjacent table. The couple's arrival disrupted the moment.

Jennifer eased back into her chair as Nicholas stared down the street. His face was clearly flushed and his jaw tightened. She placed her hand on his and presented him with a warm smile. She sat quietly listening to their café neighbors. The young woman spoke broken English through an Italian accent as she described the man's hometown of Avellino. The conversation seemed familiar to Jennifer, but she could not understand why. Jennifer drifted in thought, far from Italy. Her body began to feel almost weightless until the voice of Nicholas drew her attention.

"Jennifer?"

She could feel her body pulled back into her chair.

"Jennifer, are you still with me?"

"Yes. Of course I am," she said. "Tell me more about your Uncle ..." her request was cut short by a look of concern on her face.

"What's the matter?"

"I can't move my arm to pick up my coffee. It feels like it's going numb."

Nicholas nodded his head. "Time is never on our side, is it?"

"Nicholas, I can't pick up my coffee. My arm is paralyzed. It's starting to ache!"

"Calm down. Everything is okay. It is simply time for you to leave."

"I don't want to leave. Why are you making me leave?"

"I'm not, but don't worry; you will come back to me."

Jennifer struggled, debating her need to remain. "I haven't even finished my coffee yet."

"You can take it with you. I will pick up the tab." Nicholas smiled and leaned forward to kiss Jennifer on her cheek. "I will see you again real soon."

Jennifer's eyes opened to a view of her bedroom wall. Her senses returned to her slowly until the numbness of sleep was replaced by the numbness of low blood circulation in her arm. She moaned as she rolled onto her back, freeing the arm that had been trapped beneath her body. Staring at the ceiling, she reflected on her dream of Nicholas. It was strange having romantic dreams of a man she had never met. He seemed so real to her, and the details of Italy were so vivid despite never having been there. Her only experience with the country was through movies and television. One thing was certain her dreams had become increasingly bizarre in the past several months.

She checked the alarm clock. It was seven. The early morning daylight was scarcely enough to brighten her room. A swell of relief came over her with the knowledge of having successfully completed a full night of sleep. She glanced on her nightstand at the pill bottle next to the alarm clock, next to the steaming cup of coffee.

"I love you sleeping pills. Coffee?"

She slid across the bed to examine it closer. As she lifted her head to peer into the cup, the aroma of fresh coffee greeted her. The scent was more robust than her usual brand. She rose from her bed and gripped the cup by the handle, walking warily out of the bedroom to the edge of the staircase.

"Dad? Are you down there?"

Her words were answered by silence. She grimaced at the next thought. "Sean?" Jennifer paused, straining to hear any response, but none followed. She descended the staircase and entered the kitchen. The automatic coffee maker was empty with the carafe still in the dishwasher where she had left it. She walked into the front room and checked the front door. It was securely locked as she remembered.

She inhaled the scent of the coffee once again, this time suspiciously. She sipped it for taste. Two sugars with extra cream, just the way she liked it. There had to be a logical explanation for it, but none was forthcoming.

She sat down in the reclining chair and switched on the television. The enigma of the coffee set off a mild panic attack as her heart rate and breathing increased. She distracted herself with a reality talk show while she continued to drink from the cup. The flavor of the coffee was exquisite. She resigned herself to enjoy the gift without question. She could remember Nicholas telling her to take the coffee with her, but the idea that the cup had manifested itself from her dream seemed absurd. And yet, she was drinking the coffee.

Chapter 24

The success of the Trazodone was in its ability to provide refreshing and uninterrupted sleep. The unexpected adverse effect was the suppression of Jennifer's dreams. Since the bizarre appearance of the coffee, four nights had passed without the presence of Nicholas. In fact, no dreams had registered in Jennifer's conscious. And despite its provision of much needed rest, Jennifer had made the bold decision to discontinue her medication. She had achieved the sleep that she needed, and she was feeling stable; ready to be liberated from her reliance on the medication. She had to find out more about Nicholas.

The first evening of unaided sleep transpired as the previous three, without any recollection of night visions. Jennifer felt rested, but slightly frustrated as the morning drew into the early afternoon. She passed her time watching television and glancing out the living room window at the passing cars.

At two o'clock she switched to the Animal Channel to watch a program on canine obedience. She wondered why she and Sean had never purchased a dog for Arlen. With all his impish energy, he would have loved a puppy.

She remembered a time when he was two-years-old. She had been busy cleaning while Arlen sat in the kitchen, playing with a few pots and spoons. The backdoor was open to allow the entrance of any breeze to cool the warm summer air. She had finished rinsing her dishes while deep in thought. It seemed like only seconds had passed when she suddenly realized that Arlen was no longer in the room with her. As she frantically searched the house, the telephone rang. Her neighbor was calling to inform her that Arlen was in his backyard playing with Dino, his Golden Retriever.

Jennifer was embarrassed enough simply retrieving her son, but when she walked out onto the back porch she realized Arlen was naked. Red-faced, she explained that removing his diaper by himself was Arlen's latest trick. The neighbor laughed and reassured her that it could have happened to any parent. But she became obsessively vigilant with her son after the incident, eyeing his every move despite her housework. Even through the panic of Arlen escaping the house without her knowledge, the humor of him running nude in the neighbor's yard was undeniable. The memory provided her a rare smile.

Her attention drifted back to the television program for a few brief moments until once again, her eyes grew heavy. She closed her lids, listening to the female voice from the television. The woman was lecturing on the importance of establishing a leader in the home. The dog needs to recognize a member of the family as the pack leader, or the dog may attempt to assume the role. Jennifer found it odd that they were making references to a member of the family when speaking about a domesticated animal.

They're trying to impose our complicated world onto the animal kingdom, she thought. *All animals have to do is exist. Humans have to suffer with self-awareness. Maslow's hierarchy of needs and all of that shit. Maybe the hierarchy of needs is not a pyramid, but a circle. And the need that connects the two ends is ignorance.*

Animals have the greatest idea of living; they simply survive. Perhaps the pain they experience from the loss of someone they love is not as devastating. They're not aware of how fragile their lives really are. Ignorance is bliss.

The voice from the television grew distant as she drifted off to sleep.

Chapter 25

The large gothic basilica structure of Saint Anthony's Church had hallowed the ground beneath since 1863 - the year boldly etched into the mountain stone facade. Twin parapet towers shouldered a steep gable with heavy wooden doors. Sunlight from the south poured into a rose window above the entrance and a cross looked down from its perch high atop the gable's peak.

An awe inspiring view for Sean as a child now appeared as a welcoming home. The only place he knew that he could relieve the guilt that strangled his mind.

Inside, he was greeted by a blend of new and old smells. The scent of freshly cut flowers hung amid the dank smells of old carpet and putrefying lumber. He crossed through the portico and looked down over the empty pews of the nave. The vaulting arched high above him; the stonework ribs painted in mosaic gold. He walked down the sloping aisle and knelt in front of the altar. Staring up at the crucifix hanging in the center and the statue of the Virgin Mary to its left, he drew upon their strength. The condition of the Virgin Mother statue was nearly pristine. She wore a gown of pure white and a robe of powder blue that was lined with gold. Her eyes cast downward between outstretched arms. The only show of wear on the statue was a faint red stain below the knees of her white gown.

Sean stared at the altar, wondering if he could be emancipated from the burden of his guilt. He searched his soul for the words to confess his sins as he reaffirmed his conviction to his faith and his desire to achieve absolution.

With his eyes shut tight, he could feel the presence of the church around him. His breaths came slow and easy. His body felt lighter and stronger beneath the cloak of protection provided by his faith. He rose from the altar, signed the cross then retraced his steps back into the portico. From there a deviation to his left led him down a set of stairs to the lower level. His confession was nearly at hand.

He could still recall how frightened and intimidated he felt attending his first confession as a child. In those days, the church had its traditional confession boxes. He could remember closing himself inside the small confessional, the dark closet of repentance according to his grandfather's words. He had sat before a black screen as he waited for the father to open the window. The musty smell of the old structure filled his nostrils like the entrance to a long forgotten torture chamber. Although the torture chamber would come later, after the priest had spoken to his mother and told her what Sean had confessed. Arthur Gotaski's picture of the nude woman; he had looked at it. He and Greg Sutkins had tortured Mrs. Latimer's cat; and many other sins that he would otherwise deny. He was certain that God was already aware of his indiscretions; it was telling others who trusted him that caused his anxiety. Withholding information would have been out of the question because God had already witnessed his actions. It was better to face the temporary wrath of his mother than to face an eternity of God's disparagement.

He could recall the drive home and the family dinner that same night. His focus shifted from his plate to his mother, waiting for her to pounce on him for the sins he unveiled to the priest. When at last he was tucked in bed, he realized the priest had said nothing to his mother. He would live to commit his next sin. The priest had held his confessional comments in the strictest of confidence. It was then that the church earned Sean's undying respect and gratitude. That night, he asked God to bless his new friend, Father Anthony.

Today, the confession boxes stood as a reminder of tradition. A tradition no longer used. The church opted in favor of face-to-face confessions with the priest, performed in the crying room, which was a sound-proof room originally intended for crying children. In the past, this room was open to the parents of a rampaging youth, where they could listen to mass through a speaker system. Sean was certain he must have seen the inside of this room more than once as a toddler.

The door to the crying room was ajar, and Sean could see Father Thomas seated alone inside; confessions available, no waiting. He walked into the room and seated himself across from the priest.

"Thank you for meeting with me, Father."

"You don't have to thank me. That's what I am here for." Father Thomas responded.

Father Thomas greeted Sean in the name of the Christ. Sean responded with the sign of the cross.

"Bless me Father, for I have sinned. It has been eleven months since my last confession." Sean paused, drawing in a deep breath. "Father, I am responsible for the death of my son."

Chapter 26

The sweet smells of cotton candy drifting in a pervasive breeze; the warmth and illumination of the sun permeating down from the heavens upon a human sea. Clowns prancing in flamboyant garb, with their faces happily distorted with brightly hued paint. Neon lights flashing in exuberant brilliance as the mechanized rides spin and swoop; the exhilarated screams of their cargo emerging forcibly through the blanket of casual conversation mingling with the cries and giggles of children, the clanging of gears, and the bellowing of boisterous vendors.

For Jennifer, the thrill of a county fair was vexed by anxiety and sensory overload. The stimuli flooded her brain until it seemed to be jittering about within her skull. The overwhelming sensations caused her psyche to retreat into a shell of protection that was both a shelter and a prison. The thrill of the fair was not accompanied by the customary joy; it was nearly traumatic. It was a contradiction that she had learned to tolerate since childhood.

Young Jennifer never responded to these situations like most children. She did not scamper to the next ride nor mingle freely in the crowd, choosing instead to cling to her father; an action her mother chose to chastise rather than understand.

Jennifer's sensory dysfunction was mild in comparative cases. Had it ever been properly diagnosed, she would have recognized it as the root of her anxiety disorder. No one had ever made the connection. She was the victim of the era of her birth, and her inability to communicate what she was experiencing. She did not suffer from autism, so the problem was overlooked.

Jennifer located a lone bench beneath a tree away from the bustle of the midway, where she sat down in the cool shade. The canopy of leaves helped supply her imaginary protective shell with substance. She eased out a breath and relaxed a little, watching the people as they passed in the distance. They strode slowly along the field of grass, chatting to one another. A small child chased after a runaway plastic ball from a nearby game of chance. A towering biker dressed in jeans and a denim jacket walked with a woman under his arm - his hand thrust deep inside her jeans, exposing the tattoo on her lower back. A middle-aged man walked beside an empty stroller that he was pushing with one hand, attempting to look detached from the evidence of his domestication. They passed before her sight and then disappeared in the periphery.

The crowd gradually thinned to a few dozen - their numbers dwindling as they walked out of her range of sight. As they final remaining merrymakers faded from her sight, she spied a lone elderly man walking gingerly with a cane; his feet shuffling across the grass.

Jennifer rose from the bench and approached him. "Excuse me sir, could you tell me where the carrousel is?"

He raised his head between slumping shoulders. "The horses bring you 'round the circle to the same spot, but things still change. The faces are always different. Not always enough to notice, but different. Do you ride it for pleasure or purpose?"

"I like to try to grab the brass ring."

He shook his head in a discerning smile. "Always for a purpose; that's why we do not recognize miracles – always obsessing over our need for them. Searching for the forest and overlooking the trees." He peered up at Jennifer through squinting eyes, his skin coarse yet ruddy. His eyes twinkled in mirth beneath bushy brows. "And did you capture this ring?"

"Yes. Once I did."

"And what did you do with it?"

"I gave it back."

"Precisely!" He blurted. "They grab it, but they never keep it."

Jennifer cast a squinting glance from left to right. "Is the carrousel still here?"

"Bell horses, bell horses, what time of day? One o'clock, two o'clock, three and away. Gone dear Miss; the horses have run and the brass rings have rust." The old man pressed his hand in hers. "We can only go around once, Sweetheart. If you focus too much on the ring, you will miss the rouse of the ride."

Jennifer looked around to see the dormant fairgrounds. The rides were motionless, with the seats and trains poised on their tracks. The lot was now abandoned. Autumn leaves scurried across the ground like children left out to play, scraping and crackling upon the ground as their laughter. She turned back to the old man, "Then, is there nothing to do here?"

"Sure there is." The wet of his eyes twinkled. "When everyone is asleep in the morning, the sun still rises. And if no one attends the fair, the show must go on. I believe I saw a game of chance…down that way." He pointed an outstretched bony finger down a long aisle of empty gaming stands. The row stretched on both left and right as far as she could see. Some stands were tents that ruffled in the wind. Some were old weathered shacks with canopies.

"I don't have any money with me." Jennifer uttered.

"Money is not good here, dear Miss, only time." He patted a gentle hand against her cheek. "You go and have a good time." With a contented smile, he turned and shuffled away. His voice carried back with the wind in a sing-song chant. "The brass ring turns back in on itself to remind us all of the redundancy of wealth."

Jennifer smiled after him and then turned in the direction of the game. The path between the stands was narrow, the breadth of two men shoulder to shoulder. Jennifer followed the dancing leaves as they slid across the ground, guiding her steps. She could hear the faint sound of a Wurlitzer and the chant of a carnie as he called out, in earnest, for patrons to try their luck.

"Step right up. This is not just a game of chance. Everyone's a winner!" The shouting voice was easily recognizable.

Once again, there he was – "Nicholas," The word slipped past Jennifer's lips, leaving them with a residual smile. "So this is what you do in your spare time."

Nicholas leaned on the counter of his game booth. His impish grin annuncuated his fun. Behind him, the walls were plastered with stuffed animals, large, fluffy and colorful. "Well, if it isn't my favorite attraction - the world's most beautiful redhead. So, you have come to take your chances with me?"

"That depends." Jennifer dropped her chin and gazed up with unblinking eyes. "What's your game?"

"The game is simple. Throw the ring around the heart and you have won." Nicholas waved his hand in displaying a heart-shaped statuette. He waved his other hand and three small rings appeared in his fist.

"I love a man with good hands," Jennifer teased. "If I do it, what do I win?"

"Any prize you see before you, your host included."

"I'm tempted," She leaned in until her lips were nearly brushing his. "Tempt me more."

"You could win the gift of my heart, the gift of my undying love, and several sweet consolation prizes to be named later." Before Nicholas could kiss her, Jennifer slid to the right.

"Okay, I'll toss." She snatched the rings from his hand and leaned back, eyeing the distance to the heart. The first ring she deliberately threw too hard, as it smacked against the wall of stuffed animals and fell to the ground. She chewed her lower lip with a widening of her eyes; innocuous. "I'm sorry; my aim is a little rusty."

She threw the next ring short of the intended target. "Hmm, darn, I only have one ring left."

"Would you like me to move the heart closer?" Nicholas inquired.

"We have to play fair, Nicholas, rough, but fair." She could sense his discomfort in the air; she had flustered him. His entire being was wrapped about her finger. His body language told of his ravenous desire to embrace her. But was he ripe for picking yet? No. This was too much fun.

"Maybe," she uttered, "I should be happy to keep the ring. After all, what could a carnie provide that would actually impress me."

"I can offer you salvation. I can make your body burn cool and your spirit soar. I will show you the bluest sky against fields of fresh daisies and wrap it up for you with every sweet memory that has ever passed through your mind." His eyes softened, "I can make you happy again, Jennifer."

The passion in his speech took Jennifer by surprise. Her chest heaved in his direction, drawn to the magnet of his presence and longing for his touch. Thousands of butterflies had taken flight within the confines of her stomach. The moment had gone beyond words as she tossed the final ring over the heart. Their eyes locked.

"I guess you win," Nicholas managed, nearly breathless.

"You have made me feel alive again. I want to thank you for that." Jennifer moved closer to him, taking his hand in hers. The feeling of his touch lightened her spirit and sent pulses of pleasure rolling beneath her skin. "You make me feel warm and wonderful. I want to feel more."

Nicholas gently patted her hand. "I have something special for you; something for you to hold when I cannot be with me." Nicholas reached under the counter and withdrew a pure white Labrador puppy. A bright bow tied about the cotton fur of its neck.

"Oh, my God, he's so cute!" Jennifer accepted the gift from Nicholas and kissed the puppy's head. She rubbed her cheek against its downy fur. The pup licked her face with enthusiasm.

"It appears he likes you as much as I do."

"What's his name?"

"I thought I would leave that up to you. He is your friend now."

"Well," Jennifer curled up one corner of her mouth, "he's white, so how about Casper." She ruffled the puppy's ear. "Do you like Casper?"

Nicholas smiled, "Casper the friendly ghost. It is far more suitable than you realize."

Jennifer kissed Casper's head then returned her attention to Nicholas, "Thank you. He is a wonderful gift."

"Walk with me, Jennifer." Nicholas climbed over the counter and took her hand interlocking his fingers in hers. "Show me what you have in your mind. I want to know everything about you."

Jennifer and Nicholas strode along the empty fairgrounds for what seemed like hours. They walked between the lumber and steel structures of the still rides. The poised branches of the tall maple trees along the fairway cascaded their blessings down upon the couple. The wind brushed back the fallen leaves from their path.

Casper's tiny legs worked swiftly to keep pace with the couple's casual stroll across the down-trodden grass. Jennifer gripped Nicholas' hand, becoming distracted by the incredibly soft touch of his skin.

Jennifer's hand clutched the corner of her pillow as she awoke in her bed. The silky pillow case slipped from her palm as she sat up and stared at the far wall. She felt an ache in her heart upon the realization of her fate. The fair, the puppy, and Nicholas were merely a dream. A short film compliments of her imagination. And a story that ended, but failed to conclude.

She was peacefully relaxed despite feeling heartsick. She considered looking at the alarm clock by her bed to check the time, but why bother. Days passed like minutes and minutes like years.

Her stomach rumbled in protest of its emptiness, so she rose from bed and descended the staircase. Halfway down the stairs, the feeling subsided into a mild craving for tea. *Easier to make and less mess,* she thought.

She entered the kitchen and was greeted by a white puppy, complete with a bow. Jennifer froze. She cast a quick glance at the backdoor to see if it was ajar. Shut and locked. She looked down at the puppy, now wagging his tail wildly and whimpering for attention. Jennifer slowly knelt down and picked him up in her arms. "How did you get in here?" Following a thoughtful pause, the gravity of the situation arrived. "Holy shit! You're … holy shit!"

Jennifer licked her dry lips. Her mind worked frantically to find a reasonable explanation for the puppy's presence. "Dear God, Casper. If you're real, then …" Jennifer stepped back, her eyes darting from right to left. "Hello. Is anyone in here?" The silence was deafening. Someone, or something, could be loose in the house. Despite the absurdity of the thought, Jennifer uttered the name, "Nicholas?" A faint groan from the heating pipes beneath the house caused her to flinch, gripping Casper tighter. She was in need of some form of protection; a weapon. She shifted Casper under her left arm and reached for the utility drawer where the large knives were kept. Despite a moderate tug, the drawer slipped from its track, nearly falling out onto the ground. The metal inside rattled and clanged together as she struggled to keep it balanced. She propped it up with her knee and quickly retrieved a knife before shoving the drawer back into the cabinet. *Sean never fixed anything in this house,* she thought in frustration.

She squatted down on the floor near the entrance to the dining room, her back pressed against the wall. Holding her weapon up in front of her, she noticed it was a serrated bread knife. It would have to do. She needed to search the house, and she refused to do it empty handed. A deep breath was released to help quell her rising anxiety. She rose to her feet and began stepping quietly from the kitchen. In her years in the house, she had never noticed how much the floorboards creaked. The sound was unsettling. The old house possessed noises of its own accord and she did not like it. The knife in her palm quickly became slick with nervous perspiration.

The dining room was empty, all but the furniture. The windows all securely locked. She made her way into the living room, thrusting the knife into the curtains before using it to pull them back. All was clear. But there was still the coat closet.

She placed Casper gently onto the floor and made her way across the room. Gripping the handle, she prepared herself. She turned the knob slowly until she felt the latch spring free of the frame. With one final deep breath she flung the door open, holding the knife high above her head ready at any given second to stab; coats.

Casper wandered over and curiously sniffed at her ankles. His cold wet nose tickled her, calming her fears. She picked him up and searched the upstairs for reassurance. The puppy was small, but his presence relieved her. Certainly, if someone was in the house with them, he would respond in some manner.

When she was satisfied with her search, she entered the living room and sat down on the reclining chair as she attempted to rationalize the situation. "I have dreams about a man whom I have never met," she spoke aloud to Casper. AIn those dreams, he gives me gifts – including you. You came from my dreams. The gourmet coffee must have come from my dream also. So, you are either a physical manifestation of my sub-conscience or," she paused as a solitary tear ran down her cheek, "I've gone completely insane."

Half of her was overwhelmed with excitement of what could be the ultimate supernatural discovery. The other half was terrified beyond comprehension. She plopped Casper on the floor and dashed for the bathroom to vomit.

Chapter 27

There were times when a family tragedy could test the limits of a clergy's faith. For Father Thomas, the early passing of Arlen Bergin was one of those occasions. When he led his memorial, the memory of anointing the infant's head with holy water was still fresh in his mind. The contradiction of the two was like thousands of needles stinging the flesh of his faith.

Nearly four months removed, Arlen's father had requested a confession. Sean was now seated before him, confessing guilt for his son's death. Father Thomas could see that Sean's brow was furled from grief and guilt. Perhaps he could relieve him of at least one of those burdens.

"Why do you feel responsible?" Father Thomas asked.

Sean gathered himself and then began. "The morning was like an ugly chain of events. Arlen was playing video games and seemed to be very involved with them. So I decided to take my shower before he got his bath. Afterwards, I helped him draw the water and then went into my room to get dressed.

I'm not certain how long I waited – fifteen, maybe twenty minutes. When I went back to see if he was finished, he had only washed his hair. I lost my temper with him. He had a dentist appointment that morning - we were close to being late. I hate being late for appointments. So, I got angry and snapped at him. I grabbed the soap and was going to wash him myself." Sean paused to catch his breath.

In a conciliatory tone, Father Thomas told him to take his time.

"Father, I could see the fear in his eyes. I knew I was scaring him, but I couldn't stop myself. For some stupid reason, I was furious. That was our final moment together - my anger and his fear."

Father Thomas waited patiently for Sean to continue.

"Anyway, that's when the doorbell rang and it was Junior. I dropped the soap and handed Arlen the wash cloth and went downstairs. After Junior left, I made a business call. God only knows how long it took me to get back upstairs. I remember climbing the staircase. It was so quiet. I called his name, but he didn't answer. When I got to the bathroom, I saw him face down in the water. I'm not sure if I was in denial, not wanting to face the truth, but I thought he was just goofing around. Maybe he was seeing how long he could hold his breath under water, you know. I called his name again, but he didn't budge. I walked over and pulled his shoulders back. His skin was cold and bluish colored. I pulled him out of the bathtub and laid him on the floor. I screamed his name. Everything was so surreal; it felt like I was dreaming. I tried shaking him, but he wouldn't respond. I was panicking, not thinking clearly. I had taken CPR classes, but that was when I was in high school." As Sean spoke, tears began to trickle down his cheeks. His calm and clear voice was now rasping through sobs.

"I did what I could remember, but nothing seemed to work. I'm not sure if I was even doing the CPR properly. At some point, I must have finally called 9-1-1. I'm not sure how long I waited, because I honestly don't remember making the call. I remember kissing his little face and trying to warm his hands with my breath; they were cold. I didn't want him to be cold. Arlen always liked summertime the best. He hated the cold weather.

I felt so damn helpless. Everything I knew, any security I had with life, with myself - it all drained out of me. I kept thinking that this wasn't supposed to happen. That God had made a mistake. And as soon as he realized it, he would revive him.

For weeks after he died," Sean stared at Father Thomas with his face drenched in grief, "I would go into his bedroom and just stare at his toys, just trying to get close to him.

I can't even say I feel empty; it's something beyond that.

He was my son. I should have been the one to save him. I promised that I would always watch over him. I promised to protect him. And I failed. I had scared him. He must have been trying to hurry when he slipped on the soap, the soap that I left in the water.

I waited too long to check on him. I waited too long to pull him out. I waited too long to call 9-1-1." Sean released a tortured sigh as he stared at the ground. "Oh, God, I don't know what I was thinking." He looked up at the priest, uttering his questions in a plea. "Why didn't I act faster? Why did I even answer the door?"

Father Thomas leaned forward in his chair. He responded slowly and patiently, "Don't you think that your guilt feelings are based primarily on assumptions? You assume that he was hurrying when he slipped. You're assuming that you took a long time downstairs; yet, you don't have any recollection of elapsed time. Most of us don't expect these things to happen. Arlen was the victim of an accident. Sean, you are not confessing a sin. Even if your account is accurate; you did not injure Arlen. At worst, you made an error in judgment during a highly stressful and emotional situation. But you did not make an error in morality. An error in judgment does not always constitute a sin."

"Why then? Why did my son have to die? Why did God grant me a gift just to take him away from me?"

"Sean, God did not want this to happen. I don't believe you, nor God, had any cause in Arlen's accident. God had to bear witness to the death of His only son as well. I think He knows exactly how you feel.

God granted Arlen a place in His kingdom to relieve his suffering. God is gracious and caring to His children."

"Arlen was only five years old," Sean leaned back, eyes directed toward the ceiling then closed. "I never got to take him to a professional baseball game. I'll never teach him how to drive, see him graduate. I feel cheated. Arlen's life was wasted."

"God never promised us eternal life on Earth, only in His kingdom. Every life is precious and meaningful, no matter how long or brief." Father Thomas cast a glance to his right. A mural of a bright colored kingdom remained on the wall from the days of the crying room. It was meant to ease the children's unhappiness by reminding them of God's grace and glory. "Sean, do you remember how you felt when Arlen was born?"

"Yeah. It was the greatest day of my life. Nothing could ever replace that."

"You see, the gift that Arlen was to you cannot be measured in time."

Fingers, rough and thick from years of laboring wiped the tears from his eyes. Sean gathered himself. "Jennifer thinks I caused Arlen's death."

"She told you that?"

"She said she has doubts as to what happened that morning."

"Extreme grief can cloud our view of the world. I'm sure deep down inside Jennifer knows the truth. Unfortunately, searching for the reason 'why' can lead us to placing blame. People often search for something concrete following a tragedy. They want someone to blame; anyone. They want more black and white answers than what faith can provide."

Sean shifted in his chair. "She is looking at me trying to seek justice for something I did not do."

"Not justice. Justice implies fairness. I think she is looking to answer the 'why' just like you are. She is still full of anger. None of us can ever make sense of a senseless accident," Father Thomas paused. "Sean, no words can ever ease the pain of the loss that you and Jennifer have to endure. But I promise you, Arlen is with Him."

"It all comes down to faith, doesn't it?"

"I guess it does."

Sean picked through the flood of memories. "One of the first words Arlen learned to speak was 'more.' Whenever he wanted something, he would point to it and say, 'more.' He was only about eighteen months old at the time. One day I taught him to cover his eyes with his hands. Then when we went into a store, he naturally pointed to something he wanted and said, 'more, more.' So I told him to cover his eyes, and he did. I would say, 'If you can't see it, then it's not there.' I could get him past whatever he wanted me to buy before he would uncover his eyes. That little trick worked for a while, at least until he caught on. If you can't see it, then it's not there. I guess I was giving the kid bad advice. Your perception depends upon what you believe. I can't see him, but I know he's there. Sometimes I can feel him with me, and that feeling is more tangible than my sight." Sean suddenly fell silent.

"What are you going to do about Jennifer?" Father Thomas asked.

"What should I do? She told me how she feels. Although despite everything she said, I still love her. My heart's torn a little bit more from my chest with every second that I'm away from her."

"I think you need to do everything possible to save your marriage," Father Thomas said. "I know the love between the two of you is strong. It will pull you through this. You need to speak with her, Sean. Or, if you'd like, I could talk to Jennifer for you."

"No," Sean interjected, "I think I'll pay her a visit myself. Maybe, afterwards, we can both come and talk with you."

"Every union under God is at least worth that effort."

"I will pay her a visit first thing tomorrow morning."

"Marriage is a sacred covenant. You have to work hard to salvage it. I'm here if you need me."

"I can never thank you enough. You eased my mind. You make things seem clear and easy to approach."

"It's a gift," Father Thomas said merrily with a shrug that mocked his own success.

"I suppose I should be on my way." Sean attempted to stand until Father Thomas gripped his arm.

"Not so fast. It took eleven months to get you back in here. Are you telling me you don't have any real sins to confess?"

"Ah, give a guy a break."

"When it comes to sin, God does not take breaks, my son, so neither can we. If I have to, I will tape you to that chair." Father Thomas said with an impish grin.

Sean smiled as he slowly lowered himself back into his seat. "I hope you have some time on your hands. You are opening up a really big can of worms here."

Chapter 28

Jennifer looked at her reflection in the mirror, happily oblivious to its murky appearance. She coaxed a few curls of her long blonde hair down along her temples. She gave a contented smile and turned away to face the large dining area of her home. The walls were decorated with abstract paintings that were lined with polished, cherry wood frames. A Ming vase placed in a far corner sprouted eucalyptus. A large oak table with six matching chairs was poised in the center of the room, where the sweet scent of cherry blossoms added its gentle touch to the ambience.

Something soft brushed against her bare ankles drawing her attention. Her new puppy, Casper, was at her feet, imploring her to rub his tummy. She picked him up and cuddled him beneath her chin as the doorbell rang. She walked into the living room and opened the door. A bouquet of roses greeted her.

"I have a delivery for Jennifer Bergin," a voice behind the foliage uttered.

"They're beautiful!" Jennifer accepted the flowers, now seeing the face of the delivery person. "Nicholas."

"Having a stranger bring flowers seems so impersonal. I decided to bring them myself."

"Come in, please." She stepped back and allowed him to enter the house.

"This is a very nice home you have," Nicholas commented as he slid inside.

"Have a seat at the table. I'll go fetch a vase to put these in." Jennifer grabbed a vase from the kitchen and then returned, placing the flowers inside and adjusting the arrangement. She stuck her nose into the soft texture of the petals and drew in a deep breath. "They smell good. You spoil me." She sat down next to Nicholas and placed the vase at the center of the table.

"There's a card also," he eagerly informed her.

"Oh." She reached into the bouquet and withdrew a small floral card. *To my dream girl - believe; with all my love, Nicholas.* She lifted her gaze from the card to his face. "Thank you."

Nicholas leaned forward in his chair, "No, thank you. I have greatly enjoyed our time together. I would only hope there is more."

"There's more," she responded softly, "there's much more." She rolled her tongue across her lips. She could tell by the look on Nicholas' face that he had been enthralled by the sight. He eased himself forward, until she could feel the warmth of his breath on her now moistened lips. He closed the final distance by placing his hand gently on her chin. Their mouths came together in a deep kiss that touched every nerve in her body. His lips tasted sweet, pressing softly against hers in a passionate, yet gentle kiss. The flood of sensation nearly lifted her from her seat, to hover above him.

As he withdrew from her, Jennifer remained motionless, "Hmm," was all she could manage.

Nicholas smiled, "I guess that means you approve."

"No," she whispered, "this does." She rose from her seat, so that she could reach his lips once again. As she kissed him, she wrapped her arms about his neck and drew herself in closer. He pulled her onto his lap and held her tight to his chest.

Their rapture was unexpectedly interrupted by a flat wet tongue licking at her feet. She could not hold the moment, breaking into a frantic giggle. She pulled back from Nicholas and shifted her feet away from Casper's reach. "He's licking my feet."

Nicholas chuckled at her reaction, "Well, Casper, I believe we have found that our girl is ticklish."

"Yes, I am," she thinned her lips and narrowed her eyes, "and don't you even think about it."

Nicholas through his hands in the air, "Tell him, not me."

Jennifer slid from his lap, returning to her chair. She stared at him with a gaze that drew his soul into hers, longing to feel every nuance of his presence. It shrouded him in her desires and anticipated the entwining of their bodies.

Nicholas leaned back in his seat with a self-assured smile perched upon his face. She judged his victory to be palatable by the smacking of his lips. He seemed to be basking in her tangible display of affection. He touched a finger to the tip of her nose. "The taste of your lips was well worth the wait."

"You should have brought me roses sooner," she replied slyly. She ran her fingertips up the length of the vase and back down again, admiring her flowers. One dozen long stem, red roses softened with baby's breath - this is something I could grow accustomed to." Jennifer shifted through the roses with her hand until one particular rose caught her eye. "Oh, I'm sorry. There seems to be thirteen roses. Is this one for our love to grow on?"

Nicholas cocked his head. "What are you talking about? There should be only twelve."

"No, there are twelve red and one white," Jennifer insisted. "I must have missed it because of the baby's breath."

Nicholas looked suddenly alarmed, rising from his seat, "Jennifer, I did not put a white rose in your bouquet."

Jennifer's eyes fixed on Nicholas. He was overreacting to such a simple error. "Well, the florist must have done it for you. It's right here." With her eyes still fixed on Nicholas, she carelessly gripped the white rose. The thorns sank deep into the flesh of her finger and thumb. The stinging pain was subtle at first then grew in its intensity.

The pain in Jennifer's fingers brought her to an abrupt awakening. Confused, she found herself seated at her dining room table with her hand gripping the stem of a white rose. Gone were the abstract paintings. Gone was the Ming vase. But the roses from her dream were still present; painfully so. The thorns were buried deep into her skin, as blood trickled down her fingers. It took a few moments before she was aware enough to react to the wounds. She quickly dropped the rose onto the table in front of her and instinctively placed her fingers into her mouth. Her eyes remained fixed on the dozen red roses, neatly arranged in a vase, the roses that she was dreaming about a moment ago.

Her eyes widened as she pushed her chair back from the table. "Oh great, now I'm sleepwalking." She remembered falling asleep that night upstairs. She was still wearing the nightshirt she donned before bed. Rubbing her temples, she tried to concentrate. *Am I still dreaming? Everything is so confusing.* The sting of her fingers assured her that she was awake. Her breathing increased as panic began to set in. *This has to stay my little secret. No one would ever believe it. They would think I was insane. No one would ever understand.* Her mind worked frantically. *I won't end up like my mother.* Blind determination assumed control of Jennifer. *I'm not crazy, this is really happening! Nicholas is real. He lives in my dreams. He is in love with me and gives me gifts that transcend all barriers.* As the thoughts passed through her mind, she was unaware that she had begun to rock herself in her chair, a habit she developed as a child to replace a disconcerted mother. She wrapped her arms around her stomach. *Everything's going to be all right.* "Sssh," the sound eased from her lips.

She remembered that she had scheduled a morning appointment with Dr. Conahan. *He will calm me down.* She stood up and looked around her dining room. The morning sun was now seeping through the Venetian-blinds. *Everything is going to be all right.* She pulled herself together and went upstairs to take a hot shower.

Jennifer wrapped herself in a towel and examined her reflection in the bathroom mirror. Her hair hung wet, displaying a deeper red. She remembered the dream and her blonde curly hair. It wasn't a bad look for her. Perhaps later she may attempt to bleach her red out.

She applied her make-up and walked from the bathroom. The shower was relaxing and gave her time to reflect. She walked past the closed door to Arlen's bedroom and then paused. She needed her son, needed to be near him. She slowly opened the door and stepped inside. The room remained the same as Arlen had left it - without a toy or an article of clothing disturbed. Jennifer sat down on the edge of the bed, rubbing her fingertips gently across the exposed sheet.

"So, what do you think, Arlen? Is Mommy going nuts? If I am, it doesn't feel like I thought it would. I don't really feel any different. I still think the same way. But I can't explain what's happening to me. These dreams are scaring Mommy, but at the same time I can't get enough of them." She cast her eyes to the ceiling. "At least while I'm sleeping, I don't feel the pain. It hurts not being with you. Nicholas somehow makes me feel happy again; special. It is just so hard to tell what's real." She examined the holes that the thorns had left in her skin. 'Those roses must be real; the thorns were real enough. Did you see the roses? They are beautiful. Nicholas got me a puppy too. His name is Casper. You should come visit him." She paused through a deep and cleansing breath. "I wish I had you with me. The sky has not been blue; I'm not certain I can even see color anymore. Mommy is so sorry she didn't stay home with you that day. I know you needed me; maybe as badly as I need you now. You were all that mattered to me." She lowered her head in silence. There were no tears, only quiet exhaustion.

Chapter 29

Sean tucked his truck against the curb and shifted it into park. Easing back into the seat, he stared at his home. The spouting on the roof was coming loose, of which he made a mental note to fix. The second step on the porch was in need of repair also.

He looked up at the bedroom window where he and Jennifer once shared their bed. Sleeping close to her was near heaven, the warmth under the sheets, the fragrance of her skin, the soft touch of her flowing, red hair.

He could remember the first night in their new home. The house seemed so perfect. The trim around the windows bore a coat of fresh paint, and the siding was clean and bright. Seated outside on the porch swing on that warm summer evening, they drank wine and looked out on the peaceful street of their new neighborhood.

"Well, now that we have the home, all we have to do is have the child." Jennifer had spoken in between sips, focusing her attention on the wine at the bottom of the tall glass in her hand as she swirled it.

"I agree," Sean had answered. "I think we should get started immediately."

"How would grandpa Bergin feel about you mating with a Welsh girl?" She had smiled up at him from the nestling of his shoulder.

"I guess as long as your family didn't earn a living as mine barons, he would approve. Besides, those deep blue eyes of yours would have melted his heart just like they did mine." He had lowered his head to hers and kissed her deeply. Later, he carried her upstairs and paused in the hallway. She had never looked so beautiful. Her skin glowed with a renewed vibrancy. He pressed her back against the wall as she wrapped her legs tight to his waist. His hands slid beneath her skirt, lifting her by her buttocks. He nearly tore her shirt from her body so he could brush his lips against her creamy skin. They never made it to the bed. The hallway was the first place they made love in the house. After that, no room was sacred. He missed that life, a life that was simple and uncomplicated.

Now, the paint on the window panes were beginning to chip and the siding had been dulled from the elements. Sean ran his hands through his hair and prayed silently for this visit to go well. Repairing his marriage would be far more difficult than repairing his home. Home repairs were simple to him. But marriage repairs were something entirely new, not to mention Jennifer's sudden disdain for him. *How should I approach her? How could I make her understand?* For the first time in their relationship, he was overwhelmed with uncertainty. *What if she rejects me?* Tossing the thought aside, he climbed from the truck, stepping out into the low angle rays of the late February sun. The temperate was slightly above average; the early tease of spring gave Sean the impression of a new beginning. This was it, the moment he had spent an entire sleepless night devising. He would keep it simple; a fresh start. He would romance her back into his arms with love, patience and time. And then he would have his old life back.

He tried to open the front door, but it was locked. This was once his home. He considered using his key to enter, but he opted instead for the doorbell. Stepping back, he closed his eyes and drew a breath. *Relax. She is only your wife.*

Chapter 30

Coming down the stairs, the sound of the doorbell caused Jennifer to freeze on the final step of her descent. Her eyes shifted from the roses on the table to Casper, who was now sprawled out on the dining room floor. She went to the puppy and attempted to shoo him into the kitchen. The dog remained undisturbed even by the second ring of the door bell. "I'll be right with you," she called as she knelt down and lifted Casper in her arms. "Some watchdog you are."

She carried Casper into the kitchen and sat him on the floor. The doorbell rang a third time as she approached the roses. "Ah, shit!" She glanced about the room for a place to hide the flowers but then decided to give up the attempt. It was most likely one of the meter men from the natural gas or water companies; or even worse, a sales call.

"All right," her voice became harsh, "give it a break; I'm coming." The final words escaped her mouth just before she threw open the door. Her frustration caused her to pull on the door harder than she desired. As the door flung open wide, her eyes echoed the response when they fixed on Sean standing in the middle of the porch.

"Oh, hi," she uttered sheepishly, stepping into the door frame and pulling the door tight against her body. "Sorry, I thought you were going to try to sell me something. Salespeople are always so annoying, you know."

"That's okay," Sean replied. He stared at his wife. She was slightly gaunt, but he had not seen her in make-up for months. She looked more beautiful than he could ever remember. Her thick hair cascaded down over her breasts, and the scent of fresh perfume emanated from her pores.

He cleared his throat, searching for something to say. "Did I catch you at a bad time? You look like you're heading out."

She looked down at herself as if surprised by the news, "Oh, yeah. I have a doctor's appointment."

"Well, I guess I won't keep you."

"That's okay."

"I'm glad to see you're getting out of the house again. I saw you last week at the plaza."

"Yes. I know."

He eased out a breath. "You look great."

"Thanks. It was a quick weight loss program, but I wouldn't recommend it."

Sean responded by a nod of his head.

"What did you want?"

The question was direct. His brain suddenly froze. Sean was not prepared to respond. He stood silent for a moment waiting for his mouth to work. "I just dropped by to pick up the mail." It was the only excuse he could manage.

"It's upstairs in your office. I'll get it for you."

As she turned and pushed the door closed, Sean stepped forward. "Jennifer, I..." The door hit his foot and began to ease slowly open. He watched her as she climbed the dining room staircase. He smacked the butt of his palm against his head. *Ask her to lunch, Stupid.* He was twisting his body to gaze down the street when his brain finally registered what he had seen. He turned back and stepped into his living room. A large bouquet of roses stood proudly on his dining room table. He could hear Jennifer shuffling back to his upstairs office as he approached the table for a closer look. He found the card tucked inside and read the inscription. *To my dream girl - believe; with all my love, Nicholas.* His heart plunged into his stomach with a nauseating splash as he became gripped with overwhelming dread. Despite everything that had transpired between them, he had not come to terms with actually losing her. He looked at the staircase in the wake of her passing. He was stunned. His attention was suddenly drawn to a tiny pair of eyes staring at him from the kitchen. A pure white puppy examined him from the archway. His attention shifted back to the staircase as Jennifer descended. She paused at the bottom and returned Sean's stare from over the balustrade. She could see that his face was flush with anger.

"Who in the fuck is Nicholas?"

"He is a friend of mine." Jennifer responded, attempting to sound nonchalant on the matter.

"A dozen red roses? That is some friend."

"Well, maybe he was concerned about me. Look, don't come barging in here and pass judgment on things that you have no idea about!" Jennifer stated firmly.

"I think I have a very good idea. Is this why you wanted me out of the house?"

"What are you talking about? You left on your own accord. I did not ask you to leave."

"Who is this guy?"

"I told you. He is a friend."

"How long have you been seeing him?"

"Okay, that's it. I'm not doing this. Get out." Jennifer stepped from the stairs and pointed to the door.

"You know, I was crazy to think I could come over here and talk to you."

"What do you mean crazy?" Jennifer suddenly snapped. "Are you saying I'm crazy?"

Sean furled his brow, "No, I said I must have been. I thought we could talk things out."

"Well, I guess you thought wrong. Come back when you can be more reasonable."

"Don't turn this around on me. I'm not the one getting flowers. I suppose he got you the dog, too."

"As a matter of fact, he did."

"Jennifer, who is this guy?"

"Sean, would you please just leave." Jennifer thrust the envelopes that she had been holding into Sean's stomach. Sean spun and headed for the door. He stopped short and turned abruptly. "I'll take care of things for now. But if you're going to keep the house, you better get yourself back to work. From here on in, I'll have Angelia pick up the mail." He gripped the door handle and mumbled a final statement before slamming it behind him, "Get yourself a lawyer."

Jennifer stood in shock of what had transpired, but remained defiant. "Thanks for the visit." She shook her head in disgust. Gone were the memories of the tender man who romanced her into marriage. Gone were the memories of the strong arms that wrapped about her, keeping her safe and warm at night. He suddenly appeared smaller to her, less significant. He was nothing more than an uncouth, uncaring Neanderthal.

She drew in a deep breath. That was over, but she still had her doctor's appointment. She took a deep breath and concentrated on slowing her heart rate. She wished that she could go to bed and sleep.

Chapter 31

Sean stormed from the porch and thrust himself behind the wheel of his truck. The rage boiled over inside him, twisting in his mind like a burrowing worm. He had to release it before he completely exploded. He searched for something to hit inside the truck, something he would not damage too badly. He finally slammed his fist upward against the roof of the vehicle. He heard the metal pop. The slight pain in his fist was numbed by the adrenalin that now coursed through his veins. The sensation helped to ease his rage.

He thought about his last statement. He was not certain if he meant it as a threat, a warning, or a plea. He shook his head and released a long sigh. *So much for Father Thomas and the voice of peace,* he thought. Neither one of them had counted on Nicholas. Sean resolved that he would find out who Nicholas was. And when he did, no place on Earth would be safe for the man. He turned the key, slapped the truck into gear, and dropped the gas pedal to the floor in one continuous motion. The truck engine roared as an extension of his anger as it sped off down the street.

Chapter 32

"Vivid dreams."

The words had barely escaped Nicholas' lips before Jennifer awoke. It was 11:35. She had only dosed off for fifteen minutes after struggling to fall asleep for hours. Frustration had set in within the past hour, and now she found herself awake once again. A pale full moon hung low in the sky and seemed to illuminate the entire bedroom, making it difficult to sleep.

Her appointment with Dr. Conahan had not gone as she had hoped, despite a flawless performance. She had explained how the medications that he had prescribed were creating vast improvements in her previous condition. But for some reason unknown to her, Dr. Conahan referred her to Dr. Bomboy, the psychologist, and more importantly allowed the medications, of which she claimed to be taking, to Bomboy's discretion. She felt cornered, obligated to follow his advice. Pam, the receptionist, scheduled the appointment for her in three days. But that was a minor detail. She had already devised an excuse not to attend the appointment before the customary 24-hour courtesy deadline.

Rolling Nicholas' words over in her mind, she stared at the ceiling. *Vivid dreams? A message perhaps. Or maybe a secret code. Certainly he was trying to tell her something.* She pictured his impish grin as he stood in a patch of tall grass and wild flowers, his white shirt billowing in the warm summer breeze against his bronze skin.

Suddenly an idea rolled across her mind. She sprang from her bed and ran into the next room.

Chapter 33

Sean rolled over and looked at the alarm clock. It was 11:35 in the evening. The past hour had been spent tossing and turning in a bed that was made uncomfortable by anger and jealousy. The beer that he had consumed at the pub only intensified his rage, unleashing it by dowsing his inhibitions. Lying on his back with the ceiling as his visage, he ran his fingers through his hair then interlocked them behind his head. He tried to sort through his feelings. The anger was coated by a devastating sense of loss that turned his stomach. He exhaled through the queasiness and probed deeper. *I would have never suspected Jennifer of cheating on me. She had too much resolve to her principles and morals. She was dedicated to the institution of marriage, if not to me.* Something felt instinctively wrong about the situation, but he could not pinpoint it. He stared at the ceiling of the room that Gail had been so gracious in providing for him. He suddenly realized he had failed to offer compensation for her hospitality. He decided to remedy the oversight first thing in the morning.

The grimace on his face began to fade. He knew what would ease his mind. He rose from the bed and began to rummage through a stack of envelopes and papers that he had placed on the dresser earlier. Finding the object of his search, he sat down on the edge of the bed and unfolded a small scrap of paper. With an unsettled sigh, he reached for his cell phone. *Please answer the phone*, he thought, as he dialed Wendy's number.

Chapter 34

A new day brought new possibilities. Jennifer was in good spirits as she explored the aisles at the Med Swift Pharmacy. Her anxiety was mild, despite Sean's annoying tirade. She was determined to set aside the quandary of Sean.

'If you experience sleep disturbance or vivid dreams, discontinue the use of your nicotine patch during sleeping hours.' The label on the box was designed as a warning, but to Jennifer it read like an invitation. It was as the web site suggested, nicotine patches caused vivid dreams.

Jennifer smiled at her new prospect. The patches would be the keystone for tonight's endeavor. She was wetting her feet within the shores of discovery. She had a new-found purpose, something to be excited about. Nicholas had a message for her, and tonight it would be revealed. Last night's dreams were somewhat murky. Nicholas had only appeared for a brief moment. Vivid dreams; his words still echoed in her head as though he had just uttered them.

A quick Google search provided the answer. She typed 'vivid dreams' into the search engine and explored some of the web sites it referenced. There it was; an article on nicotine patches. It had been so long since her term paper on the psychology of resolving addictions - she had nearly forgotten. Users of the nicotine patch had reported experiencing vivid dreams when they wore the patch to bed. This seemed like a valid proposition. Her desperation transformed into sudden exuberance. She had the conquest and now the patch would grant her the means. Although another web site, dedicated to herbal medicine, suggested mugwort – the nicotine patches seemed easier to obtain. However, at a price of more than forty dollars, the patches were more expensive than she had thought. She wasn't sure how close she was to her credit card limit. She passed the candy aisle on her way and was suddenly transported to a childhood memory.

She could remember weekly visits to another local pharmacy, Tobias Drug Store, with her Dad. Jennifer's mother was one of the pharmacy's best customers, but she refused to pick up her own prescriptions - citing a need to keep up appearances.

Tobias Drug Store was a small shop, owned by an elderly pharmacist and his wife, Mr. and Mrs. Tobias. The couple worked the entire schedule of operations together, something Jennifer found to be endearing.

Mrs. Tobias was always pleasant. The woman's soft smile was angelic to young Jennifer, who fancied the woman to be her mother. Mrs. Tobias always made certain that Jennifer's dad never got out of the store without buying his daughter a Hershey chocolate bar. The kindly pharmacist's wife would always add something extra in the bag for Jennifer at no cost. Donald would argue about Jennifer's teeth and health. He worried about her developing poor eating habits.

Jennifer could still hear Mrs. Tobias lecturing her Dad. "To the devil with all those doctors. A child needs chocolate. Those doctors won't be happy until they take the youth right out of people. The only magic we ever have is our youth," she would say. "You have to enjoy it while you've got it."

Jennifer was devastated when Mr. Tobias passed away. The pharmacy was stripped to the bare walls and the doors were closed forever. She never found out what became of Mrs. Tobias. She never saw her again. And she never had the opportunity to tell the woman how much her kindness meant to a tormented little girl. In their brief meetings, Mrs. Tobias managed to be a better mother to Jennifer than her real mother even attempted to be.

The lightest touch on a life can result in an immeasurable force. And sometimes, that force is positive. While others, Jennifer thought as she approached the young female cashier to pay for her items, *are predicated to be negative.*

Jennifer was relieved by the uncommon absence of Dylan. She preferred not to have any interaction with Sean's friends at the moment. She cast an acrimonious glare at the clerk as she placed the nicotine patches, the chocolate bar and three cans of dog food on the counter. Jennifer had never read the clerk's name badge previously, but she remembered their last encounter. It was the same snippy little bitch from her previous visit.

Now, with the aid of a name tag, Jennifer could place the name Michelle to the familiar face.

Jennifer noticed that the clerk made every attempt to avoid direct eye contact with her. She could sense the young girl's penitence; she could nearly smell her discomfort. Jennifer leaned into her with a wily smile. "Well. Hello again, Michelle. Call me crazy, but I got a mad craving for a chocolate bar."

Jennifer could see that Michelle was squirming as she hedged the comment. The teen's ears and cheeks were flushed. Michelle stated Jennifer's total, never lifting her eyes from the cash register.

Arriving home, Jennifer shut the door and locked the outside world away. She breathed a sigh of relief and tried to regain her focus. She had much to do before bedtime. Casper greeted her at the door with a whimper of gratitude. "You must be hungry. Come on, I'll feed you." She entered the kitchen and glanced down at Casper's dog dish. The dish was dirty. She grabbed a soup bowl from the cupboard and emptied a can of dog food into it. She placed the bowl and empty can absent-mindedly on the floor then retrieved a tablet and pen from the utility drawer before sitting at the table. "We have a lot of things to do before Nicholas comes to visit." Casper showed no desire to partake in casual conversation. His tongue lapped hungrily against the bowl. The bowl slid forward with each lick. He chased it across the kitchen as it slid.

Jennifer removed the remaining items from her shopping bag and tossed the bag onto the floor. She tore open the wrapper of the candy and bit into the sweet chocolate. Her stomach rumbled as the first swallow reached its depths. She began writing a list of questions that she wanted to ask Nicholas. 1) *Who are you?* 2) *How did you send me flowers?* Her plan was to study the list until she fell asleep, hoping that she would remember them in her dream. The nicotine patch would elevate her dreams to a higher level of intensity. She hoped it would also heighten her awareness.

Jennifer had always believed that life possessed more magic than most people cared to acknowledge. She was convinced that there was more to Nicholas than just a dream and she was determined to uncover his secrets. She found an unnatural energy pulsing through her veins. She was restless and jittery. She feared if she did not calm her excitement, sleep may elude her completely. A cup of decaffeinated tea and some soft music soon lightened the mood.

Upon completing her list she turned her attention to another problem from the previous day. Light. The bedroom was too well lit. The windows would need covered. If she was to be in the midst of discovery, she wanted to curtail any outside stimuli that may awaken her. Some old blankets that she retrieved from her bedroom closet would suffice. Carpet tacks and a hammer helped affix them to the window panes.

Chapter 35

Dylan returned to the pharmacy counter following one of his typical ten-minute lunches. He enjoyed working with the public and wanted to be available at all times. Lunch was strictly for eating, not relaxing while on the job. He delivered his standard questions to Michelle as he checked the in-basket. "Did things go okay while I was gone? Is there anything I should know about?"

"Your friend, Jennifer, was in again," Michelle responded.

Dylan returned his eyes back to the in-basket. "Oh, is she refilling another prescription? I don't see her slip in here."

"She didn't have any prescriptions this time. She just purchased a couple items. She made an offhanded remark to me, but I was polite and courteous to her," Michelle defended herself without being reproached.

"What did she say?"

"It was something about a candy bar. But it was the tone of voice that she used. I understand now that she has a good reason to act strange. I feel bad for her, losing a child and all. And considering her current state of mind, I don't think that it's a good idea for her to try to stop smoking now." It was a well rehearsed speech, laced with pompous concern.

"Jennifer doesn't smoke."

"Well, she bought some of those nicotine patches, so I just assumed."

Dylan quietly pondered Jennifer's reasons for buying nicotine patches. Her behavior lately was certainly uncharacteristic of her, even considering what she had been through. Jennifer always appeared to him as slightly esoteric with her interests in eastern philosophy, the Druids, and even Wicca, but perhaps Sean was right. Maybe she was starting to lose her grip on reality altogether. He made himself a mental note to discuss the situation with Sean during their next conversation.

"Oh, and Mrs. Wendell called while you were eating," Michelle blurted, interrupting his thoughts. "She had a question about the cream she had picked up for her Eczema this morning."

"Did she say what it was?"

"She was concerned about going out of town for the weekend."

"So," Dylan responded quizzically, "she can take the cream with her."

"She was concerned because the directions said to apply locally."

Chapter 36

Each new day begins as an experiment in fate and faith, as a solitary event can turn the mundane into magic or the commonplace into a catastrophe. The sullen spirit of a man can be changed in the blink of an eye or in the vibration of a cell phone.

The subtle vibration against Sean's hip alerted him to an incoming call on his cell phone. Before he could pull the phone from his pocket, the vibration was replaced by a classic rock song from the band Squeeze. 'Tempted by the Fruit of Another' never seemed quite as loud as he fumbled to open his phone. He had downloaded the ringtone only days before; never considering the image it portrayed to his clients. He had meant to change the ringer to 'vibration only' mode as soon as he arrived at the Harper residence, but the thought had slipped his mind. And now Robert Harper examined the look of embarrassment upon Sean's face with mild amusement.

Robert and Harriet Harper had purchased their home eight months ago, and they were anxious to begin drastic changes to the long neglected landscape. Currently, Sean strolled the five acres surrounding the ranch-style home with sixty-year-old Robert. The two discussed Japanese maples, cherry laurels, rhododendrons, water features and retaining walls, with an eye on aesthetically pleasing functionality.

Sean politely excused himself from their conversation, stepping away as he placed the phone to his ear.

"Sean. I hope I'm not catching you at a bad time." The delicate voice would have been barely audible were it not for its captivatingly sensuous tone.

"Hello Contessa. I was just doing a site analysis for a new client."

"Oh, I'm sorry." Wendy said apologetically. "I don't mean to interrupt."

"No. It's okay. I'm glad you called."

"I've been worried about you since your phone call last night," she continued. "You seemed very upset."

"Things have smoothed out now." Sean stepped further away from Harper, motioning with his finger that he would need an additional moment for the call. "Listen. I want to thank you for being there for me. Just hearing your voice calms me down. You have a wonderful knack for lifting my spirits."

"You don't ever have to thank me for that. I always want to be here for you. But I won't hold you up. I was just wondering if you had any plans for tomorrow. I don't have to be at the hospital until four o'clock and I was hoping we might be able to meet for lunch. I'll feel better if I can look into those bright green eyes and see that you're okay."

"That would be great. I could be finished by noon and meet you at one o'clock. Is McKinney's Pub okay with you? Ed has a great sandwich menu."

"I suppose that will be okay, although I don't want to go to work smelling like a bar."

"Well, we don't have to drink alcohol." Sean paused, reassessing his decision, If you would prefer to eat somewhere else, it's fine with me."

"No. I'll meet you at McKinney's at one o'clock."

"Okay Contessa, I will see you there."

"Bye, Hon." She uttered softly before clicking the line dead.

Sean paused for a moment. His satisfaction was displayed by the prevalent smile that now spread across his lips. His heart rate increased as his mind envisioned his gracefully, beautiful lunch companion. He quickly shook the thought, reminding himself that it was merely a lunch between friends. The thumb on his left hand absent-mindedly turned the wedding band on his ring finger. He paused as he became aware that he was partaking of his compulsive habit. Robert Harper soon averted his attention.

"Is everything okay Sean?" Harper asked.

Timothy Cole

Sean turned back to Harper, slightly embarrassed by his preoccupation. "Everything is fine." He quickly moved to Harper's side and returned their conversation to the issue of landscaping.

Chapter 37

Upon completing her chores, Jennifer ascended the stairs with her nicotine patches. The sun had set, and the bedroom was near pitch black despite the attempt of a full moon to penetrate her surroundings. The old heavy blankets were working perfectly. She studied the directions and then applied the nicotine patch to her upper arm and climbed into bed with two down pillows to prop her head against the headboard. She reviewed her list of questions, studying each until they were burned into her memory. Her eyes grew heavy as her focus blurred. She studied her tablet of questions and then the interior of her eyelids intermittently, and then nothing.

Desiderio's was a five-star restaurant known for its resplendent atmosphere to romance the soul and its impeccable cuisine to romance the palate. It was an enchanted place where any man, with the wherewithal, could wisp the woman of his dreams off her feet at the sacrifice of nearly half a week's pay.

Desiderio's was located a mere fifteen miles from Honey Brook. But despite its proximity, Jennifer never had the pleasure of patronizing the establishment. Sean would say that he refused to spend the equivalent of two weeks of groceries on a single meal. She had dreamed of an opportunity to enter its pristine glass doors and now her dreams had provided that chance.

Jennifer stepped inside as Nicholas held the door open for her. The walls of the atrium were coated with a mixture of stucco and beige paint, adding texture and dispersal of the reflected light. A chair-rail of solid oak ran along each wall. The ceiling was spray coated with stucco and trimmed with crown molding, with recessed flood lights providing the illumination. The floor was covered with terra-cotta red-clay tiles for a subtle blend of color. Wrought iron benches with cushioned seats lined both the east and west walls. The front of the atrium offered three directions. Facing the doorway was an entrance to the bar area which contained several round tables, each with four wooden chairs. Matching hallways extended out to the left and right at forty-five degree angles with barrel-vaulted ceilings to add the perception of depth to the interior. Each wall that divided the hallway from the bar was adorned with a twelve-pane glass window that was framed with rich oak. The maitre d' was standing to the right of the bar entrance, greeting them as they approached. He requested the name of the reservation and Jennifer stated her name before he led them through the hallway into one of the dining rooms.

"Wow. This place is beautiful. I love the atmosphere," Jennifer exclaimed as she glanced about the decor. Beneath the bustle of the restaurant chores, the sounds of *Rachmaninoff* and *Vivaldi* filled the air.

The dining room bore a grey marbled carpet with rough-cut stained joists on the ceiling above. Curved bars strung with candescent lights hung from each joist. Plants were both hung and placed about the room adding an organic touch of color. The maitre d' led them to their table and seated Jennifer. The front waiter then approached to light the candle at the table's center and offered them water. Jennifer turned to speak to Nicholas just as the captain arrived at their table. Jennifer paused as he inquired of their choice of cocktails and presented the wine list. Nicholas broke etiquette by allowing Jennifer to select the wine. She ordered a bottle of their best Chardonnay and then, at last, she was alone with Nicholas.

"I could get used to this," Jennifer said with a sigh of satisfaction. "I've wanted to eat here ever since this place opened."

"Why is it that you never came here before?" Nicholas asked.

"Sean was not much for fancy places," she leaned forward. "He thought this place was too expensive.

When I was a little girl, my parents would take me to dine at places like this. I would always feel like a princess, having people wait on me. Everything was so proper and controlled. My mother was a little obsessive over my etiquette and manors. That added a twinge of stress to the outings, but they were still magical times for me."

"Your mother was a troubled woman," Nicholas interjected. "There were extenuating circumstances to her behavior."

"Dad never really discussed the cause of Mom's condition with me," Jennifer retorted. "I do know that we suffered as a result of it. But Dad loved her no matter what." She paused for a moment in reflection and then dispelled the thought. "I don't want to talk about my past. Today is what's important; this moment here with you is all that matters to me. This is like a dream come true … "

Jennifer suddenly straightened herself as though she were stuck by some amazing discovery of the utmost importance. "Do you know if I'm dreaming right now?"

Nicholas chuckled at her impish stare. "What do you think?"

"I am, but I'm not waking up."

"Maybe you don't wish to."

"I don't want to wake up," she proclaimed with excitement. "You have been in my dreams before. You keep giving me things. I don't even know who you are, how you got here, how you manage to make things appear from our dreams."

"One question at a time."

"Well," Jennifer was nearly stammering. "If you exist in my dreams, did I create you?"

"No. There is only one creator, the same entity who created you. It is He who created me. I have," he paused, "and do exist."

"Then what are you?" She blurted with a childish charm of discovery. "No offense. I guess that sounded bad."

"I understand this must be very confusing to you. My name is Nicholas Alfonso Feragamo. I was born in Sicily on April 12, 1928."

Jennifer chewed on the inside of her lip as his statement settled in her mind. "Nineteen twenty eight! That would make you …" she attempted the calculation, but her mind had frozen, "old!"

"Jennifer," he reached across the table and placed his hand gently on hers, "I died on August 24, 1953."

The air surrounding her carried a chill causing the fine hairs to rise with the pumps forming on her skin. She shuddered. Her mouth dried until she could no longer swallow. "I'm talking to a dead guy." She struggled to accept what she had heard. She allowed her eyes to drift away from him before flashing back unexpectedly. "Ah, and I kissed you!"

Nicholas smiled, "It's not exactly like that."

"Are you an angel?"

"There is only one angel in this room and that is you. However, I am a spirit."

Timothy Cole

"So Sylvia Browne was right!"

"Who is Sylvia Browne?"

"Never mind. Did I somehow pull you into my dreams?"

"No, I came in on my own accord. I was drawn by your essence. That is where your true beauty lies. What you see in the mirror is superficial. A shell projected by your persona; beautiful none-the-less, but no match for the elegance of your essence or spirit."

"So spirits can visit you in your dreams?" She rested her elbows on the table and propped her chin on interlocking fingers.

"Is it so hard to believe? The Bible states that when the angel told Joseph that the baby in Mary's womb was conceived of the Holy Ghost, the angelic visit was in Joseph's dream. In the Bible alone, there are countless other examples.

When I was a boy, this was after my mother and father died; I had a dream in which my mother visited me. We were by a brook. The water was running pure and clean. It was a serene setting. It was a bright, sunny, warm day in the hills of Italy.

She asked me to promise her that I would always treat people with love and respect and grow up to be the best man that I could possibly be. Before she left, she brushed the back of her hand softly against my cheek. Her skin felt like silk. I could feel her touch so vividly. And even though I knew she had died, I was not sad. Being with her in that dream was so real to me. I couldn't be sad because I knew she was right there with me. I felt her essence and the strength of her love. I never realized that the visit was real, until..."

"Can you visit me in the real world?"

"When spirits visit the natural world, the world you call real, they do not experience it the same way you do. We have no sensations in your world. We can't feel, taste or smell, not like we can in your dreams."

"In the dreams I have with you, everything feels real to me too," Jennifer commented.

"It is real. Reality is like an old man that is growing on a wart. Reality is simply a matter of perspectives. That glass seems real to you, so to you it is real. And because it's real to you; it's real to me. That's why I hope you keep dreaming."

"I stopped taking the sleeping pills that the doctor gave me. I began sleeping so soundly that I wasn't dreaming, or at least I couldn't remember the dreams I had. My doctor is sending me to a psychologist. Do you believe that?"

"You should go."

"Why?"

"It may help you to talk to him about your sadness. You should also get your medication refilled."

"But I don't need the sleeping pills. They interfere with our dreams."

"Well, you never know. You may find that you need them again."

"If you say so."

Their conversation was temporarily disrupted by the arrival of their wine. Following the tasting, the maitre d' poured the wine and then offered the menu and explained their specialties and his recommendations. Nicholas had the Bolognese tortellini in white creamy truffle sauce, while Jennifer ordered sautéed chicken breast stuffed with spinach, sauté of rapini, and baby lentils. Jennifer also ordered the fried calamari for her and Nicholas to share. The maitre d' departed with the order and once again they were alone.

'You once saved me from a nightmare," Jennifer continued, "that's why you were always so familiar to me."

"True. But I was in your dreams long before that, just in small ways."

"So, why, then, do spirits visit people in their dreams?"

"As I said, we have no sensation in your world. However, when you are in the altered state of consciousness while dreaming, we can experience what you do via the electrical impulses in the neurons of your brain. Thus the more vivid your dreams are to you, the more inviting they are to me."

Jennifer weighed the statement. "You mean you are literally inside my head right now!" She said with a slight tone of repulsion.

"Yes. And because of your dream state of consciousness, we pose no threat to each other." Slowly her repulsive expression dissipated and a smile spread across her face, "I got Nicholas on the brain."

Nicholas laughed. "I guess you could say that."

"What happens if you try to enter my mind while I'm awake?"

"For you, what appears to psychologists as Schizophrenia or Multiple Personality Disorder. For me, I would be trapped inside your mind as you assimilate my spirit into yours. Neither of us would ever be the same. We would each lose our sense of self."

"You mean like putting two spirits in a blender?"

Nicholas laughed until he experienced a coughing spell. He wiped tears of laughter from the corners of his eyes. "I love the innocent way you color things. That is why your dreams are so interesting and vivacious. Yes, like putting two spirits in a blender."

But humor was not the emotion that swelled in Jennifer; fear began to rise in her; the risk of insanity. It was the fear of losing her sense of self. Insanity robbed a person of who they were. To Jennifer, it meant a life sentence of being a zombie of incoherence, forever tortured with bizarre thoughts and images, trapped in a never-ending nightmare, and constantly exposed to ridicule.

Nicholas cocked his head for a moment as though listening to some distant voice. "I assure you, this is safe. As you awaken, your consciousness and your rationale immediately begin to dismiss me, and try to extricate me. Remaining inside your mind would be a terrible struggle for me and, as I said, it would endanger me also. I enjoy the sensation of your world, but I enjoy being free of its pain. I have no desire to return to it."

His words helped to reassure her, but she remained disquieted by the premise. "How is it that I have never been here before, yet I know what it looks like? Or, I guess maybe I don't; perhaps the real Desiderio's looks nothing like this."

"Oh, this is how the restaurant truly looks."

"But how is that possible?"

"This dream is on me. I brought you here."

"I thank you for that," she paused. "Okay, tell me something that no one knows; something about life or about God." Jennifer said persuasively.

"Alright. Do you remember when I said there was only one creator?"

"Yes."

"Well, I meant creation in more than the physical sense. He is responsible for creativity as well. Music, books and paintings have always existed since the creation of heaven and earth. Artists only channel their artwork into existence in your world. The artist is not chosen for his or her talents or creativity. But instead they are chosen for their understanding of what is trying to come through and their ability to channel it without disturbing it."

"You mean Edgar Allen Poe did not write all those stories?"

"Not in the sense that you are accustomed to. He channeled them, as only he could."

"That's amazing," Jennifer stated in astonishment. "I remember in college, I was taking some courses in psychology. The professor was a big fan of *Aldous Huxley's* work, so I read *The Doors of Perception*. You know,

I was trying to get in with the professor to earn extra consideration when it was grading time."

"Unfortunately, I died before that piece was published." Nicholas interjected.

"Anyway," Jennifer continued, "I had the same idea while I was reading that book. Huxley wrote that when he was under the effects of the drug Mescalin. He believed he was viewing the world as an artist. He considered that artists perceived objects differently than we did. Colors were more vivid to them. They were more in awe of everyday objects than the rest of us are. I guess that his reference to a creator was where my own concept came from. I wondered about creation and I wondered where human creativity fit into divinity. And my concept was exactly what you just explained to me. All works of art were created by God. I was right."

"It's humbling, is it not?"

"I would most certainly say so," Jennifer paused thoughtfully. "What is Heaven like?"

"Jennifer," he shook an admonishing finger at her. "I can't tell you everything. Actually, I have already told you too much. Eve ate the fruit from the tree of knowledge, so let us pretend that knowledge was the original sin.

The quest for knowledge is what drives life. All life is based on motion. Motion of objects, motion of the celestial bodies, and even the motion of man's evolution. Absolute knowledge would lead humankind to lethargy. No motion - no life. You are not meant to know everything. You are a small pixel in a much larger picture. Existence is attempting to understand itself. Perhaps you will get the answers that you're seeking when you finish your circle."

"What circle?"

"The one that leads you back to the beginning, to infancy, where we know everything but can communicate nothing. Or perhaps there are no absolute truths," he stated coyly, "perhaps Heaven is simply a private version of paradise for each of us, with each heaven being different, but all in the presence of God. Like I said, I have already told you too much."

"Then answer this question. Why did my son have to die?"

The sudden blunt force of the question startled Nicholas, but he recovered quickly. "You are focusing on the wrong side of the issue, Jennifer. There was no significance to Arlen's death, only to his life."

"Okay, so why me? Why do you keep coming back to me? The night must hold stronger dreamers than me."

"First, I came to you because I knew that you were in pain and that you needed me. I was here to help you during this very difficult time. But now, I must confess that I have fallen in love with you."

"Can you bring Arlen to me?"

"I wish that I could, but I can't," Nicholas responded, although he seemed agitated that she failed to react to his confession of love. "He would have to visit you voluntarily. At this point, he may not understand how to find you."

"Could you at least find him? Let me know if he's okay. Tell him I miss him."

"I promise that I will try."

Jennifer lowered her head. The yearning for her son was overpowering her sense of curiosity. Nicholas reached across the table and took her hand in his. He pulled her hand toward his body and held it to his chest. He stared into her eyes with loving concern as he slid her hand up slowly to his mouth and kissed it softly. Jennifer granted him a reassuring smile with a barely discernable quiver in her lips.

"Are you okay?" Nicholas asked her.

'Yes, of course. Please forgive me." She dabbed a tear from the corner of her eye. "Look at me; you bring me to this wonderful place, and I get all melancholy."

"Don't punish yourself. I understand perfectly."

"Nicholas, do you mind if I ask you one more question?"

"Of course you can, go right ahead."

"How did you die?"

"That is a long story, one that will make me melancholy, as you could quite imagine." He cast a coy grin. "I don't want to talk about my past. I want to know more about you now. I have answered a lot of your questions. Now, you can answer mine."

Jennifer agreed with a nod. She glanced over her shoulder and saw their waiter pushing through the kitchen doors with a large serving tray. "Oh, I hope that is for us. I'm famished."

The waiter approached; he announced each item as he placed it on the table. When he finished, he smiled a broad, peculiarly jovial smile. "Enjoy," he said as he stared at Jennifer and then disappeared from their table.

Nicholas' eyes twinkled with amusement. "Did you see him?"

Jennifer leaned in toward Nicholas. "I think he was a little odd."

"He was admiring you."

"No. He was just weird."

"I'm telling you; he was as captivated by your beauty as I."

She gave Nicholas a quasi-curtsy nod

As they ate, their conversation lightened. Jennifer spoke of pleasant memories with her father and her prospects of the future. She explained to Nicholas what had transpired with Sean. He consoled her, reassuring her that her position on the matter was the correct one. If she and Sean could not trust one another, then the marriage should be dissolved.

Jennifer awoke the next morning with her head throbbing in pain. She attempted to sit up, but the room seemed to spin lazily. "Oh, God," she uttered as she lowered herself back onto the mattress. She felt a wave of nausea swell and then ease slightly. *The squid at the restaurant must have given me food poison*, she thought, ignoring the fact that the restaurant visit had been experienced in her dream. She also failed to consider the side effects of a nicotine patch on a non-smoker.

Chapter 38

Wendy Parks paused in the process of getting herself dressed and sat down on the edge of her bed. She had donned her bra and panties, but her nursing scrubs remained spread out beside her. Across the room, the rays of the afternoon sun penetrated through the window of her second-story apartment, illuminating the drifting particles of dust into a shimmering veil that captivated her eyes while her mind wandered.

She recalled the first time she met Sean Bergin. He was strong, good looking and cocky. She was completely smitten by him until the pair started dating. Slowly she realized that Sean was too immature for her. His life was football and hanging out with his friends. She sought a more intellectual type. Now with many years gone by, she perceived his immaturity as boyish charm, a charm that she found irresistible. Sean always seemed to be looking at the world with new eyes. She recalled the first time that he saw her in a bikini. He was captivated by a birthmark just below her navel. Sean made the comment that it was shaped like a strawberry and that he wanted to see the rest of the strawberry patch. He had spoken the words as a joke, but Wendy could see the hunger in his eyes. She loved the way he looked at her. Each glance was as if he were seeing her for the first time.

Her fingertips gently stroked the strawberry birthmark on her tummy. With the memories flooding in, she slid onto the floor and withdrew a box filled with pictures from under the bed. She brushed aside some snapshots. Swing sets and picnics, Christmas trees and smiling faces, some struck instant cords of recognition while other memories were faded. The pictures fanned out against the walls of the box to reveal her high school, senior yearbook beneath. She flipped through the graduating class until she came to Sean's photo. Her fingers touched his picture as if to feel the contours of his face. She had always had a strong attraction to him, but lately her feelings had elevated to a near obsession. She had even begun to experience romantic dreams of Sean that served to solidify her desire for him.

She turned to the eleventh grade section and found the entry for Jennifer. Staring at the photo, she had to admit Jennifer possessed a natural beauty. She could plainly see why Sean was attracted to her. Her feelings toward Jennifer, in regards to Sean, were never begrudging, only that of envy. She closed the yearbook.

Jennifer had now willingly stepped aside. In the hospital cafeteria, Wendy could sense Sean's attraction to her, perhaps her return to Honey Brook and Sean's separation were a gift from God. She had stayed single long enough. The sting of her husband's betrayal had now faded along with her distrust of men. And now at the age of 35, she had begun to feel that life was slipping through her fingers. She knew that Sean could make her happy, and she knew that she could have him. If Jennifer truly ended the marriage, then she would be waiting for him. Today's lunch would be the first step of illustrating her intentions.

Chapter 39

The early afternoon crowd at McKinney's Pub was sparse at best. Sean glanced at his watch; he was early. Unable to suppress his enthusiasm, he would be forced to anxiously eye the door, awaiting Wendy's arrival. He had been talking with Wendy quite often since Arlen passed away, but this felt different. He was slightly nervous.

He pulled up a stool at the bar as Ed came down to greet him. He knew that he had discussed not drinking to Wendy, but he needed something to take the edge off. He ordered a draft and drank it quietly, trying to preoccupy his mind by staring at the television. He watched for twenty minutes without assimilating a single word or image. Several times he had heard the door open and turned on his stool, only to be disappointed by the entrant.

It is only a friendly lunch, he continued to tell himself even while he prepared for the occasion. The thought replayed while he showered and selected his gray v-neck alpaca sweater and khaki slacks. He thought it again while he sprayed cologne into the air and stepped into its mist. Gail had questioned his intentions with a discriminating tone, but he disregarded her suspicions. After all, it was merely a lunch between friends.

At last, the door opened to a tall brunette with full, curving hips swaying in a graceful stride. The standard white cotton nursing uniform rose to a higher level of fashion from the feminine delights it enshrouded. Sean slid from his barstool and directed Wendy to sit at a nearby table. As Sean pulled out her chair for her to sit, he caught the perfume of her presence. Her sweet smell was nearly intoxicating.

"Okay, now that I have you in my sight," Wendy said. "How are you doing?"

"I will be fine," Sean answered with a warm smile. He lowered himself down into his chair. "Thanks for asking. How's Gram doing? I visited her at the hospital early yesterday morning, but I may not make it out there today."

"Honey, I wouldn't really know. She was moved out of intensive care."

"Oh, that's right. I wasn't thinking," Sean admitted sheepishly.

"I can check on her if you would like me to."

"I would really appreciate that, Contessa. I would feel more secure knowing that you are looking in on her."

"It's no problem. I'll be glad to do it. I can stop by today before my shift." She brushed a strand of towel lint from the table. "So, who do you think this Nicholas guy is?"

"I don't know. Maybe someone she works with. Or an old school mate. What I do know is a man does not send red roses to a female friend unless he has something else in mind." Sean looked deep into Wendy's large sultry eyes. Wendy averted them for a moment toward the bar, in thought.

"I just can't believe that she would do that to you; especially after what you have been through already."

"She's not the same girl I married. She has put so much stress on me, both emotionally and financially. And then after I stuck by her, she turns on me. She nearly accused me of being responsible for Arlen. Hell, she almost had me believing it."

"Nothing could be further from the truth. I saw you with Arlen. And you would have never done anything to hurt him. He was your pride and joy." Sean nodded his head in approval. "I don't understand her. I mean, that takes a lot of nerve. I'm sorry, but I hate to see you treated this way. I get defensive."

"I don't want to talk about my problems. Lunch was a great idea. I'm glad you called me," Sean glanced at the table; he was remiss with his manners. "Oh, did you want something to drink?"

"I'll have a diet coke."

"Would you mind if I have a beer?"

"Of course not."

"Well I know you said..."

"Believe me, if I wasn't going to work, I would be having one too." Wendy glanced around the pub. "Gosh, I haven't been out for so long."

"Well, we can fix that problem. When is your next day off?"

"Funny you should ask. I happen to have this weekend off. I was going to drive down south to see my parents, but I can do that another time."

"I don't want you to change your plans for me. What if you disappoint your parents?"

"Are you kidding me? They would be happy to hear that I was acquiring a social life. Besides, they absolutely adore you."

"Great. I will pick you up tomorrow night at seven o'clock. We can have some drinks. Maybe I'll even take you dancing. I haven't been out dancing in forever."

"Wow, this is like a real date. I'm getting picked up and everything." Wendy gave her lashes a subtle bat and then flashed her beautiful smile.

"I guess you have yourself a date, Contessa. Does this mean I'm off the hook on the prom issue?"

"Not so fast. We'll see how much fun I have. Then I'll decide. It may take a few dates to make up for that one."

The couple ordered sandwiches from the waitress. They reminisced about high school until the food was served. They ate quickly and then decided to take a walk together. Sean opened the door for her and stepped out behind her. His hand pressed against her back as he led her out. Even the simple touch made his heart race with excitement.

They strolled casually down the street, discussing the rustic shops of the downtown area. They saw the old Laundromat, still in operation. As children, they would stop on occasion to buy soda and candy from the machines inside. Separated from the Laundromat by the entrance to a rear parking lot was Bell's Pet Shop. The pet shop was a relatively new establishment of nearly twenty years, however, the owner and proprietor was a long time, local veterinary named Ernest Bell. Bell rejected the stagnancy of retirement to re-invest his savings in a pet shop.

Ahead, they could see the hand-painted sign of the arcade, a dragon wrapping its body around a medieval castle. Magic Castle Arcade had made the transition from pinball and pool tables, to Pac-man, to the violence of modern day video games, and back to pinball and pool tables. Recently they added a few Skeeball games and a few larger video machines. The owner was known only as Zappa. He was a hippy who refused to grow up or to cut his long, and now gray, hair. Inside the glass counter at the front of the arcade, candy had replaced the pipes and roach clips that had been confiscated in the late 1970s.

"This is why I love this town," Sean commented. "Things pretty much stay the same. I like traditional values."

Wendy flashed him an admiring smile. "That sounds like you. You always reminded me of the old heroes like John Wayne - rugged, yet a gentleman."

"I like holding a door open for a lady. And I enjoy when a woman views me as her protector. I think the whole women's liberation movement got out of hand."

"Hold on a minute; I enjoy being an independent woman. I don't mind being barefoot, but you can keep the whole pregnancy thing. Of course, I also enjoy a man holding a door open for me." There was a brief moment of silence. "Speaking of barefoot, why do you call me the Barefoot Contessa?"

"Well," Sean lowered his head, staring at the sidewalk as he spoke. "You carry yourself with such poise and elegant grace that you remind me of royalty. But at the same time you are the most down-to-earth and natural woman I have ever met." Sean raised his head. His emerald eyes met the depth of her brown eyes. "You have so much natural beauty; it steals my heart every time I see you."

Wendy felt her legs weaken as the blood of excitement flowed heavy through her. Her face flushed with arousal, and her body tingled with delightful anticipation. She cleared her throat and turned her eyes forward.

Sean placed his arm around her shoulder and turned his attention in time to avoid colliding with three children as they rushed out into the street from the arcade. The eldest was a girl of thirteen. She was followed by two boys, the youngest of which had thick, wavy auburn hair. The children giggled and pushed at one another as they scurried onto the sidewalk in front of Sean and Wendy. The youngest boy, who appeared to be near the age of ten, looked up as Sean approached him. The boy's round face and warm smile struck Sean like an avalanche; a memory that jolted him instantly to a halt.

"Hello," the child said before turning his head in the direction of the arcade.

Sean heard the door open and a mother's voice, "If you three don't settle down, I'll convince the teachers to skip their in-service day and open the school. It'll give you little heathens a place to run off your energy." As the woman stepped out onto the sidewalk, her eyes met Sean's, but they quickly shifted to Wendy.

Trina Rathburn had skipped a day of work at Reiman-Fromme to spend it with her children while they were out of school. The moment of amusement that she had experienced inside the arcade quickly became uncomfortable.

Sean shook off his surprise and then suddenly realized that he still had his arm around Wendy. He slowly and discretely let it slip to his side. "Hey, Trina." Sean motioned toward Wendy, "Have you ever met Wendy Parks? She is a friend of mine from high school."

"I've heard about you. I'm Trina, Jennifer's friend from work."

Wendy nodded politely, but she could see the abhorrence in Trina's eyes.

"How did you manage to get a weekday off?" Sean asked, attempting to distract from the awkward moment.

"Actually, I took a personal day," Trina spoke blandly, her disgust apparent on her face. "Most of my days off are through the week anyway. There's no such thing as a weekend for retail people. We have a whole different perspective of weekends. If you remember correctly, Jennifer's schedule was that way too."

"Yeah."

"Well, the kids and I have to get going. You two have fun." Trina and her brood piled into a rusty old sedan that was parked in front of the arcade.

As the car pulled away from the curb, Wendy's desire to comment spilled forth, "Well, that was a little uncomfortable."

"Really," Sean said sheepishly, "I thought it went pretty well." He attempted to minimize the situation, but could feel his face flush.

"Sean, listen. I don't want to create a problem. Maybe we should just…"

"Uh-ah. Not another word. You are not getting out of tomorrow night. Jennifer and I are separated, and besides, we're only going out as friends. Unless the rules have changed, dancing is not cheating." Wendy lowered her eyes to the ground. Sean placed his hand on her chin and raised her head to meet his gaze. "Alright?"

"As long as you are comfortable with it. I don't want to be the one to put any additional stress on you."

"Wendy, just looking at you takes stress out of my life."

"I wouldn't want to tempt you." Wendy chuckled with a blushed smile.

Sanity

Sanity is only that which is within the frame of reference of conventional thought.

-Erich Fromm

Every normal person, in fact, is only normal on the average. His ego approximates to that of the psychotic in some part or other and to a greater or lesser extent.

-Sigmund Freud

Chapter 40

Ribbons away, the lady hath come out to play. Prim and proper was never a match for the luster of diamonds. And perhaps it was this latest gift from Nicholas; diamond earrings with a matching pendant that had relinquished Jennifer's guard. Jennifer was lying on top of her suitor as she hungrily explored his mouth. Her tongue tingled as it moistly brushed across the tender contours of his lips. The sweetness of Nicholas' breath and the strong yet subtle grip of his hands squeezing her buttocks through her jeans drove her passion to a fevered frenzy. Her unconstrained nipples jabbed out beneath her white silk blouse, inviting any touch or tweak they may receive. Her hips were pressed against his in an erotic primordial ritual, grinding in a palpitating rhythmic motion. The canopy bed, in which they lay, swayed with their bodies. The satiny linens glided softly against their occasional bared skin. She could scarcely catch her breath, yet her panting dizzied her in delight.

There was a faint flickering of candlelight that cast dancing shadows upon the walls. The flames twitched upon pillar candles placed about the room in alabaster holders, which rose from the marbled floor to the height of a man. Thick velvety tapestry flowed from ceiling to floor and was pulled back in their centers by ropes speckled in a metallic glitz. These tapestries accented neither windows nor apertures, only stone and mortar. The remaining decor of the room was antiquated with Baroque works of art. The colors of the paintings were only discernable to Jennifer by means other than sight. But her mind paid little attention to the fluttering details of color. She was preoccupied with the tingling sensation that was swelling in the damp region between her legs.

Jennifer began working the buttons of his shirt. With each one undone, she kissed lower on his chest and then stomach with wet lips and tongue. Once at his belt line, she trailed her tongue back up to his neck and teasingly flicked it against his ear. Nicholas moaned and stirred beneath her body. She paused for a moment, easing the fury of passion to stare into his eyes. He flashed a loving smile. The moment he had been longing for had arrived. He wanted to be close to her; to be inside of her as she gave herself to him in her most vulnerable state. He would taste each bit of flesh and enrapture each nerve until they were both left quivering in exhausted satisfaction.

Still locking her full in his arms, Nicholas rolled Jennifer over onto her back until he was on top of his prize. His eyes peered into her soul and beyond, piercing through every secret she had ever kept; the diary beneath her bed when she was a young girl, along with a long-forgotten household item that she had used in a pubescent sexual experiment, the algebra exam that she had cheated on, the swatch of cloth that she had dowsed with her mom's perfume to remind her of a time in her childhood when her mother was rational and loving. Jennifer was released from all of her secrets in his gaze and all of the discomforting pressure of their containment.

"Jennifer." Nicholas spoke in a voice that sounded distant and anomalously soft. Jennifer pressed her head back deep into the down pillow beneath her and cast a curious look at Nicholas.

"Jennifer," again his tone was that of a call rather than the natural pitch of speech. This time she recognized the oddity of his voice. It was more than soft. It was feminine.

With the front door slightly ajar, Trina stuck her head inside and examined Jennifer's living room. She had rung the doorbell and knocked twice, but Jennifer had not responded. Trina was always invited to enter the home without knocking, an action with which she was not entirely comfortable. Still, she had traveled nearly forty minutes after interrupting her day with the children. And with the information she possessed, entering Jennifer's house unannounced seemed justified.

Despite his attempt to hide it, she had seen Sean's arm around Wendy. Jennifer had a right to know and if their marriage was destined to end, she had a right to their property and much of its contents; especially if he was having an affair.

Trina spied Jennifer sleeping in the reclining chair. A few dishes rested on the end table beside her. Blankets were piled on the couch, and white hair was prevalent on the carpet. A foul odor hung in the air, part landfill and part kennel. Trina gazed at the untidy room in shock. Jennifer was a notorious cleaning fanatic.

She called Jennifer's name several times, her voice struggling against itself attempting to blend a holler within a whisper. Jennifer stirred on the chair, the muscles in her face twitching occasionally as they struggled against sleep paralysis to portray expressions.

Trina entered the room and closed the door behind her. A white puppy meandered in, sniffing at her shoes with mild interest before flopping down in front of them. This at least explained the existence of the white hair on the carpet and the kennel smell

"Jennifer, are you awake?" Trina whispered as she stepped over the dog toward the recliner.

Jennifer's twitching suddenly became more prevalent throughout her body; at times even violent. Trina could now see the sweat forming on her creased brow. Whatever she was dreaming; it was not good. Although the news Trina had to share was equally disturbing, she decided it was time to liberate Jennifer from whatever nightmare she was trapped within.

A voice to Jennifer's right drew her attention away from Nicholas. An elderly priest knelt beside the bed. Jennifer instantly recognized him from Dr. Conahan's office. The furl of concern upon his brow was softened by the compassion in his eyes.

"Nicholas," his voice wisped hollow through his dry lips. "You must set the woman free."

"No," Nicholas shouted like a defiant child, drawing Jennifer's attention back to him. "You have no right to interfere old man. She invited me in. She wanted me to help her."

A call of her name swung Jennifer's head back in the direction of the priest. "This man and his intentions are not what they seem. You must see beyond."

Jennifer turned her attention to see Nicholas' response, but instead found herself suddenly alone. "Nicholas?" Her words echoed out into the sparsely furnished chamber. A slight chill ran over her skin. The room was dank and cold. She had not noticed it before. An occasional drip of moisture could be heard as it slipped down the wall to strike the stone floor. She wrapped her arms around herself and rose from the bed. The sound of a soft repetitive creak came to her. Perhaps she was not alone after all. There was some unseen observer in the room. Jennifer squinted through the dim candlelight to see an old rocking chair in the far corner. The chair was occupied by a teenage girl with thick blonde hair that cascaded down her shoulders onto a hospital gown as she dispassionately rocked with a baby in her arms; pressing it tight to her breasts. The tiny infant remained motionless beneath a tattered and stained receiving blanket.

"I didn't know you were in here." Jennifer spoke casually as she rejected her own rising tension.

Focusing intensely on the tiny child suckling on her bosom, the teen was detached from Jennifer's words or her approach. Jennifer stood over her, looking down on the sight of maternal bliss. She could remember her nights rocking Arlen in his bedroom. In the early morning hour, it was silent and peaceful; and Arlen was the only thing in the world.

"Is that your baby?" Jennifer looked down at the teen with an adoring smile.

Slowly the teen raised her head. Her placid, emotionless features were oddly familiar to Jennifer though the face was insipidly pale and her cheeks appeared abnormally bloated for the apparent weight of the rest of her body. The shade of her dry and cracked lips nearly blended with that of her skin. Her eyes were deep and black. The veins in her forehead rippled beneath her skin like serpents in a sack. She made no effort to speak or even acknowledge the question.

Moments passed as her blank stare remained apathetically locked upon Jennifer. Finally, her lips spread apart, struggling against the restraint of black thread that held them shut; the only sound permitted to escape was a hollow wheeze.

Jennifer remained impervious to what she was witnessing, still wrapped in the warmth of her memory of Arlen. "Can I hold your baby?"

The girl's gaze remained vacant and unresponsive. Jennifer reached down, giving a corner of the cloth a slight tug. A tiny head flopped free of its nestling, the underdeveloped neck bent grotesquely to the weight. The head hung limply against the teen's arm, twisted so that the face stared lifelessly at Jennifer. The infant's veins and arteries were exposed through a thin layer of skin which covered the head. Large eyes occupied nearly half of the fetus's face, two small fissures acting as nostrils were the only indication of an undefined nose and the mouth was no more than a small slit in its friable skin. Jennifer gasped at the sight and quickly withdrew her hand. Stomach acid rose in her esophagus and the erect hair on her flesh urged her to flee. Her body refused to move - locked in a hypnotic stare of the horrific. But not at the underdeveloped fetus head, it was the other one, the prominent head which held her eyes.

This head was vibrant as it suckled wildly on a breast that had been pulled out from beneath the teen's gown. The second head was more abnormal and ghastly than the first. Its skin was serpent-like with thick overlaying scales of deep brown. Jennifer labored for breath as she watched the head ravenously wrenching at the breast. The fetus head that still hung down over the shoulder shook limply amidst the wild attack of the more vibrant twin. Its large eyes stared at Jennifer pitifully.

Another gasp from Jennifer caused the serpent head to snap around in her direction. Its face was covered in blood. The irises, green horizontal slits emphasized by piercing white sclera, dilated as they stared intensely at Jennifer. The mouth was agape, exposing rows of sharp teeth. The thin lips still rested upon the shredded, bloody flesh that was once the nipple of the breast.

The creature let out the type of screech that makes any human instinctively cower as it leapt from its nestling and flew at Jennifer's head. She could feel the rush of air against her ear as it thrust past her skin and into her tangles of red hair. Jennifer screamed and shook her head wildly, digging her fingers into her hair to free the creature. She felt a sharp tearing at her flesh as it slid down her back. She turned to see the creature scurry out of the room and disappear down a darkened hallway; a small tail slithered between the two tiny legs that propelled it, the fetus head grotesquely bobbling against its back as it ran. For a moment, she continued to rake at her hair, repulsed by the creature's entanglement. Adrenaline flooded her muscles and gushed its way into her heart like a shot nitrous into the intake manifold of a street racer. She swung back around to the rocking chair. It now glided hauntingly empty, propelling back and forth in a friction-groan of wood. The air in the chamber grew frigid, and the vapor from her warm gasps swirled in front of her vision. She stepped cautiously into the hallway keeping one hand against the stone wall for guidance. As she walked, the light that the chamber had allowed her grew faint until she found herself in total darkness. Her fingertips slid upon moist fungus as they gilded along the length of the stone wall. She could hear the distinct sound of her own breathing rising over the silence, its tone amplified as it reverberated from the corridor. The cold stone bit like a slab of dry ice beneath her bare feet as she walked. A little further along the stone path came to an abrupt end as she sank ankle deep into muddy soil.

Jennifer paused and glanced back toward the opening in the chamber but the aperture was covered by an inky nebulous. Nothing could escape this darkness; not light, not Jennifer. There was no sense of direction in this void; right, left, up, down - she was hopelessly disoriented. The mud and the frigid air suggested that she were outdoors, though no moon or stars were in sight. Perhaps she was trapped in some outdoor maze with walls that had been erected for some ill intent, to trap the wandering innocent; some ghastly gauntlet that would lead the unsuspecting to some horrific fate at its conclusion. The thought burrowed through her mind, devouring any sense of hope. She struggled against it, determined to cling to her sanity

She pressed forward down the long, dank hallway pulling her feet free of the mud as each step produced a loud sucking sound. Her fingers and toes grew numb with the chill.

Jennifer froze her advance as a sudden and inhuman shriek echoed in the confines of the stone retainers. She squinted through the darkness, attempting to capture any available light. She saw the corridor ahead as it angled sharply to the left. The sight elated her. She could see again. Light from beyond the bend was casting its flickering glow upon the protruding stones of the wall. She quickened her pace, struggling against the gripping earth; at length, she reached the wall of light and turned to see what was beyond. The breach opened up into what could be the way out, or perhaps, the entrance to another chamber. The light upon the wall writhed and twitched like the luminance from an unseen fire. This was not the fire from a candle. It was much larger, burning with a high intensity.

Jennifer stepped through the portal and into an area with no boundaries. A large bonfire blazed on the ground to her right. The flames crackled and popped, throwing sparks high into the air - to float until they were extinguished by the moisture in the atmosphere. Jennifer paused, allowing her eyes to adjust to the intensity of the light.

Following a few steps forward, her gaze fixed upon the young blonde girl standing just beyond the fire. The teen stood unflinchingly, dead eyes transfixing in an eternal stare. The area of the gown between her hips was soaked in blood and her feet were coated in a layer of clay.

Jennifer halted her advance, awaiting any movement from the girl. She was uncertain how to proceed in this eerie expanse that seemed to have avoided the usual earthly confines.

Jennifer felt a swift graze against her ankle as something rushed between her legs. The slight touch caused her skin to crawl, setting off a repulsed shiver through her body. She saw the tiny infant creature dart toward the teen as it screeched. It reached out to clutch the teen's gown as its serpentine eyes cast an evil gaze back at Jennifer.

The teen slowly stretched out her fist; within its tight grasp was a single white rose. She turned her hand over and methodically opened her fingers. The rose dropped onto the muddied soil. Trickles of blood seeped from the thorn wounds in her palm and followed the rose to the ground. Her lips struggled to part as the words "Help me" hissed from between the thread that had once sewn them shut in the confine of her earthly crypt. The vapor from her breath hitting the chilled air swirled out from her mouth, clouding the view of her face.

The infant creature flashed its razor teeth releasing another hideous shriek. It shouted in a raspy voice, "Get rid of it," before climbing up underneath the teen's gown.

Jennifer's breath came in brief pants. Her lungs felt as though they were being compressed by phantom hands. She wanted to speak, to scream, but she was barely able to breathe.

"I see you've met the little woman." The voice of Nicholas came from behind her. But this time he sounded different. His voice was hollow and strained. She turned to see him standing a few feet behind her. He was dressed in the traditional black hopsack blazer, clergy vest and white collar of a Catholic priest. His face was decayed almost beyond recognition with graying flesh hanging from his cheek bones in clinging strips.

"Sorry, I've been meaning to tell you about her, but these little things tend to slip my mind." He walked up to Jennifer and leaned in to whisper in her ear.

"I think she's okay with us. At least she hasn't said anything." He cast a glance at the teen, pausing to ponder the thought. "Could be the thread though?"

Jennifer opened her mouth to speak, but terror had parched her throat beyond its ability to vocalize. She backed away from him, keeping her eyes fixed on the dilapidated man in front of her. The foul smell of his presence now sickened stomach.

"Nicholas, please. I don't understand," she finally managed.

"Nicholas, please. I don't understand." He mocked. "Is that not the trouble with dreams - reality always gets in the way. But what the hell, lets finish what we started."

Jennifer could feel the flames of the fire burning at her back. She turned toward the teen standing motionless behind her.

Nicholas followed her gaze, "Oh, don't worry about her. I'm sure she understands my attraction to you. After all, you do bear a striking resemblance to each other."

Jennifer suddenly realized why the teen looked familiar. Nicholas was right. The girl was nearly a mirroring image of herself. She turned back toward Nicholas, barely able to hold her gaze. The sight of his decaying body was repulsive. Fear alone held her attention.

"It isn't the priest's outfit is it? I thought you would enjoy a man in uniform. Besides, I've been told it is the secret fantasy of all sluts to turn a righteous man over by their charms?" He waved his hand, motioning down the length of Jennifer's body. "And you most certainly have the charms."

Jennifer stumbled back over the bonfire. The heat flared up her calves. She allowed a fleeting glance down at the burning embers, finally seeing what had fueled the fire. Hundreds of Bibles had been tossed in a pile; Old and New Testaments burning beneath the fury of the flames.

"You like it?" Nicholas coyly commented to her. "It is my own private collection. The storylines were a little tough to follow, all those parables, but you have to admit, they sure make one hell of a bonfire."

Jennifer's mind worked frantically for an escape. She had to flee. Her heart thumped ever louder within the confines of her ribs as she prepared her muscles for the jaunt. She turned on her heels and threw herself into a run, screaming at the teen as she ran past. "Run! Get away, now!"

Her legs struggled as her feet trudged through the soaked clay. With each step her foot sunk deeper into the earth. The damp chill penetrated through flesh until the bones in her feet ached. Her pace slowed, but her effort intensified as she struggled with every muscle in her body straining to exhaustion. She could hear the padding of the soil beneath his feet; he was pursuing her. She shot a quick glance over her shoulder - the son-of-a-bitch was walking! He was walking and gaining ground on her. As she stepped, her foot sunk deep until her ankle was completely submerged in the muck. She tried desperately to step again, but her foot was held by the powerful suction of the ground. Pulling with all she was worth, she could hear the rise and fall of his approaching breathes. She shifted her weight forward, suddenly hearing a loud, sickening crack. She looked down to see her leg bent parallel to her foot. Her leg was moving, but her foot was not. She tested her ankle by pulling gently. The skin stretched just above the ankle - the bone had broken clean. There was only one option. Tears filled her eyes as an additional tug began ripping the flesh. Blood collected in a pool around her clay enrapt ankle until with a moist "thurp" her leg tore free of the foot, sending her crashing face down into the mud. Pain shot up her leg, tingling with the sting of a thousand wasps.

His feet came into view as he stood over her fallen body. He slid a foot under her hip and flipped her onto her back. His hand smacked against her throat, gripping it with crushing force before whisking her off the ground to hold her body out in mid-air. He pulled her close until her face was inches away from his.

"Well, you are kind of ugly, but a kiss is still a kiss." Nicholas drew her closer; his lips parted to apply a kiss. She gagged at the smell of his foul breath, setting off a violent fit of choking. Maggots tumbled from his lower jaw as a tongue, sticky with bile, protruded from between his lips. His grip drew ever tight about her neck, choking off her airway.

Jennifer made a desperate attempt to avoid his lips, turning her head as far she could. She closed her eyes tight to avoid the sight of his face. She could feel the trail of slime left on her cheek as his tongue worked along its contours. She chanced to open her eyes and was relieved to see the face of Trina. The view beyond Trina's face was no longer the murky chamber of her dream; instead, it was her own living room. She shifted her eyes to see Nicholas still attempting to reach her lips. His hand wrapped around her neck, squeezing relentlessly. She was being strangled and was helpless to stop it. She turned back to Trina with a pleading look of terror.

Trina's eyes were wide in shock and concern. Her lips were moving, but Jennifer could not hear the words being spoken. Her sleep paralysis had struck her momentarily deaf; a moment of silence and sight that seemed endless until at last sound burst forth into Jennifer's ears.

"Oh my God!" Trina shouted as she began to shake Jennifer's body in a desperate attempt to revive her. "Jen, wake up. You're choking!"

Chapter 41

Jennifer felt the weight of her body as gravity pressed her into the reclining chair. Her chest heaved spastically, and the sound of her own coughing now became apparent. Her lungs burned, and the blackness of a faint descended upon her. She needed oxygen fast. She bolted from the reclining chair, hitting the floor on her hands and knees and coughed violently, struggling to inhale.

At last, the spasm alleviated and she drew in a deep, cleansing breath. Cool air filled her lungs, dispersing invigorating oxygen throughout her body and as quickly as the coughing spasm began, it was over. She cast a frightened look at her foot; it was still attached, but tingled with numbness. Jennifer wiped the tears from her eyes and sat up. Her body felt stiff and clammy. The nausea that had plagued her for several days still lingered.

"Are you okay?" Trina asked.

"I'll be alright." Jennifer said, her gasps quick, her eyes glazed. "What time is it?"

"It's five o'clock," Trina responded. "You scared the shit out of me! You must have been having one terrorizing nightmare."

Jennifer flashed a brazen gaze. "Why?"

"You were thrashing around. You know … mumbling and stuff."

"Did you notice anything out of the ordinary?"

"Like what?"

"Never mind. Did I say anything?"

"Nothing that I could understand."

Jennifer stood up slowly, trying to stabilize herself on shaky legs. A sharp pain shot from her foot, extending up to her knee: she quickly shifted her weight. She raised her eyes in time to catch Trina staring at the frailty of her body and her obvious trembling.

Jennifer straightened her back in perfect posture and walked past Trina defiantly. "Let's sit in the dining room."

As she walked past, Trina noticed a tan patch stuck to the skin of Jennifer's arm. "I think you're supposed to take up smoking before you use those nicotine patches."

Jennifer reached down quickly and callously ripped it from her arm. She devised a quick explanation to avoid a potential lecture. "It is actually a vitamin patch. It's new. My doctor thought I should try it. I kept forgetting to take the vitamins he prescribed." The skin beneath the patch bore an irritated rash.

"Well, you may want to let him know that you're having an allergic skin reaction to it."

"Yeah, I noticed that." Explanation accepted, or at least unchallenged. It was time to change the subject. "So, how are your kids? I haven't seen them in forever."

"I just dropped them off at my mom's house. I wanted to talk to you without them interrupting."

Trina sat down at the dining room table and immediately noticed the dozen roses that were now wilting in the vase at the table's center. It was probably a pathetic attempt from Sean to alleviate his guilt from his affair with Wendy. And there's poor Jennifer, who can't bring herself to part with them even after they have died.

"So, what's up?" Jennifer inquired.

Trina had prepared her statement during the drive to Jennifer's house. She wanted to break the news of Wendy and Sean gently. But she was not ready yet. She would have to warm up to it.

"Well, I decided to take the day off. School was not in session today because of some teacher's in-service day. Anyway, I took the kids downtown to the Castle Arcade.

You know, that place has not changed since we were kids. Even Zappa hasn't changed. He's still the … "

Jennifer's attention began to drift. She loved Trina dearly, but was hardly in the mood for trivial chitchat. Her nightmare was still pricking at her mind, sharp needles of fear and confusion for what had transpired. *Why had the priest disrupted their dream? And what form of Nicholas was his real spirit?* She searched her instincts to discern his true persona, to no avail. While her mind drifted, Jennifer made a courteous attempt to be attentive to Trina. Bits and pieces of the story resonated, and she nodded her head accordingly.

She began to feel an irritation against her neck. The collar of her nightshirt seemed abnormally coarse. She reached her finger inside the collar and pulled out a necklace with a diamond pendant. Trina was in mid-sentence when she saw the precious stone dangling at Jennifer's neckline.

"It only took about a half hour to go through twenty bucks in that … Oh, my God! Where did you get that? It's beautiful!" Trina exclaimed.

Jennifer gave a sly smile as she pulled her hair back to display the matching earrings.

"Do you always wear your good jewelry when you take a nap?"

Jennifer bit her lower lip and dropped her chin as she looked up at Trina with large innocent eyes. "I have a secret to tell you, but you have to promise to keep this just between us."

Trina nodded. "Jen, you know me better than that."

It was true. Jennifer could confide in Trina without reservation. In the six years they had been friends and co-workers, Trina had always kept their conversations in the strictest of confidence.

Trina was apprehensive about hearing what Jennifer had to share. The purpose of her visit was to expose a philandering husband. Now it seemed Jennifer's pending confession had the potential of nullifying her quest.

A broad smile spread across Jennifer's face as she rose from her seat and moved her chair around the table, placing herself closer to Trina.

"I met this guy."

"Get out."

Jennifer nodded her head. Her mannerisms were giddy and childlike, as though she were in the midst of the ultimate crush.

"His name is Nicholas Feragamo. He is full-blooded Italian. Oh, Trina. He has the most gorgeous brown eyes that I have ever seen."

Trina was surprised by the passion in Jennifer's voice. Jennifer had always been dedicated to her marriage and Trina never pegged her to be unfaithful. She knew about the couple's separation, but it had only occurred a few weeks prior. She could not believe that Jennifer could brush Sean aside that easily. As for Sean, she began to scrutinize her memory from outside the arcade. The arm that Sean had draped around Wendy was beginning to hold less merit with the blushing of Jennifer's face.

"He's strong, but he is so gentle when he touches me," Jennifer continued. "It was Nicholas who gave me these roses. Actually, in the brief time that I've known him, he's given me quite a few gifts. Casper, that's my puppy. We even went out for dinner at Desiderio's," she added excitedly.

"Wow. This guy sounds special," Trina commented. Come to think of it, perhaps Sean only had his hand on Wendy's back. "Have the two of you … , you know?"

"Not yet. We almost did, but we sort of got interrupted."

It all happened so fast outside the arcade. Perhaps Sean was merely patting Wendy on the back. She really was not certain. And what was facing her now was a full-blown confession of infidelity from Jennifer.

"Well, when do I get to meet this Valentino?" Trina asked.

"I'm getting to that part. I have to tell you something. You're gonna think that I've finally lost my mind, but I swear to you, it's the truth. And Trina, I really need you to keep this to yourself. You have to promise me. I need to confide in someone and you're the only one that I can trust."

"Okay, okay, I promise."

"Nicholas is a ghost who visits me in my dreams." Jennifer threw open her hands as if she were finishing some vaudeville act and was now awaiting the applause.

Trina told herself to speak, but no words volunteered. She had already surmised from her surroundings that Jennifer's behavior was peculiar. But now her friend was asking her to believe that she was experiencing spectral visits in her sleep. Her brain momentarily froze until at last, it reacted in a conditioned response to the absurd. She laughed.

"I am not fucking joking, Trina. This is real," Jennifer snorted angrily.

Trina began to quell her laughter. "What?" She managed through a snickering snort.

"I know this sounds impossible, but it's true," Jennifer pleaded. "He was in my dreams a few times, but things started to get bizarre when we went to Naples for coffee."

"You went to Italy to have coffee?" Trina asked sheepishly.

"Yeah, in our dream. When I woke up, there was a cup of coffee sitting on the night-stand."

"Well, Jennifer. Are you sure that you didn't put it there? Maybe you got up in the middle of the night and made coffee, but you were too sleepy to remember the next morning."

"Come on, Trina. That doesn't make any sense. If I made coffee in the middle of the night, I would remember."

Trina stared at Jennifer in astonishment for the comment. *Was she even hearing herself?*

"The coffee pot was clean. And the coffee was fresh and hot! After that, things just started appearing. Whenever he gave me a gift in my dreams, they had materialized when I awoke; the dog, roses, this jewelry. I even got sick from the squid I ate at Desiderio's."

"You ate squid?" Trina asked, repulsed.

"That was when he told me about who he was and how he came to enter my dreams. You see, he died in 1954, but he can still experience the sensations of the real world when he is in my dreams."

Trina sat quietly, searching Jennifer's face for any sign of fabrication. Although Jennifer spoke with passion and conviction, Trina was hopeful that her friend would laugh at her for being gullible. She hoped that Jennifer would tell her it was a joke. It broke her heart to think that this lovely woman was going insane.

"Well?" Jennifer snapped.

"Well, what? What do you want me to say, Jen? This is a little hard to swallow. There has to be some explanation for this."

"There is! Nicholas is a spirit. He fell in love with me; only now there's someone who is trying to interfere with our relationship."

"Who?"

"The priest from the doctor's office."

Trina felt the hair rise on the back of her neck. The conversation was chilling and the gaze in Jennifer's eyes frightened her. *How do you tell your best friend that she needs psychiatric help?*

"The priest appears in my dreams too," Jennifer continued. "But the first time I saw him I was wide awake in Dr. Conahan's office."

Jennifer calmed her excitement, sitting in silence for a moment. "I'm sorry. I must sound like a raving lunatic. I'm just so excited about finally having someone to talk to about this. Look, if it makes you feel any better, I have an appointment to see a psychologist. Dr. Conahan thought it would be good for me to work out my depression by talking to someone.

But I swear to Heaven, I'm telling you the truth. I don't know how to explain it. I don't fully understand it myself."

Trina patted the air with her palms. "Okay. Let's look at this scientifically. I guess we don't always know what is true. I've watched my share of psychic shows, where they talk to dead people. So, I guess it's possible. Have you tried to see if this guy really ever existed?"

"Trina, that's it! I could do some research. If I can prove what he says is true then I'm not crazy."

"Where was he born?" Trina asked.

"He was born in Italy."

"That's going to be difficult. Why don't you get dressed and we'll go to the library and see what we can dig up on him?"

Jennifer snickered. "Or try to dig him up." The two laughed for a moment and then fell silent. Jennifer suddenly rose from her seat and wrapped her arms tightly around Trina. Trina could hear gentle sobs as she returned the embrace.

"Thank you," Jennifer managed.

"Thank me for what?"

"Thank you for believing me."

Chapter 42

Jennifer placed her new diamond jewelry carefully into her armoire and ran her fingertips over the stones in the necklace. She desperately wanted to speak to Nicholas, in hopes that he could explain what had transpired. But at the same time, the very idea of dreaming frightened her.

Trina's presence in the house provided Jennifer with much needed comfort. And the visit to the library could provide some much needed answers to the bizarre occurrences in her life.

Exiting the bedroom, she made her way down the hallway to the staircase. She had taken a few steps when a shadowy object darted from the bathroom, crossed the hallway and disappeared under the door to the hall closet. Her stride was instantly frozen. Currents of fear pulsed through her body and electrified her skin. She had caught a glimpse of the object but was uncertain of its appearance. It moved too swiftly to identify. She eased back a step and pressed her shoulder into the wall for support. For a moment she thought of the demon fetus from her dream. *Oh, please no. The creature manifested itself in the real world like the gifts from Nicholas?* The thought chilled her blood. She attempted to calm herself by rationalizing a more logical explanation. *It happened so quickly; it was just a shadow. Maybe it was my imagination. Or this old house has finally succumbed to a mouse invasion. No. The object was too big. A rat! Oh God, please don't let it be a rat either. Maybe I should open the closet door to investigate. No way. They do that stupid shit in the movies. I am not that brave.* Finally, she decided to press her body against the opposite wall, slip past the closet and then make a run for the downstairs to grab Trina and a tennis racket.

She eased herself along the far wall, keeping her eyes fixed on the bottom of the closet door. Her shoulder slid along the support until it reached the doorway to the bathroom. She was as close to the closet as she would be. Another ten paces to the staircase. Her heart pulsed in her temples with each breath. She hated little things that moved swiftly, especially when it was too dark to see them. She had only enough light emanating from the downstairs to outline her surroundings. With her eyes fixed on the closet door, she reached inside and flipped the bathroom light switch.

The glow from the bathroom illuminated the closet. All was still. The closet door was shut tight. There was no evidence of a tiny intruder. She took a single step. A sound from behind her once again froze her retreat, the sound of water; not just dripping, but shifting in subtle splashes. Her eyes remained fixed on the closet.

She turned slowly, wary to peel away the stare that had been assigned to the crack beneath the door. She chanced a glimpse at the tub. It was filled until its contents nearly spilled from the rim. She labored for breath as she stepped cautiously into the room to examine the drain. There beneath the ripples; pale skin, the body of a young female was submerged inside her bathtub. Jennifer's breathing increased to a near pant; her muscles atrophied with terror refused her order to flee. The teen from her nightmare had manifested in the real world. Her eyes, black and void, fixed on Jennifer's position. A hand slowly rose from the waterline, reaching out as tiny droplets spattered upon the floor. Every ounce of will screamed within Jennifer to move, but instead, she was locked in a dumbfounded paralysis; her body refusing to react to what her mind could not comprehend.

The hand gripped Jennifer about the wrist. The feel of the cold, grey flesh caused an involuntary shudder down Jennifer's small frame.

Jennifer heard the bathroom door slam shut behind her as the teen began to tug at Jennifer's arm, attempting pull her into the tub or pull herself out. Jennifer wanted neither. Her body trembled and her mind convulsed without definitive direction. She could not move. She could not scream. She could only manage a mild resistance to the tug.

"No," Jennifer managed beneath her panting breath. She flexed her hand and wrist in an attempt to slip from the teen's grasp; the cold, dead fingers gripped tight. She pulled against the corpse's demand, attempting to free herself from the lifeless touch; free herself from the death. At last, Jennifer's moistened wrist slid free, sending her stumbling backwards and crashing into the bathroom door.

She reached back and frantically tried the doorknob. Her hands quivered with such intensity that she could barely control their actions.

The teen began to rise from her submergence, without bending joints – she rose as a rigid board being lifted from behind. Water ran freely from her ears and mouth, no sign of life in her body; no motion of her lips or heaving of her chest; only black eyes that peered out from pale, grey flesh.

"Come on," Jennifer spat in frustration as she struggled with the doorknob. She took her attention from the teen to use both hands. She pulled frantically back on the door and willed her hands to obey. The latch clicked free, the door swung in on its hinge and Jennifer nearly tumbled into the water. Wet, cold hands grasped the back of her blouse. She never chanced a look back as she pulled free and stumbled into the hallway. Her constant panting had dizzied her. She could feel herself losing consciousness as she swooned. She was fainting. Her last thought was of what her fate would be. Her last image was of a quickly approaching floor. Her last verbalization was the desperate cry of "Trina!"

Chapter 43

The elevator doors opened to the third floor and Wendy stepped out into the hall. She walked with a purpose, turning right when the hallway formed a T. Her break was limited to fifteen minutes so she had to return to the ICU as quickly as possible. She had promised Sean she would check on Grandma Bergin. She had planned to arrive twenty minutes before her shift, but her plan had been thwarted after she went to the intensive care unit first to see what to expect for the evening. The unit was full, and as usual, the staff was short-handed. She immediately threw herself into the fray, helping the current staff by checking vitals; before she was even aware of the clock, her evening had already descended.

She made a turn to the room marked 326, but her entrance was halted by the exit of Arlene Bergin from the room. Arlene looked up with that typical snide glare. Wendy was never certain why Arlene seemed to dislike her, but the dislike was purposefully displayed.

"Hello Wendy," Arlene spoke first. "I think it's a little unusual for a nurse to follow a patient to their next level of care?"

"Actually, I'm on my break. I promised Sean at lunch today that I would check on her." *Oops, that information could have remained unveiled.* The gaze now changed from snide to penetrating.

"Nice. Well, she's fine. She is sleeping right now." Arlene's vocal cords were tight. *Prepare for the first volley.* "You know it's a shame what is happening to Sean and Jennifer. I was there when that relationship started. I was there when they exchanged their vows. There is a lot of love between them. Sean needs to wake up and remember what they have together. I'm sure Arlen would have hated to see his parents fighting."

"In the first place, why are you assuming that the problem is Sean?"

"Oh, do you know differently? Why don't you enlighten me?"

Wendy wanted to unload; she wanted to tell this judgmental little bitch the truth about Jennifer. She wanted to explain how Jennifer was seeing a man named Nicholas. But she knew it was not her place to come between Sean and his family. "I am not going to get into that with you here. Why don't you ask Sean?"

"Oh, I'm sure I'll get a straight answer from him. He has been great with his responsibilities of late." Arlene spat.

"Your brother is a great man. Okay, he made a mistake, but haven't we all? Your grandmother would have fallen and broken her hip whether he visited her that day or not. That was not his fault. It was an accident. Arlen was not his fault, and neither is the decline of his marriage."

"Of course Arlen wasn't his fault!" Arlene snapped. "I just want you to remember before you go polishing your stilettos; that he is still married."

"Are we finished?" Wendy was quickly losing her patience with the conversation.

"For now," Arlene pronounced in defiance.

"Well, if you will excuse me, I have a promise to keep."

Arlene made a small step to the side, "Well, don't wake her up. She needs her rest."

The pair exchanged glares, but the verbal battle had ended. Arlene stomped away down the hall as Wendy slipped into Meagan's room. She pressed her back against the door as she closed it behind her. She tilted her head back and closed her eyes. Her nerves were frail from the hectic pace of the ICU. The last thing she needed was an encounter with the miniature Medusa. *How can Arlene judge what she can't possibly understand?* One day Arlene will push her too far and even the thought of upsetting Sean won't stop her from fighting back.

Chapter 44

The raindrops served only as a minor annoyance. The intermittent wipers cleared the water from the windshield with an occasional squeak. However, the wet road cast moistened reflections from the headlights of passing cars; diminishing night vision. It was the first rain the town had seen, breaking the grip of a snow-heavy winter. The wet streets and walkways cut through the layer of snow which still held dominance over the lawns and landscaping.

Trina glanced across the tattered front seat of her sedan at her friend next to her. Jennifer's hair was pulled back in a lose ponytail. Her t-shirt and jeans seemed oversized as they hung from her frail, thin body. The image nearly brought Trina to tears. Jennifer quietly nibbled on the chicken burger that Trina had purchased for her at a local, drive-through restaurant, despite Jennifer's objections. Trina had been prepared to force-feed Jennifer if necessary.

Trina steered the car into the twelve stall parking area of the library. It was getting late, and the library would close in an hour. She was not overly optimistic about finding any information on Nicholas Feragamo. Nonetheless, when the search turned up empty- handed, Jennifer would begin to recognize how irrational she was behaving.

Trina put the car in park and killed the engine. "Have you ever done this type of research before?"

"Somewhat," Jennifer shifted in her seat and slipped the half eaten sandwich back into the empty take-out bag. "But that was back when I was in college. The library has old newspapers on microfilm. Nicholas said he was born in Italy in 1928, so we won't find a birth announcement. He moved to the U.S. when he was ten-years-old. We may find him in

Timothy Cole

the census listings after that. But the easiest reference will be his obituary. I remember him telling me that he died on August 24. The year was 1954."

"How do you know that he was even from this area?"

"I'm certain he once told me he lived in Honey Brook. And when he took me to Desiderio's he seemed familiar with it. So this is worth a try. I would not even know where to begin to research a birth from another country."

After they entered the library, Jennifer retrieved an intake reel from the librarian at the front desk. They entered a small room off the main atrium where three Eyecom microfilm readers lined a desk pressed against the far wall. A young man in his early twenties was busy scanning a roll at the far end. The sight of the man brought back memories of reports and deadlines to Jennifer. She had loved college for all of the non-social reasons; late-night library invasions, term papers and classroom discussions. Her classmates would tell her that she was insane to get so excited about research and reports. But it was discovery that fueled her interest, along with an intense drive for the perfect grade average that her mother had drummed into young Jennifer's head.

Trina took a seat at the first reader while Jennifer searched the cabinets for the appropriately dated microfilm. The rolls were stored in small boxes with labels marking the first and last dates of the newspaper editions on each film, which contained approximately two months of every pressing of The Morning Sentinel. During the 1950s the local paper ran Monday through Saturday, with no Sunday issues; the presses had begun to run a Sunday edition in the early 1980s.

Jennifer retrieved the appropriate film and fed it into the machine, wrapping the blank lead around the intake reel. After a few turns, she sat next to Trina and used the fast-forward button on the automated system. The pages of the newspaper flashed quickly by in a grey smear. The chronological events of the past whirled across the screen as the machine hummed and the film flipped. All of the headlines that had held the attention of the readers of the day were now blurred to the eye. She paused several times to check the date at the top of a page until she had advanced to the desired month. She then used the slow advance button to slide past each page, stopping at Tuesday, August 24, 1954. Jennifer adjusted the focus and began scanning up and down each page, at last reaching the obituaries.

She released a sigh and shot a glance at Trina. "This is it."

The pair drew closer to the screen as they read each headline. Trina was always a swift reader and reached the bottom first. She sat quietly awaiting Jennifer's response. Jennifer's eyes lifted back to the top and scanned down a second time. She then sat silently staring for what seemed an eternity to Trina.

Trina parted with a breath that seemed to be held against her will. "Jennifer, maybe there's another explanation for what's happening to you."

"Trina, I'm not going insane." Jennifer leaned back in her chair, her eyes remaining fixed upon the screen. "I know what's happening to me is real. I need something to verify it."

"It's okay." Trina rubbed Jennifer's back lovingly. "Everything's going to be okay." The words were spoken without conviction, and both of them knew it.

"You can just take me home." Jennifer rose from her chair. "This is worthless."

Before Jennifer could turn away, her face suddenly brightened. "Wait a second! The Sentinel is a morning paper. If Nicholas died on August 24, it would not have made the paper until the next day."

The young man, who had been sitting at the distant machine, cast an aggravated glare at Jennifer's outburst. He quickly gathered his notes and excused himself around Jennifer; the two investigators were left in private.

Trina wanted to stop her. She had brought Jennifer here to expose the truth; this dream guy does not truly exist, but her efforts were falling hopelessly short. She tapped her fingertips on the desk and gazed blankly at the microfilm cabinets as Jennifer paused on the front page of August 25th and stared at the headlines.

The glow from the Eyecom reader cast a glow on Jennifer's pale face as she eased back into to her seat, still transfixed to the screen. "**Ike Signs Anti-Red Bill**. President Eisenhower. It is strange to see these old events like this. I am more accustomed to seeing them in documentary films from high school. Oh, my gosh, look at this," Jennifer continued. "**Honey Brook Teen Found Dead Following Illegal Abortion**. I guess some issues never change."

Trina made no response beyond the increased rhythm tapped out by her digits; until a sustained silence from Jennifer drew her eyes. The final swirls of pigmentation had drained from Jennifer's face as she unwaveringly locked her eyes on the monitor.

Jennifer wanted to speak, but the words lumped in her throat. Her lips parted without oration as she stretched out a finger toward the lower part of the screen. Trina turned to see a photo of a handsome priest.

"That's him," Jennifer finally managed. Her body shook with a sudden chill.

Even Trina began to feel the hair on the back of her neck rise as she read the accompanying headlines aloud. "**Local Priest Commits Suicide.**" She continued reading the story, "The body of a 26-year-old priest was found at the foot of the Virgin Mary's statue at Saint Anthony's Parish yesterday evening. Father Nicholas Feragamo was pronounced dead at the scene by county coroner James Feely. The exact cause of death has been withheld pending further investigation. However, officials have stated that the death appears to have been a suicide. Feragamo was a priest at Saint Anthony's where he was found. He shared his duties with Father Anthony Feragamo who was also the uncle and legal guardian of the deceased. Father Anthony was not available for comment. The local diocese has announced intentions of conducting their own investigation into the incident."

Trina slowly shifted her eyes from the screen, her features now as ashen as the light that illumed her. "Holy shit, Jen. This guy was real."

"This guy IS real. Rewind that," Jennifer commanded flatly. "I don't even want to touch it."

"My mother used to tell me stories about the Incubus of Honey Brook." Trina said.

"Those were just ghost tales mother's used to scare their daughters into obedience. This isn't just an urban legend; this is real life."

Despite receiving the verification that she had desired, Jennifer was still unsettled. She had been so headstrong to confirm her story that she was unprepared for the truth. The existence of Nicholas was nearly as disturbing as if she had only imagined him. Insane or haunted was not exactly a palatable choice. He was real, and he had been a priest. Not only a priest; a priest who committed suicide. The existence of Father Anthony provided additional fear. He was real and he had also paid her a visit in the flesh; twice.

Jennifer thought of her appointment with Dr. Bomboy scheduled for the next day. She wondered how the psychologist would explain this.

"Trina," Jennifer spoke through dry lips, "do you think that your mom could keep your kids overnight? I don't mean to impose, but I don't want to be alone tonight."

"I understand." Trina's voice was subdued with shock. "I'm sure she will be fine with it."

"The sleeping pills that the doctor had prescribed have a tendency of suppressing my dreams," Jennifer stated. "I guess it's time to pull them back out."

Trina stared at the screen as the news pages rushed backwards in time. Her empathy toward Jennifer had faded into a fear of the unknown. *What have I gotten myself into?* Not wanting any part of Jennifer's haunting, she worried that being in the same house as Jennifer could draw the spirit in a different direction; perhaps her direction. She had heard Jennifer's discountenance, but the fireside yarns of the Incubus resurfaced like a pale moon over a pallor ocean; slipping into her thoughts in waning sentences fraught with warnings.

"Could you spare a couple of those sleeping pills for me too?" Trina asked finally.

Chapter 45

The gently rolling profile of Resurrection Cemetery was mantled by a crust of rain-polished snow. Even in the thick, grey morning, the hills glistened like the tops of crystal balls that offered an occasional glimpse into the past via granite monuments that thrust themselves skyward, longing to be read so the occupants of the hallowed ground beneath would be remembered. Lines of swirling fog levitated above the icy mantle and etched the arcing surfaces of the basal slopes. Last evenings warm front had forced its way up from the south bringing rain and the promise of melting the remaining snow as Honey Brook attempted to free itself from the doldrums of winter.

Jennifer maneuvered her car along the narrow, blacktop road that snaked a course between the clusters of grave markers and ornamental trees. This was an unscheduled stop. Her excursion to the psychologist's office had brought her within two blocks of Resurrection. By then, the visit had to occur. She eased off the road as the tires crunched their way to a stop on the snow-covered ground. The warmth of the blower at her feet made her pause before killing the engine and stepping from the car.

Only the soles of her tennis shoes sank into the frozen crystals as she attempted to tread lightly in hopes of keeping her feet dry. She had donned an old heavy parka to curtail the chills which seemed to reverberate through her body even before she left the house. The sleeping pills and the presence of Trina had granted her a restful night's slumber, but her body was still weak and it quivered in protest of her neglectful treatment of herself.

A rose, itself in the final throes of death, hung limply in her palm; the once silky, white petals were now stained brown. Dark lines of decay webbed across each petal, giving it the appearance of a specimen ready to undergo the scrutiny of a botanist's microscope. The leaves on the stem were wilted and curled in on themselves as if attempting to hide from some horticultural grim reaper, but it could not escape the inevitable truth; it was time to return the elements it had borrowed from the bank of organic molecules, so that another rose could sprout-forth. For Jennifer, this was not a place of renewal - it was a place of somber goodbyes.

The icy hill sloped downward, keeping Jennifer mindful of her steps as she passed through the rolls of monuments. The grave marker she would attend bore distinct features. Made of smoothly polished green granite, the monument was an oblong sculpture with rounded corners, adorned with a Celtic cross. The base of the cross was etched into the main stone, but pulled itself free of the monument as its intersecting bars and trademark circle reached to heaven. As she approached, the encryption that she would never truly accept came in to view. **'Arlen Thomas Bergin. May God hold you in the palm of His hand.'**

Jennifer collapsed to her knees, feeling the cold moisture permeate her jeans as she stared despondently at the final acknowledgment of her son's existence. She reached inside her pocket and withdrew the three pennies she had saved from her visit to the pharmacy. She placed them on the base of the headstone and arranged them; two with heads up and one with tails up. Fragments of information about the accident fired across her mind in rapid succession. *Blow to the head. Child asphyxiated. Slumped forward into the tub. Accidental drowning. Father cleared of negligence. A blow to the head. Father cleared of negligence? How negligent do you have to be? He was there. He was right there.*

Jennifer's grip on the wilted rose intensified with each thought. Warm blood seeped between her fingers as the thorns bit into her skin. The sting of the puncture wounds liberated her. *I need to feel pain for you. I need to bleed for you.* She tightened her grip on the rose.

With tears streaming from her eyes, the words surfaced on her tongue, "I need to bleed for you. I need to bleed for you."

A blow to the head.
"I need to bleed."
Child asphyxiated.
"I need to bleed…"
Father negligent.
"…for you."

As though she had suddenly returned from a transient out of body experience, she released the rose and sat back on her feet. Her hands shook as she examined the blood that trickled from numerous prick-holes in her palm. Then, leaning forward, she touched her palm to Arlen's headstone, leaving a trail of blood as she let her hand slip back to her side. The crunch of footsteps on the snow behind her drew her attention to an approaching figure that halted as their eyes met.

"I'm sorry," Sean muttered uncomfortably. "I didn't realize you were going to be here. I can come back if..."

"No." Her clenched teeth made the word hiss from her lips. "I was just leaving."

Jennifer rose to her feet and examined her possible routes of retreat; with grave markers on either side of a narrow path, she had no choice but to walk around him. And as she did, a hand reached for her elbow.

"Lass, I..."

"Don't touch me." Her eyes were brilliant with fury. "Don't you dare fucking touch me."

Sean withdrew his hand and stepped aside as she scrambled quickly up the incline. When she reached the edge of the roadway, she shot a glance back down the slope. Sean was shaking his head in apparent disgust as he turned to make his way to Arlen's grave. The sight of his cynical gesture brought her anger to an immediate boil. She spun on her heels, noticing that Sean had parked his blue pick-up truck behind her car. She stormed around the truck's rear bumper and up along the driver's side. As she neared the truck cab, she thought of grabbing something to slash his upholstery, but as she reached the rear window, her eyes fell upon an open tool box wedged in the front corner of the truck bed. The handle of a steel hammer with a black rubber grip poked out from the mass tangle of plastic and metal implements. Jennifer slowed her pace and looked down the hill to see Sean knelling at Arlen's headstone, lost in prayer. *Father negligent.* She could see him examining the three coins and the blood flecked rose she had left behind. *A blow to the head.* Her features darkened as she made her decision. She reached carefully into the tool box, mindful not to create undo clatter, and retrieved the steel, claw hammer. Hefting it in her hand, she tested the balance of the tool, now a weapon.

Her approach would have to be silent. If she drew his attention he could easily overpower her and use the weapon against her. Her grip on the handle was made slick with blood, but anger gave her the strength to hold it firmly. She eased her way back to the rear of the truck, never removing her eyes from the crouching man in front of her son's grave. Her arm was parallel to her shoulder with the weapon brandished high. Arlen would be avenged and at the same time she would rid herself of Sean's impetuous meddling.

The air was still and a somber quiet lay void to the desolate place. Not even the slightest whistle of wind existed to mask the sound of her methodic footsteps - they echoed down the hill with the crispness of a Boise radio. Her target cocked his head and lowered his chin as though he were requesting a direct blow to the temple in hopes of making it a quick death. His shoulders then drew back. *Did he hear me?* Her breathes came uncontrollably heavy as she fought against the hammering of her heart. As she rounded the corner of the truck, a shift in the body weight of her prey froze her approach. She considered throwing herself headlong into a brazen assault - the element of surprise as her ally, but she knew he could not be taken that easily. He rose to his feet. This was the defining moment. She had to make a decision.

The slamming of the car door was the second sound that Sean heard, or was the second sound merely an echo of the first. Jennifer's car sped away as he traversed the snow covered terrain to get back to the warmth he was sure to find in the cab of his truck. He and Jennifer's inadvertent encounter made their separation seem all the more plausible. Obviously, they could not get along, even when he attempted to remain civil. Her mannerisms were becoming increasingly deranged - he could no longer reason with her. He pulled his keys from his front jeans pocket and flipped through the crowded ring to find the one to his ignition. As he moved along the side of the vehicle, his eye caught a glimpse of something out of place. His favorite hammer - perfectly balance, durable, made of high-grade steel - had been bounced from his tool box to the very edge of the tailgate. As he reached to retrieve it, he noticed the rubber handle glistened with thick moisture. *Oil?* He touched his fingers to the substance and examined the stain on his fingertips. *Blood?* He shot a glance at the rear of Jennifer's car as it disappeared in the distance. A cold chill ran the length of his spine.

Chapter 46

Jennifer sighed as she finally shifted her weight in the large brown leather chair. Dr. Bomboy was seated across from her reviewing the contents of a file folder; she stared at his appearance in mild amusement. Dr. Bomboy was a balding, bespectacled man in his mid-fifties, with a strip of thick brown hair wrapped around the back of his head, running from ear to ear. The top of his head was smooth and came to a near point. He was short and jovial. His protruding stomach seemed to continue around his back like a ring. Perhaps his body was fond of hoola-hoops and decided to grow a permanent one. Perhaps he was prepared for a splash in an indoor pool after work and had already donned his duck-ring floatation device under his shirt. Or perhaps God had decided that he should be a walking, astronomical teaching tool, so He created him to be the human paragon of the planet Saturn.

A full beard sat upon his ruddy face. It was as though he had been drawn by some demented Warner Brothers cartoonist - prepared at all times to deliver his infamous catch-phrase; 'En my opinion, you are a cazzy wabbit.'

"So, I don't get to lie down on a couch?" Jennifer questioned with a smile.

"Are you uncomfortable?" Dr. Bomboy asked.

"No," she replied flatly. He must have heard that comment many times before.

"Why don't you start by telling me a little about your recent past? What are some things that are currently troubling you?"

"I've been having trouble sleeping."

"Uh huh. Can you attribute that to anything?"

'We may as well get right to the heart of the matter." Her voice softened, and she began turning her wedding bands, staring at it as though it would provide her with a script. "In October, I lost my son, Arlen. He was at home with his father. It was an accidental drowning."

Jennifer paused.

"That must have been extremely difficult for you." Dr. Bomboy commented.

"He, huh…he meant the world to me." She dabbed a tear from the corner of her eye with an errant fingertip. "My world just stopped; caved in on itself. That morning he wanted me to stay home. I could see it in his eyes. It was as if he knew something bad was going to happen. But I told him work was important. And I left anyway."

"How do you feel about that?"

"Guilty and sad. You cry. And you cry. Until it seems that you have no more tears. Your heart gets so sick, and then before you know it; you're just empty inside." She displayed a calm, nearly defiant stare as her body rocked subtly in her seat. Then turning abruptly in her chair, she stared out a distant window. *This is going nowhere,* she thought. She had covered and recovered this ground and her feelings would never change. The pain would always be there and no one could ever possibly understand it. It simply hurt too much to discuss.

"Doctor, do you believe in angels?"

"Do you?"

"I think angels are like snowflakes through a window. The snow is cold; and yet, through the window you can't help but feel some arrant warmth. You watch them drift slowly. They come down to earth soft and silent; silent and soft. When you're outside, they land on you. You can see them; feel them, but only for a short while until they melt into your skin. Soft and beautiful. And you just want to hold them forever. But they always go away. Angels and snowflakes," she paused. "Dreams are like that also."

Dr. Bomboy quietly jotted notes on a legal pad as he listened, looking up at Jennifer occasionally, although her attention remained on the window.

"Dreams are real. Dreams become a part of you.

I like to sleep and dream. Sometimes in there, it doesn't hurt. Sometimes in there, I can feel good again." The room was gone now. Her mind had levitated her body through the glass and into mist of the morning. "Have you ever had a dream about someone that you have never met before?"

"Have you?"

"Someone that you don't recognize from any part of your consciousness?" Jennifer continued, ignoring his response. "A person you feel a love or a special bond with. And when you wake up, you wonder why your mind would create such a connection. You know, a connection to someone that you have never seen before. But you rise anyway to go about your day; your day in reality. Or at least what you think is reality. Maybe we're all just dreaming, all of the time. All of this pain is not real. We're all tucked in some cozy bed after Daddy tells us a bedtime story. And there is no pain. What do you think?" She asked, finally shifting her attention back to Bomboy.

"This is not about what I think - it's about what you think."

"Okay, then what do your books say about dreams?"

"Dreams can be wonderful expressions of our inner creativity. Some believe they can even provide us with our own personal brand of psychotherapy."

"You mean like the mind trying to heal itself?"

Bomboy nodded.

"Maybe the dead, ghosts and spirits visit us in our dreams."

"Is that what you believe?"

"I don't know.' She glided her fingertips along the smooth, cool leather of the armrest. "Maybe."

"That's a very spiritual point of view."

"Is it?"

"That particular belief can be found in most Native American cultures, in their legends and folklore."

"And in the Bible."

Bomboy did not respond. He sat across from her, looking at her. She was being judged, and it frustrated her. He was attempting to assess her symptoms. He was deciding how crazy she was.

"Sometimes you see places in your dreams that you have never visited before. Maybe, C.G. Jung's collective unconscious theory was right." Jennifer stated pompously; deliberately displaying her knowledge of the reference in order to impress. "Perhaps that is where the strange faces and places come from."

"I see you've done some homework in my field."

She brushed a finger across her cheek and cast her eyes to the ceiling. "I've dabbled in psychology."

Dr. Carl Jung was a colleague of Sigmund Freud in the early 1900s. He was best known for his collective unconscious theory, in which archetypes and visual patterns are stored in the human unconscious mind that allow us to view similar things which we have had no previous contact. Dr. Jung theorized that the main lightning rods for these images were dreams.

Jennifer had studied his theory while attending college. She had originally entered Bloomsburg University seeking a degree in psychology. Her sophomore year was the most exciting and intellectually stimulating time in her life. Psychology and Philosophy came naturally to her. She poured herself into countless books and theses; her mind chewed upon each fact and theory as though it were dining on fine cuisine. During her studies in psychology she happened upon a book by Dr. Jung and became an instant fan of his work.

But fate had other ideas for Jennifer. Jennifer watched as the costs of her education took its toll on her father. He was being forced to juggle the mortgage and living expenses without an income from her mother, Sue Ellen. Jennifer knew that an eight-year degree would have placed tremendous strain upon the family's single income and her part-time job did little to help. She applied for some school loans, but in the end compromised on a two-year associate's degree in interior design and merchandising. She approached her father with the excuse that her interest in psychology was more casual than professional. And with that, she officially left behind what she knew to be her calling in life. She became the tree that saw fit not to flourish for the betterment of the forest. That was when something inside of her snapped, and her feelings for her mother changed from intimidated to contempt.

"Would you like to tell me about your dreams?" Bomboy asked.

"No. I don't want to talk about them right now." She chewed on her lower lip. She knew he was trying to structure the conversation in an indiscriminate manner.

"Okay. I want you to set the pace, Jennifer. The important thing is that you feel comfortable talking."

A long period of silence followed. Jennifer became aware of a clock ticking in the background; their silence magnified its rhythm.

"Dr. Conahan tells me that you and your husband have recently separated." Bomboy said, breaking the silence.

"Yes."

"How do you feel about that?"

Jennifer emitted a sarcastic snicker, "Oh, sometimes I think I love him. Sometimes I know I hate him." She shot Dr. Bomboy a cynical glance. "But most of the time I really don't give a shit."

"I don't want you to use the word hate. Let's use the word anger. Okay?"

Jennifer shrugged.

"Why are you angry with him?"

"I'm angry with him," she enunciated, "because he's a self-centered Neanderthal. He was home. He should have been with Arlen - watching him. Or maybe he was with Arlen at the very second he died."

"Have you expressed your feelings to your husband? Rationally, of course."

"Yes and no."

"What do you mean?"

"Yes, I told him. No, not rationally. We're getting a divorce."

"Jennifer, during this grieving, I would advise you not to make any unnecessary life-altering decisions. You should focus on healing."

"Well, this divorce seems necessary." Jennifer paused. Tears swelled in her eyes. "Every time I look at him I see my son. I don't want to equate Arlen with my disdain for him. Can you take that away?"

"I'm going to try to help you heal yourself. We're going to work through some of those feelings. Our goal here is to allow you to function in society and help you cope with your loss. We can work together to make this better."

"The only way to make this better is to give me back my son. Can you do that for me?"

"No. I'm afraid I cannot."

The answer came to Jennifer. He could not, but she knew someone who could. It was time to force the issue. She would have to swallow her fear. Nicholas and Father Anthony were real. There must be a way for them to find Arlen; to bring him back to her. She would sleep forever if it meant reuniting with her son. She was not sure if she could trust Nicholas or Father Anthony, but one of them had to help her, and once she had Arlen in her arms; she would be safe. She had foolishly allowed herself to be wooed by Nicholas and she was acting like a frightened little girl with a teenage crush. Her ultimate objective was clear to her now; Arlen was the only one who could heal her.

The session with Dr. Bomboy continued, but Jennifer's mind was preoccupied. In the end, Bomboy requested another session as soon as she could arrange it. He was to telephone Dr. Conahan to have both of her prescriptions refilled.

"I could have those prescriptions phoned in to your pharmacy if it's more convenient."

Jennifer agreed. She would have complied to any request or suggestion, but not for her own benefit. The answers did not lie with a psychologist. He had no idea of the real world or the possibilities it held. She would have to finish the journey that she had started; alone.

Chapter 47

Sean gave his appearance a final inspection as he stood in front of the full-length mirror in Gail's bathroom. The gray dress shirt with his black pleated casual slacks seemed painfully devoid of color, so he had opted for a slate blue sweater. The anxiety bug fluttered in his stomach. He could not remember how long it had been since he was out on a date. *Too long for comfort*, he thought. His rugged face stretched into a smile, his dimples now fully visible. He was ready.

He bounded down the stairs with the energy of a teenage boy. As his feet landed on the floor, he nearly collided with Gail who was coming from the kitchen.

"Oh my, you smell good." Gail commented. "Did you get all dressed up for me?"

"I'm going out tonight," he announced. Sean had not mentioned his date to Gail- better to be silent than to be lectured. After all, he was still married and Gail was still the sentinel of his honor.

"Well, I imagine you're not going to McKinney's Pub with that cologne on. Do you have something to fess up to?"

Always prodding. "I'm going to dinner with Wendy Parks."

Gail dropped her chin and looked up at him over top her eyeglasses. "Sean, don't you think it's a little too soon to..."

"Mama Gail," Sean looked directly into her eyes, "it's just a dinner date with a friend. Okay? Nothing more. I may be home a little late. We are going out dancing afterward." He added firmly. "Angelia will be stopping by later to drop off some mail. I haven't gotten the mail from the house for a few days, and I'm sure Jennifer has not bothered to check it. She has been preoccupied lately."

"What's that supposed to mean?"

"It's a long story; one that will go great with tomorrow morning's coffee."

"Speaking of tomorrow; I was wondering if you would like to spend the day with me. I have a few errands to run, and I thought we could have lunch together. You're living under my roof, but I never get to see you."

"I like the idea. It's a real date." Sean leaned down and kissed her cheek.

"Imagine that, your second one this weekend," Gail commented slyly.

Sean pulled his head back to cast an impugning glance. "I have to go. Don't wait up for me. I will give you all of the gory details in the morning."

"Be prepared to be interrogated."

Sean stepped from the house with a deep sigh. He could not expect anyone to understand his position. The evening had barely taken seed and already he felt a bounce in his step. Something he had not felt in years. He felt alive again. And his heart thumped with romance.

He decided to take Wendy to Desiderio's Restaurant. It would be his first time there. Going beyond the safety net of their home was difficult for Jennifer, thus having a night on the town was not a part of their routine. Her battle with anxiety would usually bring an abrupt ending to any engagements they attempted. During their courtship Jennifer was much more relaxed in crowds; however, the freshness of courtship turned into the mundane of marriage. And before Sean had even become aware of the transformation, Jennifer had changed. Somewhere along the way Jennifer had become a recluse, and Sean had suffered as a result. He remained patient and supportive, but he often missed their evening excursions.

Conversely, Wendy was comfortable with the hordes of celebrants at any gathering. This night was a long time coming; a night in which Sean could relax and have fun with a woman on his arm. This night would be magical.

Chapter 48

Jennifer stepped back and admired her work. She had previously covered the upstairs windows to prevent light emission; now the first floor windows were covered. If her plan were to succeed, she could not risk waking up prematurely. Nicholas and Father Anthony seemed to be aligned against one another. She would use that to her advantage. She had been able to control her thoughts during her visit to Desiderio's, and she could do it again.

Casper paced the floor at her feet. He had been whiny and nervous since she returned from Dr. Bomboy's office. She knelt down and stroked his pudgy body.

"What's the matter little guy? You can sense them, can't you? The spirits are here."

She would not use her sleeping pills on this evening; however, she was concerned with her ability to fall asleep. She was excited and nervous. Perhaps a drink would stave off the nerves. Sean had left some beer in the refrigerator; with her low body weight and the absence of food in her stomach, one should do the trick.

She retrieved a bottle of beer from the kitchen and returned to the dining area. She put her lips to the bottle and took a deep swig. *Oh, that's nasty! How can he drink this stuff?* She looked at the bottle knowing she must press on. It was a means to an end. She chugged half the bottle before coming up for air.

A few more details to attend to and she would be off to bed early. She made her way back into the kitchen and nearly stepped in a pile of dog crap; a thoughtful gift from Casper. She did not have the time or attention to house break the puppy. She was relying on old newspapers that she had strewn about the floor of the kitchen. He had been good up until now. He must have missed the paper. Perhaps it was from the nervousness that he had been portraying. She stepped around the mess to lock the backdoor before turning her attention to the front of the house. She entered the living room and knelt down by the telephone stand to pull the plug from the wall. The sudden ring from an incoming call caused her to jump. Her free hand clutched to her chest as she stood up and stared at the phone. She was slightly jumpy already and that only exposed the frailty of her nerves in theatrical style. She envisioned a call from some strange, maniacal agent within the house. Although in Hollywood, they only seem to prey upon the babysitter.

She pondered letting this call go, but decided, at length, to answer. "Hello."

"Hi, Mrs. Bergin," the voice of Angelia came through the receiver. "How have you been?"

"Fine. And I've told you before to call me Jennifer." Jennifer's voice came far more brazen than she had expected or desired. Angelia's polite manners were rare among her peers, a quality Jennifer had always appreciated, but not within her current circumstance; her nerves were frail and ready to erupt.

"I'm sorry to bother you." Angelia sensed the anxiety in Jennifer's voice. "I wanted to make sure that you were going to be home this evening."

"Yes. Why?"

"Well, Mr. Bergin asked me to stop and collect the mail from your house. I am sorry. I hate doing this. I feel like I'm being trapped in the middle of something."

"You don't need to apologize, Angelia. He never should have bothered you with this." Jennifer scrapped her fingernails across the top of the telephone stand. "I desperately need some sleep, so I will put the mail on the end table near the door."

"Okay. I'll be quiet."

"And Angelia; do not wake me up under any circumstances. I don't care if I'm sleepwalking. Do you understand?"

"I know you're not supposed to awaken a sleepwalker." Angelia responded.

"That's right. So don't worry about me. Just grab the mail and go. Okay?"

"I understand. I should be there in about two hours."

"That will be fine. And lock the door on your way out."

"I will. Bye."

Jennifer set the receiver down and quickly unplugged the phone from the wall. She looked down at Casper in frustration. "Why do I always have to get interrupted? Oh, and thanks for the gift in the kitchen, mutt." She patted his head and then snatched him up into her arms. "You're sleeping with me tonight, but you're not allowed on the bed. I have to count on you to keep me safe, so if you could muster up a little watchdog; that would be great. If everything goes right, you should sense the presence of your brother Arlen tonight as well." The night would bring the answer that she had longed for. She would make it happen by sheer will.

Chapter 49

Desiderio's bustled with its usual Friday night flare with only the reserved tables empty. Sean and Wendy had already been seated and were awaiting their drinks. The butterflies had not left Sean's stomach; in fact, Wendy's presence had intensified them into a full blown swarm. Although in this case, considering the ill feeling welling inside his gut, calling them a murder of butterflies would be more appropriate.

The anxiety shivered his body slightly as though he were cold. He tried hard to control it, hoping Wendy had not noticed.

She was dressed in a navy colored sweater with three-quarter-length sleeves. The sweater exposed a sliver of her belly when she raised her arms; the tantalizing bare part of her ensemble. A long flowing beige skirt provided her with the Contessa aspect. She wore dress sandals with her toe nails painted to match her sweater and a thin gold anklet above her right foot. Her thick mane of auburn hair flowed about her shoulders and breasts. The delightful sight of her intensified Sean's trembling.

He broke from his gaze to glance over his right shoulder in time to see a familiar face approaching them.

"Hey, Sean; I thought that was you." Evan Kershaw said, approaching the table. "My wife and I frequent this place, but I've never seen you here before."

"Yeah, this is my first time." Sean responded, flatly.

"I saw your wife in here the other night."

Sean attempted a cordial smile at Evan and then averted his eyes across the table toward Wendy. Evan took the cue.

"Oh, I'm sorry. I..." There was something he desperately wanted to add, but he knew it would have to wait for another time.

Timothy Cole

"There's no need to apologize." Wendy responded.

"Wendy, this is Evan Kershaw. Evan, this is Wendy Parks."

Wendy nodded. "I've heard your name quite often, but never had the pleasure."

Sean said. "Evan here owns half of Honey Brook."

Evan's smile bore a hint of self-assurance. "Well not half, but I have acquired my share. And speaking of which, I never got a chance to tell you what a fine job you did on the addition to the plaza, Sean. I appreciate your eye for detail." Evan cast a glance at Wendy's face that trailed down her body until the remainder disappeared beneath the table.

"Not a problem." Sean spoke the phrase and then fell into silence. At length, Evan picked up on the hint.

"Well, I guess I better be getting on. The wife and I are heading home for the evening." He motioned across the room to a beautiful tall blonde seated at a distant table. "There's no place like home." Evan, who had recently turned fifty-six, was married to a woman who was twenty-five years his junior. Sean noticed that the marriage had brought some roseate tone to Evan's pale cheeks.

"It was nice meeting you, Wendy. Watch this guy." He commented pointing an accusing finger in Sean's direction. "He is as smooth as they come."

"Oh, I'm well aware of that." Wendy responded.

"You folks have a good evening." Evan turned and walked across the room.

"He is quite a character," Wendy commented.

"He can be. He can also be the most brutal businessman that you will ever meet."

Their drinks were served as they continued their conversation. "I ran into your sister, Arlene, at the hospital yesterday." Wendy announced.

"Let me guess, she was rather rude to you."

"Well, now that you mention it."

"Don't let her get to you, Wendy. She has no right trying to judge me or my friends. She's all bark and no bite. I apologize for her on behalf of the rest of my family. We are not all that nasty."

"I know."

"I hope that you're well-rested tonight." Sean jibbed. "I plan on dancing into the wee hours of the morning with you."

"Irish Eyes," Wendy brought her glass to her lips and ran her tongue discreetly along the rim. "I am ready for anything tonight."

Chapter 50

Jennifer's dream began as a disjointed mix of past and present. Seated in the rear seat of a car, her view was obstructed by a thick layer of frost on the window. She could make out the subtle glow of multi-colored Christmas lights on the houses as they passed before her. The uncongenial cold of the leather seat numbed her buttocks and the back of her legs. From the front seat, a single antiquated speaker rattled as Chuck Berry rolled through his version of 'Run, Run, Rudolph.' Jennifer had to strain to hear the conversation taking place between the driver and passenger in the front seat which appeared to be hundreds of feet away.

"I don't know why we have to go to church this evening. It's Christmas Eve. We should be at home." The female passenger said.

"Christmas Eve is the most important time to attend church. Honestly Sue Ellen, I don't know why you insist on putting up such a fuss. It never bothered you before. You always loved these services." The image of her parents came into focus; Don was young and vibrant, dressed in his favorite pin-striped suit. In contrast, Sue Ellen was pale and displaying signs of aging. She wore a heavy, double-breasted trench coat which was unbuttoned to expose her hospital gown beneath.

In the seat next to Jennifer was Dr. Bomboy. He was scrutinizing a file that he held on his lap. His round body swayed with the motion of the vehicle; Saturn in orbit. "So, Casper is currently troubled by the persistent arguing from your parents?" He asked.

"Yes. He has been really whiny and frightened lately." Jennifer responded.

"A dog can provide himself with psychotherapy." Dr. Bomboy commented.

"I hate attending this church. I don't like this church." Sue Ellen continued from the front seat.

"Mother, you have attended this church all of your life. It would be crazy to change now?" Don questioned.

"Are you calling me crazy?" Sue Ellen shouted.

"How are you feeling?" Dr. Bomboy asked Jennifer.

"I'm nervous. I have to dream soon," Jennifer responded.

"Don't worry Jennifer. It is magic. Remember? It is all smoke and mirrors."

Jennifer's body jolted forward as the car came to an abrupt halt. Jennifer opened the door and saw the enormous stone structure of St. Anthony's Church. The flecks of snow that drifted and swirled around the peak of the cathedral illuminated the night sky. Jennifer began to climb out of the car before being momentarily drawn back by Dr. Bomboy's voice.

"Don't focus on the church; focus on healing." He instructed.

Jennifer nodded as she pushed the large car door closed with a prominent metallic groan.

"Do not get that dress dirty! You fucking worthless brat!" Sue Ellen shouted as the car sped away.

Jennifer walked up to the stone stairs that stretched to the oak door of the church. Despite the wintry scene, she felt the comforting warmth of anticipation inside of her as she ascended the steps. The snow danced in the air guided by a swirling breeze, landing on her nose and eyelashes, tickling as it melted. Before she could reach the top step, the door swung open and Father Anthony stepped out.

"Hello, Jennifer." His greeting was as warm as an old friend. Jennifer did not respond, keeping a wary distance. "There was a time when my nephew was quite a young gentleman. I fancied him to follow in my footsteps, as fathers often do. He would be the closest thing that I would ever have to a child of my own. But perhaps I pressed too much. The calling was mine, not his.

It was not long before I sensed that something was amiss, but I did nothing. I turned my head and prayed that my intuition was wrong." Father Anthony gazed down the street, exhaling a deep sigh causing a halo of breath vapor to rise and dissipate above his head. "Carol was only a child. After what happened to her, Nicholas could not live with the consequences of his actions. But you don't have to hear this from me. The door is open for you to bear witness personally. I want there to be no doubt remaining in your mind. Step through the door, Jennifer; step into 1954."

Jennifer turned her attention to the open door in front of her; the church inside was dimly lit. She stepped forward without hesitation. Despite the foreboding of Father Anthony's words, her heart was still filled with warmth and longing for what was beyond the door.

Once inside the portico of the church, she veered to the right before entering the nave. A small mirror was hung on the wall. She stood before the mirror, unable to see her reflection in the murkiness of the dim light. She stepped closer and leaned in. The reflection of the face staring back was a beautiful teen with a face as smooth and flawless as a fine porcelain doll. Her golden blonde hair was pulled back into a ponytail and held in place by a chiffon scarf. She wore a tight sweater with three-quarter-length sleeves and a long pleated skirt with a leather cinch.

She turned and walked toward the entrance. She was to visit someone here. She had wonderful news to tell, the excitement of which tickled her tongue as she walked down the aisle and stopped three pews short of the altar. This was a seat well known to her, though she could not remember why. She sat quietly, smiling as she gazed at the statue of the Virgin Mary. Off to the right of the altar, she heard the sound of a door close softly. Her excitement intensified, and her legs quivered in anticipation. He was here. A young priest walked toward her, glancing over his shoulder as he approached. As he drew within her light she recognized him as Nicholas. He appeared to have a surprise for her as well, for one of his hands was tucked behind his back. He slid into the pew next to her and presented a gratified smile.

"Hello, Carol," Nicholas greeted her. "I have something for you." He withdrew the arm that had been concealing the surprise. He extended a single white rose to her.

"Oh, thank you!" She squealed.

"Ssh!" Nicholas warned, turning away to glance nervously back at the altar.

She giggled and held her hand over her mouth as she spoke. "White roses are my favorite. It symbolizes innocence and purity, and in some cultures; secrecy. They say the first rose was white. Some myths say it was stained by blood; some say it blushed after being kissed."

"This one symbolizes your beauty." He gazed down over her body, his eyes – lustful pools of urgency.

She reached over and held his hand in hers, "Nicholas, I have wonderful news."

"Are you going to tell me, or keep it to yourself?" He quipped with a smile.

She lit up with excitement and she bounced in her seat. "We are going to have a baby."

The smile wiped instantly from his face. "What?"

"You and I; we are going to have a baby!"

He pressed his finger to her mouth and shushed her with a scowl. "You must be mistaken." He growled in a whisper, "I have only been with you once."

"Maybe once is all that it takes."

"Carol, do you have any idea what this means? I am a Catholic priest! I will be removed from the church, and my uncle will disown me. And you; you're only fifteen years old..."

"But you said I was already a woman." Her face was a cauldron of confusion.

"You may never get your chance to be a woman. Your father will kill us both."

And he was right. Carol's father was a strict man and a devout Catholic. A man who earned the thick skin on his large hands working in the coal mines. But the strength of her love for Nicholas had eradicated that thought before it presented itself.

"Carol," he gripped her shoulders firmly; his eyes wide and intense, "you have to get rid of it."

"I don't understand."

"You must get an abortion."

"You want me to kill our baby?" The perfection of her smooth brow dissipated in deep creases.

"Carol, please understand. If we allow this to happen it will destroy both of our lives. We could never remain together after the fallout from this. Do you understand me?" His voice was rising in agitation. "You will lose me if you have that baby."

She began to cry softly, giving every attempt to remain quiet. "But it's our baby."

"I said get rid of it!" Nicholas thrust himself from the seat. And following a glance around the chapel, he retreated to the door from which he entered.

Jennifer wanted to leave; she wanted to run out of the church, but her legs were too weak to stand. Her body shook as she sobbed. She sat crying while the minutes ticked past endlessly until a gentle voice called to her and a hand rested upon her back.

"Why, Carol. What on earth is the matter?"

She looked up to see Father Anthony leaning toward her with an expression of concern. She shook her head and slid from her seat, pushing him aside as she ran up the aisle to the front door. She grabbed the door and pulled. She needed fresh air. She wanted out of that church more than she had ever wanted anything. She stepped through the doorway, but instead of being surrounded by the evening sky, she found herself in a tattered living room.

The room was sparsely furnished with a couch and matching chair, both of equal dilapidation, accompanied by a narrow coffee table. The rancid air within the house was stale and heavy. Jennifer looked around frantically. The outside world was gone and terror twisted her insides into knots. The room spun, and her stomach heaved. She collapsed into the arms of a thin, man with a hawk nose. His pale complexion only served to intensify his dark sullen eyes.

"It's okay Carol," he said. "Let's just have a seat for a moment. You look very pale. Have you eaten today?"

"I think I'm going to be sick." A gag replaced her words. Her body recoiled and her mouth sprung open to release a spray of putrid vomit. The contents of her stomach spilled onto the floor and sprayed the shirt of the hawk-faced man.

Clumps of food particles and stomach acid dripped from Hawk Face as he stood with his arms spread in disgust. "I guess that would be a yes. I don't have time for unforeseen cleanups. I have other places to be this evening. Are you quite certain no one saw you enter?" There was a weak shake of her head. He continued. "I need to do a few more preparations before we begin. But first I will need the money. We had agreed upon one hundred dollars."

She nodded as she withdrew the cash from her purse. The payment was made. There was no turning back. She could barely hold herself together as he walked to an adjoining room that was separated by a thick curtain. Hawk Face disappeared, leaving her alone in the room. She wanted to run, but her body felt heavy and cold; though her face was flush and hot. She could barely move her arm to wipe the sweat from her brow. Whatever was about to happen, she was powerless to stop it.

Chapter 51

Hawk Face led Jennifer into the room beyond the curtain. It was a small kitchen with a table and chairs pressed haphazardly against the far wall. A few appliances, including an old stove and a tiny ice box, rounded out the customary gadgetry.

In the center of the room was a narrow three-foot high table made from rough-cut lumber that had been haphazardly constructed. Two wooden studs were fastened to adjoining corners of the table, rising two feet above the tabletop at 45 degree angles on each side of the table. A beige canvas material, spotted with fades of crimson, covered the table top. The entrance to the scullery on the far right was also covered by a blanket.

"Go in there and remove all of your clothing from below your waist," he instructed. "There's a bucket in there also. I will need you to empty your bladder. I think one mess from you this evening is enough. I should charge you an additional twenty dollars as it is now."

She complied as though she were a marionette with an unseen force controlling her strings. She reappeared in the kitchen holding her clothes in front of her pelvic area. An ashamed vulnerability stirred within her rising fear. He was in control. And she would obey.

He yanked the skirt and underpants from her hands and tossed them callously on the floor. "We won't need those. Climb on the bench and lie down."

"There are blood stains on there." She spoke softly.

He ignored her comments as he retrieved a metal tray and leather pouch from the pantry.

She could hear the metal clanging of the instruments within the tray as he approached. Surrendering what now remained of her dignity, she rested back onto the canvas. Thin, elongated fingers gripped her knees and spread her legs apart. Each foot was placed against one of the studs at the base of the table.

Hawk Face positioned the steel surgical tray between her legs and withdrew a swatch of cloth and a dropper bottle from the small leather pouch. He squeezed a few drops of liquid onto the cloth and offered it to her. "There's some chloroform on that cloth. Hold it up to your nose and breathe. It will take the edge off."

Tucking the cloth to her chest, she stared at the rotted ceiling, picking out a small area where the paint had been chipped away in the form of a butterfly and focused intently on it.

She felt the bite of cold steel as he inserted a speculum to open the walls of her vagina. An inadvertent glimpse of the next instrument caused her eyes to shut tight. It appeared to be a long spoon with a tiny round bowl at its end. Suddenly she felt the scrapping inside of her stomach. She fought the urge to lurch; instead she buried her face deep within the chloroform cloth. She could feel intense pressure against her bowels and the unnatural sensation as inner organs not normally associated with touch were pushed against. A tinny 'splosh' echoed in the room as fluids spilled into the tray. She opened her eyes and made a desperate attempt to focus on her paint-chip butterfly as tears trickled from the corners of her eyes. Its wings spread across the water-stained ceiling and its body now drifted and rolled under the dizzying effect of the chloroform. She fought against another wave of nausea by clenching her teeth. Sweat beaded on her forehead and a black, fuzzy ring formed on the periphery of the undulating butterfly. Her arm draped down, and the cloth floated to the floor. She was dizzy but still conscious. A sharp, stabbing pain deep inside of her caused her to flinch, drawing an immediate response from Hawk Face.

"Damn it! Hold still. I am almost finished. I hope you brought your sanitary pad. You will have some bleeding after you leave."

The pain grew to a consistent numbing burn until she was unable to judge when the scraping had stopped. The metal instruments fell into the surgical tray with a grotesque splash, and then everything was still. Jennifer, still in the embodiment of Carol, blinked her eyes several times as she regained her senses. The butterfly was once again nothing more than paint chips on a kitchen ceiling.

"It is finished." He quickly wiped her legs with a cold, damp rag, then picked up his tray and disappeared behind the curtain into the scullery. He reappeared to collect his leather case. "Get dressed. You can stay here for a short while, but the owner will be home in fifteen minutes. I assured him that the house would be in order, so you will need to leave before he returns. You will be bleeding for awhile, so don't panic and run to a doctor. What happened here tonight will seem pleasant compared to what will happen if I get caught because of you. Understand?"

She nodded, rolling off the table with her hands pressed to her stomach. She whimpered as she knelt down to retrieve her skirt and underpants. Her legs wobbled, and she nearly collapsed onto the floor. She dressed herself and then stumbled out into the night. The pain was intense, and her sanitary pad was soaked before she could reach the sidewalk.

Nicholas had only provided her with enough money to pay for the abortion and one-way cab fare. She would have to walk three miles to get home.

Within two blocks, the stabbing pain had grown too intense for her to stand. She slipped into a dark, deserted alley and crouched against a wall. Warm blood trickled down her thigh as she clutched her stomach. She was too weak to continue. The temperature outside must have lowered dramatically while she was in the house; her body was shivering cold. She leaned her head against a wall, weeping in gentle sobs. Alone and frightened, she longed for home and a warm, safe bed. The dark alley loomed ahead, swallowing her up and bringing dread in its shadow.

Chapter 52

Seventeen-year-old Angelia Eckley had stepped upon the porch of the Bergin household on countless occasions as their babysitter; happier times when the house glowed with the love and warmth of its family members. That glow had been extinguished, and her visits were now cloaked in anguish. She was relieved that this particular visit would be quick and uneventful.

Angelia had a pleasing girl-next-door appearance. Her short, brown hair touched upon an olive complexion. She was an intelligent, audacious teenage girl who ranked in the top five in her junior class as she prepared for her collegian agenda in biology. She was highly active in high school athletics, playing both soccer and basketball, and the strength of her conditioning was evident on her body. Although, these visits to the Bergin house since Arlen's death left her weak in mind and body.

She quietly opened the door and slipped inside. The interior of the house was as black as pitch. A foul odor hung in the air, instantly clinging to her clothes and hair - a repulsion that was unusual for the Bergin home. The windows were covered by heavy blankets as though the occupants of the home were hiding from daylight. Home decor compliments of Count Dracula. An ominous weight of suffering could be easily felt and the hairs upon her arms rose in protest to it.

A thin sliver of illumination from the streetlights came in through the cracked door. She remained still while her eyes adjusted to the low-light. The mail was resting upon the end table, just as Mrs. Bergin had promised.

With the mail in her hand, she turned and flipped the lock on the door, but a loud crash from the kitchen prompted her to spin on her heels. Frozen, clutching the stack of envelopes as though it were a shield, she peered into the darkness. She strained her eyes for what seemed an eternity, but no further sights or sounds were given up by the home that now appeared more like a black hole were nothing escapes.

She was instructed not to intrude no matter what the circumstances. She pondered her next move, hearing her own heavy breathing echo in her head. She was frightened; a feeling to which she was unaccustomed. If Mrs. Bergin was in trouble and she failed to investigate the noise, she would never forgive herself. Stress was a way of life for Angelia. Whether it was an important final exam that would affect her impeccable grades or the final shot to win the basketball game, she accepted the pressure with great bravado. *Suck it up, wimp. You can't leave. You need to investigate.* If Mrs. Bergin was sleepwalking, she could simply turnaround and quietly walkout. Her heart raced. If Mrs. Bergin was in trouble, she needed to help.

Angelia began edging her way into the Black Hole. As she maneuvered her way around the dining room table, she could see a subtle red light emanating from the microwave in the kitchen. The light would be enough to be her guide.

Chapter 53

Jennifer, now a puppet helplessly carrying out Carol's life, completely collapsed in the alley. She did not control her own thoughts and actions; instead, she seemed to be a participating witness to a horrible act. Her breathing had become shallow. The cold and the dark were taking her as her bleeding now rushed out of control. Alone as the life drained from her body, she hated Nicholas for abandoning her, and hated herself for abandoning her baby. She closed her eyes and parted her dry lips. Her words escaped in a low whisper as she inhaled in quick pants between each line she spoke, "The Lord is my shepherd." She gasped. "I shall not want."

Angelia's hand felt her way along the wall of the kitchen. The brush of something across her right ankle froze her approach. She peered down through the low light to see the white fur of a puppy - its tail thrashing wildly in ignorant glee. The kitchen smelled of garbage and shit; her lungs nearly seized as she attempted to breathe. A mumbling voice came from across the darkness, near the backdoor. Her steps were placed methodically as she maneuvered herself across the room with nothing to guide her advance. She began to see a dim light shining from the backdoor window - the only window in the house that appeared uncovered. She could make out a shadowy figure stretched across the floor. As she drew closer, she could see the face of Mrs. Bergin. The woman's head was propped against the wall, her neck bent at an abnormal ninety degree angle. The eyes were wide and sunken, surrounded by blackened flesh as they stared blankly into space. The face was pale and gaunt, nearly grey in color. The skin was stretched tight to the jaw and cheek bones, giving the face a skeletal appearance.

Angelia could barely catch her breath as she stared in disbelief. Her heart thumped like a stampede of cattle escaping a predator. The freakish apparition was barely recognizable as Mrs. Bergin; it could hardly be recognized as human. Mrs. Bergin spoke as her head wobbled against the wall. The lips moved frantically through each line spoken and the chest heaved with each breath. "He maketh me to lie down in green pastures. He leadeth me beside the still waters."

Angelia slowly knelt down beside the woman who once helped her with her Psychology homework and listened while Mrs. Bergin continued to mumble her prayer. Mrs. Bergin's head snapped suddenly toward Angelia causing her to tumble onto the floor. Angelia flopped down hard on her butt, scrambling backwards until the backdoor blocked her retreat. Mrs. Bergin's eyes grew even wider, and her voice changed from a mumble to a projected gruff, "I walk through the valley of the shadow of death."

"Mrs. Bergin," Angelia's voice came out in a whimpering plea, as terror instantly drained her of her strength.

"I walk in the valley of the shadow of death." Mrs. Bergin's hand shot out, grabbing Angelia's leg. The fingernails dug deep into her flesh. Angelia let out a painful cry as Mrs. Bergin's lips moved as if she were a ventriloquist's doll. "And death brought evil with it."

Angelia pulled her leg free, grabbed the stack of mail and scrambled to her feet. She had only run a few steps when she felt her footing loosen on the laminate floor. By the time she realized an unseen substance had caused her to slip, she was falling toward the ground. Instinctively her hand lashed out, desperately searching for something to break her fall. Her fingers grasped a small metal handle that yielded to the pull. She could hear the rattling sound of metal on metal as she hit the ground. Her ribs crashed down hard, and the air was knocked from her lungs. Silvery blades darted the ground around her head casting off glimpses of reflected light. For a moment, she remained motionless, taking stock of her condition. A sharp sting on her cheek told her that one of the knives had sliced her. Pressing her hand to the wound, her palm dampened with warm blood. A stabbing pain rushed through her chest with each breath she managed.

Mrs. Bergin continued her rant which had now escalated into a shrill screech. "And death brought evil with it." Angelia climbed back to her feet and stumbled through the dining room. Her pulse pounded in her throat as she hurried through the living room and out onto the porch. She pulled the door closed behind her with both hands, leaning back to hold it shut. She held tight to the doorknob until the blood from her palm caused her hand to slip free. Crying in fear and gasping for breath, she backed away from the door. That thing was not Mrs. Bergin. It could never pass as the charming mother she had once shared affection with. She chanced turning her attention away from the door as she leapt from the porch. The landing reminded her of the pain in her ribs. Holding her right arm gingerly across her chest, she made her way to her car. As she steered away from the curb, she glanced in the rearview mirror at her cheek. She had gotten lucky; the cut was not deep and the blood was beginning to clot. She had to get help, but her parents were gone for the evening. She used her cell phone to contact Sean, but there was no answer. There was only one person left who could help. The woman was difficult to approach, but possessed a strong bond with Mrs. Bergin. Uncertain of how she would be received, she headed for the residence of Sean's sister, Arlene.

Chapter 54

Speaking any softer than a shout was futile as the house band at a club called The Mouse Trap revved up to play rough shot through their next set. The band played dance-driven pop songs along with some classic rock selections that the crowd danced to anyway. Wendy managed to limit her number of drinks by dancing almost constantly, while over-consumption was never a problem for Sean. The seven beers that he had downed between the breaks in the music had little, if no effect, on him. The force of the bass was thumping hard into his chest, and he loved it. Watching Wendy's body sway and shake was an added allurement; the motion of her body was sexy, while the uninhibited grin on her face was adorable. As the band closed out their rendition of Roadhouse Blues, Wendy leaned in to Sean and requested a break. The couple retreated to their table in laughter and perspiration. No sooner had they taken their seats when the band ripped into the next number. Soon all normal audio pitches were reduced to background noise.

"This is so much fun. I'm having a great time." Wendy shouted.

"Huh?" Sean replied.

"I'm having a great time," she repeated with a shout, but this time leaning across the table to project her voice. Sean smiled and gave a nod.

He lifted his mug of draft and took a deep swig. The glass was still pressed to his lips when he heard what seemed to be a female voice. In the split second that it happened, the raucous music was instantaneously muffled. It was a blip so fast that he was not entirely certain if he heard a voice or simply a sound that mimicked one. But he was almost certain he heard the words *"tempt you"* spoken. He pulled the glass away from his lips to gaze across the table at Wendy, who was immersed in the band and the action on the dance floor.

Sean leaned across the table and tapped her arm. "Did you just say something?" He shouted.

Wendy's lips turned down while she gave him a shrug and a shake of her head. "No."

She saw the expression of confusion on his face as he rested back into his seat. "Are you okay?" She asked with a discomforted chuckle.

"Yeah," he paused. "Do you want to get out of here?"

"I'm happy with anything you want to do, Hon."

"The dancing was fun, but I want to go somewhere we can talk."

They finished their drinks quickly and headed out the door. Their ears still rang as they stepped out into the relative silence of night. Wendy slipped her arm through his, "It's only eleven o'clock. Why don't we head back to my apartment?" She spoke softly, a welcome change from the shouting of the past hour. "I have some beer, and we can play some soft music on the stereo." Sean agreed as he opened her door and helped her into his truck.

Chapter 55

The first foreign sound jolted Arlene from her light slumber. The second was recognized as a knock at the front door. She gave her husband a sharp elbow into his ribs, a message to get out of bed and see who is knocking.

"Alright! I'm going," Patrick snapped. He pulled on a pair of sweat pants and groggily exited the bedroom. Arlene glanced at the alarm clock; it was 11:15. A third knock caused her to wrap her pillow around her ears. She could hear the muffled voice of Patrick's bark, "I'm coming!"

The door opened and then came the chatter of distant voices. Curiosity finally won her attention as she threw the covers aside and wrapped herself in a robe. As she neared the foot of the stairs, she saw Angelia Eckley slip inside, her face dampened with tears, her cheek brushed with blood. "Angelia. What the hell happened to you?" Arlene demanded as she reached her side.

Angelia took a deep breath in an attempt to calm herself, but when her mouth opened she began to rant. "I was on my way home, but I had to pick up Mr. Bergin's mail. I found Mrs. Bergin on the kitchen floor. She looked like she was sleeping, but she's acting weird. She's talking like she's possessed or something."

"Whoa. Hold on there, girl," Arlene took Angelia by the arm. "Come into the living room and sit down. Now repeat that again, a little slower."

Angelia sat gingerly on the couch, desperately trying to protect her ribs. "Mr. Bergin..."

"Sean," Arlene instructed.

"Sean," Angelia continued, "had asked me to collect his mail this week so he wouldn't have to face Mrs... I mean Jennifer." Arlene's face drew into a scowl. "Jennifer told me to simply walk in and grab it. I wasn't supposed to disturb her because she would be sleeping. But I heard a loud crash in the kitchen so I went in to check it out. She has all of the windows covered with blankets and; forgive me for saying this; her house is an absolute mess. And that's just not the Mrs. Bergin I know.

Anyway, I went into the kitchen and found her lying on the floor, and she looked really bad. She was talking nonsense. She grabbed my leg and tried to hurt me before I could run out of there."

"Did she do this to you?" Arlene barked the question.

"Sort of, I got hurt when I fell in the kitchen."

"Okay," Arlene rose from her seat on the sofa, "this has gone far enough. I'm tired of that son-of-a-bitch avoiding his responsibilities. First of all, my brother should never have positioned you in the middle of his domestic disputes, just because he's not man enough to face his own wife."

"I don't want Mr. Bergin to be angry with me," Angelia pleaded.

"I'm going over to Gail's house to put my right foot up his ass, and if he so much as says 'boo' to you over this, I'll insert the left one later! I'll take the mail with me and see that he gets it."

"What about Mrs. Bergin?" Angelia asked.

"You don't worry about Jennifer; I'll see to her. Where are your parents?"

"They are in Philadelphia for my father's conference."

"Can you get in touch with them? I think you should go to the emergency room and have your ribs checked."

"I have the telephone number of the place where they're staying. I can call them on my cell phone."

"Patrick will take you home and stay with you until they arrive. You should not drive anymore tonight in your condition. Besides, you still have your junior driver's license."

"I'm really sorry about waking you up."

"Don't you dare apologize; you did the right thing. I'll call you tomorrow and let you know that everything is okay."

Arlene returned to her bedroom to change clothes, reminding herself to grab her brother's precious mail from Angelia's car so that she had something to throw at him. The showdown with her baby brother had been on slow boil for weeks and tonight, it was about to boil over.

Chapter 56

Sean drove to Wendy's apartment in apprehension. The void of losing Jennifer was growing in his gut no matter how much he attempted to subdue it. It twisted and ate its way through his already thin soul. He glanced across the seat at Wendy. She was beautiful; her charms hard to resist. The answer would have to come soon. Wendy's body language was clearly inviting him to make a move for her affections. But he would have to break through his own feelings of love, guilt and responsibility to get to her.

Wendy stepped through the doorway into her apartment and displayed a sultry smile as she held the door open for Sean to follow. He stepped inside, glancing around the house without moving beyond the threshold.

"So this is how the Barefoot Contessa lives," he commented.

"You also called me the Strawberry Princess in school. Do you remember that?"

Sean thought for a moment, then the dawning of recollection made him smile broadly. "Oh, your birthmark; I could never forget that." The memory of Wendy's strawberry birthmark made his face warm. The birthmark rested at the very top of her bikini line, eliciting fond memories of the public swimming pool. Wendy's body could always turn heads, and the tall brunette's long smooth legs could turn a boy's gym class into a drooling kennel.

Wendy bit her lower lip with a girlish grin, "I still have it. Do you want to see?" Before Sean could respond, Wendy pulled down on her skirt with one hand and lifted her top to expose her tummy with the other. The birthmark was clearly visible, along with a glimpse of a neatly trimmed patch of velvety hair below. His face flushed, and his eyes widened. Wendy giggled slightly at his gaze, straightened her garments and walked into the living room. Sean eagerly followed.

"Sit down," she motioned toward the couch, "I'll get us a beer."

Sean watched as her hips swayed their way into the kitchen. *If a man failed to get aroused from that motion, he would most definitely become seasick.* He tried to relax, but guilt burned his stomach, branding him with the word *infidelity*. Wendy continued to speak, projecting her voice into the next room.

"Do you remember John Morrison?"

"Wasn't he that crazy kid in Mr. Burke's chemistry class?"

"That's him."

"I remember Burke had to move his seat away from the wall because Morrison kept sticking a paperclip in the electrical outlet."

Wendy returned to the living room in laughter. "That's the John Morrison that I'm talking about. I ran into him at the hospital the other day. He hasn't changed a bit. He still looks like he never combs his hair. And, as a matter of fact, he became an electrician. He was in the ER because he grabbed hold of a bare two-twenty electrical line and jolted himself off a ladder. Luckily he came out with just a sprained ankle."

Sean laughed, accepting the beer bottle from Wendy as she took a seat next to him on the couch. "Didn't he date that girl with the horn-rimmed eyeglasses who couldn't speak without snorting? I think her name was Amy Weaver."

"Yeah. I don't think that ever worked out for them though."

"I haven't seen either one of them since the prom."

"Let's not bring up the prom again."

"I thought I made up for that tonight."

"You're working on it. Would you like some music?"

"Sure," Sean cleared the discomfort from his throat; "preferably something very soft."

"That band was awfully loud, but the lead singer was cute."

"You noticed that too, huh?" Sean said with a smile. Wendy turned her attention away from the stereo to make certain that Sean's expression was one of jest. She tried to play the jealousy card. He was too slick for that. Wendy placed a CD in the stereo and pressed play. The sound of the 1959 instrumental hit, 'Sleep Walk' emanated through the speakers.

"I love this song," Sean commented.

"When I was a little girl, my dad would play this for me and we would dance together." Wendy stood in the middle of the room, hips swaying gently to the melodic steel guitar. "This song has such a haunting sound. It's reverent and tormented at the same time."

She watched Sean's eyes lock onto her body, which increased her own level of arousal. The desire in his eyes made her feel seductive. She allowed her head to roll from side to side, freeing her long hair to slide across her cheeks. He was hooked.

"When Daddy danced with me," she continued, "I always felt safe and secure. I knew that he would always protect me." She paused with a glance. "You make me feel secure like that too."

"I'm glad that I remind you of your father," Sean chuckled.

"You remind me of a man who could protect a woman." She pandered. "Sean, please come and dance with me."

Sean nodded, staring into her eyes while still entranced by the provocative swaying of her shapely hips. "I guess I can stand in for your Dad in his absence." He rose from the couch and positioned himself in front of her. The tip of her tongue swept across her lips in anticipation of his embrace.

Sean reached out slowly to take her hand - the sensation of which was felt long before skin touched skin. His other arm reached slowly around her until at last drawing in to wrap about the small of her back. Wendy was startled by the overwhelming sensation of his touch. She inhaled a soft trembling breath as her hips instinctively thrust toward him. She averted her eyes downward, exhaling slowly through pouted lips, hoping he had not noticed her overreaction to his embrace.

As their bodies drew near, she could feel the enticing brush through her sweater as her nipples glided gently across his chest. She felt a sudden flash of warmth and a delightful flow of moisture between her legs. Her face was flush and tingling, and her body delicately quivered. She could feel his strong hand pressed firmly on her lower back. In her mind, the desire to be touched attempted to will his hand lower, begging it to slide downward. She rested her head on his shoulder and closed her eyes, breathing in his scent. Their bodies swayed to the music as the world seemed to revolve beneath them, adding twirl to the dance. His hips pressed hard against hers, and she could feel the swelling of his own arousal.

Wendy's long wavy hair tickled against Sean's cheek; the smell of vanilla filled his senses. He pressed his hand adamantly against her back, drawing her closer. There was no hiding his arousal; he could barely contain himself. He was dizzied by a blend of smells: her hair, her vanilla body spray and the scent of her own oils. He wanted her, and she wanted him. He did not want to complicate their lives, but what if no one found out? After all, it was Jennifer's affair that had driven him into Wendy's arms. He began to pull his head back, and she mimicked his movement. Their cheeks brushed against each other until their eyes met. Each drew in closer to the other until the warmth of their breath blended as one.

Her lips touched his in a soft kiss, parting to invite his tongue inside her mouth to explore. He had forgotten how tenderly she kissed. Her body pressed hard against his, tempting him to pursue her delights. Tempting him. The gravity of the situation nearly buckled Sean's knees as he abruptly pulled away from the kiss. He had heard those words before. The memory of their whisper blew through him like a strong wind through a hollow hall. Wendy appeared shocked and confused.

"Wendy, I can't do this. I'm frustrated as hell with Jennifer, but the truth is... I love her. I always will."

Wendy pulled away from him, returning to the stereo to shut off the music. Then she turned abruptly. "You know, I'm not some evil witch trying to break up a marriage. You asked me out."

"I know. And I'm sorry if I led you to believe that this was something other than friends."

"Friends!" She huffed, "I don't think the bulge in your pants agrees with you."

"I didn't mean for things to go this far. But it's not too late to stop. Whether we like it or not, I'm still married."

"Oh, don't worry, I know my place. Just here to massage your ego, you self-centered prick!"

"Contessa, I'm sorry. I didn't..."

"Didn't what, Sean? Didn't mean to lead me on? Hey, don't feel sorry for me; I knew this would end like this, as soon as it started."

"Then why did you ride it out?"

"Because I had hope; I hoped that this time would be different. But you're still the same juvenile that you've always been. You tease and lead women on for the good of your almighty ego. Perhaps you should take more care of the hearts you take hold of."

Sean fell silent. There was nothing left to say. He had hurt his friend, but he was doing what he knew was right. He had to stop the moment before it escalated into something that they both would regret. Quietly, he turned and headed for the door. The door had barely swung open when he heard her approaching from behind.

"Sean wait," she reached him and wrapped him in a tight embrace. "I didn't mean what I said. I'm not a victim here. We both got caught up in a moment that never should have happened. I don't want to lose your friendship." Her tears released as her voice cracked. "God, I don't want to lose your friendship. You go and save your marriage no matter what it takes. And if you need me," she sobbed, "I'm still your friend."

Sean held her for as long as she needed. All of the years and the memories between them erased away. He knew that they would never be the same again. If he was lucky enough to rekindle his marriage, his guilt would keep him from Wendy. She was a beautiful woman, and most men would give anything to be in his place. But she was never intended for him.

Wendy pulled back from Sean and wiped the tears from her eyes.

"Are you okay?" He asked. "I hate to leave you alone like this."

"Do you have any idea the number of guys that have asked me out this week? Believe me; I won't end up an old maid."

"I do love you, Wendy."

"Please, Sean, don't say that."

Sean lowered his eyes and turned to leave.

"I'll always be here for you," Wendy said at his back, "so don't hesitate to call me."

"I will."

"You promise?"

"I promise." A promise he did not intend to keep.

Chapter 57

It was shortly after 11:30 pm when Arlene arrived at Jennifer's door. Rain had fallen earlier in the evening, and the moisture seemed to prevail in the chilled winds. She turned her back on the damp black sky and stepped onto the porch. Through the window, she could see the heavy blankets that Angelia had described; an eerie and unsettling sight. She knocked lightly at the door before gently trying the doorknob. The door was locked. She knocked more forcefully several times, at last hearing the distant sound of footsteps as they shuffled across the floor inside. The door cracked opened slightly; the streetlights invaded the pitch inside the room, and the smells inside spilled out into Arlene's nostrils. Jennifer's head suddenly slipped through the aperture.

Jennifer gawked at Arlene through blackened eyes and cheekbones etched through tight, emaciated skin that looked inhumanly pale in the surrounding light. "What do you want?" She snapped.

Arlene was taken aback by the snide tone of Jennifer's tongue. "Is everything okay?" She asked sheepishly.

"Why wouldn't it be?" Jennifer asked.

Her voice was sharp. Every blink of her eyes; every subtle movement was twitchy as though the film of Jennifer's life bore imperfections and only a fraction of the images were being projected. A chill shook Arlene's body. She was uncertain if it was from the cold or the atmosphere surrounding her friend. "Well, Angelia was here a little while ago. She was concerned about you. She said that you were sleeping on the kitchen floor."

"And?"

"And that you were acting a little peculiar."

"She said that, did she?"

"I just wanted to make sure that you were okay. Do you mind if I come in for a moment?"

"I was sleeping. And I should be sleeping right now, but I'm answering the door. So quite frankly, you are bothering me."

Arlene's mouth was agape in shock. She was unaccustomed to rash tones coming from the otherwise polite and demure Jennifer. Of all the possible scenarios of this encounter, she had not expected hostility to be one of them.

"Oh, I'm sorry. I didn't mean to bother you," was all that Arlene could manage.

"Of course you didn't," Jennifer commented, then abruptly slammed the door. Arlene's anger toward Sean was now completely drained from her. It was a rare occasion when the feisty woman was driven to tears, but her eyes filled quickly. She was hurt by her sister-in-law's actions; but moreover, she was concerned for Jennifer's mental health. This was not a simple case of depression. The situation had escalated into something bizarre - something dangerous. It was clear that Jennifer had lost all control of her senses. Arlene had to find Sean and convince him that Jennifer was in trouble. He would have to witness this for himself.

Jennifer slammed the front door and turned to come face-to-face with Father Anthony. In the pitch black of her living room his features were barely discernable, but his identity was unmistakable from a distance of mere inches. She could feel no warm breath escape his lips for he was clearly not breathing. He glared at her with a firm and unrelenting gaze; his face was bluish and stoic. Jennifer remained undaunted by his sudden appearance. She cocked her head in defiance.

"Do you have something to say?" She snapped. But within a blink of her eyes the image of Father Anthony had disappeared. "I thought not," she murmured. She spun on her heels and made her way back into the abyss that she had created; the abyss that was once a warm and welcoming home.

Chapter 58

Gail had habitually left the porch light on for Sean when he was out late, but this time a lamp also glowed in the window. He had told her not to wait up for him, perhaps she was preparing the spot lights and polygraph machine for her volley of questions. His spirits had lightened on the drive home. He was proud of himself for resisting the temptation of Wendy. For the first time in weeks, he knew that he had done the right thing. When he entered the house he was greeted by a female seated on the couch, but it was not Gail.

"Arlene, what are you doing here? Is everything okay?"

"No. Everything is not okay, and you need to do something about it."

Sean walked over to the couch and dropped his keys on the coffee table before flopping down next to his sister. "Talk to me," he said.

"It's about Jen. And don't give me any lip this time." Sean stared blankly, awaiting the news. "Angelia stopped by my house with your mail." She motioned to a stack of envelopes on the edge of the coffee table. "Jen frightened the poor girl out of her wits; she was sleeping in the kitchen and then hurt Angelia."

"What?" Sean said, aghast.

"That is what Angelia claimed. I think she may have bruised her ribs. She fell in the kitchen trying to get away from your wife. She said Jen was speaking strangely and when Angelia tried to get out of there, I guess, Jen tried to stop her. Did you know that Jen has all of the windows in the house covered with blankets?" Sean shook his head. "Well, she does. I saw it firsthand tonight. I went over to your house to check on her, but she wouldn't let me in."

"Maybe she had someone inside with her."

"It wasn't like that. I really think she has snapped, Sean. She looks like hell. Her face is so pale and drawn, and her eyes are black and sunk in. She was nasty to me, but not like she was covering up anything. I was clearly annoying her just being there." Arlene paused. "I'm really worried about her."

"The last time I was there, I found a dozen roses on her table from some guy named Nicholas."

Arlene felt as though she had been punched in the gut. "I'm sorry, Sean. I didn't know."

"Well, I'm not sure what's going on, but I am planning on paying her a visit tomorrow."

"Maybe that's why she acted so strange towards me, but it doesn't explain what happened with Angelia." "No, it doesn't. But maybe I can find out..." He lowered his head and fell suddenly silent. He could feel a flood of emotions swelling inside of him. He wanted to release them, but he had learned from a young age to steel his emotions; a lesson he had learned from the absence of his father. Sean was a man long before his body fit the role. He looked up into his sister's eyes. Arlene was patiently waiting for him to continue. She could tell that he needed a moment to compose himself. Something that she fully understood, she too had learned to be strong as a child. "I can't," he paused. "I can't just walk away from her, no matter what. If there is another man involved, then he's going to have one hell of a fight on his hands. I just want to hold her and make all of this pain go away. I want to be in her arms again, then the rest of the world can fall away. I love her; she is all that matters."

"I know things haven't been good between the two of you," Arlene intervened. "But you and Jen belong together. What happened to Arlen took its toll on her, so we have to be there for support. I would do anything for Jen; she's like a sister to me."

"I have to take Gail to a few places tomorrow morning, but as soon as we're finished I'll stop by our house."

"Please let me know how she is. And if there's anything that I can do, call me."

"I will, Sis."

Following a rare embrace and a slight show of emotion, Sean walked Arlene to the door and thanked her for coming to him. He had broken the heart of one woman tonight, but had reacquainted with the heart of another. Arlene had always been Sean's favorite, but tonight they seemed to connect on another level. He knew that he would not be alone in his battle for Jennifer. And that thought brought him solace.

Perspective

Everything we see is a perspective, not the truth.

-Marcus Aurelius

Chapter 59

Sunlight spread across the fields, the farms and the mountains of eastern Pennsylvania. As a new morning arose, life stretched itself and shook free from the sleep that had entranced it. People began to busy their lives with appointments and deadlines, affairs and daycare, the nearly unwavering cycle of society. The acrimonious reassurance that no matter what ills befall any of us, life goes on.

Sean was behind the wheel of Gail's car while Gail rested in the passenger seat, peering out at the passing scenery. They both sipped coffee from individual travel mugs, enjoying the aroma and the silence. Before departing on their errands, the pair had conversed over coffee at the kitchen table. The conversation had focused primarily on Sean's date with Wendy. Gail had questioned Sean extensively, as promised - though not all of his answers were taken at face value.

Their first stop was the Med-Swift Pharmacy to refill a prescription for arthritis medication for Gail. The stop would give Sean a chance to catch up on current events with Dylan, who had been absent from his life since the night of Mincy's party.

Inside the pharmacy, Gail presented her prescription bottle to a middle-aged woman behind the counter while Sean strolled down to the opposite end where Dylan was studying a computer screen.

"Excuse me," Sean said. "Do you have anything for anal warts?"

Dylan looked up from his work. "Hey! What's up, Slugger?"

"Come on. I feel bad about hitting Mincy."

"You shouldn't," Dylan commented bluntly.

"Have you been busy?" Sean asked.

"Are you kidding me? We're at the height of the cold and flu season. Half of the population is taking one form of antibiotic or another. And I can't seem to keep enough cough medicine in stock."

"In other words, you're happy as hell that everyone is sick."

"I'm happy about the sales of tissues and the over-the-counter medications. I just wish that I made more money off of these prescriptions, for as much as they cost me."

Dylan looked around the store and then leaned toward Sean. "By the way, I've been meaning to call you. Jennifer has been in here a couple of times. Did you know that she's on anti-depressants?"

"Good, I think she needed them," Sean responded.

"Yes, but she's acting very strange." Dylan crinkled his brow. "When did she take up smoking?"

The right side of Sean's lips curled into a brief half-smile. "Jen doesn't smoke."

"Well, she made a purchase of nicotine patches."

Sean responded to the news with a bewildered gaze and a shrug of his shoulders.

"That's what I thought. It didn't make much sense to me either. Michelle Kenrick said she was even talking to herself."

"I'm going over to the house to check on her after I drop Gail off at home."

"Hold on a second," Dylan began flipping through a basket of bags with prescriptions in them. "Yeah, here it is. She also has a refill of some sleeping pills to pick up."

"Sleeping pills," Sean remarked in surprise. "Maybe it's worse than I thought. I might as well pick them up for her."

"Okay. Just let me finish refilling Gail's prescription."

Sean wandered back down the aisle to Gail, who was waiting patiently for her pills. He smiled at her and rubbed her back gently. She had been a godsend to him. It was comforting to know that he was always welcome in her home. Dylan came down to the cash register with the prescriptions and rang them in personally. He gave Sean the total amount for both, and Sean handed him a credit card. Gail attempted to protest Sean's generosity, but Sean told her to shush. Dylan slid the credit card through his electronic authorization machine. After a moment, he pressed the clear button and swiped the card again. He then brought the card back to Sean and whispered, "Your card was declined."

"What?" Sean spoke loudly, surrendering his right to privacy. "That has to be a mistake."

"I'm sorry, Sean. I tried to run it through twice, but it was declined both times."

Gail stepped forward with her purse, "What's wrong?" She inquired, pretending not to have overheard, although she had already withdrew her wallet.

"Put your wallet away, Mama Gail. I told you I'm paying for it."

"You do still accept cash here, don't you?" Sean joked, trying to conceal his embarrassment.

"Of course. I wouldn't be too concerned about it. It's probably some computer error." Dylan frowned and shook his head in anti-establishment disgust.

Sean retrieved his change and the pills, thanking Dylan for the service and the information about Jennifer. As they exited the pharmacy, he remembered the stack of mail sitting on the coffee table at Gail's. He knew that it was time for his credit card statement to arrive and there had better be a logical explanation for the problem. He shook off the incident and promised himself to make the best of the day ahead.

Their next and final stop was Bell's Pet Shop where Gail purchased all of her supplies for Sweetheart. She spoiled her parrot as one would a child, so Gail was one of Bell's favorite customers.

Old man Bell was a kindly spirit and a lifetime native of Honey Brook. Bell began his working career as a veterinarian some thirty years before he created Bell's Pet Shop. The store was not intended to be a cash cow, simply a means to escape the boredom of retirement. Bell had a busy life as the only vet in town for his first twenty years in practice. He was an upstanding member of the community, donating his spare time in the summer to organizing the animal show at the annual county fair. Bell would borrow most of the animals from local farmers and often times import exotic specimens from his friends at distant zoos. He would oversee the animal's transportation and care personally, being trusted by all parties involved. But as his body began to deteriorate with age, he established his shop to keep close to the people and the animals of his community.

A loud cow bell clanged as Sean and Gail opened the door and stepped inside. They were greeted by an antique carousel horse whose bright colored paint had worn over time. The wooden horse was a good-luck gift from the county fair for the grand opening of Bell's Pet Shop and had adorned its foyer ever since. The original hardwood floor was still intact, although it showed the wear of its years. It creaked as they walked back between the three aisles to the rusted metal and glass counter toward the rear of the shop. The air was thick with the smells of cedar chips and food pellets with a slight detection of vinegar. Old man Bell was seated behind the counter at a redwood desk that was once the focal point in the office of his practice. He looked up when he heard them approach. His thin lips curled into a smile, and his trademark twinkle danced in his bright blue eyes.

"Well, if it isn't the prettiest feather in the flock. And look at this! She's brought trouble in with her."

Sean smiled, "I haven't snuck in here to release your animals from their pens since I was fourteen years old. Are you still mad at me for that?"

"How could I ever be angry with such an outstanding young gentleman? Besides, liberating animals seems to be a well respected endeavor these days."

"It wasn't for the sake of freedom as much as it was the amusement of anarchy. How are you Dr. Bell?" Sean asked.

"Oh, good as ever - bad as never, I suppose. Did you know I handled all of the animals for every county fair for almost fifty years? Do you believe that?"

"I don't know where you got all of your energy, Doc." Sean commented, aiding the old man's need for recognition.

"Yeah, I'm not that young man anymore. I'm a young old man now." He turned his attention to Gail, "So, what brings the sunshine out today?"

Gail smiled at the elderly man. "Sweetheart needs some of your special blend of seeds."

"Do you want the eats or the treats?"

"Make it both," Gail responded.

Bell rose slowly from his chair, gripping the armrests for leverage. His old body shook as it righted itself onto his feet. He peeled two small brown paper bags from a stack beneath the counter and walked slowly over to a group of plastic bins on the right. Sean stared at him, wondering what the brisk young Alfred Bell must have been like. He had more life in his old bones than Sean had on his best day. In his prime, Bell must have been a force to reckon with. Now his bouncing stride was replaced by a steady shuffling of his feet.

Bell scooped some of the contents of two of the bins into the paper sacks, then shuffled back to place them on the counter.

"So, Sean, how's that new pup behaving for you?"

Sean smiled with a widening of his eyes, excusing away the comment as an old man's failing memory. "I don't have a puppy."

"Well, your misses was in a little while back and bought one from me."

Sean looked puzzled, remembering the small white puppy that was a gift from Jennifer's friend. "Do you remember if she had someone else with her?"

"Nope, she was alone."

"Are you sure it was Jennifer and not some guy?"

"Hells bells, man! These eyes are old and stricken with cataracts, but they can most certainly discern the difference between a man and a woman. She picked out a little white Labrador retriever and paid for it herself by credit card. Although she sure didn't act like herself that day. I remember her paying by credit card because of what I noticed when I balanced my books that evening."

"What?"

"She didn't sign her name. She signed a man's name. Nathan, I think."

"You mean Nicholas?"

"That's it. I was going to call you but now-a-days with this automation you could sign your name as Mickey Mouse and the banks don't care; numbers mean more to these scoundrels than a man's mark!"

"Do you still have a copy of the signed credit card slip?" Sean asked.

"I should. I keep a copy of each week's slips in a separate envelope in one of my desk drawers." Bell shuffled back to his desk and slowly leaned down to rummage through the top desk drawer. The desk appeared to be in absolute disarray; however, his mind's eye viewed it differently; to Bell it appeared to be completely organized. He had fumbled with opening several of the envelopes before announcing his success.

"Here it is." He boasted, holding the slip up in his hand. "She signed it as Nicholas Feragamo. I never thought to look at it when she handed it back to me. Seeing as it was Jennifer and all. I trust you folks. You're both good people."

"Do you think I could get a copy of that from you?" Sean requested.

"Well, I ain't got no copying machine around here."

"Would you mind if I borrowed the original? I would be willing to leave my credit card with you for collateral."

Bell's wrinkled old face stretched into a broad smile. "Now that's being real trustworthy. Hey, Sunshine," he called to Gail. "How about you and I go on a wild rendezvous? I just acquired me a credit card."

Gail smiled, although she was preoccupied with Jennifer's bizarre actions.

Bell handed over the receipt, but he refused to take Sean's credit card. "I trust you," he said.

Sean examined the slip and recognized his wife's penmanship. "I can't thank you enough for this."

"I hope I didn't start no trouble between you and the misses. Her mind was probably elsewhere when she signed it; happens to me all the time lately."

"No, you didn't start any trouble. On the contrary, you may have solved a dispute."

"Well, that I'm glad to hear then."

Gail paid for her seed and gathered her bags. As they walked out of the store, Bell hollered his goodbye, "Even if it's not worth your while, it's at least worth your smile! You folks have a fine day!"

Chapter 60

Jennifer's face bore a catatonic expression as she sat slumped in her reclining chair. She had been frozen in the chair for nearly seven hours, struggling to regain focus. Her mind was a tangle of broken thoughts, and her eyes stung to a squint from lack of sleep. She had a brief period of restless slumber, the results of which left her dazed and confused. A phantom residue seemed to have remained behind following her dream. Carol was clinging to her like an annoying song stuck in her head, unwilling to let go. She could feel the other identity attempting to gain cognizance as it fought to orient itself in a new realm. Jennifer battled to maintain control of her thoughts. She could scarcely feel the rest of her body. Not due to numbness, but due to insignificance. Her mind was all that remained with the tug-of-war that raged inside.

It was late morning by the time Sean arrived at the place he once called home. The desire for his wife had grown into concern as the pieces of a twisted puzzle began to fall into place. He grabbed Jennifer's pill bottle and an envelope from the passenger seat before heading to the front porch. As he stepped toward the door, he never considered knocking.

He stepped inside a dreary version of his living room where he finally became a witness to the stories he had heard. A foul odor hung in the chilled air, the kind that seems to stick to your skin. His eyes traversed the room as they surveyed the surroundings. Heavy blankets were tacked haphazardly to the window panes blocking all but the light that seeped in through the fabric. On the floor, fine white hairs covered the hunter green carpet. A few unwashed dishes sat on the end tables, one a coffee cup with mold forming within. His eyes fixed upon the reclining chair, which was faced away from his view. Female arms were slung out over the armrests, hanging limply to each side of the chair. Sean walked slowly around to the front, staring at the person resting in the cushions. A thin female body dressed in a sheer night shirt and panties. The hip bones protruding far out beyond the stomach pouch. The arms looked frail with the elbows unusually pronounced. The face was all but covered by a thick mane of knotted red hair. As he moved around to face her, she raised her chin from the nestling of her chest. Her eyes were dark and sullen as they peered up at him.

"What do you want now?" The woman spat defiantly.

"Christ, Jennifer, you look sick."

"Rough night," she murmured as she slowly rose to her feet and walked across the room, away from him. "You know you shouldn't just barge in here. This is not your house anymore. We don't need you here."

"What do you mean, we?"

The hard glare cast over her shoulder took a defensive posture to his question. She slid properly into a chair at the dining table. "What are those?" She nodded toward the bottle of pills in his hand.

"I stopped at the pharmacy this morning and they told me that you had a prescription there, so I thought that I would bring it by."

"That was thoughtful of you." She spoke in a monotonous voice. "You can just put it on the table." She waved her hand like a princess directing a loyal subject.

Sean walked forward and placed the bottle on the table, never unlocking his gaze from her. He quietly stood in front of her, searching for something to say.

Jennifer tilted her head with a smirk. "Is that it?"

"I spoke to Dr. Bell this morning. He was wondering how the puppy Nicholas bought for you was working out."

"That was so nice of him to ask. Casper the spook is fine"

"Look Jennifer, I'm worried about you." There appeared to be no other way of approaching the conversation, except bluntness. "Dr. Bell gave me a copy of the credit card slip." Sean walked around the table and placed the slip on the table in front of her.

Jennifer examined it momentarily. "And?"

"It's signed Nicholas Feragamo."

"So?" She looked up, blinking her eyes in dramatic fashion

"Jennifer, that is your handwriting. And the credit card number matches ours."

She threw her head back in riotous laughter. "You are pathetic. You just can't handle the thought of another man's interest in me."

Sean pulled a folded paper from an envelope and spread it out in front of her. "Do you know what this is? This is our credit card statement. Look at the purchases, Jennifer. Read the entries; Bell's Pet Shop, A Touch of Class Florists," Sean read down through the list, "Miosi's Jewelers, Desiderio's restaurant."

She stared down at the statement and then slowly lifted her head in a defiant stare. "Wow, you've been spending a fortune." Her voice was smooth and her face a totem of expression. "Buying stuff for your precious friend Wendy, I'll bet."

Sean ignored her comment. "There is no Nicholas Feragamo. You are buying this stuff for yourself."

"You think you have it all figured out, don't you. You have no idea. No idea how close I am."

"Close to what, being institutionalized?"

"Get the fuck out of my home." Her words wisped through clinched teeth.

"Lass, please. I'm worried about you. You need help."

"You are playing in something that you have no clue about." She rose to her feet. "I am this close." She shoved her hand in his face with her index finger and thumb sampling the distance, "to succeeding where you failed me. And now you want to step in here and fuck it all up!"

Sean stepped back from her approach, "Look, you can either go willingly now or..."

"No. I think you're going to go willingly now; out of my house. And next time you decide to come barging in here," she paused with a deep cleansing breath and a smile, "kindly wipe your feet. I adhere to strict cleaning standards."

Sean retreated to the front door in exasperation. He decided that a battle between the two of them was futile. He had no experience with mental illness, but he knew someone who had. He turned to look at her once more. "I will be coming back, but I won't be alone."

"Bring 'em. Bring all your little friends. We'll all have a party."

Sean released a deep sigh, and his eyes filled with tears until they spilled over onto his cheeks. "I love you, Lass."

Jennifer fell silent. Deep within the twisted remains of her consciousness the sight of Sean's tears turned back memories. She had only seen him cry on two other occasions; once for the loss of his grandfather and once for the loss of Arlen. The old Jennifer longed to reach out for him, but she couldn't gain control of her arm. Instead, she stood by solemnly as he closed the door behind him. She turned her attention to the pill bottle that rested on the table. She would have to risk the dream dampening effects of the Trazadone to get back into the dream world. She had to find Nicholas. She had questions that would behoove him to answer. And this time, he had better produce Arlen to appease her.

Sean stepped down from the porch and withdrew his cell phone. He dialed his father-in-law's number as he walked back to his truck. After five rings and a moment of hopeless desperation, Donald's voice sounded on the other end. *"I'm sorry I can't come to the phone right now. Please leave a message after the tone."*

Sean left a message requesting a return call to his cell phone and then ended the call. He sat in his truck for a few brief moments. His hands shook uncontrollably, and tears blurred the vision of his home. He pressed back into his seat and wiped his eyes. He had to remain calm. This was no time to lose himself in emotions. But his nerves refused to cooperate. He desperately wanted a drink; something to take the edge off. He decided to make a stop at McKinney's Pub while he waited to hear from Donald.

Chapter 61

The volume on the television above the bar was barely audible, and the occasional clink of glass muffled what remained. No matter. Sean had little interest in what he was unable to hear. Nor was he interested in the images as they flashed across the screen. Fortunately, the other two patrons at McKinney's never attempted conversation with Sean. One sat quietly sipping a beer three stools down. The other, a middle-aged man in a bright silk shirt, was pressing for a conversation with the attractive barmaid about a topic she showed little interest in.

Sean had been so distracted since leaving Jennifer in her deteriorated state that he had no recollection of the drive to the pub. He had ordered a beer upon his arrival and thus far had only managed a single sip from the mug. One would assume that he was enthralled with the television program of which he stared, but his thoughts were miles away. The sound of the door pulled him momentarily from his trance. A figure walked behind him to the far end of the bar. Nevin Mincemoyer sat down next to the silk shirt guy who was attempting to converse with the barmaid. Mincy's presence caused the man to bid a temporary retreat to one of the tables.

Sean caught Mincy's gaze from the corner of his eye. The gaze was not one of fear or anger, but more pouting in nature. Sean sighed. He was in no mood for Mincy at the moment; no one was ever in the mood to deal with Nevin Mincemoyer, but he needed to call a truce. He owed Mincy a peace offering.

With the concession that he would only have to tolerate him for one drink, Sean motioned for Mincy to join him. Mincy slowly sulked down to Sean.

"Have a seat, Mincy," Sean ordered. The pouting Mincy obliged. "I just wanted to apologize for my actions at your birthday party," Sean continued. "I didn't mean to come at you like I did. I've had a lot on my mind."

Mincy displayed a yellow-toothed smile. "That's okay Buddy. I knew you didn't mean it."

"I'll feel better if you let me buy you a drink."

"Well, if that's what it takes," Mincy rubbed his palms together, "okay."

Sean motioned for the barmaid, who had been pounced upon once again by Silk Shirt Guy. She was happy to come to Sean's end of the bar. Sean ordered Mincy a mug of beer. Mincy grabbed the handle and motioned toward Sean, "No hard feelings." And within one swallow the mug was half empty. Sean returned his stare to the television, trying to plot his next encounter with Jennifer.

He lifted his mug to his lips when a soft whispering voice sounded in his ear. It took a few seconds before the apparent words registered in his mind, "Daddy, don't drink." *Please tell me I'm not hearing voices. Why does this keep happening to me?* He glanced quickly at Mincy, then down the length of the bar. Mincy was busy staring off in the distance at the attractive barmaid. Sean was desperate to rationalize what he had just heard.

"What did you say to me?" He questioned Mincy.

Mincy was immediately panic-stricken. The last ounce of color emptied quickly from his face. "Jesus, not again," Mincy pleaded. "Sean, I swear to God I didn't say anything this time!"

Sean shook off the comment, blinking his eyes in confusion. "No Mincy, it's okay. I just thought I heard you say something. Don't worry about it. Go ahead and finish your beer."

Mincy eyed him suspiciously.

"Seriously," Sean commented, lifting his own mug to demonstrate a truce. "Everything is alright."

Mincy kept a weary eye on Sean as they both lifted their mugs to their lips. But before the mug reached his mouth, Mincy abruptly stopped. He slowly replaced the mug onto the bar, glaring at it, as if it were filled with some rancorous witches' brew. Sean's mug had also stopped short of its target and was placed back onto the bar. Sean turned to Mincy, "Aren't you going to finish your beer?"

Mincy seemed stunned by the question. He stammered to produce an answer, "No. I guess it's just too early to drink beer."

Sean glanced back at his own mug, now realizing he had also failed to drink. Mincy rose quietly from his seat and headed toward the door. Sean turned on his barstool to watch in wonder as Mincy exited the pub. Before his mind could prepare a reaction to what he had just witnessed, his cell phone alerted him to an incoming call. Donald's name and number appeared on the digital screen. Sean threw a few dollars onto the bar and hastened outside to answer.

"Hello Dad. I'm glad you called." Sean spoke while he made his way toward his truck. "I'm worried about Jennifer. She is doing some pretty bizarre things. I was wondering if you were free today."

"Sure," Donald responded.

"I'll fill you in on all of the details when I arrive." Sean turned off his phone and climbed behind the wheel of his vehicle. Perhaps Jennifer's father would have some answers about some of her peculiar behavior. The truck jumped into gear and sped away from the pub.

Chapter 62

The darkness of Jennifer's surroundings seemed to close in on her, pressing against her skin like damp linen. She stood in front of the same bonfire where Nicholas had threatened to strangle the very life from her body. The fire burned low. The orange flames crackled, popping an occasional spark into the air. A dark figure was approaching from the distance. Her fear rose quickly, choking off any ability for rational thought. Her muscles knotted, preparing to flee. As the figure stepped into the light, she could see the white of the collar beneath the black suit. And the face that smiled above was Nicholas. A face not decayed and hideous as before, but more handsome than she had ever remembered. He ceased his approach to stand at arm's reach in front of her.

"I am so happy to see you again," he confessed. "I realize things have been confusing. I assure you that I can explain everything that you have witnessed. I am sorry that my uncle has tormented you so. But I promise he won't bother you again."

"I see that you have come dressed as a priest this time." Jennifer commented.

"I never meant to mislead you. Yes, in my lifetime I was a priest. But I was also a man. And from the moment that I saw you, that man wanted to be free. Free to love and enjoy all of the pleasures with which God has gifted you. I have witnessed much of the world. But no sight has ever moved me more than the sight of you. You are God's work at its finest."

"You're not real, Nicholas."

"Don't say that."

"I made you up to help me cope with the loss of my son."

"No. You're wrong. I came to help pull you from the depression that threatened your life. I can provide you with solace and salvation. A salvation found only in the arms of a man who truly loves you."

"Is that why I purchased all of those wonderful gifts for myself? Is that why I took myself to a fancy restaurant?"

"I am in no condition to simply walk into a store and make a purchase," Nicholas spread his arms from his body. "I am a ghost, remember; one that can only exist in the world within your dreams. I cannot manipulate objects in the material world. I needed you to do that for me. I guided you to those items. I meant those gifts most sincerely."

"No, Nicholas. You are my imagination at its best; at its most bizarre." Jennifer studied his features. "I must admit; my work is rather impressive. You are a gorgeous creation. A painting perhaps that I could never otherwise put on canvas; but not real."

"If you shun me now, I can no longer help you. And you will never know the truth about Arlen."

"What do you know about my son?"

"I know the cause and effect that stole your son's life. I tried to warn you, but you failed to listen to me."

"I don't know what you're talking about."

"Do you remember your nightmare? The one that took place inside the store where you work; the dream during which you first laid eyes on me?"

"Yes. But I still don't understand."

"I didn't want to be the one to tell you this, but you caused your son's death."

"That's a lie! I wasn't even home. He was with Sean."

"You sinned against your son, Jennifer. It was your greed that took you away from him that day."

"That's a stretch."

"I guess dying comes in somewhere beneath the importance of work for you."

"Go to hell."

"Your son died because of your neglect, because you were too lethargic to stop it. And the answer was right in front of you that morning."

Jennifer eyed Nicholas with suspicion.

"But don't take my word for it. Why don't you see for yourself?"

Jennifer was blinded by a brilliant flash of white as she tried desperately to shield her eyes. She lowered her hands slowly, blinking in an attempt to refocus. Her sight cleared peripherally, working toward the center of her vision until at last she found herself standing in the hallway outside of her bathroom. She could hear the distant sound of voices coming from the kitchen on the first floor. The smell of coffee and french toast sweetened the air. She recognized Arlen's voice and turned to advance toward the staircase, but a sudden jolt thrust her body forward. She could feel something pressing in on her from behind; pushing right through her. Her body recoiled as the object moved out through her chest and into the bathroom. She could now see that it was a healthier and more robust version of herself. The robust Jennifer was dressed in a silky midnight blue gown as she stared at herself in the bathroom mirror, admiring the body that she worked so hard to maintain. She then became enamored by the sight of a copper-colored glass sphere that rested on the edge of the sink. The weight of which depressed the towel on which it rested. Robust Jennifer then wrapped herself in a robe and moved toward the door. Before she could step out of the way of herself, the robust Jennifer was once again moving through her body. The experience was nearly painful. Pulling back through her until it felt as though her spine would be pulled from her back, and then abruptly another brilliant flash of white.

As her eyes cleared, she found herself once again standing in her hallway facing the entrance to her bathroom. This time her eyes focused on something that she had not expected. Arlen was seated in the bathtub, playing with his action figures.

"Oh, my baby," Jennifer managed, as she stepped gingerly inside the bathroom to stand within the door frame. Tears streamed from Jennifer's eyes as she had finally achieved her goal. She had been reunited with her son. She stared at the angelic face that had provided her world with such warmth and happiness. Tiny droplets of water hung from his long eyelashes, making his eyes appear an even brighter shade of blue. His round, jovial face concentrated on the figures as he submerged them under the bathwater. His tiny body once again glowed with the life that she held so precious.

He abruptly lifted his head and stared directly at her. She stepped back, stunned by his sudden awareness. She stammered. "Arlen?" He sat poised for a moment in silence, as he gazed at her, through her.

"Dad?" Arlen called out. He raised one of his action figures to his sight, staring at it momentarily. "I bet you're a seraph," he whispered.

Jennifer began to turn to view the surroundings behind her when, once again, her body was jolted forward as something passed through her.

This one felt different. It was painful and yet joyous at the same time. Her mind could only equate it to the feeling of giving birth to her son. As the object moved out of her, she could see that it was Sean. He towered over Arlen, standing in exasperation with his hands on his hips.

"Stooge, have you washed up yet?" Sean barked.

"I washed my hair," the tiny boy responded.

"Well, come on Arlen. We're running out of time." Sean grumbled. "We have to get to your dentist appointment. We can't be late."

"Sorry," Arlen said quietly.

"What have you been doing all of this time?" Jennifer could see the anger on Sean's face.

"I don't know," Arlen said.

"I hate it when you screw around like this. Where's the soap?" Sean snapped at the child as he stepped toward the tub. His feet suddenly slipped out from under him, sending him crashing to the floor. Sean's face became intensified with fury. His body trembled as he growled in pain, grasping at his knee. "How many times have I told you about getting water all over the floor?"

"Don't you hurt him, you son-of-a-bitch," Jennifer snapped as she swung her hand to slap Sean upon the back. Her hand passed through Sean, disappearing until her follow-through brought it away from his body. The ring of the doorbell halted both of their actions.

"Wash up quickly," Sean snapped. "I want to get out of here in fifteen minutes. I have to go downstairs and see who's at the door."

Sean stood and spun on his heels, passing through Jennifer once again; a sensation to which she was nearly growing accustomed. She watched as Sean disappeared down the staircase behind her, then she returned to Arlen as he sat in the tub staring at the action figure of Queen Amidala.

"I love you, Mommy." He gently whispered as he placed his lips upon the figure in a kiss.

Jennifer sobbed, "Mommy loves you too, Baby."

Arlen washed his upper body, never bothering to clean anything below his waist. It was a typical unaided Arlen bath. He reached behind him and haphazardly gripped the towel that rested on the edge of the sink. Time slowed to a crawl as Jennifer's gaze moved to the towel, watching as the heavy glass ball shifted on top. "Baby, No!" She attempted to shout, but her words drifted from her lips in a hollow echo.

Arlen yanked at the towel and the sphere sprung free from its nesting, flinging through the air. It hung in space like the bubbles within its own glass, spinning; descending. Jennifer watched in hopeless disbelief as the air pockets within the sphere spun within its confines. The sphere dropped down toward the tub with malice intent, finding its mark on the back of Arlen's head. His head bolted forward by the force of the blow as the sphere ricocheted off, flying from the area surrounding the tub to quietly bounce again on a throw rug on the floor. Aided by the pitch of the old floor, the sphere rolled between Jennifer's legs. Jennifer turned her head in time to see it disappear through the slightly opened door of the linen closet on the other side of the hallway. She turned her head back to the sight of Arlen, face down in the water. She reached out to pull him free when the brilliant flash of white light blinded her vision.

She awoke on the floor of her hallway. Tears stained her cheeks as she lifted herself onto her elbows. She could now feel the weight of gravity as it held her frail body to the floor. It was only a nightmare; a painful twist of her unconscious imagination. She pulled herself up on her knees and stared into the bathroom. The tub was empty. She turned her head toward the linen closet to see that the door was firmly shut. She released a long sigh. Her imagination had pulled a horrid trick on her, yet she had to erase any lingering doubt. She reached up slowly and turned the knob on the closet door. The door sprung free and obediently swung open to her gentle tug. The interior of the linen closet had three shelves; the bottom two were stacked with towels and wash clothes while the top shelf supported the weight of various cleaning products. A large wicker laundry basket had been tucked under the bottom shelf.

Jennifer reached in slowly and pushed the basket to the side to see the wall behind it. Her heart thumped, and her blood chilled as her gaze fell upon the copper sphere which was lodged in the corner at the back of the closet. With one shaking hand, she reached out and lifted the sphere from its resting place. She raised it to her eyes searching the circumference. Her eyes stopped when she saw a few matted hairs stuck to the sphere by a nickel-sized smear of a dark substance. Jennifer swallowed hard and tried to stand, but the wobble of her legs wouldn't allow it. Her stomach turned with anguish and anger. Her mind could not lock itself onto any thought as a flood of activity shook the foundation of her sanity.

The vision was real, and the scathing words that Nicholas spoke rang true. Her failure to retrieve the sphere when she saw it had brought about a deadly result. Her son was gone, and the very thing which tore him from this life now rested on the tips of her fingers; the sphere with which she had allowed him to play, the sphere that was not a toy. Not a ball with a rubber core, but a solid chunk of copper-colored glass as large as her fist.

Jennifer's confusion turned to rage as she spun on her knees and hurled the object at the bathroom mirror. The sphere struck the mirror, shattering it into hundreds of glass shards. The sphere bounced back, unscathed, while broken pieces of mirror sprayed out from the sink and sprinkled the floor in front of it. Jennifer's hands reached for her head, each gripping a fist-full of her knotted hair. Her forehead dropped to rest on her knees as she released a violent scream. The scream turned to a deep-throated growl then finally into wrenching sobs.

She had found her answer to the lingering doubt surrounding the events of Arlen's death. The gut feeling that had been gnawing at her insides for months had come into focus amidst an eerie light. Sean had been pulled away from Arlen that morning by circumstance, but she had been overly passive to an unforeseen danger that ultimately took her son's life. And that brought a pain that rushed through her blood and jabbed at her from every point.

She dropped to her stomach and crawled into the bathroom, picking up the largest shard of mirror glass from the floor. Her grip caused her palm to be sliced, something that she should have felt, but did not. Her blood squeezed through her fingers as she moved her hand to her other arm and placed the sharp edge of glass to her wrist.

She swallowed hard. She could no longer live with the pain that burned so hollow in her soul. The months of desperation and loneliness had taken a grave toll. She was frightened, but longed for release. In the back of her mind a memory flashed. A distant memory faded by many years that separated it from her consciousness; faded by a shroud that her mind had pulled over the incident to protect her from the pain; vision of blood that flowed from a wrist and stained the sheets beneath it. Perhaps she had done this before, but her mind had blocked out the memory. A flood of emotions roared through her. Her hand shook as it pushed the shard down until it depressed the skin beneath. A small trickle of blood ran down her arm as she struggled with herself to finish the cut.

"No," Carol's voice reverberated in her mind like the memory of a past conversation. The sound of the voice never reached Jennifer's ears. "This is not the answer." Carol moved inside of Jennifer's mind to take control of her arm. The tug-of-war between life and death raged for what seemed an eternity, until at last fear decided the outcome. Jennifer dropped the shard of glass and pulled herself to her feet. She staggered into her bedroom and fell onto the bed. The room about her appeared to be spinning, and darkness descended upon her. She fought against the encroachment until she wondered why she was fighting at all. After what she had just discovered, unconsciousness would be a pleasant relief.

Chapter 63

Sean's only memories of Jennifer's mother were derived from two occasions; once as a young teen, he and his friends were meandering through the neighborhood when a few of the boys chanced to walk through the Langdon's front lawn. Sue Ellen had burst forth from the house to berate them for what she called trespassing. Sean and his friends were more amused than terrorized as they trotted away down the street in laughter.

The second occasion was on his wedding day. Sue Ellen was in attendance for the ceremony, but she appeared sedated and oblivious to the festivities. She was not placed in the receiving line; instead, she was escorted out by a caretaker as the line was being formed. Sean had stopped her and placed a kiss on her cheek, but she never spoke nor acknowledged his existence. Jennifer, on the other hand, had made every attempt to avoid her mother throughout the ceremony.

Sean knew very little about the woman's condition. Only that she revolved in a system of state mental hospitals and personal care homes known as Community Residential Rehabilitation homes or CRRs. Sean had attempted to discuss Sue Ellen's condition in casual conversation with Jennifer; however, she had always skirted the subject. He eventually dismissed it entirely as private family business. But the current situation warranted further pursuit of the issue. He had to investigate the possibility of Jennifer's actions as being some form of hereditary mental illness. He was uncertain if heredity was a contributing factor, but it was a place to start.

He arrived at his father-in-law's home while the afternoon sun fought to penetrate a heavy layer of rain clouds that had moved into the area.

Donald ruefully listened as Sean laid out some of the events surrounding Jennifer's peculiar behavior of the past few weeks. Sean was fully aware that Jennifer was a vital part of Donald's life, a fact that led Sean to withhold the most disturbing details of her condition. If Don became aware of Jennifer's imaginary romance and the lavish gifts she had bestowed upon herself, he would panic. A decision he would later regret. He only disclosed that she was not eating and was prone to fits of temper.

Sean thought he noticed a glimmer of guilt in Donald's eyes. Donald must have recognized Jennifer's symptoms also, but he failed to act accordingly. Perhaps Donald was praying that his suspicions were incorrect, silently hopeful that he would not have to endure losing another loved one to a disorder which delineated the inflicted from familiar faces.

Following his explanation, Sean revealed the impetus of his visit. "Through all of these years, I have never been exactly clear regarding your wife's condition. I'd like to get as much information as possible."

"Sue Ellen's psychiatrist, Dr. Heggenstaller, and I have become acquaintances," Donald said, "I could call him and request a meeting. I'm not certain if he works on Saturday, but I do have his home telephone number. I would like to get his opinion on Jennifer's behavior myself."

"That is exactly what I was hoping."

Donald's phone conversation was brief. Dr. Heggenstaller was to meet with them in one hour at his office in the staff development center at the state mental health hospital. Sean insisted on driving to keep his attention from the concern that loomed ever-ominous in his mind. Donald conceded the comfort of his Lexus to ride as a passenger in Sean's truck despite the thirty-mile drive.

Jennifer faded in and out of sleep so often that she was no longer certain when she was experiencing either state of consciousness, even while on her feet. Her mind worked in broken lines of thought, with blackouts in between. Carol's incessant humming was a constant reminder that the teen was still trapped within Jennifer's mind. Her presence was growing ever stronger. Her humming was not audible, yet it echoed unrelentingly through Jennifer's mind, and it was beginning to grate her nerves. The hum was soft and soothing to Jennifer at first, but now she wished that Carol would grow tired and sleep. Perhaps she could think clearer if the teen were unconscious. Their catatonic stare spread out across the front lawn and down the street as they gazed from Jennifer's bedroom window.

Jennifer contemplated jumping through the window and smashing Carol's skull upon the pavement below, but Carol refused to let her budge.

"Jennifer?" A voice came from the rear. Nicholas stood behind her in the bedroom. Carol crouched in a corner of Jennifer's mind with her hands covering her face, releasing any control that she had over the motion of Jennifer's body. Jennifer could sense that the girl was frightened. Carol was hiding from Nicholas.

Jennifer's muscles relaxed as she was no longer fighting to maintain control. She turned her body with ease now and faced the man who had been tormenting her dreams. But this time he was standing in her bedroom.

"I didn't want to hurt you," he said. "I only wished you to know the truth. I want us to trust each other, hide no secrets."

Jennifer sensed a sudden fearful glare from Carol, *"Don't tell him about me."* The words expressed in thought.

"Jennifer, I can ease your pain if you will only give me the chance." Nicholas extended his hand to her.

"What do you want from me?" Jennifer managed.

"I want you to join me; to join us. We can be a family; you, me and our son. We can all be together for eternity."

Tears swelled in Jennifer's eyes. "I don't know how to do that."

"The sleeping pills on your table," Nicholas responded. "If you take enough of them, you can dream forever."

"I'm scared, Nicholas."

"Don't be scared. I'll stay right here with you. I'm never going to leave you alone again. I'm not like the people in your world. I won't ever leave you and neither will your son."

"I want my baby," she cried.

"You can have him. He's waiting for us even as we speak."

"No, don't do it," Carol's words came to Jennifer in a panicked whisper, *"You mustn't; we'll be trapped again!"*

"I'm afraid to die," Jennifer uttered.

"I'm not speaking of death," Nicholas responded, "I'm speaking of eternal life. Go downstairs and get the pills; I'll wait here for you. I'll prepare a note for your father. We can tell him that you left to be with me and that he should punish Sean for it."

Jennifer walked from the bedroom. Carol thrashed about in terror, but she was too afraid to attempt to take control. She had been under the restraint of Nicholas long enough to know his capabilities. She flashed images at Jennifer of the life that they were about to step into, but Jennifer was no longer heeding her.

The Pennsylvania State Mental Health Hospital was located on nearly 300 acres of land. A private road off of a four-lane highway led up through a wrought-iron gate entrance. The gate remained open under normal circumstances. Once inside the complex, the road forked with signs directing the traffic to the desired sections. The road to the north was used for admission and administration while the road to the south was used for maintenance and access to the facility's power plant. The Staff Development Center was located on the far northern fringes of the hospital.

Sean steered the truck into the visitation parking area. The sight of the main building made Sean's skin crawl, but he knew not to voice his opinion to Donald. The old building was worn and weather-beaten. Tan painted stucco walls bore several color variations where sections had peeled or chipped, but Sean decided it was the windows that gave the structure its creepy appearance. Tall, thin, arched windows were paired along the walls with a lintel of brick curving up above each arch. The lining of brick gave the appearance of an eyebrow above each window, and each pair of windows appeared as a set of eyes peering out over the free and roaming countryside from the small and twisted world within their walls.

A sidewalk guided them along the building and into a brief open field where the Staff Center was located. They saw several patients along the way who had earned a pass to roam the grounds. The presence of the patients made Sean uneasy as he kept his eyes fixed on the building ahead while Donald acknowledged each with a nod or "hello."

The Staff Center was a modern structure of red brick that had been built within the past few decades. A small, unassuming man stood at the entrance cupping a lit cigarette in his hand. He took a deep drag as he eyed their approach.

"That's Dr. Heggenstaller," Donald informed Sean.

Heggenstaller was a meager, loutish man in his mid-thirties. His long, black, curly hair was tossed chaotically about his head, and his face bore a full beard that was in desperate need of trimming. His persona was more patient than doctor. His head slouched forward so that he had to crook his neck to simply see what was in front of him.

"Good afternoon, Donald," he spoke after another drag on the cigarette.

Copper Dragons

"Thanks for meeting with us on such short notice," Donald responded.

"Not a problem. I'm on call 24-7, whenever I'm needed. I get bored sitting around the house."

"Trevor , this is my son-in-law, Sean Bergin," Donald announced.

"Pleasure," Heggenstaller smiled and shook Sean's hand. The shake was limp. Sean would have preferred one of Junior's vice-grip handshakes. In Sean's culture, a limp handshake was a sign of weakness or insincerity.

"C' mon into the office; I have Sue Ellen's file pulled." Heggenstaller led the two men inside and down a zig-zagging hallway with rows of office doors. Picture frames were hung between the doors, each with a historic photo of the hospital. One photo caught Sean's eye. The black and white image of the area which led to the Staff Center had been taken over one-hundred-years ago. The image appeared more black than white. A full moon glowed just above the main building, while women dressed in the long, white gowns of the period strode through the courtyard. The brilliance of the white dresses against the surrounding darkness gave them an iridescence that made the women appear like ghosts as they wandered about the grounds. The photo only added to the uneasiness that had blanketed Sean since he and his father-in-law arrived.

Sean's pace slowed as he became mesmerized by the image. Suddenly he found himself alone in the hallway. His walk turned into a trot as he moved back and forth across the hall, trying each door. All were locked. An unusual wave of panic flooded him. His normally smooth demeanor changed to the look of a lost child, clumsily searching for his mother. He was quickly running out of hallway and doors to test when a voice called to him from behind. Donald had his head poked out of one of the offices, calling to him. Sean's face reddened as he meandered back down the hallway to where Donald now held the door open for him. He averted his gaze from his father-in-law as he slipped into the room, hoping that Donald would not notice his embarrassment.

The interior of the office was not what he would have expected. Judging by Heggenstaller's unkempt appearance, Sean was expecting to see total disorganization. To the contrary, the desk was clear of any stray papers or books. A few 5x7 picture frames, a name plate, a double pen holder and a large inner-department envelope were the only items on the desk. Long rows of neatly arranged books lined the shelves of a bookcase against the far wall. The office was complete with a television and video player on a portable metal stand. The AV stand reminded Sean of the ones he had seen in high school. The sight of them in the front of a classroom always made him happy. A film in a class meant no notes or quizzes.

Dr. Heggenstaller offered them seats, and then he sat down behind the desk. He carefully unwound the string on the clasp of the envelope and pulled out the contents.

Donald rested his elbows on the desk and leaned in toward Heggenstaller. "We are having some problems with my daughter, Jennifer."

"Oh, I'm sorry to hear that." Heggenstaller responded.

"Sean felt that it would be helpful if he fully understood the circumstances of Sue Ellen's disorder."

"I'm not sure it will help, but I can most certainly provide you with Sue Ellen's case history."

"She was difficult to live with, but I never wanted her institutionalized," Donald interrupted. "It wasn't until Sue Ellen's suicide attempt..."

Sean creased his brow. "Sue Ellen attempted suicide? Jennifer never told me."

"Honestly, I'm not surprised. Jennifer was the one who found Sue Ellen. Jennifer was only eleven at the time. She came home from school one day and found her mother on our bed. Sue Ellen had used a razor to slit her wrists. That was when we brought Sue Ellen here. The staff psychiatrist of the hospital at the time also provided some sessions for Jennifer as well. After the sessions, Jennifer refused to talk about the incident even to me. In time, I just let her bury it." Donald paused with a contrite look poised on his face. "When it came to my little girl, I was never one to push things, even when I should." Don nodded toward Dr. Heggenstaller.

With the nod, Heggenstaller began his presentation. "Sue Ellen was admitted in 1986 under the care of Dr. Wesley Kieser. Dr. Kieser was well respected among his peers and had a high success rate in the hospital.

Sue Ellen was highly depressed and seemed to be suffering from episodic memory loss. She was unresponsive to drug therapy, and her condition deteriorated in the first month of her stay. She began to demonstrate the traits of a multiple." He paused, looking up at Sean. "Multiple Personality Disorder. MPD was typically attributed to some form of physical or sexual abuse from childhood, although no evidence emerged during her therapy. However, there did appear to be evidence of a childhood trauma.

Dr. Kieser noted that she appeared to have three individual personalities including her own. But MPD is very controversial now. During the time when Sue Ellen was first admitted, there was a proverbial witch hunt for 'multiples.' Several books and movies had been produced on the subject, and some therapists began routine examinations that included searching for signs of MPD on all patients, neurotic or psychotic. In an overwhelming number of cases, the therapists were the ones who actually named the personalities. It was almost like the disorder was manufactured by the therapists and then forced on the patients.

Because of this, a second witch hunt began with the State Mental Health System carefully reviewing any case of MPD in their hospitals and weeding out the therapists who acknowledged their existence. The condition had become one of such controversy that the Health System wanted to distance itself from those who believed that the condition actually existed at all. Dr. Kieser and the hospital parted ways in 1995, stating professional differences.

When I arrived to take over Dr. Kieser's patients, Sue Ellen was displaying what appeared to be severe symptoms of the disorder as a new and individual personality manifested itself daily. She displayed hundreds of personalities without repetition, except for a single male persona that Dr. Kieser had referred to as 'The Conduit' in his notes. I have been attempting to treat her underlying problems without focusing on the personalities that she displays. We don't wish to acknowledge them in fear of providing those delusions with any validation, thus perpetuating her disorder. I discovered an interesting video of one of her early sessions. Donald, this is the tape I spoke to you about. I guess we can all watch it together."

"That's fine." Donald answered.

"It shows Sue Ellen speaking in a child-like voice. She is claiming to be five years old. Well, I think the video speaks for itself. Let's take a look. I'll answer any questions when it's finished. It's approximately ten minutes in length. But it explains a section of Dr. Kieser's notes when he attempted to gain access to an old police file. The sound quality is a little low so I'll turn up the volume."

The image was shot from above. Two people were seated across from each other with the camera angle directed toward Sue Ellen. Dr. Kieser sat across from her, but he was only visible below the waist. Sue Ellen was wrapped in the solitude of her own arms with her knees drawn up to her chest. She was clutching a sheet of paper and a crayon in her hand.

"Who are you?" Kieser asked.

"I'm Suzie," she responded

"How old are you Suzie?"

"Five."

"Is she under hypnosis?" Sean asked in a whisper.

"Not by her file. Very few therapists use hypnosis anymore. A subject under hypnosis tends to try to respond in a conciliatory manner. Subjects wish to obey the hypnotist, so they provide what they think are the desired answers. It is primarily used now for arresting habitual mannerisms, such as smoking or obsessive compulsive disorders."

"I guess I should stop relying on Hollywood for information."

"You and millions of others." Heggenstaller commented quickly.

"Suzie," Kieser continued in the video. "Do you know where you are?"

"I'm at the church. It's getting close to Christmas time."

Kieser paused to adjust his questioning. "Is anyone with you?"

"My Mommy. We're parked in her car in front of the church. We have a Christmas present for Father Nicholas."

"Did she just say Nicholas?" Sean asked.

Donald shushed him and leaned forward, listening intently.

"Mommy is putting on make-up," Sue Ellen continued. "She always has to make herself pretty for Father Nicholas. I'm tired of waiting. I'm going in by myself. Mommy yells at me, but I don't listen."

"Can people have regressive memories without hypnosis?" Donald asked.

"There have been instances where patients hypnotize themselves; either accidentally or with intention. This episode could have been sparked by trance writing. Notice the paper and crayon in her hand. Trance writing is another method of drawing out repressed memories."

Suddenly Sue Ellen's brow creases, and she begins to pant in soft whimpers.

"What's the matter Suzie?" Kieser asks in a calm and monotone voice.

"Something's wrong in here. There's blood. He's on the floor."

"Who's on the floor? Father Nicholas?"

Sue Ellen nods her head, "He's on his knees in front of the altar. He's naked. He's yelling at Mary. He's mad because somebody's dead." She sobs. "There's blood all over Mary. He keeps rubbing blood all over Mary. Why is he doing that?"

"I assume that she is referring to the statue of the Virgin Mary." Heggenstaller commented.

"He fell down!" Her voice now comes in panicked bursts. "He fell down! His wrists are bleeding. I'm grabbing them and holding them as tight as I can. The blood is seeping through my fingers. I can't hold it in!

There's blood everywhere!" She begins to scream. "He won't stop bleeding! He won't stop bleeding!" Sue Ellen leaps to her feet and runs out of the camera's view. Kieser now steps into the picture and glances up at the camera long enough for his face to be seen. He moves toward her direction. Sobs and voices are heard, but there is no verbal comprehension. Following several minutes, the image abruptly ended in static.

    Jennifer stared down at her vanity through a mist of tears. She must have blacked out. For how long, she was not certain. A note had been written on a legal pad, the handwriting of which she did not recognize as her own. Her bottle of sleeping pills rested with a glass of water next to the pad. She heard a whispering male voice say it was time. She mechanically obeyed. Lifting the pill bottle and removing the top, she emptied the bottle's contents into her palm. She spread the pills out on the note pad and then scooped up a small handful. She stuffed the pills into her mouth and chased it with a mouth full of water. She gagged and coughed a spray of water out against the mirror of the vanity. She hated swallowing pills. She finished the pills and walked stoically to her bed. She slid under the covers and rested her head back against her soft pillow.

    Carol had become silent and even Jennifer's own thoughts fluttered across her mind in brief, pale flashes. There were no final words nor profound thoughts as her peripheral vision became fuzzy. She felt an unexpected sense of normality as the room began to spin and the fuzziness faded to blackness. Apathy was the last word to cross her mind before it surrendered itself to the encroaching blackness.

Chapter 64

There was a moment of stunned silence until Heggenstaller stood up to switch off the television. It was a moment for the raised hair to fall back to their skin. Sean was not only chilled by the images, but by the reference to Nicholas. Perhaps Jennifer somehow knew what happened to her mother as a child or perhaps the choice of the name was pure coincidence.

"I've watched that tape several times," Heggenstaller released a sigh, "and it still disturbs me. I've seen many unfortunate cases, but there is something here I can't put my finger on." He finished his sentence and walked over to the window, staring down at the courtyard below. His urge for nicotine was growing, but all building interiors of the hospital were smoke-free environments. "Children are forced to endure thousands of other scenarios much worse than what Sue Ellen describes; still something never sat right with me on this one. I don't believe that her disorder stems solely from the incident, but the story was a place to begin so I took the time to research it. I wanted to validate it. I quite honestly was surprised when I found out that a Father Nicholas Feragamo had indeed committed suicide in the year that Sue Ellen would have been five."

"Father Nicholas, huh? Is that where the name Nicholas came from?" Donald questioned Heggenstaller.

"You knew about this Nicholas guy?" Sean interrupted with his question before Heggenstaller had a chance to respond.

"Sue Ellen mentioned a Nicholas in her suicide note." Donald had no sooner spoke the words when the door to the office swung open.

The face of the horse was hideous despite the brilliant colors of which it was painted. Its lips were drawn back into a sinister sneer, displaying white gnawing teeth. The horse drew upward away from Jennifer only to fall back toward Earth until its features eclipsed the rolls of chase-lights beyond. The raucous sound of the Wurlitzer blared its song into the twirling winds. Jennifer was lying upon the spinning platform of a demented carousel with a wooden horse prancing above her. She turned her head to see what was beyond the carousel, but she discerned nothing except utter darkness. She struggled to stand amidst the disorienting spin of her world as she gripped the golden pole that guided the horse. She could now see many pairs of horses all following one another around an endless circle. As the carousel turned, she saw the familiar bonfire as it passed before her vision and then disappeared once again behind her. The carousel slowed as if on cue as she stepped to the edge of the platform. She waited until the fire was within her sight and stepped down.

A heavy balding man stood in the doorway of Heggenstaller's office, "Hey, Doc. Are you here on your day off again? You need to take up golfing."

"Afternoon Harvey," Heggenstaller responded, noticing the man's eyes averting to Sean and Donald as he awaited an introduction. "Harvey, this is Donald Gray and his son-in-law, Sean." Heggenstaller then turned to the men in his office. "Gentlemen, this is Harvey Burke, he is the superintendent of the hospital."

"Gray?" Burke said thoughtfully. "Your wife's name is Mary, right?"

"No, Sue Ellen," Donald corrected him.

Heggenstaller was visibly frustrated by the intrusion. Burke had a distinct ability to butt his nose in everywhere possible. He would pretend to remember the names of every patient in the hospital, but Heggenstaller had yet to witness him being correct.

"Of course, Sue Ellen," Burke responded pompously.

Heggenstaller recognized the look of utter confusion welling under Burke's self-assurance and decided to bail him out; yet again. "Sue Ellen returned to us just after Christmas," his comments were directed toward Burke. "She had been doing well at the Timberland Residential, but she seemed to experience a severe relapse. She was originally diagnosed with Multiple Personality Disorder."

"Dissociative Identity Disorder," Burke corrected Heggenstaller with the modern terminology, casting him a sharp glare. "A load of crap. Excuse my language. We've made remarkable strides with Sue Ellen. We never feed into that multiple garbage. My hospital focuses primarily on proven diagnosis and field tested treatment, along with several programs that I have developed myself. The first thing I did was to nearly eliminate the use of restraints. We have had only one incident when we had to restrain a patient in the entire ten years of my watch."

Heggenstaller was nodding his head approvingly. "The only incident was Sue Ellen, when she was readmitted in January."

Burke's glare would have sliced through Heggenstaller like razors if he had not noticed that Donald was watching his reaction carefully.

"Well, if there's anything I can do for you Dan, just let me know."

Donald nodded in appreciation - never bothering to correct the name - as Burke closed the door behind him. All three men were thinking the same thing, but thought best to refocus on the discussion at hand.

"As I was saying, there was a suicide during the year when Sue Ellen was five-years-old," Heggenstaller continued. "She had been interviewed as an eye witness; however, her statement was later dismissed. It did not collaborate with the statements made by the church or her mother. Her mother claimed that the child remained in the vehicle. I did, however, find a few strange details in the file. Father Nicholas was clutching a white rose in his hand. I'm not certain if that pertains to the gifts that Sue Ellen and her mother had brought. He was pronounced dead at the scene. But despite a complete bleed out, it was noted that there was an unusual lack of blood at the crime scene."

"The church was covering up the suicide to dampen the exposure," Sean reasoned.

"It would appear so," Heggenstaller added. "The last thing the church would have wanted was to be responsible for exposing a five-year-old child to this type of atrocity. So it is quite possible that what we have seen on this tape actually occurred."

"I need to know more about this suicide note," Sean requested.

"Yes, I actually have it in the file." Heggenstaller walked to the desk and rooted through the paperwork. "Donald was foresighted in bringing it to the hospital with him when Sue Ellen was first admitted."

Sean reviewed the brief letter, pausing at the part which read: "We will both have what we want. You will have your precious daughter. And I will have Nicholas."

"Did Jennifer say that she read this note when she had found Sue Ellen?" Sean asked.

"I'm not sure," Donald responded. "Jennifer shut down for quite some time after the incident. As I said before, she won't talk about it, which is why she never told you. It must still haunt her."

Sean turned his attention to Heggenstaller. "Would it be possible for me to see Sue Ellen?"

Heggenstaller looked at Donald for approval; Donald shrugged. "Sure." There was a pause as all three men awaited for one of the others to take the lead. Heggenstaller said finally. "We will have to walk over to the main building." *At last*, he thought, *a chance for a cigarette.*

Jennifer walked with a slight waver, still dizzy from the spinning. A crowd had gathered around the bonfire some fifty yards ahead; the bodies stood motionless in a semicircle. The crowd consisted of dozens of females, all staring blankly at the raging fire before them. Their skin shined waxy gray and their bodies were as motionless as mannequins. As the details of the faces and the bodies glowed within the bounty of the blaze, silent tales of anguish were told. One woman bore a red scar about her throat; countless others stood with their wrists slit open, their wounds too dry to bleed. A fowl stench rose in the air and choked off Jennifer's breath. The crowd parted as Nicholas pushed his way through and stepped into the clearing, a broad smile spread across his decaying face.

The dancing light of the fire cast a twisting shadow upon him like a writhing soul seeking to remove itself from his hideous flesh.

"Welcome home," he said timorously.

Jennifer's body froze. She gathered her strength and firmed her resolve, "Where's my son? You promised me my son."

"Of course," Nicholas turned and shouted back through the crowd. "Mommy's home!"

The serpentine fetus lashed through the women, slashing their legs open with the claws of his grotesque hands. The under-developed fetus head that had haunted Jennifer's nightmare bobbled wildly against its driving legs. Jennifer stepped back in retreat as the strange creature closed in quickly, gnashing its teeth at her feet.

"You promised me my son," she uttered.

"I promised you our son. Did you think for a moment that I didn't know where that little bitch was? I knew Carol was with you. And now, we're all together again."

Jennifer sensed Carol pressing to the back of her mind, desperate to hide from the fetus that had terrorized her. Jennifer swallowed hard, mustering every ounce of courage that remained in her frail body. "I won't let you do this, Nicholas." Jennifer spat.

"You won't let ME do it?" Nicholas replied quizzically. "You're the one who took the pills."

"I won't let you trap us here. Bring me my son like you promised, and let us go."

"Let me consider the proposition." He paused. "No."

"You can't keep us here. We won't let you." Jennifer spoke her words to Nicholas, but hoped that Carol was discerning them also. She wanted to rally the teen to stand up and fight for her soul.

"Okay, I'll reconsider." He paused again. "No." Nicholas released a sinister chuckle. "Did you really think that you were that special to me? Allow me to introduce you to the rest of my coven." He waved his hands in display of the women surrounding the bonfire. "All tormented souls that I have collected along the way."

"You have preyed upon the minds of the suffering," a distant voice projected from within the crowd.

Nicholas spun in the direction of the voice just as Father Anthony pressed through the crowd. "I have saved these women," Nicholas retorted. "I saved them from the loss of their children, from abusive husbands and raping fathers. I have granted them eternal life!"

"You have done nothing except drive them to suicide. You have drawn them into your own damnation! You will not take another soul." Father Anthony's face was flush with anger. He thrust his hand out, gripping Nicholas by the throat. Nicholas stumbled back, surprised by the action.

Nicholas frantically reached for Father Anthony's throat, waving his hand through the air. The bonfire leapt and thrashed the sky in response to the men's fury. The surrounding women stepped back away from the heat of the flames. "It is time, Nicholas. It is time to face your retribution."

"You and your church always meddle in the lives of men," Nicholas spat. "Trying to shape us into something that we were never meant to be. We are not holy; we are men. The way God created us. The way God wanted us to be."

"You have gone far enough, Nicholas."

"You made me do this," Nicholas replied. "You forced me into the church and deprived me of my needs. Natural desires that rush through the blood of every man."

"I provided you with the discipline and structure that you so desperately needed."

"You led me into the church as your sacrifice to God. I was to be your testament to the faith; an endowment of your convictions, by converting a troubled teen into a pillar of Catholicism. You were focused on your needs as a priest and not on my needs as a man! Your ego is inflated, old man. You have stepped into my realm and, once again, you attempted to save me," Nicholas sneered. "Now, who is going to save you?"

"This ends now, Nicholas," Father Anthony commanded.

"I was a fragile child when I lost my parents in that fire," Nicholas continued. "I know that you always thought that something inside of me died when I escaped from that burning house as the only survivor. But I think that particular something died a little before that. Your brother always told me not to play with matches," Nicholas paused with a smirk. "But I failed to listen. You know, I'm pretty sure that I heard them screaming when I ran from the house. I could hear the flesh sizzling. I could smell it. My mother's beautiful face simply melting away," he paused thoughtfully. "Incidentally, you always had eyes for your brother's wife; didn't you?"

The words struck Father Anthony like a fist; a moment when a man's deepest desires; even those previously unbeknown to him, are revealed. In his moment of revelation, Father Anthony loosened his grip. Nicholas seized the opportunity to make a successful lunge at Father Anthony's throat. The force of the strike now turned the offensive to the side of Nicholas as Father Anthony stumbled backwards.

Father Anthony could no longer maintain his grip on Nicholas' throat. His hand released and dropped to his side. "Yes. I can see it in your eyes." Nicholas peered into the eyes of his uncle. "You yearned for the life that he had; lusted for it. You lusted in your heart for your brother's wife. How does it feel to be human Uncle Anthony?"

"Please don't do this, Nicholas," Father Anthony rasped.

Anthony's eyes grew wider through shock and strangulation. Jennifer's mind had clouded into a trance as she watched the two priests struggle, but with a shake of her head, she returned to her senses. Nicholas' back was to her and he was preoccupied - this was her chance. She let out an angry scream and leapt onto his back. Her fingernails sank deep into the decaying flesh that hung from his face. Nicholas struggled to maintain his grip on Father Anthony against the force of Jennifer's pull.

"Let him go," she demanded.

Nicholas writhed in pain. Despite his already deteriorated condition, her attack was having some effect. He thrust his head forward until her fingers scraped up to his hairline. Jennifer could feel the slime of his skin accumulating beneath her nails. He exerted a great deal of force to simply turn his head as she strengthened her clasp.

"Junior," Nicholas uttered to the fetus that crouched in the mud next to the fray. "My hands are a little full. Would you mind getting this off of me?"

The beast scrambled up Jennifer's back, lashing its claws deep into her flesh upon his ascent. Jennifer arched her back in pain, trying desperately to keep her hold on Nicholas. Suddenly the fetus drew back his hands and thrust his claws into her temples. Jennifer threw her head back in a wail as the pain shot through her skull. She stumbled backwards before falling onto the platform of the merry-go-round; the fetus scrambled on top of her, holding her down with a force larger than his tiny body suggested. The pain stabbed sharp in Jennifer's head from the wounds the fetus' claws had left, robbing her once again of her balance. She laid upon the ground whimpering in her discomfort.

Nicholas straightened himself, still maintaining his death grip on Father Anthony's throat. Until, at last, Father Anthony's body lay motionless on the ground in the fetal position. Jennifer watched helplessly as Nicholas towered over his prize in a satisfied moment of redemption. Her mind worked frantically to conjure an escape. The effects of the sleeping pills were flooding her thoughts. It would not be long before she could no longer dream.

"Please God, help me," she sobbed. "I don't want to die."

Nicholas turned abruptly to her. "Just relax. It will all be over soon."

Chapter 65

Heggenstaller eagerly lit a cigarette and drew in a deep breath of nicotine-enriched smoke. The jitters that had begun to plague him in the office subsided as he led the party to the hospital's main building. He set the pace to a half stride, not being in any great rush to arrive anywhere.

Sean's pace was set on autopilot, his mind - far too indulged to focus on body mechanics. The connection of Nicholas between Jennifer and Sue Ellen's abnormal behavior was not coincidence, but was it plausible? The human mind is intricate when functioning within the boundaries of normality, but it appears enigmatic when that function goes awry. Yet Sean could not help but feel that there was something unearthly stirring beneath the existential psychology of Jennifer's condition. He eyed Donald's mood as one of introspection. He was hopeful that his father-in-law was reliving some important pieces of his wife's history. A history that could lead to the answers that Sean was seeking.

"Donald, Sue Ellen seemed almost romantic in her explanation of Nicholas," Sean commented.

"Oh, I think you are reading far too much into it," Donald responded. "After all, remember, Sue Ellen knew Father Nicholas as a guide to her faith. I suppose her depression led her back to the very origin of that faith, where Nicholas had helped to initiate her journey. Don't you think?" He asked, looking to Heggenstaller for confirmation.

"She simply longed for relief of her pain and viewed suicide as her only way out," Heggenstaller added. "An unfortunate message that Nicholas had inadvertently conveyed to her when she was an impressionable child."

Sean had been prepared to discuss Jennifer's strange purchases under the name of Nicholas with Donald, but Donald's dismissal of the charge of romance stifled his approach to the subject. He allowed the conversation to fall away.

The trio stepped into the hallway of the main building where twelve-foot-high walls rose to an arched ceiling. The place bustled with its normal flood of activity, despite the weekend's allure. Heggenstaller nodded to the woman at the front desk before she stopped them, insisting that Sean and Donald sign in and obtain visitor passes. He then led them down the hallway where a staircase awaited to guide them to their desired floor. The third floor required the ascent of six flights of stairs, as Heggenstaller was noticeably wheezing before the completion of the fourth.

At the top of the stairs, he unlocked a large steel door with a tiny window whose glass appeared as thick as it was wide. They stepped into a brightly painted hallway that was cleaner and more inviting than most hospitals. Heggenstaller paused to poke his head into the television room to see if Sue Ellen was present. He withdrew and motioned for his companions to follow him down to the end of the hallway where one of the open doors led into an eight by twelve foot room furnished with a portable closet and a narrow single bed. Sue Ellen was standing before a narrow window, gazing out as twilight settled over the area. Nature's silence was about to be disturbed - a powerful storm was advancing from the western sky.

"Sue Ellen." Heggenstaller announced their presence. "You have some visitors."

Heggenstaller pressed his body against a wall to allow the two men passage into the tiny room. Donald stepped in first and walked cautiously toward his wife. "Hi, Sue Ellen. I brought Jennifer's husband, Sean, here to see you."

Sue Ellen turned slowly. Her body was gaunt despite the protrusion of a stomach pouch. Her elbows pressed out against time-worn skin, and her eyes were dark and sullen. Her lips were thin with age, and her cheeks drew in to display the bone structure beneath. Sean noticed a rash present on her neck surrounded by blotchy skin patches.

"Sue Ellen, do you remember Sean?" Donald inquired.

"I'm not Sue Ellen," she commented blandly.

"Sue Ellen," Sean interrupted, maneuvering himself in front of Donald, "I wanted to talk to you about Jennifer."

"I said I'm not Sue Ellen," she repeated. "I am Rachel."

Sean turned his head to cast a glance back at Heggenstaller who shook his head disapprovingly at what he sensed was Sean's intentions.

"Rachel," Sean spoke, "Jennifer has been visiting with Nicholas." His words quickly snapped Donald's attention, who cast Sean a confused gaze.

"What are you talking about?" Donald demanded.

"Rachel, I think Nicholas may be leading Jennifer down the same path that he led you and Sue Ellen," Sean continued, ignoring Donald's question.

Donald grabbed Sean by the wrist angrily and turned to face him. "That is enough. You heard what was said; don't play into the multiple delusion. I want you away from my wife. And you're gonna tell me what is happening with my daughter on the drive home."

Sean pulled his wrist from Donald's grasp and reached out suddenly to Sue Ellen, causing her to retreat toward the window. "Rachel, please. If you have any information that may help me to understand what is happening to my wife, I need you to tell me."

"I said that's enough!" Donald's face reddened with anger.

Sean clutched his hands to Sue Ellen's frail shoulders and gave her a slight shake to force her attention to him. "Did Nicholas coerce Sue Ellen into the suicide attempt? Did he do the same to you?"

Donald wrapped his arm across Sean's chest and began pulling him back toward the door, "Trevor! Help me get him out of here!"

Heggenstaller stood frozen in the doorframe amidst the unexpected commotion. Age had robbed Donald of too much of his strength to pull Sean from the room, but his attempt was valiant.

"Just relax," Sue Ellen's words rolled softly from her lips.

The tension of the struggle deflated like the air from a balloon. Donald paused, loosening his grip across Sean's body enough for Sean to spring free.

"Just relax," she repeated. "It will all be over soon."

Chapter 66

Once again, Jennifer suddenly found herself lying on the platform of the carousel, the fetus creature still holding his post as he rested on her chest, peering down at her through the thin slits of his irises. The horses that had once adorned the ride in eerie fashion were gone. Nothing remained except the platform and the roof that seemed to press ever closer down upon Jennifer. Looking off in the distance, she could see the bonfire and hear the cackling laughter of Nicholas as he tormented Father Anthony. The carousel spun faster than before, and her sense of direction was swiftly becoming tainted. The roof above the platform was alive with swirling colors and mist that occasionally took shape in the form of moving images and then returned to swirl in a twisting blend of hues. Jennifer watched the images playing out above her as if they were being projected against a movie screen.

She could see the image of her bare legs spread out before her, her feet resting in stirrups as a pair of hands pulled her baby from her womb. Arlen nestled quietly in the hands as he was lifted up into view. The umbilical cord stretched skyward, still attached within her uterus. Jennifer felt a sharp pain deep within her abdomen as the cord strained to hold onto the child that was being taken from her. The image then spun until she could no longer discern its contents - swirling faster and seeping forth a thick mist.

The colors twisted, slowly taking shape in the form of Father Anthony's face. His skin was flushed with beads of perspiration seeping from his pores. His expression was that of distress as he spoke in his native tongue, "E beheld un'altra bestia che esce in su la terra; ed ha avuto due corni come un agnello ed ha parlato come drago." And as quickly as it appeared, the face twirled away into a stream of flowing color.

The next display was the edge of a river, the waves of which rose in choppy peaks of gray. Jennifer could sense herself standing along the shore as she watched Arlen desperately attempting to row a small vessel across the dangerous water. On the opposite bank, Sean sat comfortably upon a tall metal stool with a matching table before him, serenely sipping on a cup of tea. The image shifted and reformed into Jennifer's legs as she rested upon the delivery table. The pain in her abdomen returned as the serpentine fetus clawed its way through her stomach, shrieking loudly as it tore her skin.

The swirling colors returned, and the pain subsided as the image of Father Anthony's face took shape above her. The distress upon his face had now intensified with blisters rising on his skin until they burst with seeping fluid. His voice rose as he shouted in English, "And I beheld another beast coming up out of the earth, and he had two horns like a lamb, and he spoke as a dragon."

Another swirl led to the image of her mother stretched out across a bed, blood flowing from wide gashes in her wrists. Her mother's head lifted with a wild-eyed, eerie stare. "You will have your precious daughter. And I will have Nicholas." The words were cast from her mouth in Jennifer's voice.

The image suddenly disappeared, and the swirling colors faded to black. All that remained of the display was a prevailing mist. Slowly another image appeared out of the darkness - an angel with three sets of wings that Jennifer recognized to be a seraph. The seraph covered its face with one set of wings and its feet with another, the final set spread wide from its body. Slowly it separated the wings that covered its face, unveiling the likeness of the elderly woman from Jennifer's nightmare. The same woman who had haunted her dream, shouting at her to get rid of the copper sphere before Nicholas awoke her. The seraph held out its hand to reveal a white rose clutched within its palm. It tossed the rose which fell from the roof and landed upon Jennifer's chest behind the serpentine creature who had been obliviously keeping his guard. The image disappeared, and the spin of the platform slowed to a crawl.

Within her mind, Jennifer turned to Carol. "Carol, you have to help us. You are our only hope." Carol quivered and buried her head between her knees.

Outside Jennifer's mind, Nicholas was putting the final touches on his catch. "You tried to bury me beneath the Word of God," he spat at Father

Anthony. "Now, I'll return the favor. Lusting for your brother's wife is pretty serious. I think you need some more Bible study." Nicholas gibed. "Let me help you." Thousands of bibles rained down from above, piling on top of Father Anthony until his body could no longer be seen.

"Carol, please. You have to act now while he is still distracted. That fetus out there is not your baby." Carol's head rose slightly at the words. "Your baby is still inside of you, nursing on the goodness of your soul. It will always be there for you. That thing out there is the anger and guilt that you are carrying, but it is not your child. Your anger and guilt will trap you here. Get rid of it! I promise you, God has already forgiven you; all you have to do is forgive yourself. You were not alone in that abortion. Nicholas betrayed you. The man who performed the abortion betrayed you. But Carol, the story of your tragedy helped to dissuade many women from making the same mistake you did. In some small way, you actually saved the lives of many children. Now it is time to stand up against the man who drew a young teen into a horrible mistake. For God's sake, help us, Carol!"

Jennifer could feel Carol's movement as she rolled from her nestling. She could feel Carol's presence slowly pulling free until, at last, she could no longer feel her. Above Jennifer the serpentine fetus glared down upon her - its tongue lashing out occasionally, rolling over lidless eyes. It never realized that Carol stood above him until it was too late.

Carol snatched the creature up in her hands. The creature shrieked in a pitch that would rupture the average eardrum. It clawed at Carol's hands, trying to get a grip on her, but its attempt was fruitless as she leapt down from the carousel and raced to the bonfire. She held the fetus high above her head and hurled him into the raging fire; the creature hit the flames in a bright spray of sparks. It screamed and thrashed about wildly as its flesh burned from its torso. Nicholas spun in time to see Carol's jaunt across the mud in his direction. She slammed into him head-on, driving his feet back in the soft soil toward the rising flames. The flames lashed out igniting loose threads from the black cotton of his garments.

"You killed my little boy!" Nicholas caught his footing and began driving her back. The flames leapt high behind them, licking the air and longing for fuel. Nicholas felt the heat of the flames ease as he pushed back Carol's advance. "You're gonna pay for this, you little bitch." Carol's feet slipped backwards despite exerting the entire force of her small frame. Jennifer rolled off the carousel and tried to struggle to her feet, but her limbs were heavy and void of strength. She dropped to her knees, sinking deep into the cold earth. She could only watch helplessly as Nicholas gained the upper hand.

Chapter 67

Just relax. It will all be over soon. The words had been delivered with more callousness than calm. Sean eyed Sue Ellen suspiciously, wondering what the deranged woman had meant by the statement. "What will be over?" Sean asked. But no response came from Sue Ellen who had fallen into a catatonic state. Sean's voice elevated into a shout, "What will be over?"

"Damn it, Sean. What the hell are you getting at? Leave her alone!" Donald snapped.

Without warning, Sue Ellen cast an insidious glare at Donald, "You're a liar!"

"Sue Ellen," Donald said lovingly, "everything is alright."

"Those flowers are from him!" She spat.

An ominous vacuum seemed to suck the air from the room, leaving an uneasy aura in its place. Donald stammered for words, but his lips could barely release sounds. Sean spun on his heels and gripped Donald by the arm. "What does she mean?" Sean demanded.

"On the morning of her suicide attempt, I had confronted her with a bill I received. She had telephoned a local florist and had roses delivered to herself." Donald explained. "I always felt guilty about that. I think it may have triggered her attempt."

"We have to go, now!" Sean tightened his grip on Donald's arm as he led him from Sue Ellen's room. Heggenstaller followed quickly on their heels.

"Would somebody please explain what is happening?" Donald questioned in astonishment.

Sean spoke quickly as he led Donald down the hallway. "I'm not really sure I fully understand, but I have to get to Jennifer."

Jennifer's eyes searched the coven of women who watched in apathy. She prayed someone else would step through the crowd to save them. Her eyes stopped on the face of a woman whose neck bore the burns of a rope. For a brief moment, Jennifer found her face familiar. A mother that she nearly forgot had once existed, but the familiarity seemed to flex in and out of the woman's features. The woman stared at Jennifer almost lovingly. Then her face tightened with determination. The woman stepped from the pack, sprinted around the bonfire and slammed her full force into an unsuspecting Nicholas. The tide of the struggle had turned once again as Nicholas was thrown off balance by the additional force. The two women worked as a single unit, driving their antagonist back toward the flames. A third woman broke from the ranks of the coven and sacrificed her body to the fray. He had only moments to avert his attention to a fourth woman as she ran headlong at him before he felt the force of her blow. "What the fuck are you doing?" He winced as he struggled against their insurgence.

One by one the women of the coven that Nicholas had coerced into death joined Carol in driving their tormentor toward the flames. Behind their frail bodies was the puissance of vengeance along with the anger of betrayal, the pain of their losses and the longing for the loved ones they had left behind; victims all - victims of the reality of their own nightmares that had brought substance to their suffering in the form of a haughty man; a heathen who was choked by his own collar of goodwill until it spilled forth his true nature.

"You stupid bitches are going to kill us all!" Nicholas gasped.

The flames thrashed about like the tongue of a hungry puppy when its master is filling its bowl. Nicholas could once again feel the flames licking against his back. His face curled into a sneer of anguish. "But I loved every one of you! Why are you doing this to me? I granted you salvation from the lives that you could no longer endure!"

The crowd of women that had gathered now eclipsed Nicholas from Jennifer's sight. The pile pushed until, at last, all resistance from Nicholas ended in a single leap. The mass of human forms slammed down into the bonfire. The orange flames burned higher as each girl and woman fell unto the pile, until the fire burned white. The flames leaped with hunger, engulfing all in a white light that grew quickly in intensity. The light flashed its brilliance in a sunburst until all the surrounding darkness had been chased back. Suddenly with a loud 'swoosh' the white flame rose into the air in one final surge. Jennifer shielded her eyes from the radiance as the flame shot from the soil and trailed upward from sight.

Moments of darkness followed with only Jennifer's shallow breathing to denote any form of presence. She strained her eyes to capture any available light, to no avail. Her struggle was near an end. A calming peace fell over her as she released herself from the anguish that had devoured the last months of her existence. She let go of all of her anger and guilt until at last all that remained was the relaxing comfort of a strange inner peace.

She rose to her feet, standing blind in the engulfing darkness, when she suddenly felt something moist on her eyelashes. Had she been crying without realizing her tears? She reached up and touched the moisture from her lash; it held the warmth of tears. But soon all questions subsided as she saw the origin of the dew, a large snowflake floated down in front of her. It glowed with its own iridescence. The purest white light she had even seen. She turned her attention skyward to see dozens of large snowflakes floating down toward earth; each one possessing its own light. The souls of the women had been released. *Soulflakes*, she thought. Soon the air surrounding her was alive with glowing snowflakes as they drifted and danced their way down from the sky. The flakes felt warm as they brushed softly against her cheeks. Time slowed as she basked in the serenity of their presence. Jennifer brushed the air as the snow swirled around her outstretched hand. "You are free now. We are all free now."

Chapter 68

The glowing spectral snowflakes covered the ground and spread their luminescence about Jennifer's dark world. But despite the warmth of the snowflakes, Jennifer's body grew steadily chilled. She spread herself out upon the ground, embraced by the souls that surrounded her. Lives once separate now became sisters in a fellowship of redemption and healing. Jennifer rested her head upon the soft pile of flakes and closed her eyes. Moments passed as her breathing became shallow. Her eyes parted slightly to squint across the vast field of snow. In the distance, a dark figure approached her, shuffling gently along an unseen path.

A downpour of gray seemed to wash the color from the landscape as Sean's truck roared down the highway in the direction of Honey Brook. The visibility was sparse at best through the rain's slanting assault against the windshield. The headlights were barely cutting through the drenched night to illuminate the turns in the road in time to react at this speed. Strong gusts of wind shifted the path of the heavy truck as if it were nothing more than an autumn leaf.

Sean gripped the steering wheel, squinting steely-eyed with the resolve of a man possessed. His personal safety meant little against the growing concern for Jennifer's life. As he drove, Sue Ellen's words ate through his confusion like cleansing acid, awakening every nerve and sensation of his being. His senses were highly acute and no match for the treacherous driving conditions.

Dr. Trent Heggenstaller and Donald Gray, however, did not display the same assurance. Donald was scrunched in the middle of the seat while Heggenstaller rode shotgun. Donald clutched the dashboard in panic as he stared at the madman beside him who was wielding the truck as if it were a child's toy. But he was far too bewildered and frightened to utter any objections. The pragmatist in Donald had been unseated by Sue Ellen's sudden flashback. He was physically and emotionally plunging headlong into something he could not see.

The approaching figure stepped softly, but with purpose. Finally, in the surrounding glow appeared the warm smile of Father Anthony as he knelt beside Jennifer.

"You have done well, Jennifer," he commented as he brushed his palm along her cheek. "Your journey here is nearly at an end. But first, this realm holds one more surprise for you."

Father Anthony rose to his feet and slowly backed away from view. At that, another figure approached in the distance. This one was barely half the height of Anthony. The round and shining face of Arlen leaned down to kiss his mother's cheek. His long lashes spread wide like wings above his azure blue eyes that danced with the same fervor they possessed in life.

"Arlen?" Jennifer uttered through quivering lips as she lifted her head from the ground.

"Hi, Mommy." He spoke casually as he sat down next to her, gazing at her with a broad smile.

"Oh, my God," she gasped as her fingers ran along the contours of his face. "Mommy missed you so much." Jennifer took his hand, bringing the soft skin to her lips, and kissed his palm. A salty droplet released from its well and trickled down her cheek. Overwhelmed with joy and pain, her heart was breaking as she began to sob. Once again, she found herself giving birth to her son. "I don't know where to begin," she muttered. "I have so much to ask you. So much I need to say. Mommy is never going to leave you. Not ever."

"I'm okay, Mommy. Don't cry," Arlen pleaded. "I've been staying with Father Anthony. He teaches me things."

"I am so sorry about what happened." Jennifer tried to lick her parched lips. "I didn't know. I never knew you would get hurt."

"You couldn't have. And Daddy didn't, either. It was an accident," he paused thoughtfully. Reaching into his pocket, he pulled out three pennies and displayed them to her on his palm. Two of the coins were heads and one was tails. "Mommy, do you remember my story about the two-headed copper dragon?"

Jennifer's lips quivered as she reached out and brushed her fingertips against the coins. "Of course I do, Sweetheart."

"Well, I never got to finish it. You see, the two dragon heads soon realized the spilt milk wasn't anybody's fault. It was only an accident. They never forgot their longing for the milk, but they decided to allow the love that they felt for one another to quench their thirsts. And they lived happily ever after. And you and Daddy can too."

Jennifer's hand quickly covered her lips in an attempt to subdue an emotional outburst as tears streamed down her face. Arlen smiled and took her wrist, pressing the three coins into her palm.

"Thank you for playing Copper Dragons with me," he said. "Thank you for all of the time you spent with me. And all the time you made sure I was happy. Thank you for being my mommy."

"Thank you Arlen Bergin," she sobbed. "Thank you for being my son."

Time froze as mother and son held tight to each other in an enchanted embrace; an embrace that transcended the ages and embodied the love of generations past and those to come. With each beat of her heart, Jennifer could feel Arlen's heart match the rhythm, to remain one beat for all eternity.

"Mommy, you can't stay here with me," he said as he pulled back to gaze into her face. "It's not time for you to join me. Daddy needs you." He patted her face gently.

"No. I'm not going to leave. I want to stay with you forever," Jennifer argued.

"It's not your time yet. You have to go back."

"But Mommy doesn't know how," she uttered in confusion. Her eyes squinted, nearly blinded by sleep and weeping. "I'm so cold and tired."

"You have to go back."

"No. Please. Not yet."

"You and Daddy need to be together. Mommy, you have to listen to me."

"Okay. Okay," Jennifer struggled to remain cognizant.

"I want you and Daddy to have a baby brother for me."

Jennifer nodded yes, unable to vocalize her thoughts as she cried.

"Could you have a baby brother for me? I always wanted that."

"Okay. We will." She brushed the back of her hand upon his cheek. "We will." Jennifer lowered her head into the snow. "But Mommy needs to sleep now, Honey."

A warning light on the dashboard drew Sean's attention. Low fuel. In the haste of all of the day's concerns, he had forgotten to fill the gas tank. He cursed his weak memory.

The needle inched lower as the old truck ravenously consumed the gas amidst the revving of the inefficient motor. But there was no time to hesitate. He had to push on and pray that the remaining fuel would hold out. The situation drew out Sean's anger, and his anger depressed the gas pedal further. The engine sputtered then jerked the truck forward at a higher rate of speed. Heggenstaller reached for the overhead handle, gripping it until his knuckles shone white. He was certain he felt the tires sliding on the wet roadway.

Arlen gently brushed the hair from his mother's eyes with the softness of his little hands. Jennifer's head pressed instinctively into the touch. The flow of tears eased as she began to fade from the dream. "No Mommy," his voice remained calm. "You have to wake up. Daddy's coming. He is going to help you."

Jennifer's lids blinked lazily. "I'm so tired. I can't go on."

"Mommy, stick your finger down your throat."

Hydroplane. The word flashed across Sean's mind as he felt the tires of his pickup lose their traction, gliding upon a film of water. Before he could react, the truck was fish-tailing on the road. He worked the steering wheel frantically trying to control the skid. His stomach twisted into knots, and sweat quickly seeped from his brow. With his foot off the gas, the truck had slowed. But it was now across the dividing line and threatening to turn sideways. Sean knew at this speed, they would never survive the roll. His face became flooded by the headlights of a diesel truck that was approaching in the opposite lane with no time to stop. The blare of the semi's horn ripped through the sounds of the pattering rain.

"Huh?" Jennifer's mind was spinning, and she could barely make sense of Arlen's request.

Arlen clutched her hand and extended her index finger. "You have to stick your finger down your throat. It will help you get some of the pills out of your belly."

Jennifer groggily placed her finger into her mouth. Arlen suddenly pushed her elbow so that the finger rammed deep inside her throat causing a gag reflex.

Lying on her bed, Jennifer's actions mimicked her dream. As her finger suddenly shoved deep into her mouth, her frail body tightened, and her belly quivered in retching heaves. The contents of her stomach now spewed forth across her pillow. While in her dream, Arlen rubbed his palm lovingly across her forehead as she vomited.

The headlights from the diesel momentarily blinded the trio, washing them in a horrid, white glow. Two screams of primal fear filled the cab of the truck. The night had suddenly erupted in a flash of bright halogens and a blaring horn blast that rousted every hibernating demon in hell. The men in the pickup truck braced themselves for the impact. It was a moment of chaos that seemed to last an eternity. The rain splashing against the windshield. The truck sliding from side to side.

"Shit!" The word hissed through Sean's clinched teeth. He frantically worked the steering wheel. His right elbow inadvertently slammed into Donald's ribs. Donald groaned as the air was pushed from his lungs. The force of the jar ripped Sean's hand from the wheel. The pickup truck was now headed straight for the guardrail lining the opposite side of the road. Sean grabbed the wheel and seized the opportunity to accelerate, pressing the men back into the seat. The truck roared across the opposing lane in the direction of the brim of the road. The rear tires loosened as the rush of wind from the passing semi nearly lifted them from the macadam. Sean jumped on the brake and turned the wheel hard to the right. Gravel flew out into the night. Some clanging against the guardrail, others disappearing down the steep decline beyond. At last, the truck straightened and after a brief skid, came to a bone-rattling halt. The bodies of the three men lurched forward in their seats and then were slammed back.

The engine sputtered once again then settled into a low hum. No words were spoken. No gazes were met. Heggenstaller watched in the rearview mirror as the taillights from the diesel rig disappeared down the road. Thankfully, the driver of the semi never overreacted to the near collision. Any attempt to avoid them could have caused his truck to jackknife. The outcome for both vehicles could have been worse. After a few deep breaths, Sean signaled to reenter the roadway and calmly directed his truck into the proper lane. He matched his speed to the posted limits and tried to ease his nerves.

Despite the chaotic muscle spasms of the regurgitation, Jennifer's body quickly fell limp once again. The sight of Arlen's face dimmed until all that remained was darkness. Until the muffled sound of a distant voice sounded in her ear.

Sean's heart thumped hard against his ribs as he pulled the truck to a quick halt along the curb in front of his house. His adrenalin-filled muscles nearly ripped the truck door from its hinge when he swung it open, the metal groaning in protest. If Jennifer was in trouble, he could not be too late - not again. He had been too late to save Arlen; he would not allow that to happen to Jennifer. He crossed the lawn swiftly and traversed the porch with one stride. His momentum drove his shoulder into the door, never pausing to turn the doorknob. Despite the door being locked, it swung free of the frame; metal and wood splinters sprayed across the living room from the broken lock and surrounding door frame.

"Jennifer!" His shout echoed in the dark house. Without a pause in stride, he reached the staircase to ascend.

Donald followed shortly after, running with more vigor than he had displayed in years. Sean's imperative pace was only serving to elevate Donald's fear as well. As Donald stepped through the threshold of his daughter's home, his pace was slowed by the unexpected disarray of the interior. A rancid smell hung heavy in the air and the glow of the streetlights that managed to slip through the blanket-covered windows made the rooms appear surreal. His heart beat in his throat, and he silently cursed himself for not returning sooner to check on her. When he reached the bottom of the staircase he could hear Sean's panicked cries in the level above him. Donald's heart quickly sank.

Arlen's head suddenly averted from his mother as he focused on the sounds beyond his realm. "Dad's here. Everything's going to be okay. I love you, Mommy. Father Anthony says we have to go meet Jesus now. But I'll come back to visit you and my new baby brother." He paused with a warm smile. "Please. You need to wake up."

Sean burst into the bedroom, seeing the thin limp body of his wife lying motionless on the bed. His eyes quickly surveyed the room until they fell upon the empty pill bottle on her vanity. "Jennifer! Oh, God no, Lass!" His vocal cords tightened from the overwhelming anxiety, and the pitch of his voice slid occasionally into a slight shriek. He rushed to the bed and pulled her frail upper body into his arms, crying as he called out to her. "No, not this way, Lass! Why?" He gently kissed her forehead, leaving a glistening stain of tears behind. "Oh, please Jesus, don't do this to me! Jennifer, I love you. Please. You need to wake up! You can't leave me." For a moment he patted her cheek. He shook his head clear and forced himself to act rationally. He pulled his cell phone from his pocket and dialed 911 as Donald entered the room.

"She took pills," was all Sean could manage to say.

Heggenstaller finally entered the room in a loutish trot. He quickly retrieved the pill bottle from the vanity and brought it over to the side of the bed as Sean was giving the emergency dispatcher his address. Sean read the type of medication that Jennifer had taken and explained that she had vomited. The dispatcher reassured him, saying that an ambulance was already in route to the home. She requested him to remain on the line until they arrived. As she spoke to Sean, his thoughts raced in a panic.

His inner voice of damnation silently screaming in his ear, *"I bought the pills for her! Why didn't you think?" I can't be too late this time. I can't be too late."*

Chapter 69

Jennifer's dreams became flicks of senses that seeped through the darkness, all attempting to disrupt her slumber; an irritating alarm clock that tried to awaken her with a high-pitched siren; a room full of people all talking on cellular phones saying, "Jennifer, can you hear me? Can you wake up for us now?" Lights bright enough to penetrate through tightly shut eyes twirled and danced with one another in the darkness. Her nose was stuffed to the point that she labored to breathe, accompanied by a horrible chalky taste prevailing in her throat. She witnessed the shining green eyes of her husband, his cheeks dampened with tears as he spoke. "The doctor says you're going to be okay. I love you so much, Lass. I'm never going to leave your side again." And then a calm, deep sleep.

The next afternoon Sean sat in a small office within the hospital with Dr. Bomboy, who was seated behind a desk. Dr. Bomboy reviewed his notes momentarily and then began speaking.

"How are you holding up?" He asked.

"Pretty good," Sean responded.

"That's a frightening thing to go through."

"I went home for a little while this morning. It felt so strange walking through that house. I gathered an outfit for Jennifer to wear home when she's released, but I couldn't stop feeling like I had actually lost her. I mean, I know she's okay." Tears filled his eyes, and he averted his face from sight, "But it's like I'm mourning a death that never actually occurred. Why does it hurt so much? I feel like my heart has been broken."

"You went through a traumatic experience. Give yourself some time." He paused. "I spoke with her this morning. She told me about some very strange dreams that she was experiencing. The dreams could actually have been a self-imposed therapy to help her work through the loss of her son. Quite honestly, her sense of reality seems more stable than my first meeting with her. She was suffering from severe depression, but I think with a short-term medication and continued sessions, she'll be fine."

"Will I always have to live with the fear that she may try this again?"

"I wish I could say no, but we'll have to watch her closely. Make certain that she is communicating her feelings. She is still harboring an underlying guilt for what happened to your son. I understand she discovered a glass sphere that was left in a bad place and that somehow aided in his death."

"Yes. She mentioned that to me when she woke up last night," Sean responded. "I found it lying in the bathroom this morning. She had smashed the mirror with it. I turned it over to the forensic investigators who had worked on Arlen's case. I told them they could get rid of it when they were finished."

"Good. That would be something you wouldn't want to keep around Jennifer. It will be best to bring your lives into some form of normal routine as quickly as possible."

"What do you make of this guy Nicholas?"

"A bit of a mystery, but the trauma of what her mother witnessed as a child very well could be tied in with her mother's suicide attempt. I will keep in touch with Dr. Heggenstaller as we move through Jennifer's recovery. I believe Jennifer now understands that the presence of Nicholas was a result of her imagination. When a person becomes desperate to feel good and normal about life, they can cling to strange things - repressed memories or even dreams."

Sean listened to Dr. Bomboy, but he continued to feel something bizarre beneath the surface of the events that transpired on the previous evening. He was not certain that Dr. Bomboy's dream therapy idea could explain what he had witnessed at the State Hospital. Dr. Bomboy went on to explain his course of therapy before excusing himself from the meeting.

Sean returned to Jennifer's room. She had been sleeping so soundly when he first entered the hospital that he did not want to disturb her. This time she was propped up in bed with several pillows. He was greeted by the warmest, most welcoming smile he could ever recall.

"Good morning," she said sheepishly. "I guess I kind of made a mess of things, huh?"

"You don't worry about that. I'm just happy you're okay." Her pouting face appeared more adorable to him than ever before. Last night he had lost her; today he would never let her go again. "I'm sorry that I left you the way I did. I was angry."

"Sean, I was wrong for what I said about you being responsible for Arlen. I never really believed that. I was confused."

"I am glad to hear you say that," he said softly. "Lass, I want our marriage to work, and I'll do anything to keep it."

"I want that too," she consented. "No more harsh words." She gave him a gentle smile, "I love you."

Sean walked to her bed and kissed her lips, a sensation he had taken for granted until he lost it. He pulled his head back and ran his fingers through her thick red hair.

"Dr. Bomboy said I wasn't crazy," Jennifer suddenly commented, "just really depressed. I guess a part of me was trying to make you jealous. Maybe that's where this whole Nicholas thing came about."

Sean smiled, "Don't over analyze this, Lass. Why don't we trust Dr. Bomboy to do that?"

"I'm glad you convinced me to see Dr. Bomboy. I'm really comfortable talking to him." Jennifer commented followed by a moment of silence. "How does the house look? I made a mess of that too."

"You have a lot of people who love you. As a matter of fact, Gail, Arlene, June and Angelia Eckley are there now cleaning up the place; they wanted you to come home to a fresh house - a fresh start."

"Oh, but I don't want them cleaning up after my mess," Jennifer argued.

"Just let it go," Sean answered, "they wanted to do something to help. So I let them."

"I'll have to do something nice for them when I get out of here."

"Lass, you don't owe anyone anything. Relax. Let people take care of you for a change. Just let us love you." He could no longer restrain the lump that was expanding in his throat, choking off his words as he attempted to speak them, "okay?"

"Okay. I'm sorry I put you through this. And I'm so sorry for everything I said. You were right. Life isn't always a magic garden."

He bent down and kissed her full on the mouth and then whispered in her ear, "I love you. And that's all that matters right now."

The opening of the door made Sean straighten up as Donald entered the room. "Well, caught in the act," Donald joked. "It's like the two of you are back in high school."

"Hi, Daddy," Jennifer greeted him.

Donald walked to the edge of the bed and embraced his daughter tightly, wincing slightly from his bruised rib. "I'm happy to see the two of you together again. Sean is a good man." Donald made the comment and looked over his shoulder at Sean.

"I know he is." Jennifer's eyes twinkled with emotion.

"You gave us quite a scare last night," Donald said, redirecting himself to Jennifer.

"I gave myself one too," Jennifer responded.

"Jen," Sean interrupted, "I'll walk down to the vending machines while you visit with your Dad. Do you want anything?"

"A chocolate bar," she answered with the impishness of a child.

"You can have whatever you want," Sean promised. His eyes lit up as he stared at her. *Adorable*, he thought.

Donald stepped to the door with Sean, "I'll be right back, Princess. I just want to talk to Sean for a moment." Jennifer nodded her response.

The two men stepped into the hallway and closed the door to her room. Sean was taken by surprise when Donald suddenly latched onto him in a sincere embrace. Donald then stepped back, looking embarrassed by his own actions. "I went out to visit Sue Ellen this morning. She seems alright. In fact, she seemed more in tune with reality than I've seen her in years."

"That's good news." Sean commented. "I'm sorry about the way I handled the situation."

"You don't have to apologize. You saved my daughter's life last night. But I'm still a little cloudy on how you knew she had taken those pills."

"A few facts and some intuition, I guess. Jennifer is of the opinion that it was all devised in her head. We need to allow her that."

"I won't say anything, but this whole Nicholas situation is amazing, yet frightening at the same time. It makes you wonder if we explain away too many paranormal incidents."

The two men fell into a moment of silence which was at length broken by Sean. "Well, I'll go get her chocolate bar. I'll be back shortly."

Sean walked slowly down the hallway, his eyes staring down at his feet as he strode. White Adidas sneakers now became the canvas for deep thought as he watched them flopping against the tiled floor. He was no longer sure what really happened in that mental health hospital. Perhaps it was just the heat of a stressful moment that made the events more surreal.

He could hear someone approaching as he raised his head in time to see Wendy walking toward him. He was about to say hello when she averted her eyes to avoid speaking to him - an uncomfortable moment in a friendship destroyed by a romantic encounter that was never meant to be. Sean made the decision to respect her desire for silence, but as he passed he was halted by the sudden sound of her soft voice.

"Sean? I heard about what happened to Jennifer. I'm sorry. I hope the two of you can work through all of this."

"Thanks, Wendy," he turned to reply. "We're going to try."

She turned and continued down the hallway. Sean watched her as she departed, thankful that he had averted a mistake that could have cost him his marriage. He wished they could remain as friends, but he knew he had to let her go. He stopped at the elevators and pressed the button to go down to the lobby.

As he entered the lobby, he spotted Father Thomas walking toward the hospital's parish. Sean increased his pace to catch up with him.

"Father Thomas," Sean called.

Father Thomas turned to him, but with a face more somber than he usually displayed, "Hello Sean. How is Jennifer doing?"

"She's going to be okay."

"Thank our Lord. And how about you; how are you doing?"

"I'm fine." Sean glanced at the floor for a moment. "Father, something happened with this. I haven't figured out what yet, but I believe it wasn't normal. The only thing I know for sure is that I'll never look at this world the same again."

"What happened?"

Sean glanced around to make certain he wouldn't be heard. He moved closer so he could speak softly. "Do you remember the story of a Father Nicholas Feragamo?"

"That name again," Father Thomas replied. "I've heard that name many times over the years. Some called him The Incubus. He had already passed away long before I arrived at Saint Anthony. From what I understand, Father Nicholas was quite a charismatic man, but it still amazes me how folks seem to be obsessed with him after all these years."

"He committed suicide, didn't he?" Sean asked.

"Yes," Father Thomas raised his chin. "Why are you asking about him?"

"Jennifer imagined that she was dating him; in her dreams none-the-less."

"Huh? I don't know what to think of that. I trust Jennifer will be seeing a psychiatrist?"

"She is, and he thinks it was a strange mental response to her depression, but I can't help feeling that there may have been something substantial to her original claim," Sean pondered. "Do you believe in possession, Father?"

"In the ancient times, many people who were suffering from mental illness were mistakenly accused of being possessed by demons. I believe that could work both ways." He grappled with the thought. "Are you suggesting that Jennifer is possessed?"

"If she was," Sean responded, "it appears to be over for now. Listen to the way I'm talking. All of this supernatural stuff - I'm beginning to sound like Jennifer."

"Life isn't always black and white, Sean. God's miracles can work in wondrous ways. Don't always discount those things which seem beyond belief. If logic fails you, then consult your faith for the answers."

Sean nodded his head thoughtfully. "What brings you out here?"

"Actually, I'll be up to visit Jennifer shortly. I just have a few items that I promised to gather for the family of a departed member of our congregation."

"One of our members died last night?"

"Yes. Unfortunately, we lost Rachel Simmons," Father Thomas said somberly.

"Oh, God. She was only a little older than I am. Gail had told me about what had happened to her; about her attempt to hang herself."

"She was in a coma for quite some time." Father Thomas wiped his hand across his mouth. "Last night, she lost her battle." His eyes welled at his next thought. "I had been counseling her."

"I heard about that also," Sean admitted. "Word travels fast and far in a small town."

Father Thomas sighed. "I wish that I had seen what was coming."

"I could say the same. I guess there is only one God, and we are not Him." Sean shuffled his feet uncomfortably, not knowing what else to say to console Father Thomas. He was also feeling a sudden mixture of sorrow for the family and relief that Jennifer was safe. But after his experience, he was certain that Rachel Simmons lived on in a place far from the abusive husband who had haunted her.

Timothy Cole

"Well, I guess I should be on my way; Jennifer is waiting on a chocolate bar. You know how women can get if they don't have their chocolate when they want it."

Father Thomas responded with a smile then suddenly remembered a question that he had for Sean. "Guess who showed up for church this morning."

Sean shrugged.

"Nevin Mincemoyer. He was all cleaned up and sober; said that he decided to quit drinking."

Sean grinned with a shake of his head, "I'll be damned."

Father Thomas eyed Sean's impish grin suspiciously. "You wouldn't know anything about that, would you?"

"Who me?" Sean responded coyly. "Nah; can't figure that one."

Father Thomas released his stare with thoughtful caution. "I will stop by Jennifer's room on my rounds. We can pray together. I will also drop by the Assisted Living Community to visit your Grandmother later this week." He paused. "Do you think that perhaps you will see your way back into church next Sunday?"

"You can count on it." Sean walked away from the conversation with more questions than answers. Perhaps some knowledge was never meant to be revealed? Perhaps, the mysteries that surround the human mind and the afterlife are beyond human comprehension. Perhaps we should allow magic and miracles to be themselves without explanation? Life is not always black and white. He suddenly realized why his favorite color was gray. The thought left him with an unexplained craving for a chocolate bar.

Epilogue

"Wake up, Mum" The voice started out faint to Jennifer's ears, but grew in its intensity.

Jennifer regained complete cognizance from her slumber and became instantly aware of a beautiful pair of jade green eyes gleaming down at her. The eyes were set in a round face with soft angelic features, outlined by flowing curls of red hair. Her four-year-old daughter, Carol, was a beautiful replica of her mother, but boasted her father's Irish eyes. The morning summer sun came through the curtains to further illuminate the child's eyes. *Dawn in a child's eyes,* she thought, *there's no better promise of the future.* Six years had reconstructed Jennifer, who now felt healthier than she had since her youth. Her longing for the future could only be surpassed by her longing for the present. God had truly blessed her.

Jennifer brushed her palm across the subtle cheek of the toddler and smiled from the wonderful awakening. "The little angel of the white rose," she said softly.

"Daddy said it is almost time for church," the precious child spoke, struggling to perfect her pronunciations. "We cooked breakfast."

"I can smell it," Jennifer commented. "It smells absolutely delicious."

Suddenly a jolt of the bed silenced Jennifer, and her smile slipped into a look of contrived fear. "Did you feel that?"

"Yep," the tiny girl giggled.

"Did you come in here to distract me while he snuck in?" Jennifer asked suspiciously.

"Yep," again Carol responded with a giggle.

"Ah ha! I caught ya." The voice shouted as Jennifer felt a thump against her chest. Jennifer rolled over to rest on top of Carol's now squirming twin brother, Anthony. Anthony had the same hue of hair as his sister, but his eyes were a soft blue.

Carol wasted no time in leaping onto her mother's back and squeezing her in a tight embrace. "We caught you, Mummy!" Carol shouted.

"Oh no, I've been captured by the two-headed dragon!" Jennifer exclaimed. "Help me, Daddy!"

The sound of bounding footsteps could be heard seconds before Sean burst into the room and belly flopped onto the bed. He began wrestling the children free of Jennifer until each took a child, tickling them until both toddlers gasped for breath from laughter. The parents occasionally exchanged smiles of broad contentment and love as they basked in the rejuvenating giggling of their children.

At the foot of the bed, the family dog, Casper, leapt and barked, his tail waving frantically through the air as he watched his two masters happily frolicking with their three pups.

Made in the USA
Monee, IL
07 February 2024